Flashover

Other Books by Suzanne Chazin

The Fourth Angel

G. P. PUTNAM'S SONS

New York

Suzanne Chazin

Flash over

G. P. Putnam's Sons
Publishers Since 1838
a member of
Penguin Putnam Inc.
375 Hudson Street
New York, NY 10014

Library of Congress Cataloging-in-Publication Data

Chazin, Suzanne.
Flashover / Suzanne Chazin.
p.   cm.
ISBN 0-399-14850-7
1. Women fire fighters—Fiction.   2. New York (N.Y.)—Fiction.
I. Title.
PS3553.H3468 F48   2002   2001048772
813'.6—dc21

Printed in the United States of America
1   3   5   7   9   10   8   6   4   2

This book is printed on acid-free paper. ♾

Book design by Victoria Kuskowski

FOR KEVIN,
for the boy you are, for the man I know you'll be.

Acknowledgments

There are times when an event eclipses all that came before it—when heart and nerve and sinew are all that's left to carry us through. That happened tragically, on September 11, 2001, when two hijacked jetliners crashed into the World Trade Center towers, taking the lives of some three thousand civilians and rescue workers, including three hundred forty-three members of the Fire Department of the City of New York. My husband, FDNY Deputy Chief Thomas Dunne, was fortunate to avoid the same fate because of a reassignment that occurred barely two months before the disaster. Our family is eternally grateful. However, no words can express our profound sorrow and heartache for the firefighters and their families who were not so lucky. We will never forget their courage, devotion and sacrifice. It has been estimated that those three hundred and forty-three men helped save the lives of twenty-five thousand New Yorkers that day. Though the world at times may be short of heroes, the FDNY never is.

· · ·

I would like to offer my condolences to the members of the FDNY as well as my deepest gratitude for their efforts—both large and small—in support of this book. In particular, I'd like to thank retired FDNY Fire Marshal Gene West, whose enthusiasm and expertise in arson investigation are equaled only by his intellect and instinct for story. I owe all my best material to him. I'd also like to thank FDNY Supervising Fire Marshal Randy Wilson for his patience and good humor in orchestrating all my firsthand research. A special thanks as well to several current and retired members of the FDNY for their generous efforts on my behalf:

··· Acknowledgments

Louis Garcia, Vincent Dunn, Denis Guardiano, Neil McBride, Arthur Parrinello, and Brian Dixon.

Thanks, too, to the following people for their technical expertise: Roy Haase, Jr., Salvatore Oliva, Richard Gehlhausen, Ned Keltner, Edward Scharfberg, David Djaha, Robert Dosch, Jr., Jessica Gotthold, Rip Gorman, and especially my agent, Matt Bialer, and my editor, David Highfill.

A special thank-you to Susan Stranahan and Larry King, who sparked my interest in the subject of toxic fires with their wrenching eight-part series in the *Philadelphia Inquirer* about a fire in Chester, Pennsylvania, that was responsible for the deaths of dozens of emergency personnel over a two-decade period.

And finally, thanks to my parents, Sol and Lillian Chazin, to my dearest friends, Janis Pomerantz, Sharon Djaha and Warren Boroson, and most of all to my husband, Tom, for being the pillar of my life. I couldn't imagine going on without you.

A final note about the badge number on the cover: 594. It was my husband's number when he was a firefighter. It also belonged to my late father-in-law, FDNY Lieutenant Frank Dunne. The cover is in tribute to him.

Beware the fury of the patient man.

—JOHN DRYDEN

Flashover ··· a transition phase in the development of a contained fire in which surfaces exposed to thermal radiation reach ignition temperature more or less simultaneously and fire spreads rapidly throughout the space.

FROM THE NATIONAL FIRE PROTECTION ASSOCIATION'S
Guide for Fire and Explosion Investigations

Flashover

Everyone called him Bear, even his four-year-old. Six feet four, 240 pounds, he towered over the other men in Ladder One-twenty-one. "You're gonna be tall yourself one day," Bear promised the child.

"And a firefighter, like you," the four-year-old vowed. When Bear talked about fighting fires, the child pictured cartoon flames shriveling like day-old balloons with just one swipe of Bear's callused paws.

For all his size, Bear was a quiet man. His hands did the talking. He built things—a wooden race car for the four-year-old, a jewelry box for Mommy, a crib for the baby growing inside her tummy. He'd come home from work, a lollipop tucked into the right front pocket of his uniform shirt. The child loved to climb all over him, patting his chest for the telltale crinkle, breathing in the smell like burned pork chops that radiated from his hair and skin. Bear always smelled like that when he came home from the firehouse. Even after he showered and put on clean clothes. Mommy said fighting fires did that to you—got under your skin. In ways you couldn't imagine.

The youngster didn't mind. On Bear, burned pork chops smelled good, especially when you rode his broad shoulders and buried your face in his thick hair, the color of fresh wood shavings. Up there, the world was a safe place. Monsters didn't dare crawl out from under your bed, and bad guys didn't jump out at you from inside your closet or from the stairs to the basement. Nothing was brave enough to mess with Bear.

The summer air was as thick and sticky as cotton candy when Bear came home from work early one morning. It was barely light out yet. He always bounded into the kitchen, but this time, his footsteps trudged straight to the basement. "Don't touch me," he yelled at Mommy as she came down the stairs in her robe. He'd never yelled like that before.

He ordered Mommy to get him a garbage bag and hot soapy water and bring it down to the basement. Maybe Bear had found a puppy. He was always promising they'd get a puppy. Maybe they were going to give it a bath. The four-year-old stumbled out of bed and toddled toward the shaft of bright light coming from the open basement door. A puppy was worth getting up early for.

Bear was coughing—a hoarse walrus bark that resonated throughout the row house. Mommy was talking in a high, excited voice. Then there was a sort of slippery sound, like the time the four-year-old ate all those jelly beans and threw up on the living-room rug.

The child took one step down. Then two. Something was pooling on the basement's beige linoleum tiles. Something black, but reddish, too. Lumpy. Gooey. Like bits of rotten strawberries in Hershey's chocolate syrup. The four-year-old shivered in bare feet, fighting a sudden urge to pee.

The youngster took one more step and froze. At the bottom of the stairs, Bear, naked and trembling, was doubled over. His soot-stained body was covered with oozing red sores like the ones cousin Johnny had when he got chicken pox. Only this wasn't chicken pox. Mommy wouldn't be crying about chicken pox. And Bear—big, strong Bear— wouldn't be on his hands and knees, retching up this foul, dark liquid that even then, the youngster knew, was something to be feared.

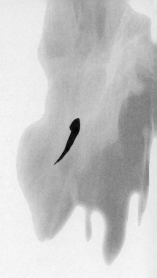

. . .

AT FIRST, she was aware of nothing. Not the feathery darkness that stole across her closed bedroom window. Not the bitter smell that blanketed the lilac potpourri on her dresser. Not the odd way shadows seemed to flicker up her heavy floral drapes and across the dentil moldings on the ten-foot ceiling. Hers was the perfect blackness and stillness of deep sleep. The sleep without dreams. The sleep of death.

But gradually, something hot permeated that cocoon Dr. Louise Rosen found herself in. She felt the heat pressing down on her with physical force, tunneling into her unconscious. It curled the downy fluff on her arms until each hair felt as coarse as a steel scouring pad. She coughed violently, as if someone were trying to shove a towel down her throat. Her nostrils stung. Her airways began to spasm. She forced her eyes open. She saw what instinct had already told her: her bedroom was on fire.

Get out. Get to the door. Actions came slowly. Words, not at all. The smoke blackened, eclipsing everything in the room, sealing off the Manhattan streetlights below. She couldn't see the bedroom door, couldn't even recall closing it. She didn't have the energy to crawl to it, much less open it. Wisps of flame darted across the ceiling. There were jagged fingers of orange climbing up her drapes, devouring a padded chair in the corner. She tumbled off the bed, hoping to hide from the heat. Even here, on the floor, it bore down hard on her tender skin, blistering it.

Her hair became as coarse and brittle as straw. She felt as if nails straight from a blast furnace were being driven through her flesh.

Got . . . to . . . got to—what? She couldn't remember the sequence of steps needed to get to the bedroom door. Fifty-six years of living, a Columbia University medical degree, and it had all fizzled in the space of a heartbeat. She wasn't even sure, if pressed right now, that she could remember her name. The pain was excruciating, tearing into her flesh like a pack of wild dogs. A dress she had tossed near the windowsill burst into flames, as if an invisible hand had just taken a blowtorch to it. She wanted to scream, but her throat had swollen up too much to make a sound. Skin hung from her fingers like wet tissue paper.

Hide. Got . . . to . . . hide. She rolled under the bed and lay on her stomach, her hands protecting her face. She was playing a deadly game of limbo now, trying to make her body as flat as possible to escape the descending curtain of heat. It banked lower and lower, like a murderer working his way down a flight of stairs. First the paint on the ceiling blistered. Then the pictures on the walls began to melt. Next came the lampshades. Then one by one, the bottles of perfume on her dresser began to shatter as if they were being picked off in a shooting gallery. The heat was on top of her now, sizzling like hot butter across the surface of the mattress. Soon, there would be nothing in the room that wasn't burning up. Nothing.

And then she heard it—a popping like gunfire, then cracks like footsteps on a frozen lake. Her bedroom window had shattered. The smoke, so black before, began to thin. The heat seemed to hiccup for a moment. But it lasted for less than half a minute before a new and louder roar took its place. A fiery cyclone. She couldn't see it, but she knew by the sounds of breaking glass that nearly everything in the room was igniting. The bed frame collapsed and the box spring ticking pressed down into her seared flesh.

She became vaguely aware of another noise beneath the roar. Someone was kicking down her bedroom door. She heard a whoosh like a huge wave. It hit the ceiling then fell like rain upon the floor. Then the wave subsided. The heat should've washed away as well, but it had crawled so deep inside of her, she felt branded on the soul. Before that moment, she believed the pain could get no worse. But she was wrong.

Someone doused the mattress and box spring with water, then lifted them off the floor. There was a tearing sound, like a Band-aid being ripped off hairy skin. The ticking had melted to the flesh on Louise Rosen's back. The movement of the box spring ripped it off her, right down to the nerve endings. Pain tore through the synapses of her brain, wiping out all other sensations. She knew no past, no future. She felt no joy or sadness, no hope, no will to survive. There was only a silent, unbearable agony. She couldn't even scream. Her throat had swollen up too much to make a sound.

"Hey, Cap, you better get on the radio. We got somebody," said an excited voice.

There was a murmur of other voices, a shuffle of heavy boots and then a long, slow, exhale before another, older voice spoke.

"Not for long."

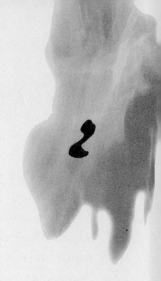

. . .

JUST A FEW misplaced embers from a smoldering cigarette. Fireflies on a hot August night. That's all a mattress fire was. A belch of black smoke. A long, slow burn. And pretty soon, someone was dead. Or in this case, damn close to it.

Georgia Skeehan gazed up at the apartment building from her fire department Chevy Caprice. Four stories above the hunter green entrance canopy, two upturned braids of soot streaked the white marble façade. It wasn't often she and her partner, Randy Carter, got called to a Park Avenue address.

On the sidewalk, a doorman in epaulettes watched a firefighter hose something down. Georgia didn't have to see what it was to know: the victim's mattress. It was a common sidewalk site in poor neighborhoods. Here, beside the prewar buildings of Manhattan's elite, it attracted ghoulish curiosity from spectators.

"Lady can afford Park Avenue," said Georgia. "She should be smart enough not to smoke in bed."

Carter ran a long, bony thumb and finger down the sides of his graying mustache and gazed at the crowd behind the police barricade. The pulsating red lights of rescue vehicles washed out the color of his dark, lined skin like overexposed film.

"Lady can afford Park Avenue," he shrugged. "She should be smart enough to get out of the city on a ninety-five-degree weekend."

"What does that say about us?" Georgia jabbed her finger at the air-conditioning button on their dark blue Caprice. Lukewarm, moldy-smelling air continued to pour from the vents. Even the silver chain she always wore was sticking to her skin. "Record-breaking heat wave and we get stuck with a November vacation slot and a toaster oven of a car."

"You think this is bad?" said Carter. "Wait 'til you step outside."

Georgia opened the door of the sedan. It was four-thirty in the morning and, still, the mid-August temperatures hovered near eighty degrees and the city's nicotine breath coated her skin like Vaseline. Static-filled voices from one of the fire engine's radios cut through the dark, humid night as sharply as a welder's torch. When she turned her head, Georgia caught the moldy cheese smell of ripe garbage from a can on the corner of Seventy-fourth Street. The contents of her stomach rolled about like marbles in a tin can. She hoped it was just the heat making her nauseous. Her period, which you could set a detonator by, was a week overdue. *Don't even think about it,* she told herself. She hadn't seen Mac Marenko in three days. She wouldn't begin to know how to tell him.

She and Carter made their way through the crowd just as two fire department EMTs emerged from the building wheeling a woman on a stretcher. The woman was badly burned and writhing in pain. She lifted an arm. It was black and flaky in some places, bright pink like chewed bubble gum in others. If the rest of her looked like that, she'd be dead within hours.

"Can she talk?" Georgia asked, hustling over to the EMTs as they loaded the victim into an ambulance.

"Honey," said one of the EMTs, a heavyset black woman, "She's lucky she can breathe." The EMT adjusted an oxygen mask around the victim's face. Her partner, a slight, Latino-looking man, injected a clear liquid into the victim's veins. Her burned skin balled up on his powder blue latex gloves like a label on a wet shampoo bottle. The smell of it—an odor like burned sugar and copper—hung in the air.

"You probably wouldn't have gotten much out of her anyway," said the man. "There were a lot of empty liquor bottles in her kitchen. A and E was looking at them."

"Dang," said Carter. He slapped his thigh in disgust at the mention of the Arson and Explosion Squad, a rival unit in the New York City Police Department. "Maybe we could actually *do* our jobs if the PD didn't always get there first." Although only fire marshals are allowed to examine physical evidence and make a determination of arson, nine-one-one dispatchers typically notify the NYPD of an emergency first. In higher profile cases, the resulting scramble over jurisdiction can turn into a political slugfest.

An urgent beep pierced the close air inside the ambulance. The Latino EMT furiously began chest compressions on the victim.

"Gotta go, guys," he said. "She's falling fast."

Georgia and Carter stepped back as the doors closed and the ambulance took off, cutting across a wide, nearly empty stretch of Park Avenue, lights and sirens at fever pitch.

The waterlogged queen-sized mattress lay behind them on the sidewalk, next to a pile of what looked like charred red blankets. An unburned area, resembling the shape of a body, marked the center. On each side of the unburned area, great wads of foam padding erupted like volcanic lava. Georgia pushed a foot on the mattress's edge, expecting the springs to have annealed—collapsed because of extended exposure to high heat. But the springs rebounded perfectly.

"Couldn't have been a very hot mattress fire," Georgia noted to Carter.

Carter shrugged. "If it was a mattress fire at all."

"What do you mean?"

"Look at the burns," he said. "They're even on both sides of the body outline."

Georgia could see Carter was right. If the victim had been smoking in bed, the burns should have been deeper on the side of the mattress where the cigarette fell. The victim's body would have acted as a firestop and kept the other side of the mattress from burning as badly. Georgia could think of dozens of explanations for the unusually even burn, but they were all conjecture at this point. If eighteen months as a fire marshal had taught her anything, it was not to get too caught up in the "what ifs" so early in a case.

She walked ahead of Carter into the lobby, past firefighters carrying out tools. The fluorescent yellow stripes on the men's bulky black turnout coats reflected the gleam of the chandelier, silently mocking its elegance like a pair of fuzzy dice in the window of a Mercedes. Georgia overheard snatches of conversation above the piecemeal crackle of radios. The rumor mill was going strong this week. The police commissioner had resigned to take a job in San Francisco and word was that William Lynch, the fire commissioner, might take his place.

"They could hold his freakin' farewell party in a phone booth," she heard one of the firefighters say. Lynch, a lawyer, was not a popular man with the FDNY's rank and file. Georgia always knew he'd move on. It was one of the reasons she'd kept her distance from him since her last big investigation in April. She knew she'd have to work with the people he'd alienated long after he was gone.

Georgia and Carter got the name of the victim from the doorman. It wasn't until they looked at the mailboxes in the lobby, however, that they realized she was a doctor. *Louise Rosen, M.D.,* read her mailbox.

"She was burned so badly, it was hard to tell even how old she was," said Georgia.

"Mid to late fifties," mumbled Carter as they walked across a Persian rug and past two cream-colored damask couches. Carter pushed the elevator button.

"You know her age just by looking at her?"

He shrugged. "She's a doctor with bread, Skeehan. She's not twenty."

The elevator doors opened and Georgia found herself staring at two vaguely familiar, rough-hewn faces in silk-blend suits. Detectives from Arson and Explosion. The older detective, Phil Arzuti, was a lean, dark-haired man, a little on the haggard side, with a crooked, world-weary smile and bags under his eyes. He was reputed to be a first-rate poker player, and the few times Georgia had worked with him, she could see why. He exuded an air of nonchalance that made it impossible to tell what he was thinking. Georgia racked her brains to remember the name of his younger partner. Chris something. *White? Williams?* She saw Carter stiffen as the younger detective stepped out of the elevator and rocked on the balls of his feet.

"Well, whatta ya know. It's the Mod Squad," said Chris loudly. He was probably only in his mid-thirties, but he already wore the waistband of his pants at a downturned angle to accommodate the overhang of his gut. His blond hair had begun to recede at the temples. It contrasted oddly with his thick red mustache. "Hey, Pops," he said to Carter, "I thought they'd have put you out to pasture by now."

Carter's dark, basset-hound eyes seemed to crawl deeper into their sockets, and the lines on his face tightened as if attached to a winch.

"Somebody's got to get their hands dirty, Willard," Carter drawled as if he'd just come up from North Carolina last month instead of thirty-three years ago. "Can't all of us be worrying 'bout mussing up our hair"—he made a point of looking at the top of Chris Willard's head—"or what's left of it, anyway, for a collar."

"Collar? The Bureau of Fire Investigation's got no collar here, old man," said Willard. "Chick got tanked on Jack Daniel's, then roasted herself smoking in bed, pure and simple. Casework on this baby wouldn't fill a pencil box."

Georgia flinched. Cops and firefighters talked this way all the time—but not within earshot of civilians, some of whom were being allowed back into the lobby now. Willard either didn't have the smarts to understand this, or he didn't care. Either way, she disliked him. She stepped into the elevator and Carter followed, but he made a point of giving a backward glance at Willard's shoes. The detective followed his gaze, though his gut was probably beginning to get in the way of it.

"What?" asked Willard, self-consciously lifting a sole. Probably thought he'd stepped in dog shit. Georgia stifled a giggle.

"Gucci, Willard?" asked Carter.

"My shoes?" The detective frowned as the door started to close.

"I need to know so that when the lab tells us some horse's ass walked all over our crime scene in expensive Italian shoes, I can tell them which horse's ass to look for."

The doors closed, and Georgia bit back a grin as they rode to the fourth floor.

"What's up with you and that jerk, Willard?"

Carter pulled at the cuffs of his gray pinstriped suit. "Nothing that five minutes in a dark alley couldn't cure."

There was no door on Louise Rosen's apartment anymore, just a steel frame that was compressed in two places like a crushed tin can. The fire was out and the smoke had cleared, but the taste of ash settled at the back of Georgia's throat. Her tongue felt as if it were coated with road tar. A layer of oily residue covered the teak furniture in the living room. Soot shaded the white plaster walls and a set of heavy, floor-length red drapes drawn across a window. The hallway mirror was opaque enough from the fumes to write on. Yet, in the living room at least, there was no burning. Lamps hadn't shattered. Even Sunday's *New York Times,* scattered in a corner, lay intact, opened to the crossword puzzle.

A row of photographs on a huge, well-stocked bookshelf sported an oily layer of soot but hadn't gotten hot enough to melt. One woman was in enough of the shots for Georgia to assume it was Louise Rosen. She was a slim, middle-aged woman with a short helmet of dyed-blond hair and a penchant for ice pink lipstick. A closet drunk, Georgia supposed, as she glanced into the kitchen where two empty fifths of Jack Daniels and six crushed Michelob cans sat on a solid granite counter.

Georgia and Carter followed the tamped-down carpet, blotted black like the brushstrokes in a Chinese watercolor. It grew darker with soot as they neared the bedroom. Here, the fire told a different story. There were scorch marks along the walls. The bedroom door, now open, was burned heavily on the inside, especially along the upper half. There were sharp demarcation lines between the burned and unburned areas, suggesting it had been closed at the time of the fire.

Inside, the walls were black and powdery like coal dust. The floor was soggy from hose runoff and littered with plaster and debris. A chair in one corner had burned so thoroughly, it no longer had any legs. The finish on the dresser had blackened, and everything on top had charred or cracked. The window glass had either shattered or been broken and the wall next to it was so badly burned, Georgia could see the original wood studs beneath, now segmented like logs left overnight in a fireplace. The mattress was in the street but the box spring was still in the center of the room, surface burned. The air had a close, heavy smell of ash, sweat, and the sickly sweet stench of fried skin.

Carter ran a gloved hand over the burns on the door. His eyes tracked the blistering on the ceiling.

"Looks to me like this place was cooking," he said. "The hot gases were collecting on the ceiling and radiating back down fiercely, judging from the damage."

"Then how come the mattress springs weren't annealed?" Georgia noted. "A fire that causes this much damage to a room should've done a little more damage to the mattress."

"Maybe the captain can tell us," said Carter. He nodded to a far wall where four firefighters from a ladder, or "truck," company were punching holes in the plaster ceiling, looking for pockets of fire that could smolder and reignite, a task called "overhauling." Georgia saw Carter cringe. Overhauling was hell on a crime scene.

The truck captain slogged through the muck to greet them. Hagarty was his name. He was a doughy man with washed-out brown hair and pale skin. Carter and Georgia nodded to him, and Georgia pulled out her notebook.

"What've you got?" she asked the captain. She had to shout over the noise of the falling plaster.

Hagarty tipped back the brim of his black helmet and wiped a sleeve of his turnout coat across his sweaty brow. The air-conditioning was off in the apartment, and the temperature hovered around ninety degrees.

"Routine smoking in bed, as far as I can see," said Hagarty. "Looks like she got drunk and fell asleep. Her bedroom door was shut. When we arrived, there were already flames rolling across the ceiling. A couple of minutes longer, and everything in the room would've ignited, for sure."

"A flashover," Carter mumbled, his eyes scanning the scorch marks that traveled three-quarters of the way down the walls.

"You vented the window?" Georgia asked Hagarty.

"Didn't have to break it," said the captain. "It broke before we got into the room." Hagarty shrugged. "Not that it's my call, but those

A and E detectives did a walk-through and came up empty. It's a mattress fire—in an upscale neighborhood maybe, but still in all, a mattress fire."

Georgia turned to Carter. "What do you think?" she asked him.

Carter shrugged and said nothing. He'd never done that before. They'd been partners for a year and a half now—ever since Georgia left the firefighting arm of the FDNY to become a fire marshal. Although they always took turns running investigations, and this one was Georgia's, Carter—with sixteen years as a marshal—was usually the guiding force.

But since that serial arson investigation in SoHo last April, Georgia had noticed Carter hanging back more. On the one hand, she welcomed it as a sign of his increased regard for her abilities. But there was a bittersweet side as well. Carter was fifty-nine years old. He had nearly thirty-one years in the FDNY. One of these days soon, he'd probably put in his retirement papers. In his own quiet way, he was forcing her to become less dependent on him.

Georgia put away her notebook and scanned the room. There was something wrong with this smoking-in-bed scenario. Carter was right—the mattress burn was too even. And the springs hadn't annealed. But there was something else, as well. She pulled out her flashlight and shined it across the blistered ceiling, bringing the beam to rest on the blackest part in the far corner, directly above what was left of the chair. She walked across the room and moved the chair frame aside. The floor was badly burned underneath.

"If Rosen was smoking in bed," Georgia wondered aloud now, "how come the lowest, deepest burns are in this corner?"

Beneath Randy Carter's mustache, Georgia thought she saw the hint of a smile. They both knew that because fire typically travels in a V pattern, upward from the base, the lowest burn point is often the point of origin.

She walked past Carter and Hagarty to a floor lamp five feet from the burned-out chair. The metal had oxidized—rusted—because of the heat. The lampshade had burned away. The lightbulb underneath had melted and elongated as if made of Silly Putty, a process known as "pulling." Carter had taught her that when lightbulbs melt, they have the odd habit of pointing in the direction of the heat.

"The bulb is pointing to the chair in the far corner, by the window, not the box spring," Georgia noted.

She turned to Carter, waiting for a reaction. She thought she'd done a thorough initial sizing up of the fire. But instead of looking pleased, he was frowning in the direction of the living room.

"The front door," Carter asked Hagarty. "It was locked when y'all arrived, right? That's why you took the rabbit to it." The rabbit is a twenty-five pound hydraulic wedge so named because it looks like a rabbit's foot.

The captain rubbed the back of his grimy neck and shifted his feet. His eyes flicked to the firefighters at the wall behind them. They were nearly finished. "We're not sure," he admitted.

Georgia started. *The firefighters broke down the door without first trying the knob.* It happened all the time in the adrenaline rush of the moment. Only in this case, an unlocked door could be significant because it signaled the possibility of an intruder. She couldn't believe she had missed it. *What else am I missing?* Georgia wondered. She scanned the charred top of the dresser, noting the shattered perfume bottles and a three-candle, wrought-iron candelabra with two melted orange blobs still in their holders. She kicked at the debris surrounding the box spring with the tip of her crepe-soled black work boot. And then it hit her. She scanned the floor of the room.

"Where are the ashtrays?" she mumbled.

Carter gave her a puzzled look.

"Maybe we wouldn't find cigarettes or matches in a fire this hot," said Georgia. "But I don't see anything that would pass for an ashtray— not even an empty glass or bottle or beer can."

Carter straightened. He started to speak, then swallowed the thought. He walked the perimeter of the box spring, nudging soggy bits of wood and plaster. When he met her gaze, his deep, soulful eyes held a mixture of pride and something else she couldn't quite read. A sadness, perhaps. He wasn't ready for this shift in their relationship.

"So she ditched her ashtray and neatened up before she passed out," said Hagarty. "She's a regular eighty-proof Martha Stewart—so?"

"Maybe," said Carter. "Then again, she'd be the first one I ever saw who was."

. . .

NOBODY REALLY KNOWS what's under the concrete and asphalt of New York City. Way, way down, there are graveyards of slaves from the seventeen hundreds and scattered timber remnants of houses that haven't stood since sailing ships called New York home.

There are elegant subway stations with fresco murals and mosaic tiles, miles of tunnel and track that were begun with great optimism, then simply abandoned when the money ran out or the politician in charge couldn't get his kickback.

There are water tunnels blasted out of the granite bedrock big enough to drive a semi through that connect reservoirs upstate to water-processing plants in the city. And there are pneumatic tubes that once delivered mail between New York office buildings at nearly the speed of the Internet.

People live in the bowels of the city, too. "Mole people" they call themselves—mostly drug addicts and crazies, but some children as well. Robin Hood knew why they came. Down here, it was peaceful. Damp, glistening bricks. Puddles of water that pooled like quicksilver in the light. Down here, the oppressive August heat was but a memory, the city noise, a rumble like distant thunder. Only the splash of water on boots and the jingle of Hood's tool belt passed for noise. It was the city of a hundred years ago—fashioned not by silicon chips, but by bricks and mortar and the sweat of men. A good place, thought Hood, for hiding just about anything.

Hood rubbed two grimy gloved hands down a pair of baggy blue jeans. It was done now. One way or another, there would be justice— not the formal, antiseptic variety, perhaps. Hood had seen men die waiting for the formal, antiseptic variety. This was something better— something befitting a Robin Hood.

At a juncture where a wall of bricks had turned white with lime and decay, Hood felt for the familiar rusted rungs of a ladder and slipped through the porthole that separated earth from sky. Dawn would come within the next ten minutes; the eastern horizon was already the color of faded denim.

Hood removed a hard hat and slipped off the tool belt. An oily stench hung low in the air, as heavy as wet canvas. In the distance, cars rolled over the steel plates of a bridge and a police siren wailed until it was out of earshot. Hood surveyed the landscape, amazed that in a city of eight and a half million most people still went about their daily routines giving very little thought to what lay beneath the paper-thin façade of glitz and power that passed for civilization here. New York City could be like a teenager in that regard: vain, full of hubris, clinging to a faith in its immortality, yet defiantly naïve when you came right down to it.

That surface toughness and razzle-dazzle soothed the bankers down on Wall Street, the press with their minicams, the tourists ogling the Broadway marquees. But it remained an act, a sleight of hand from the men who really kept the city together with tape, glue and prayer. Hood knew it. And so did they.

And what's more, thought Hood, stretching with satisfaction, those men would pay a lot of money to keep others from figuring that out.

4

. . .

THE TASK BEFORE Georgia and Carter was dirty and brutal—equal parts muscle and precision. They were alone in the apartment now. Just the two of them, a couple of shovels and a large stainless-steel toolbox known as a PET kit—PET being short for Physical Examination Tools. The box was filled with pliers, screwdrivers and claw tools—everything necessary to pull apart the wreckage to figure out how and where the fire had started. Called a Cause and Origin determination, or C and O, it was the first step to any fire investigation.

Georgia slipped on a pair of navy blue coveralls and opened the red drapes across the living room window. The air-conditioning was off in the apartment. Sweat ran in rivulets down Georgia's body as she and Carter shoveled plaster dust off the box spring. Dawn was breaking outside and the heat of the day was coming on strong. Carter's breathing became ragged.

"Take a break," she urged him. "I can do this."

"Y'all gonna start treating me like Chris Willard now?" he choked out. "I ain't ready for a nursing home yet, you know." He leaned on his shovel for a moment and wiped the sweat that coated his face like butter. Georgia could see he was hurting, no matter how much he pretended otherwise.

"I think you're right, by the way," said Carter between gulps of air. "About Rosen not smoking, I mean. There are no ashtrays or matches or lighters in this place. No cigarettes in her garbage, either."

"None of that proves she wasn't drinking, though," said Georgia.

"She's got two bottles of good Chardonnay—not the cheap stuff—in her refrigerator. One of 'em's open."

Georgia stopped shoveling and wiped her brow on the sleeve of her coveralls. "So?"

He took a deep breath. "Y'all ever seen an alcoholic who could open a bottle of *anything* and not drink it all?"

"You've got a point there." Georgia turned her attention to the chair in the corner. It sat legless on the scorched floor like a beggar.

"Randy? Do you remember that seminar we went to at the crime lab last May?"

"The one given by that Indian chemist with the towel on his head?"

"*Turban,* Randy." Georgia rolled her eyes. "They call it a *turban.* Anyway, I seem to recall him saying that once a room passes through the flashover stage and becomes fully involved, it can be very difficult to determine whether a fire was accidental or incendiary."

"But this fire didn't reach flashover," Carter reminded her. He bent down by the box spring and picked up a nickel-sized piece of half-melted red plastic. A bottle cap of some sort. "Every burn is still in a condition to tell us something."

"Exactly," said Georgia. "So what do you make of this?" She squatted behind the charred chair frame and ran a gloved hand over a heavily blackened section of the wall a foot or so off the floor. The wall, once plaster, was burned right through to the wooden studs. "You've got a low burn here—lowest burn in the room," said Georgia. "In a corner where there are no electrical outlets or other obvious sources of combustion. If the fire had gone on a minute longer, the whole room would have looked like this. We might never know about this low burn."

Carter dropped the red plastic cap into an evidence can. Then he squatted beside her and scraped a gloved finger across the blackened floor beside the chair. A waxy orange residue came off on his glove. He nodded to the wrought-iron candelabra on her dresser.

"She burnt one of those candles over here by the window," he muttered.

"But it's too far from the chair to be the source of ignition," said Georgia.

Carter straightened up with effort and frowned at the room.

"Rosen's a common Jewish name, right?" Carter mumbled. "Got to be hundreds in New York—a lot of 'em doctors."

Georgia shrugged. "I guess—why?"

"Just wondering."

He sealed the evidence can. Georgia studied him from behind. His breathing remained uneven, and he looked shaky from the heat. His hand slipped as he wrote the case number, time, date and his name on the top and sides of the can. When he reached for his shovel, Georgia thrust an arm across the metal grip.

"Not now, Randy. I need you to talk to witnesses."

His dark eyes narrowed. He saw what she was doing. "Ain't nothing wrong with me, girl," he protested. "I was prying doors off their hinges by *hand*—none of these rabbit doohickeys—when you were still in diapers."

"I know," she said gently. "But *somebody's* got to charm those old society matrons. And I'm not the charm half of this duo."

He made a face. "Seems to me, y'all doing a pretty good job of it right now."

A ghostly quiet descended on the apartment after Carter left. It seemed to settle in the air and thicken it with a morbid replay of the terror and mayhem only hinted at in the carbonized ruins. Even with the windows open, the ash and plaster dust were like a fine gauze blanket to the lungs. Georgia fought back a cough the way she used to as a kid when she'd swallowed too much powdered sugar on a doughnut.

She sifted through the debris on her hands and knees, searching for evidence of shorted wires, blown fuses and unexplained burn patterns. She took samples of the floors and walls, the mattress on the street and the box spring in the room. She snapped her own black-and-whites after putting in a call to Herb Moskowitz, the department's sole forensic photographer, and discovering he'd been pressed into taking pictures of Mayor Ortaglia's breakfast with members of the Hispanic Coalition.

No one needed to tell Georgia that in city politics, photo ops took precedence over crime scenes.

She was struggling to maneuver the box spring to one side of the room when she heard a set of footsteps in the living room.

"Randy, can you give me a hand?" she called out.

The footsteps clomped toward her in the bedroom.

"Hey, Scout, you're looking radiant today."

Georgia turned. Supervising Fire Marshal Mac Marenko slouched in the bedroom doorway, his tie loosened, his white shirtsleeves rolled up and his strong, sinewy arms folded across his chest. When they were alone, Marenko always called her "Scout," a nickname he'd coined after once complaining that she was as naïve as a Girl Scout. The name stuck, in part because it was a lot better than other things he'd called her when she first joined the bureau. In front of the other marshals, however, he always called her by her last name. Marenko was terrified of anybody finding out they were dating.

Marenko pulled a set of latex gloves out of the back pocket of his dark blue trousers. "You want some help?" he asked. At six feet two, he towered over Georgia.

She brushed her gloved hands down the front of her baggy coveralls. "I can handle it."

"My ass, you can." Marenko grinned, yanking the box spring and tossing it halfway across the room. "Anything else you want me to move?"

"Yeah. You." She pulled a black twin-handled gadget from a leather pouch on her duty holster—the belt around her waist that held her Glock nine millimeter—and extracted a small screwdriver from the gadget's attachments. Then she crouched down and began to pull apart some wiring on a burned lamp.

"You're carrying a Leatherman now, huh?" asked Marenko, referring to the small tool—part pliers, part Swiss Army knife—that a lot of fire marshals carry. "I thought you were partial to screwdrivers in your purse."

"I broke down and got a Leatherman instead," said Georgia. "The pliers come in handy."

Georgia gestured to the bags and cans she had stacked on the dresser. "I'm nearly finished with the evidence collection. Did you see Randy in the lobby?"

He nodded. "Carter asked me to come up and have a look at this place, see what I think." Marenko was one rank higher than Georgia and Carter. He oversaw arson investigations rather than conducting them himself.

"So"—Georgia straightened up—"what do you think?"

Marenko let his blue eyes, the color of an oven pilot light, travel the length of her body. "I think my mechanic dresses better." He reached out and wiped a smudge of soot from her face. "Then again, I wouldn't ask my mechanic what he was doing for dinner tonight."

She shook her head. "I can't. I promised Connie I'd help quiz her for her sergeant's exam." Connie Ruiz was a detective with the NYPD, assigned to the Arson and Explosion Squad. She was also Georgia's best friend. "You can come help, if you want."

Georgia caught the change in Marenko's expression, the momentary embarrassment in his boyish features, then realized why. Randy Carter was ducking under the crime-scene tape in the living room.

Though Georgia had told Carter about her relationship with Marenko, Carter, always the gentleman, never let on. He simply nodded to Marenko as he entered the bedroom. But Georgia also caught a shade of wariness in their exchange of glances. The two men had different, if at times competing, roles in Georgia's life, and they seemed to dance around each other now, like two similarly charged force fields that repelled each other if they got too close.

"You were right, Skeehan," said Carter, flipping through his notes. "Dr. Rosen doesn't smoke. Seems she asked the super to unclog her sink a couple of months ago, then complained when she came home and smelled smoke from his cigarette in her kitchen."

"That doesn't mean jack." Marenko dismissed Carter a little callously with a wave of his hand. "The chick could've quit, then gone back to it. I've done that myself maybe twenty times."

"You stack your empties neatly on the kitchen counter before you get tanked, too?" asked Carter.

Marenko's jawline hardened. "I don't *get* tanked," he said stiffly. "But I *do* call the shots 'round here, and it looks to me like a routine accidental fire you're wasting too much time on." He pulled off his gloves and checked his watch. "Wrap this up in the next hour and send me the report by Thursday." Marenko started for the door.

"You're wrong, Mac," said Carter.

Marenko turned. His eyes became slits. "Excuse me?"

"I don't mean about whether the fire's accidental or not. I mean about whether it's *routine.*" Carter softened his tone. "Mac, listen to me for a moment. You're thirty-eight, right?"

"Thirty-nine," Marenko said defensively.

"And Skeehan's thirty. You haven't seen too many of your friends on this job come before the One-B Board." The One-B Board: the fire department medical board, the all-powerful panel of doctors who decide whether or not a firefighter gets "three-quarters," the coveted line-of-duty pension, if he becomes disabled because of a job-related injury. A "three-quarters" is just that: three-quarters of a firefighter's last year of salary, tax-free, every year, for the rest of his life. Firefighters whose injuries are not considered job related get smaller, taxable pensions depending upon their length of service.

"What the hell's the One-B Board got to do with this?" asked Marenko.

"Louise Rosen, man," said Carter. "In the nineteen eighties and nineties, she made a career out of turning down injured firefighters for line-of-duty pensions. Some of those guys . . . they never forgave her."

Georgia frowned at Carter. "That's why you asked me about the name Rosen earlier, huh?"

Carter gave her a sheepish look. "I didn't say anything before 'cause I didn't want it to color your findings," he explained. "I'm not even sure it matters. Rosen's been retired for maybe five or six years."

They were all silent for a moment. Then Marenko ran a hand through his thick mane of blue-black hair and cursed. "Did you tell Arson and Explosion any of this stuff yet?"

"I figured I'd leave that to you," said Carter. "I know you have to tell them, but I was hoping you could hold back a day, maybe buy us a little time." He nodded to the living room. "Dr. Rosen kept two big boxes of patient files in the basement. I got the super to give them to me. They're out there, by the door. I figured Skeehan and I could look through them later—see if any names pop out."

"Jesus." Marenko ran a hand down his face. "I don't want this. And I know Brennan won't." Arthur Brennan was chief fire marshal of the city of New York and every member of the Bureau of Fire Investigation's ultimate boss.

"All right." Marenko sighed. "I'll hold back as long as I can. Look through the boxes. Visit Rosen at the burn unit. But don't get carried away. I'd like to step *around* this shit if possible, not in it."

5

. . .

THE TEMPERATURE WAS almost chilly inside New York Hospital on the Upper East Side of Manhattan. Even so, Georgia felt a trickle of sweat creep down the silver chain tucked inside her shirt as she pushed the elevator button. She didn't want to be here, at the Cornell Burn Unit, one of the most advanced burn-treatment centers in the world. But then again, neither did Louise Rosen.

"What odds of survival are the doctors giving her?" Georgia asked Carter as they stepped off the elevator and walked down the window-less seventh-floor corridor, polished to a blinding sheen.

"Not good," he said. "She's got burns over sixty percent of her body. And you know the rule . . ."

"Age plus burn equals the likely percent of fatality," Georgia said grimly.

"Fifty-four plus sixty," said Carter, shaking his head. "I don't think she'll last long."

"Seems horrible for someone to suffer all this only to have no hope of survival."

"Gives her family a chance to say good-bye, at least," said Carter. Georgia caught the wistful note in his voice. His own estranged daughter had died four months ago in a monstrous blaze. There had been no prolonged suffering, as far as Georgia could tell. But there had been no opportunity for a farewell, either.

"You wouldn't have wanted this for Cassie," Georgia offered softly.

Carter shrugged but said nothing. Georgia could talk to him about almost any subject—except Cassie's death. At times like these, his grief danced around them, a black hole that Georgia could sense, yet not see.

She was concentrating on her partner's reactions so intently, she didn't notice the two familiar figures in silk-blend suits walking toward them until they were practically on top of her. Chris Willard's too-tight Italian shoes squeaked on the shiny white linoleum. He walked a little ahead of his partner, his gut jiggling over his downturned waistband. He spoke first. Georgia got the impression he always spoke first.

"Hey, Pops," said Willard, stroking his red mustache. "You're wasting your breath if you think the nurses will let you talk to this chick. Those bats won't let you get within half a mile of intensive care."

Carter gave Willard a long, stony stare—long enough for Willard to feel the heat of his gaze. Then he shifted his eyes to Phil Arzuti. "I thought y'all had no interest in Louise Rosen," said Carter.

Arzuti offered up his trademark poker player's smile. "A formality," Arzuti assured him. "It's been a slow tour."

A good feint, but Georgia wasn't buying it. "Your CO sent you back out, huh?"

The bags under Arzuti's eyes tightened slightly in surprise. He opened his palms. "Marshal"—he sighed, like a man just following orders—"we have a very thorough commanding officer."

Damn, thought Georgia. *The cops know about Rosen's connection to the FDNY.* She noted the sudden military erectness in Carter's posture—a vestige of his days as an army drill sergeant. Clearly, he was thinking the same thing.

"Did you find out anything?" Carter kept his eyes on Arzuti. Willard answered.

"The chick can't talk," said Willard sourly, waving his hand about as if swatting a fly. "You won't get past Nurse Ratchett there at the main desk."

"Watch me." Carter turned toward the entrance of the burn-care unit. Georgia began to follow. That's when Chris Willard looked at her for the first time. He had eyes the color of soggy cardboard—flat and muddy. But there was a glimmer of something else, too—something sharp and unseen, like a knife in the silt of a riverbed.

"You like seeing crispy critters, Marshal?" Willard asked her now. "The ones still walking and talking with their faces hanging off?"

"I've seen plenty of burned people," Georgia reminded him. She tried to sound firm and in command, but the raggedness of her voice betrayed her. In nearly eight years in the fire department, she'd encountered more than her share of burned bodies—some fatally. As a fire marshal, she'd taken statements from severely burned victims. But she never got used to it. There was nothing as horrific as a burn. She hated Willard for uncovering this chink in her armor.

He smiled wickedly at his victory. "You'll see her in your dreams," he promised.

"Are you okay?" asked Carter. "That moron didn't get to you, did he?"

"No," she lied. "I'm just not very good with burn victims."

Carter exhaled. "Okay, look—you'll be fine," he assured her. "A couple of rules. Go in and suit up without being asked—cap, gown, booties—the works. It's a sterile environment, and the nurses won't even talk to you if y'all don't respect that. That's why Arzuti and Willard got thrown out."

"I understand," said Georgia.

"Remember that Louise Rosen doesn't know she's checking out of the picture, so don't say anything to her to suggest that. She's not a perp. And we're not doctors. We don't tell people whether they're gonna live or die."

...

Kathleen O'Meara, the head nurse in the burn unit, looked to be in her late forties, with the sinewy arms and hollowed cheeks of a long-distance runner. Her moss-green eyes held a mixture of kindness and determination. She hugged Carter as soon as she saw him.

"I haven't seen you in ages," Kathleen scolded. "Not since that fire department fund-raiser for the burn center."

"I've been sort of . . . preoccupied," Carter said thickly, and Georgia thought again about his daughter, Cassie. Carter introduced Georgia and asked Kathleen if they could talk to Rosen. "We'll be quick and compassionate, I promise," he added.

Kathleen looked over their clothes. They both had donned white smocks and masks from a sterile bin. Georgia had tucked her curly, reddish-brown hair under something that looked like a shower cap. She and Carter had slipped clear plastic booties over their black-soled work shoes.

"I'd like to, Randy. Really, I would," Kathleen explained. "But it's like I told the detectives—she can't talk. She's got inhalation burns and she's on a ventilator . . ."

"—Can she blink?" asked Georgia.

"Yes . . . of course," Kathleen stammered.

"Perhaps we could ask her yes/no questions and she could blink her answers," Georgia suggested. "One blink for yes, two for no."

"No," Kathleen said sharply. "Look, Marshal, you won't get answers to those kinds of questions with a blink."

Georgia and Carter exchanged puzzled looks.

"Kathy," said Carter gently. "What do y'all think we're gonna ask?"

"The same as the detectives, of course." Kathleen played with a small gold post in her ear. Her face went pale. She leaned closer. "You know— the bomb," she whispered.

"The *bomb?*" asked Georgia. Carter's eyes were as wide as hers.

"You mean a bomb in Rosen's apartment?" They had done a thorough physical examination of Louise Rosen's apartment. If there had been a bomb there—or evidence of a bomb—they should have found it.

"No . . . I don't think so," stammered Kathleen. "Somewhere else, I guess. I . . . I thought you knew."

"It's all right, Kathy," Carter said soothingly. "We know those detectives. We'll probably get briefed about it later." It was a lie, Georgia knew. Whatever made Arzuti and Willard do a one-eighty on this case, they weren't sharing it with the FDNY. Only civilians believed that all the good guys were on the same side.

"We'd really be grateful if you could give us a heads-up on this bomb thing," Georgia coaxed Kathleen. "It could take hours for the information to come through official channels. By then, the trail could be cold."

"No one has to know where it came from, Kathy," Carter assured her.

"But I don't know anything else," said Kathleen. "Really—that's the truth. The detectives asked me if Dr. Rosen had mentioned a bomb. I don't think the bomb was supposed to be in her apartment. I got the feeling it was somewhere else. But as I told you, Dr. Rosen can't talk. She never mentioned a bomb. She never said anything."

"Kathy"—Carter put a hand on hers—"please let us visit with her and see if there's anything we can find out. We won't cause any trouble."

She hesitated a moment, then sighed. "Come on, then."

They followed Kathleen O'Meara through a set of double doors. The temperature on the inside of the hallway was at least fifteen degrees hotter than it was in the waiting area. Georgia had forgotten that burn victims have no skin to help them maintain their body heat. She swallowed back a sudden, metallic taste in her mouth and searched for a comfortable way to hold her hands. To her relief, she noticed that even Carter got quiet. Maybe no one really became accustomed to seeing people horrifically burned.

In a large room to their left, Georgia could hear screaming and moaning above the white noise of a pounding shower. An ear-piercing shriek echoed above the thrumming of water, followed by whimpers that didn't sound human at all—more like cats in heat. Kathleen must have seen the discomfort in Georgia's face.

"The tank," she said evenly, answering Georgia's unspoken question.

"The tank?"

"Nurses have to scrub off a burn patient's dead skin so that infection doesn't set in and the doctors can do skin grafts," Kathleen explained. "The scrubbing's done under a high-pressure shower. It makes removing the skin a little easier, but it's hard on the nerve endings." She smiled sadly. "The patients'—and the nurses'," she added.

Georgia heard the unmistakable cries now of a young child and winced. "Can't they give him morphine to make the pain go away?"

"Oh, we do," said Kathleen. "Those cries? That's *with* morphine. If the nurses give that child any more, they'll kill him."

A male nurse doing the morning rounds nodded to Kathleen, then tousled the nappy hair of a black boy of about three, wearing a diaper, his legs encased in gauze bandages. The boy clutched a metal walker to help him get around, like an old man in a nursing home. His large, soulful eyes looked far too old for his years.

"How are you doing E.J.?" said Kathleen, giving the child a big smile. The boy did not smile back. They were at the other end of the hall before Kathleen spoke.

"E.J.'s mother got mad because he wet his bed. So she gave him a bath—in one-hundred-and-forty-degree water."

"Is he going to recover?" Georgia asked.

"Physically? Yes," said Kathleen. "Emotionally? How do you ever get over something like that? We get a lot of children through these doors. Some are just unlucky, but a lot of them are either burned intentionally or left alone for hours, even days. They get into matches or try to cook something to eat and next thing you know, they're here. Or dead."

Kathleen pointed to a glass door at the end of the hallway. The three-bed intensive-care unit. She opened the glass door and led Georgia and Carter to the nurses' station. There was a printout on the desk, and Kathleen picked it up and read it.

"This is interesting," she said. "The hospital did a toxicology screen on Dr. Rosen when she was admitted. The lab results just came back. They found no alcohol or drugs in her system. Even her carbon monoxide readings aren't exceptionally high."

Georgia raised an eyebrow in Carter's direction. He'd been right about Rosen not being a drunk. But that only made her injuries more perplexing. *If she hadn't been drugged or drunk or near death from CO poisoning,* thought Georgia, *what had kept her in that bedroom for so long?*

Kathleen led them past the nurses' station now and into intensive care. Along one entire wall, machines encased in black plastic and stainless steel beeped and whirred and whooshed like a NASA space station.

In the center of all this gadgetry, a bloated figure lay motionless, swathed in gauze bandages. The sickly sweet odor of burned hair and flesh permeated the room.

Louise Rosen was unrecognizable by age, race or gender. She was hooked up to at least two dozen tubes and wires. Feeding tubes. Breathing tubes. Cardiac and blood-pressure monitors. A morphine drip. Antibiotics. Electrolyte fluids. But her eyes were open. She was awake and alert.

"Can she tell we're here?" asked Georgia.

"She sees you," Kathleen explained. "But she's been given drugs to paralyze her because she's on a ventilator. She's suffered tissue damage to her lungs, and the doctors don't want her to move and make them worse. She's on sedatives, too, so she won't panic about being temporarily paralyzed."

Georgia willed herself to step close to the bed. Her eyes settled on Louise Rosen and she swallowed hard. A burn—even a very severe one—often doesn't look that bad when it first happens. The body may be all red or charred or even milky white. The person is often in shock and doesn't feel much pain. Sometimes they're walking and talking. But a few hours later, it's an entirely different story. Like taking the peel off a banana and then watching it rot.

Louise Rosen looked as if she'd gained a hundred pounds from the pictures Georgia had seen of her in her apartment. Her eyes were nothing but two slits in a face as plump and red as a tomato. Her nose was black, and blood seeped from her lips. Her right arm, which Georgia hadn't noticed before, lay unbandaged. A deep gash ran the length of the blackened skin, exposing bloody, pulpy tissue and muscle. The gash wasn't a trauma—it was a surgical incision, an escharotomy, performed by surgeons on severely burned tissue to ensure that the swelling didn't cut off blood flow and invite gangrene.

Georgia cleared her throat and tried to appear relaxed, though she felt as if she were about to pass out in the overly heated room. "Dr. Rosen? My name is Georgia Skeehan and this is my partner, Randy Carter. We're with the fire department, we're marshals and we'd really like to talk to you." She spoke to Rosen the same way she interviewed children and older people—burying her title and authority in an effort to humanize the encounter. This was particularly necessary for a fire marshal because, unlike police officers, fire marshals have the legal power to take sworn affidavits—admissible in court—on the spot. This upped the stakes on interviews because a well-prepared witness statement could make or break a case.

"May we sit down?" asked Carter, dropping his voice an octave, turning it softer and more southern. It was a rhetorical question; Louise Rosen could neither invite them to sit nor prevent them from doing so. But the politeness of it was all part of what made Randy Carter so effective. People *wanted* to tell him things—even criminals tended to confess in his presence.

Georgia pulled up two chairs by her bedside. The ventilator pumped out a rhythmic whoosh while other machines hummed and beeped their white noise. It was like listening to the engines in the bowels of a huge ship. A phone rang at the nurses' station, and Kathleen walked back to answer it. Georgia took a deep breath.

"Dr. Rosen?" she began. "We want to find out what happened to you. We know you can't talk, but if you can blink your eyes, we can help. Can you do that? Blink your eyes? Show me a blink, Dr. Rosen."

Rosen's eyes looked tight and fearful. Georgia had a sense the woman knew she was going to die. She was a doctor, after all. Still, very deliberately, the woman shut her eyes tight, held them a moment, then opened them. Georgia smiled.

"That's great, Dr. Rosen. Now, I'm going to ask you some questions. Blink once for yes, twice for no—got it?"

Rosen blinked once again.

"Y'all doing real good, ma'am," Carter offered.

"Were you smoking when this fire broke out?" asked Georgia.

Two blinks—no.

"Were you alone in your apartment?"

Kathleen O'Meara interrupted their session. "I'm sorry," she said. "You're going to have to leave."

"But why?" asked Georgia.

"I just got a call from my director," said Kathleen. "Those two detectives lodged a complaint about not being able to interview Dr. Rosen. My director said we could be in legal trouble if we allow one law-enforcement branch to interview a patient, but not another. She said we have to let everyone in, or no one. I'm sorry. The interview is over."

Georgia looked over at Louise Rosen. Rosen blinked twice. *No. No. Don't go.*

"Two more questions—just two more questions," Georgia pleaded.

"I'm sorry, Marshal. I could lose my job if I let you stay." Georgia looked over at Louise Rosen's bloody, pulpy face and saw her blink twice again. Georgia tried to manage an encouraging smile.

"You rest up, Dr. Rosen," she said. "We'll do this another time." But the woman didn't blink. She knew as well as Georgia: there would be no other time.

. . .

"WE HAD HER—she was ours," fumed Georgia as they left New York Hospital. "And Arzuti and Willard blew it for us."

It was almost noon when Carter began the drive back to the bureau's base in lower Manhattan. Georgia rolled down her window. She wasn't in the mood for air-conditioning today. She wanted to feel the breeze on her face and rejoice in being alive. Along the avenues, Asian and Latino men stood at the top of cellar hatch doors to restaurants, fanning themselves in the heat. There was music from passing cars and open windows. There were the smells of the city: urine and sweat, garlic and soy sauce, diesel and garbage, all rolled into a thick, gritty paste that settled like flour on her skin.

"It's no use writing out a subpoena, either," said Carter. "The hospital can stop us from talking to Rosen just by saying we're putting her life in jeopardy. We haven't got a legal leg to stand on." He hit the steering wheel in frustration. "This bomb stuff's out of left field. Louise Rosen was a doctor. There was nothing in that apartment to suggest she knew about bombs or was the target of one. What would make Arzuti and Willard ask about such a thing?"

"They'll never tell *us*. That's for sure," said Georgia.

"And our guys don't know, or we'd have heard by now," said Carter.

"There is another way," said Georgia. She fished out her cell phone from a black hip bag around her waist.

"Who are you calling?"

"Only person I trust at A and E." She punched in the numbers from memory and heard Connie Ruiz's voice come on the line. Georgia didn't identify herself. She didn't have to.

"You don't have to do this," she said by way of greeting.

"Uh-oh. Should I hang up now?" Connie teased. She had the kind of bright, breathy voice that would've made her a great radio announcer. Georgia had heard of cops who called A and E's squad room just to hear her voice.

"We're working a case that Willard and Arzuti are working on, too," said Georgia. "We're hearing some strange rumors on your end. Have you heard anything?"

"Jesus, don't tell me," muttered Connie. The lightness left her voice. "Step back on this one," she said tightly. "It's bad."

"How bad?"

There was a pause on the line. "She's dead, you know," said Connie. "Died about fifteen minutes ago. I just took a message from the hospital for Arzuti. He and Willard are out."

"Aw, man." Georgia felt the air leave her body. She cupped a hand over the receiver and broke the news to Carter. He clenched his fists as if he wanted to hit something.

"Can you talk?" asked Georgia.

"Not here."

"Can we meet for lunch?"

They ruled out meeting at a downtown deli—too many chances of running into cops Connie knew. Ditto for the Chinese restaurants, hot dog stands and pizza joints.

"There's a great Indian dive on East Sixth Street that's strictly vegetarian," Connie suggested. The odds of running into a cop or firefighter chowing down sprouts were about the same as finding one at a foreign-film fest during the Super Bowl.

"Vegetarian Indian it is," said Georgia. Randy Carter groaned from the driver's seat. His concept of ethnic food was a slice of pizza and an egg roll.

· · ·

The New Delhi Delight was in the semi-basement of a brownstone on East Sixth Street. Sitar music played over the speakers and peppery incense filled the air. A waiter put two dishes of yogurt and chutney in front of Carter, and he stirred them with a fork as if looking for something that would—once and for all—convince him to forgo the meal.

Connie arrived late. With the exception of her job, she was always late. Georgia expected Carter to tap his watch and frown when she arrived. But he just stood and grinned like a schoolboy at the tall, buxom, butterscotch-colored woman in the brown silk pants suit. Clothes hung on Georgia. On Connie, they cleaved, and she knew it. It was rare for Connie not to walk into a room and leave a trail of men wanting her phone number.

"Hey, girlfriend!" Connie called out. She gave Georgia a hug which, given Connie's seven-inch height advantage, caused Georgia to be dinged in the chin with a shoulder bag large enough to carry the GNP of a small Caribbean nation.

"You're looking mighty fine, Detective," Carter offered shyly. He held out a chair for Connie, something he never did for Georgia. Not that she wanted it, but *what the hell?*

Georgia looked down at Connie's open-toed Ferragamo pumps. The color of desert sand, they were shiny and faceted like the skin of a lizard. They were among Connie's favorites. Georgia couldn't resist a dig.

"What is it with you A and E cops?" she ribbed, feeling very short and pale and ordinary, as always, in her best friend's presence. "You wear shoes like you're walking a fashion runway instead of working an arson beat."

"These?" Connie took a seat and pointed her toes so that the small gold shoe buttons above her Day-Glo orange toenails caught the light. "You've seen them before. Besides, the only place I'm going after lunch is up to Rodman's Neck. I don't need combat boots for that."

Rodman's Neck was a jetty of land off the tip of the East Bronx. The NYPD's firing range was up there. It was also where the police bomb squad disposed of illegal fireworks and explosives—a fact not lost on Georgia.

"You confiscate some M-eighties today?" Georgia asked, hooking her own thick black work shoes around the legs of a chair. They were still filthy from the morning's predawn romp through Louise Rosen's apartment.

"And a whole lotta stuff besides," said Connie.

The waiter came, and Connie ordered for all of them. Although she never cooked—even microwaving was beyond her—she was an adventurous eater, and she relished explaining the dishes. When the waiter left, Georgia laid out the morning's events—the fire in Louise Rosen's apartment, Arzuti and Willard's unexpected change of heart about the case and the rumor about the bomb. She said nothing, however, about Rosen's connections to the FDNY, her negative tox screen or the boxes of medical records Carter had taken from her apartment. Nor did Connie pump her for information. They were both cops. They knew the ground rules here: the Rosen fire wasn't Connie's case, so technically, she couldn't compromise it. But it *was* Georgia's, so anything Georgia shared was a definite breach of confidentiality.

Fifteen minutes into their discussion, the waiter brought over a tray of food. Carter frowned at the white cubes of goat cheese floating in a curried broth of broccoli rabe, chick peas and curry.

"It's *supposed* to look like this?" he asked the waiter. He poked a fork at the goat cheese as if it were alive.

"Yessir. It's very good, sir."

Connie shrugged off her jacket and shook her head at Carter as the waiter left. "There's life outside of barbecue, you know, Randy," she teased him. She took a few bites of her eggplant dish and nodded with satisfaction. Then she put down her fork and leaned forward.

"Willard and Arzuti don't talk to me, so what I know, I just overheard," explained Connie. "Seems after Willard and Arzuti left on the initial call, word came down that the mayor's office had received a tape in the mail—from someone threatening to blow up the Empire Pipeline."

They all took a moment with the news. Mention fuel pipelines to average New Yorkers, and they'll picture miles of steel snaking across the Alaskan tundra or fanning out over dry, dusty plains in Texas and Oklahoma. They can't conceive that the same line of liquid fire could gush just a yard beneath their feet.

But it could. And Georgia—like every firefighter and cop in A and E—knew this and was trained in it. Empire carried two fuels over its lines—gasoline, and something even hotter and more tenacious: JP4. Jet fuel. A highly refined form of kerosene. As a firefighter, Georgia had sat through endless drills about how to stop a pipeline leak and fight a flareup. You could never be too prepared when it came to a river of gasoline or jet fuel that could take out an entire city block on the embers of a cigarette.

Connie finally said what they were all thinking. "Man, that's always been one of our worst fears at A and E. That pipeline's a disaster waiting to happen."

"Are they taking the threat seriously?" asked Georgia.

"From what I can tell, yes," said Connie. "Lots of meetings between our commander, Lieutenant Sandowsky, and the mayor's office. Lots of conferences with pipeline engineers."

"But I still don't get it," said Georgia. "What's this threat against the pipeline got to do with Dr. Rosen?"

"I think the blackmailer said something like 'Ask Dr. Rosen about me.'"

"Could be any Dr. Rosen," noted Carter.

"I know," said Connie. "There must be at least a hundred in New York. I think Willard and Arzuti are spending the afternoon tracking them down. But when *this* Dr. Rosen turned up badly burned, it kinda gave them pause."

"How are they figuring her?" asked Georgia. "As the target? Or part of the plot?"

"I don't think they've gotten that far yet," said Connie. "All I know is, nobody wants to take any chances in the city these days."

They all went silent. No one touched the food.

"I wish we knew if Louise Rosen was the 'Dr. Rosen' from that bomb threat," Georgia said finally. "If we could've talked to her before

she died, maybe we could've narrowed down the possibilities. She's retired, so it's not even like we could check with her patients or col-
leagues . . ."

"Dana," Carter muttered, as if in a trance. Connie and Georgia gave
him puzzled looks, so he elaborated. "Charles Dana—Louise Rosen's
former medical partner. The name just came to me."

"You *knew* Louise Rosen?" Connie asked Carter.

He shook his head and fumbled about for an explanation. "Just something I saw in her apartment." Carter wasn't about to mention the fire
department connection to Connie—not without more evidence, at least.

"Excuse me, ladies," he said, rising from the table. "I need to make
a call."

Carter left the table, and Connie studied Georgia. "You all right,
baby girl? You look exhausted."

"It was a tough night," Georgia admitted. "And it's not over, I guess.
But I still want to help you study for your sergeant's exam later." She
noticed a Band-Aid on the inner crook of Connie's left arm. "You give
blood today?" she asked.

"Give it every day," said Connie, shrugging off her concern. "Don't
worry about my exam. You need rest more. Or a little road therapy with
Dr. Harley."

Georgia smiled at the thought of her Harley-Davidson Softail Cus-
tom, parked in the narrow lot next to Manhattan base. Then she shook
her head.

"Actually, Con," said Georgia, playing with her fork. "I kind of need
to talk to you more."

"Uh-oh," said Connie, tucking a wad of frothy black hair behind one
ear that sported three or four pierced earring holes. "Man trouble, job
trouble, mother trouble or kid trouble?"

"Is it always one of the above?"

"No. Usually, it's three out of four."

Georgia felt herself bristle slightly at the truth behind Connie's
words. It was Georgia who usually ran to Connie—not the other way
around. Though Connie was a year younger than Georgia and childless,

her toughness and self-assurance made her seem so much older and wiser. There was an effortlessness to Connie that Georgia envied—not least of all because Georgia found that kind of decisiveness and grit so hard to muster in herself.

Connie pressed a glass of water to her full, cocoa-colored lips. "It's Mac, isn't it?" she asked, putting the glass down without drinking. "What's he done, the pig?"

"Maybe everything. Maybe nothing," Georgia sighed. "I think I'm pregnant."

"You take a test?"

"The kits say you have to wait ten days after a missed period. I'm only eight days late."

"Eight days doesn't mean you're . . ."

"—I'm never late. And my breasts are sore. And I've got this funny tingling around my nipples that I haven't experienced since I was pregnant with Richie—"

"But you're on the pill, right?"

"No. It makes me gain weight. I've been using a diaphragm, but one night, I forgot and I didn't want to tell Mac, so I just winged it and . . ."

"—Shit," Connie muttered. She played with the Band-Aid on her left arm.

"Yeah. Shit."

"Have you told him?"

Georgia shook her head. "We've only been together four months. Aw, man." Georgia held back a catch in her throat and massaged her temples. "I can't go through with another man what I went through with Rick. It was horrible. I can't raise another child alone."

The two women sat in silence for a moment. Finally, Connie spoke.

"It's not the Dark Ages, girl," she offered gently. "You're not trapped— you know that, don't you? I . . ." Connie fiddled with the leather wristband on her watch. ". . . I've been there. I'd help you through it."

"You've *been* there?" Georgia stared at Connie, unable to conceal her astonishment. They'd been friends for eight years. Hell, the word *friends* didn't even begin to cover it. One weekend, when Richie was two and a half and Georgia's mother was away, the child had a temper tantrum over a bowl of peas. Georgia, physically and emotionally exhausted from being a brand-new firefighter, lost it. She screamed and cried and seriously considered giving Richie up and just walking away from the idea that she could ever cope with being a single mother.

It was Connie who saved her that night—Connie who came over, scraped up the peas and broken dishes, gave Richie a bath and put him to bed, made Georgia go for a run and then talked to her until three that morning. Since that time, there was nothing the two hadn't shared with each other—or so Georgia had thought. Yet here was something Connie had chosen to hold back.

Did she think I would judge her? Georgia wondered. She longed to ask her friend a million questions: *When? How old were you? Was it with your ex-husband?* Connie had had a brief, childless marriage at nineteen that she seldom spoke about. And there had been one other serious love in her life—a man she'd met through her job, about two years ago. But that, too, was short-lived and had hurt Connie so deeply, she never told Georgia his name.

Georgia started to speak, but Connie cut her off. She seemed to know what was coming.

"The details don't matter, baby girl," she said gently. "It was a long, long time ago. I'm just trying to tell you that I'll be here, no matter what." She patted Georgia's arm and smiled. "That's more than either of us can say about the men in our lives."

Carter walked toward them now, grinning and waving a piece of paper in their faces. Like most men, he had trouble picking up cues between women and simply assumed that his mood would be theirs.

"Got it," he said with satisfaction. "Rosen's old medical partner, Charles Dana, lives in Riverdale, up in the Bronx."

Georgia pushed her plate aside and tried to do the same with her jumble of emotions. "Did you call him?"

"Yes. There was no answer. But I understand he's not in great health, so the odds are good he's probably close to home."

"Let's take a ride up," said Georgia.

Connie rose from her chair, looking alarmed. "Girlfriend, you go up there and start asking this Dana guy about a bomb on the Empire Pipeline, Arzuti and Willard will have my head. They'll *know* where you got it from."

"We wouldn't do that," Georgia assured her. "Not that way. And besides, you didn't tell us about Dana."

"But you don't know what you're walking into," Connie argued. "You don't know how or even *if* Rosen's death is related. It's dangerous—and it's going to come back to me. I just know it is."

"You have our word," Georgia promised. "We won't mention this lunch to anyone."

Carter frowned at the dishes on the table. "This was lunch?"

. . .

RIVERDALE IS A tiny enclave in the Bronx, hemmed in on the south by Manhattan and on the west by the sheer cliffs overlooking the Hudson River. Though it occupies acreage within the city limits, Riverdale shares little else with the rest of the borough. Its citizenry is largely white and affluent, and they live in a mix of stately homes and elegant high-rises.

Georgia consulted her Hagstrom's map of the borough now, and cursed the roads that seemed to meander and dead-end without warning. "I like Manhattan and Queens," she muttered. "The street numbers make sense. You turn right three times, you're back where you started. Here, we do that, we could be in Jersey."

"The scenery's pretty, at least," Carter noted as they drove along narrow streets filled with ancient oaks and a profusion of rose vines and lavender wisteria. Each house was different and more magnificent than the last: palatial Tudors with their dark timber beams and slate roofs. Spanish villas decked out in red tile. Brick Georgians with palladium windows and gated entranceways hemmed in English boxwoods.

"Tell you one thing," said Carter. "Dr. Dana had bread *before* he started doing One-B Board medicals for the FDNY. Which just burns me up when you think of all the guys on the job he shafted—guys who didn't have enough disability pension to pay their mortgages."

Georgia nodded. Like most marshals, she was occasionally assigned to guard the One-B Board hearings—a precaution installed back in 1987 after a distraught firefighter, turned down for three-quarters, fatally shot one of the pension board doctors. Some of the firefighters who came before the board were schemers and drunks—people who never deserved the job in the first place. But there were others who stuck out in Georgia's mind long after their rejections: haggard men who shuffled and limped, who were swollen up on steroids or rail thin with cancer. She recalled the wives most of all. Many left crying.

"Did you know any hard-luck cases personally?" asked Georgia.

Carter was quiet for a long spell. Georgia assumed he wasn't going to answer the question. Then all of a sudden, he murmured a name. "Danny Maguire."

"You worked with him?"

"Uh-huh. When I was a firefighter up in Harlem in Twenty-eight Truck. Salt of the earth, Danny. First in the building at every fire. He couldn't cook worth a lick—typical Irishman that way. But he treated me right—never cared that I was black—not like a lot of the others back then. Danny spent his whole career in Harlem and the South Bronx. And that was when the Bronx was burning, man. Twenty, thirty fires a night. No mask, nothing. One day, Danny started having trouble swallowing. Doctors diagnosed esophageal cancer."

"Isn't that line of duty?" asked Georgia.

"Not before the Cancer Bill back in ninety-four, it wasn't," said Carter. "Maguire wanted to stay on the job, but in the end, he couldn't. He went before the One-B Board. Rosen and Dana found out he smoked. They told him that those twenty fires a night he inhaled for years had nothing to do with his cancer. It was that itty-bitty cigarette he puffed a few times a day. "

"Did he appeal?"

"What was he going to do, Skeehan? Civil service law is plain here. The city can pick any doctor it wants to do the medical evaluation and even then, it can veto the findings. The city picked Rosen and Dana, and hundreds of men ended up just like Danny Maguire. They gave their lives and their health to this job, and the job gave them nothing in return."

"C'mon, Randy. A lot of guys get out on three-quarters, and not all of them are legit. What about that marathon runner a few years back? He was a firefighter on three-quarters. And remember when the city cut back on desk jobs, and all the brass at headquarters suddenly came down with job-related injuries?"

"You know the right people, you get the right pension." Carter shrugged. "You're a chief at headquarters shuffling papers, you got a whole lot better chance of getting three-quarters than a guy like Maguire, sucking up smoke every day, doing his twenty in Harlem and the South Bronx."

They found Charles Dana's house at the next bend in the road, behind a dense hedge of forsythia and lilac. Three stories high, it exuded New England charm with its white clapboard siding, columned front porch, hunter green shutters and brick chimneys rising solidly at each end. On the right side of the house, a large oak tree graced the lawn. On the left, set back about twenty feet from the house, sat a two-car garage topped by a cupola with a rooster on a weathervane.

Carter pulled into the driveway, and Georgia noticed now that there were three days' worth of *New York Times* newspapers still in blue plastic wraps at the Belgian-block inlaid foot of the driveway.

"Think he's away?" asked Georgia, nodding at the papers.

"He's not supposed to be well enough to travel."

Georgia raised an eyebrow. "Exactly *how* do you know all this?"

"From a buddy of mine in fire department personnel," Carter explained. "I got Dana's number from him. The less A and E knows about the fire department connection right now, the better."

They got out of the car, and Carter walked over to Dana's mailbox. It was overflowing with bills and supermarket flyers.

"Guess my friend was wrong about Dana being sick and all." He sighed. "Still, we're here. Might as well ring the doorbell."

They followed a brick path onto the front porch. Georgia pressed the doorbell button and peered through the side panes of glass. She saw a large foyer with a sweeping center staircase. The lower half of the walls was covered in white bead board; the upper half in bold red floral wallpaper. No one came to the door, yet she could hear a television blaring. Georgia and Carter traded puzzled looks. The mail suggested he wasn't home; the television suggested he was. Carter tried the handle. It was locked.

Georgia and Carter walked around to a flagstone patio in the rear. Except for the rumble of a lawn mower on the next street, the yard was as silent as a cemetery. No sirens. No car alarms. No teenagers' boom boxes. Just the buzz of cicadas and the caw of black crows at a birdbath. Georgia never realized how much she took the white noise of the city for granted until there wasn't any. The stillness that replaced it had an edgy quality to it, like an amusement arcade off-season.

On the patio, Georgia cupped her hands over the panes of glass at the back door. On a kitchen counter, she spotted a ring of keys with a small black clicker beside it. *The garage-door opener.*

"Who goes away and leaves their keys at home?" asked Georgia.

"Maybe he has two cars and two sets of keys," said Carter. He banged on the back door and tried the handle, but there was still no answer. "Let's go check out the garage."

Dana's two-car garage sat about thirty-five feet from the back of the house. It was sided in white clapboard, with eight windows the size of place mats across the door in front. The windows provided very little light, and it took Georgia a moment to focus. One bank of the garage was filled with old furniture and bicycles; the other, with a black Mercedes sedan. The driver's-side door was open. There was a figure in a short-sleeve collared shirt slumped over the wheel.

"Dana?" said Georgia. "Oh, my God."

Carter whipped out his radio. In a calm voice, he asked fire dispatchers to send an ambulance and a fire truck to Dana's address. Georgia wasn't waiting, however. She ran back to the kitchen door. The garage-door opener was right there—right on the counter. All she had to do was slip the lock on the door and press the clicker to open the garage. If Dana was still alive, maybe she and Carter could start CPR. Maybe they could save his life.

It was a flimsy push-button door lock. *It wouldn't last two minutes in Queens,* thought Georgia. From the corkscrew-sized case on her duty holster, Georgia extracted her Leatherman. She pulled the black handles open and searched through the array of gadgets for the flat blade of a file. Then she slipped the edge of the instrument in between the door-jamb and the wood frame and slowly pushed up. She felt the button give way. With her other hand, she turned the knob.

She grabbed the opener, ran outside, pointed it at the garage door and pressed the big gray button in the center. There was a momentary rumble and clatter as the door started to rise. And then suddenly, after lifting about five inches off the ground, the motor cut out. The door froze in the semiclosed position. Georgia tried the button again. There was a jolt, but no movement. She pressed the button several more times. Nothing happened.

"It's jammed," she told Carter, shoving the clicker in her pocket. She got down on her stomach, hoping that she'd be able to squeeze under the door. But five inches just wasn't enough space.

And then she saw it, in a corner of the garage: a finger's worth of flame. It was dancing across a foam-rubber mattress that was leaning upright against an interior wall. Her heart quickened. She got to her feet. Carter turned and looked at her ashen face.

"What?"

"Fire," she sputtered. Carter looked in the garage windows.

"Lord almighty," he said softly, drawing the words out. He pulled out his radio again. "Ten-seventy-five," he said, giving the code for a working fire and updating dispatchers on the situation. Then he turned to Georgia.

"Give me the clicker," he demanded. Georgia handed it to him. He pressed the button frantically. Nothing happened. Through the garage-door windows, Georgia could see the flames tearing up the center of the foam-rubber mattress now, growing into a plume of bright orange that fanned out across the ceiling of the garage like a palm tree. Gauzy gray smoke danced like fog, filling the upper reaches of the interior in a matter of seconds. Georgia could see Dana's head resting on the steering wheel. *He's dead. He's got to be. He hasn't moved.* The smoke thickened, blanketing the top layer of the ceiling, feeding off the air that was being sucked in under the five inches of door that Georgia had managed to open.

Georgia scanned the patio. There was an outside spigot for water, but no hose. All the hoses were in the closed garage. Carter seemed to be realizing the same thing.

"There's a halligan in the trunk of the Caprice," he grunted as he gave a futile tug on the handle of the garage door. "Bring it to me."

Georgia ran to the car and popped open the trunk. She grabbed the halligan—a crowbarlike prying tool used by firefighters—and brought it back to Carter, along with a shovel for herself. Carter first tried to jimmy the door back onto its gliders. When that failed, he swung the halligan and tried to splinter the door open while Georgia did the same with the shovel. Sweat poured off both their bodies, but the door didn't move. Nothing, it seemed, could compensate for the jammed or burned-out electric motor. The eight windows across the garage door were too small to get into or out of, and breaking them would only feed oxygen to the fire and make it hotter.

The entire mattress was now engulfed in flames, and smoke was banking down as if someone were pumping it with an enormous set of bellows. Soon it would be so thick, it would bury Dana and his car in darkness. Georgia squinted into the car now. Smoke was pouring in through the open driver's side, encircling his body like an enormous python. And then she saw it—a twitch in Dana's right shoulder. The barest tremor in his right arm. He seemed to jolt his head up suddenly, and Georgia thought she heard a raspy, throaty cry.

"He's alive," Georgia choked out as her partner kicked at the door. "Dana's alive. Dear God, what do we do?" Georgia picked up the shovel and bashed it against the door. The garage was surrounded by concrete. She couldn't even tunnel under the five inches of doorway to get Dana out. The heat was building, radiating from beneath the door like an open oven. A curtain of smoke dropped down from the ceiling, blotting out light and air.

Dana tumbled out of the car to the concrete floor of the garage. It looked like an effort for him to move and Georgia couldn't tell if it was the smoke and heat, or some prior condition that was making his actions so limited and jerky. He was a heavyset man, perhaps about seventy years of age with thinning gray hair that was already starting to frizz in the elevated temperatures. His eyes were wild and disoriented, as if he had no idea what he was doing in that garage, much less what was happening to him now. He gagged up black phlegm, then called out in a cry so high-pitched, it sounded like a child's. The skin on his arms began to blister, and his shirt began to melt into his back. Georgia got down on her stomach and reached a hand under the garage.

"We're here, Dr. Dana. Here's my hand. Crawl to my hand," Georgia shouted. But within seconds of sticking her hand underneath the garage door, Georgia felt a sudden, geometric rise in the heat. The pain drove her back.

"What do we do, Randy?" she asked, getting to her feet. "What do we do?"

"I don't know," he said.

Dana, disoriented, began crawling in circles. The smoke had turned black. Already, visibility in the room had dropped to knee level. Chest-high temperatures appeared to hover around five hundred degrees, judging by the mass of metal cans and glass jars on the shelves Georgia could hear popping inside. A broom ignited spontaneously in a corner. So did a lawn-chair cushion and a calendar tacked to the wall. Ghostly wisps of flames flew like lightning across the ceiling, multiplying in number with each passing second.

"He's burning up. He can't find his way," said Georgia. "We've gotta break the windows. He'll die if we don't."

"He'll die if we do," Carter shot back, then looked at her gravely. They both knew that breaking the windows was a two-edged sword. On the one hand, it would temporarily vent some of the smoke and heat trapped inside the garage, and improve Dana's immediate chances of survival. But it was also true that firefighters vent—break windows, cut holes in roofs, open doors—only when they can follow up their actions with water to cool a fire's gases and smother its flames. Here, without a hose line, it was a gamble that would only pay off if the engine company arrived within fifteen to thirty seconds of venting.

"We don't have a choice," said Georgia. She heard a siren rounding the corner. Carter heard it, too. If they broke the windows now, the engine might make it in time to save Dana. "He's dying, Randy. We've got to do something."

Carter swung the halligan and delivered one swift blow to each of the eight single panes of glass. The windows shattered easily. Black smoke streamed out of the interior. For the moment, at least, the heat would abate and visibility would return. Dana might have a chance. Georgia looked to the street, expecting to see a big, fat red fire engine pulling up to the hydrant by the curb. But the siren she'd heard wasn't attached to a fire engine. It was attached to an FDNY ambulance. *Of course,* Georgia realized suddenly. *Carter called for an ambulance first. Dear God. We blew it.* I *blew it.*

She turned back to the vented windows. Black smoke belched from the interior. And then, suddenly, something else began to stream from the garage: jagged orange flames. They crackled and spit as their fingers curled upward to the gutters along the roof. The temperature spiked suddenly, pushing out of the garage with physical force. Georgia heard a roar like a hurricane from inside. Carter hooked his arms underneath Georgia's armpits and dragged her back, away from the doors just as an explosive plume of gas and flames tore through the garage roof, climbing ten feet into the air. In the distance, an air horn sounded a throaty bray. Fifty-two Engine and Fifty-two Truck were finally here.

And it was all too late.

· · ·

ROBIN HOOD FINGERED the grave blanket on the passenger seat of the car. Red carnations, white hollyhocks and yellow freesia—no lilies. Bear hated lilies. Roses, too. They reminded him of funerals. He'd been to enough in his day.

Hood set out on the worn and treeless footpath along an unbroken line of headstones that seemed to tumble right down to the East River, like rows of dominoes just waiting for a push. Calvary Cemetery was quiet on this late Monday afternoon. The grass was so brittle and dry, it crunched underfoot. The sun, so intense earlier, was locked in a prison of clouds, but the glare beneath was enough to make Hood slip on a pair of mirrored shades and a baseball cap.

At the crest of the footpath, Hood cradled the grave blanket and stared out past the field of headstones. Across a thin strip of tin-colored water rose the skyscrapers of midtown Manhattan, undulating in a coating of ozone and radiant heat. Here was the picture-postcard view of the city—the slanted roof of the Citicorp Center, the filigreed Art Deco peak of the Chrysler Building. Here was the whole of Manhattan strutting its lithe and leggy curvature like a bunch of beauty queens at a pageant. For an audience of the dead. Bear would laugh at the irony. He'd spent his whole life in a Brooklyn row house with a view of a granite-block school and a neighbor's jerry-built laundry line. And now that he was dead, he had a panorama any developer in New York would kill for.

Hood squinted down the military-straight row of gray headstones for

Bear's grave and noticed a familiar face squatting before it. Alan Levine. He was barely forty, but he already possessed the round-shouldered slouch and lumpy body of a man much older.

Levine rose slowly, grunting with the heat and the effort. He had large, pale gray eyes that seemed to bulge slightly from behind his thick glasses. When he smiled, as he did now, his full lips, normally compressed into the center of his face, spread like ink on wet paper and tended to sag. The effect was very much like staring at a chameleon.

"Beautiful view, isn't it?" asked Levine, inhaling a deep breath of air that was too still to be refreshing.

"Yeah. Makes you want to croak just to enjoy the scenery."

Levine's bulging eyes crinkled in appreciation. But he wasn't here to shoot the breeze, and they both knew it. If he was trudging around a cemetery in Long Island City on a hot summer afternoon, it was to deliver bad news. Good news, he could've called in over the phone from his air-conditioned office in Brooklyn Heights.

Levine kept his back to the water and stared at the gridlock of cars sitting end-to-end on the boxy gray trusses of the Kosciuszko Bridge. Their honking horns and rumbling engines were far off and dreamy from here, as if this land were already a transport to another world.

"I knew you'd be here today," he said softly, kicking at a small pebble beneath his polished black wing tips. Lawyers' shoes. That was the problem with Alan Levine. Much as he cared, he was, in the end, an outsider. He could never really understand firefighters.

"It's Bear's birthday," Hood grunted.

"I know." Levine eyed the grave blanket. "I debated about waiting a day because of it."

"Bad news is just as bad a day later."

Levine studied the Maltese cross chiseled into the top of the shiny dark gray headstone. Four fluted inverted triangles projecting from a center disk. It was the symbol of firefighters everywhere. He was silent while Hood squatted down and put the flowers on Bear's grave. When Hood rose, he spoke.

"I really tried on this one," Levine began. "It just can't be done. It's been too many years. The paper trail is lost."

"You mean *they* lost it."

Levine offered up a sad, chameleon smile. "Maybe. Then again, everything was filed by hand in those days—medical records, personnel files, work charts, fire reports. There were no computers. Things *can* and *do* disappear. I've seen it happen in other cases."

"No paper trail, no lawsuit—is that what you're telling me?"

"It's more than that." Levine sighed. "After it happened, two of the four companies were closed and the men were scattered. How do you prove that one fire did them all in?"

"Nineteen men are dead, and the twentieth ain't far off."

"Yes," Levine acknowledged. "But dead from what? We've got six different kinds of cancers. We've got Parkinson's and multiple sclerosis and Lou Gehrig's disease, too. And five of those nineteen didn't even die of illnesses you could trace to exposure. Lopasio died in a fire. Parrietto and Sikorsky had heart attacks brought on by clogged arteries. That proby, Mickey, shot himself. And you know about the hit-and-run."

"But all of them were already getting sick. Their autopsies and medical records show that."

"Doesn't matter. They didn't *die* of injuries that can be directly linked to their work as firefighters. That's what a judge will say. And besides, sixty-five other men who fought that blaze are alive and kicking."

"They weren't inside the warehouse. These men were. You sound like the fire department," said Hood.

"I sound like a *judge*," said Levine. "Because I know what a judge will say. He'll say, 'show me the proof.' And there is none."

Hood nodded at Bear's grave. "You're looking at it."

"I'm looking at the grave of a man who suffered and died. And I'm sorry. Truly, I am. But the man in that grave also drank and smoked and went to many, many fires—in the days before most firefighters wore masks. I need more than your grief to make this case stick."

Hood picked up a rock and threw it down the crest of the hill just to see how far it would go. It bounced off a headstone somewhere below. The *plink* echoed across the cemetery. The air was heavy with the odor of rotting vegetation.

"Bear loved the summer—didn't matter how hot it got. He'd take me to Mets games and at night, we'd lie on the roof and count stars." Hood stared out at the East River now, at a passing garbage barge encircled by seagulls, cutting a wide strip through the still, concrete-colored waters.

"They say you can't see most stars in the city sky—they say the lights wash 'em all out. But I remember seeing hundreds." Hood gave a small shake of the head. "Funny, now I look up at night, and all I see is darkness."

"I'm sorry," said Levine. "I know you wanted justice. I wish I could give it to you. But you have to understand that there is no such thing as justice in the abstract. It is merely a compact between men."

"Says you."

"Said the Romans more than two thousand years ago," Levine corrected. "Cities weren't built on justice. They were built on compromise—and the bodies of just men."

A red carnation bud had tumbled on the path. Hood picked it up and used it to make the sign of the cross over Bear's grave, then squeezed the bud so tightly, the red petals oozed through Hood's fingers like blood, dropping at Levine's feet.

"There are other kinds of justice, you know."

. . .

"ALL RIGHT, let's go over this again before Brennan shows up," said Mac Marenko. "I want to be real clear on what happened here."

Marenko paced Charles Dana's kitchen. The house was the only part of the property not crawling with emergency personnel. Georgia was wrapped in a blanket—courtesy of the EMTs who thought she might go into shock. Her blouse was filthy, her pants had a hole in the knee from crawling on the driveway, and the back of her right hand was red with first-degree burns from sticking it under the garage door to try to rescue Dana. She didn't really need the blanket anymore, but like a child, she was afraid to give it up—it was all the security she had.

"You." Marenko pointed at Carter, all business. "You saw Dana in the garage, slumped over the wheel of his car, so you called dispatch—correct?"

"Affirmative," said Carter stiffly. He could be all-business too. "I requested an ambulance."

"And you." Marenko pointed at Georgia. "You were where?"

Georgia gritted her teeth. The bastard hadn't even asked about her burned hand.

"I was with Carter," she said coolly.

"The *whole* time?"

"You want to polygraph me?"

"This isn't personal," he said, fixing his bright blue gaze on her.

"So I've noticed."

"Aw, Jeez," said Marenko, throwing up his hands. "You don't get it, do you? You're in a shitload of trouble for coming up here without authorization. Look, I don't know why, but A and E's crawling all over this one. As is the mayor. They've got special branches of the PD out on the front lawn *I* haven't even heard of. Nobody's telling me anything. And if you hadn't tried to open that garage door, Dana would still be alive."

Georgia shot Carter a nervous glance. In it was an implicit question: *Should I let Marenko know what Connie told us about Rosen and the bomb threat to the Empire Pipeline?* Carter offered the faintest shrug of his shoulders. Georgia read the gesture: *It's your call. Connie's your friend.*

One minute, Georgia felt certain she should tell Marenko. After all, two people were dead. The gravity of that certainly outweighed all else. *And besides,* Georgia reasoned, *I don't have to tell him the information came from Connie.*

But Georgia also reasoned that there may be no connection between these deaths and the bomb threat. And even if there was, A and E was already working it. Telling Marenko—and by extension, Chief Brennan—wouldn't shed any new light on the case. No matter how much Georgia protested, everyone would know the information came from Connie. It would destroy her best friend's career. Georgia couldn't take that chance—not for such a vague and uncertain payoff.

"We were following up on the Rosen case," she told Marenko soberly now. "Rosen and Dana used to be partners." She caught Carter's eye, and he nodded that he understood. There would be no mention of their lunch with Connie Ruiz.

"You couldn't run it by me before you came up here?" Marenko asked.

"You weren't in."

"There's a thing called a pager, Skeehan," he said, tapping the device on his belt. "Use it next time."

"Look, Mac," Carter interrupted, "whether Skeehan paged you or not, I think given the chain of events, our actions were reasonable."

"Reasonable, huh?" grunted Marenko. He peered out the kitchen window at the garage. The little white, clapboard-sided building was a charred, crumbling hulk of its former self. The roof had partially burned away, leaving only blackened rafters. The cupola had collapsed into the garage. The rooster weathervane had somehow disengaged and was lying on the driveway, bent and oxidized orange. Firefighters had finally managed to get the garage door off its hinges. Now, scorch marks wreathed the entrance.

"Where's the garage-door opener?" Marenko muttered without taking his eyes off the garage. Neither Georgia nor Carter answered. Marenko turned to face them.

"What?" he asked. "You gonna tell me the door just decided to rise by itself? Where's the opener?"

Carter shrugged. Georgia knew he still had it. He was trying to protect her.

"It's okay, Randy," she said softly. Then she looked at Marenko. "Carter had nothing to do with this. It was my idea."

Reluctantly, Carter pulled the opener from his front pants pocket and handed it to Marenko. Marenko examined it for only an instant, then tossed it on the counter and cursed.

"Make the explanation good, Skeehan," he said, folding his arms across his chest. "'Cause Brennan is gonna nail our asses to the wall on this one, if A and E and the mayor don't get there first."

"It was on the counter," said Georgia, nodding to the gray granite surface Marenko was leaning against.

"And the kitchen door just *happened* to be unlocked?" Marenko drummed his fingers along his biceps. "It *was* unlocked, right? Please don't tell me you broke in on top of all this."

Silence.

"Look, Mac," Carter pleaded, "forget about the door for a minute. We had a man in a locked garage, slumped over the wheel of his car. It's a clear-cut case of exigent circumstance . . ."

"—In a court of law, maybe," said Marenko. "In a court of law, you can throw around a term like 'exigent circumstance'—tell a jury that life and safety issues overrode any constitutional concerns. But this ain't no court of law. A and E finds out we did anything questionable here, they'll leak it to the media. The press will have a field day telling the

public how a couple of firefighters went to interview a prominent doctor and ended up torching him instead."

Georgia looked at her partner. Carter had nothing to do with her
choice of breaking in. But if she told the truth, Marenko would have to
take it to Chief Brennan, and they would both hang. Carter was maybe
a year away from retirement. She couldn't do anything to jeopardize his
career, any more than she could Connie's.

"The door was unlocked," Georgia blurted out. Marenko looked at
Carter.

"That your story, too?"

Carter froze. Seconds passed.

"It must've been stuck when I tried it earlier," he said finally.

"So," Marenko exhaled, "now all I have to do is make you two look
like you can find the right end of a matchstick."

Carter stiffened. "I've been investigating fires for fifteen years, Mac,"
he said tightly. "I was doing it when y'all were still figuring out which
end of the ladder was *up*."

"Guys, c'mon," said Georgia, stepping between them. "Both of you
go get some air." She practically pushed them out the door, then hung
back in the kitchen, thankful for a few minutes of privacy to try to get
her own emotions under control. Then she walked across the lawn to
the garage. Melted cans and shattered glass littered the concrete floor.
The surface of the Mercedes was now a dull blue-black, pitted and
rusted from oxidation.

There was a dirty white sheet over a figure about five feet from the
garage entrance. Herb Moskowitz from the photo unit was behind it,
snapping pictures. He was a heavy man, and as he trudged across the floor,
it oozed with a slimy mixture of half-melted furniture cushions, paint
cans and leaking fluids from the burned-out sedan. Moskowitz noticed
her looking on just as he was about to remove the sheet covering Dana.

"Hey, Skeehan." He smiled darkly. "Nice day for a barbecue."

"Don't start, Herb," said Georgia.

Moskowitz snapped a flash photo of the hole in the roof. "Hey, if it's
any consolation, the guy was probably a goner no matter what you

did." Moskowitz stepped back for a moment and surveyed the chaos of uniforms and suits trampling across the front lawn, every last one of them with cell phones or radios in their hands.

"I know this guy's a doctor and all, but what gives?" he asked. "I mean, you'd think he was the president the way A and E's going at this thing."

Georgia shrugged, hoping to sidestep the question. "Do our Bronx guys have any idea what started it?" she asked.

Moskowitz snapped some photos of a blackened, pitted metal box on the ceiling. The motor for the garage-door opener. "They're speculating that the tracking for the pulleys got bent somehow and the door jammed. Then the motor overheated and a stray spark found its way onto some scrap pieces of lumber stored above the door, then over to the foam mattress in the corner. Once that happened—with the air coming in from under the garage door, the fuel load of furniture and paint supplies—the conditions were just about perfect for a flashover."

Moskowitz removed the sheet covering Charles Dana. His clothes had mostly burned off, and the heat had turned his skin powdery black. Here and there, the skin had split, showing a pulpy red as bright as a child's cherry popsicle beneath. He was on his stomach, his hands covering his face, his legs and arms bent as if ready to box. The "pugilistic pose," they call it, the result, not of an attack, but of muscle contractions caused by intense heat.

"Too bad whatever made the poor bastard collapse in here in the first place didn't just kill him," said Moskowitz. He snapped a picture of what was left of Dana's face. The eyes resembled overcooked egg yolks.

"'Cause the way he died," added Moskowitz, "I wouldn't wish that on my worst enemy."

Georgia felt her stomach slosh about with queasy uncertainty. The heat, the humidity, and the bitter smell of burning plastic all contributed to her nausea. But none could account for it more than her terrible sense of guilt.

"I've got to get some air," she said, backing out of the garage. At the entrance, she felt a hand on her shoulder. It was Randy Carter.

"Brennan's here," he said tightly. He didn't have to say more. She followed Carter through a tangle of cops and firefighters to the front lawn. A beefy figure in a white helmet barreled toward them.

"In my car," barked Chief Fire Marshal Arthur Brennan, pointing to a black Crown Victoria parked on the front grass with the motor running. Behind it, the crowds and camera crews were two feet deep. The chief caught Marenko's eye across the driveway, where marshals and detectives were scouring the wreckage. "You too, Mac," he called out.

Georgia and Carter trudged as sheepishly as two kids going to the principal's office. At least the car would be air-conditioned. Not that it mattered. They'd be sweating bullets anyway. Marenko fell in behind them. When Georgia looked coldly at him, he gave her the barest wink. She scowled.

"You're not on my list of favorite people right now," she told him.

"I'm trying to save your ass, in case you haven't noticed," he muttered.

Brennan removed his white helmet and got in the front passenger seat. He had a crew cut of thinning silver hair that reminded her of newly seeded grass, and a pro-wrestler's snarl. He ordered Marenko, Georgia and Carter in back. The car was ice-cold, the leather upholstery as chilled as a mountain stream. Georgia wished she could have enjoyed the sensation more.

The chief loosened his tie around his fire hydrant of a neck. The rosacea on his pale, pudgy face was florid in the heat and he looked barely able to contain his rage.

"You two"—he pointed at Georgia and Carter—"are in some serious shit." At least Georgia knew where Marenko got his nifty management style from: the Arthur Brennan School of Charm. "This whole excursion should've been cleared through channels. Now, a prominent doctor is dead, A and E is breathing down my neck and I've got to do the mea culpa shuffle with the commissioner and the PD. You're lucky the door to Dana's kitchen just *happened* to be open, Skeehan. As it is, I'm considering departmental charges."

"Chief?" Marenko interrupted. Anyone else would be shot for doing that, but Brennan was a mentor of sorts to Marenko—in department lingo, his "rabbi."

"I told Carter and Skeehan to interview Rosen at the hospital," Marenko explained. "Carter knew Rosen's history with the department. It wasn't that big a leap for them to track down Dana . . . Hell, I'd have probably given them the go-ahead anyway."

Brennan was silent for a moment. He seemed to be trying to read his protégé. Marenko silently held his ground. The chief rubbed the chapped palms of his hands against each other. The sound of skin on skin was the only noise inside the car.

"I'll take that into consideration," Brennan muttered. "In the meantime, you two"—he pointed at Georgia and Carter—"are going to wrap up the Rosen investigation ASAP. I've seen the medical examiner's report. Rosen wasn't beaten, raped or strangled and we've got no evidence of forced entry. So I want a nice, simple report about a woman who died from smoking in bed."

"But, Chief," said Georgia, dumbfounded, "surely you can't . . . I mean . . . there are some inconsistencies in Rosen's death that we still need to investigate . . ."

"—Skeehan," Marenko cautioned under his breath, "you heard the chief."

Brennan's face turned a hypertensive shade of red. He looked like a balloon that had been overfilled and was ready to burst. "Are you *actually* telling me how to do my job, Skeehan?"

"No, sir. It's just that we don't yet know what started the fire. And with Dana now dead and . . . and . . ." *And the possible bomb threat connection,* Georgia wanted to say, but couldn't. ". . . I just think Carter and I could use some more time to put together our investigation, that's all."

"Well here's a news flash for you, Skeehan," said Brennan icily. "Rosen isn't *your* investigation anymore. As of this time tomorrow, it belongs to the NYPD. Dana's, too . . . So unless you've got some really strong evidence I don't know about, you will write up your cause and origin determination the way I tell you to."

10

. . .

"I'LL DRIVE YOU HOME," Marenko offered. "Carter can take the Caprice back to Manhattan."

"My motorcycle's still at base," Georgia said coolly. "And I can drive myself home, thank you."

"C'mon, Scout." Marenko frowned, then looked around to make sure no one was listening. "Don't get all sore on me here. If this is gonna work between us, you gotta learn to separate what happens *on* the job from what happens *off* it. Hey, I saved your butts back there with Brennan. You should be thanking me, not pissing on me."

"Yeah, well, don't count Carter in your fan club, either." She went to turn away.

"Georgia," he said. He rarely called her that, and the sound of it always brought shivers to her spine. She looked at him now. The bluster was gone. His jacket and tie had been ditched in the car, his white shirtsleeves were rolled up, and there was soot on the cuffs. He looked pretty spent himself.

"C'mon, don't be this way," he pleaded. "You're in no condition to ride tonight. Let me drive you home. You can get your bike tomorrow. You have to come into Manhattan anyway to write up the C and O on Rosen and attend that task force review."

The task force review. Georgia had almost forgotten. Back at the beginning of his administration Mayor Ortaglia had charged the NYPD with the job of tightening security and procedures at city landmarks.

The monthly briefings were held all over the city and attended by a rotating cross-section of area law enforcement personnel. Tomorrow's little shindig was at Grand Central Station, and was run, as always, by A and E. *Oh, joy.*

Still, Marenko was right about the advantages of getting a ride home in his car—she'd be able to split those case files of Louise Rosen's with Randy. The case was theirs for one more night, at least. The two boxes were still in the trunk of their Caprice. She couldn't have gotten a big box like that on her motorcycle.

"I guess I can leave my bike at base tonight," she said.

It was 5 P.M. when Marenko and Georgia left Riverdale. Traffic on the Major Deegan Expressway was bumper to bumper. Georgia stared out the window of Marenko's seven-year-old silver Honda Accord. The late-day sun colored the crumbling facades of the tenements and warehouses a warm shade of ocher. Emaciated models decked out in Benetton and J. Crew floated on huge billboards overhead, oblivious to the gritty streets below.

Marenko cursed the congestion under his breath and fiddled with the radio. The Yankees were playing a doubleheader. Georgia sensed he wasn't really listening, though. From the corner of her eye, she saw him sneaking glances at her, inhaling as if to say something, then tapping his hands nervously on the steering wheel. When he finally did speak, it was with such force that she nearly jumped out of her seat.

"You aren't responsible, Scout," he blurted out. "I know you're feeling pretty down on yourself about Dana right now. But believe me, you didn't do anything wrong."

"Yeah, right. That's not what you said back there." Georgia gave a hard laugh and kept her gaze on the window. They were passing Yankee Stadium now. She could see the white, horseshoe-shaped stands glowing peach in the sunlight, and the flags flapping softly over the blue stadium lettering.

"Listen to me—that was heat-of-the-moment stuff. Truth is, he'd have probably died no matter what you did."

"Forget it, Mac. You wouldn't be so charitable if you knew the truth."

"You think I don't?" At a merge in the traffic, he reached across Georgia's waist, and slipped the Leatherman from a pouch on her duty holster. Then he rolled down his window and tossed it onto the pavement beside the expressway. It landed in a heap of broken bottles and crumpled newspapers. "It's gone now," he said. "Don't do that again."

"Randy told you?"

"He didn't have to." Marenko shrugged. "I figured Carter would have tried the doors to Dana's house. So either a shrimp like you was strong enough to open what Carter couldn't, or"—he winked at her—"you had a little help."

"I'm not a shrimp."

"A cute shrimp." He grinned, the first smile he'd given her all day. She'd almost forgotten how different he looked when he smiled. "Anyway, it's over. And whether you forced the back door—or used the garage-door opener or vented the windows—the results would've been the same. Somebody would've gone in there at some point and started the ball rolling. Or Dana might've pushed the interior button and done it himself. Like Carter said, it's exigent circumstance. So stop beating yourself up."

They snaked past a fender bender in the right lane that had been snarling traffic and picked up speed.

"Mac? Do you *really* believe that two doctors who once worked for the One-B Board could burn to death accidentally in less than twenty-four hours?"

"I *want* to believe it," said Marenko. "Or I want to have a damn good reason *not* to believe it. It's like Brennan said: Either come up with some hard evidence to the contrary, or write up Rosen as accidental."

"But it can't be accidental," Georgia blurted, then caught herself. "I mean . . ." she stumbled about for the words. ". . . what if there's more to it?"

Marenko rested his eyes on her now. "More what, Scout? Such as?"

Georgia unbuckled her duty holster, trying to avoid his questioning gaze. "I just wish we'd had more time, that's all."

"If something's gonna come out that's embarrassing to the FDNY, I'd rather know about it before the cops do." He paused a beat to make sure his words sank in. "But I don't want to hand them *suspicions—okay?* That makes us look bad, and it doesn't catch perps."

Georgia threw her duty holster in back. She didn't want him to read her eyes just yet, so she shifted them to a piece of paper on the rear seat. An invitation of some sort. Printed on a home computer. Pink ice-cream cones and yellow flowers. She picked it up and studied it.

"A party on Labor Day, huh? At your brother Pete's house in Jersey." Georgia did a quick mental calculation. Labor Day was less than three weeks away. "I think I'm off that Monday."

Marenko cleared his throat. "Great. You know what? Right afterward, I'll come see you."

"Afterward?"

"Sure," said Marenko. His voice sounded stiff. "I'll take you and Richie out to eat."

"Oh." Georgia stared out the window. The silence in the car was palpable. Georgia waited for Marenko to say something more, but he didn't.

"Why won't you take me to your brother's house?" she asked finally.

"C'mon, Scout." He made a face. "It's just family stuff—you know, kids, relatives, that sort of thing."

"I wouldn't know about kids, I guess. Or relatives, for that matter. Certainly not yours, anyway."

He missed the dig—or pretended to. They were on the Triborough Bridge, heading into Queens. Georgia saw the low-lying buildings of the Fire Department Training Academy below, next to the smokestacks of the Wards Island Sewage Treatment Plant. A faint smell of rotten eggs permeated the air.

"What's the matter?" Georgia asked finally. "Ashamed of me?"

"Huh?" He frowned at her. "You're talking nonsense."

"You son of a bitch," she said. Tears began to well in her eyes. She tried to blink them back, but that just made them stream down her face.

Marenko looked around, panicked, as if she'd just been shot and was hemorrhaging all over the upholstery. He was definitely one of those men who didn't know what to do when a woman cried. They were a hundred feet in the air, over the East River, heading into Astoria, Queens. Hardly the ideal spot to pull over. "What the hell's wrong with you?"

"Forget it." Georgia palmed her tears and hid her face by looking out the window. "Just forget we ever knew each other."

"Hey!"

On the other side of the bridge, Marenko made a sharp turn off the exit ramp and onto a patch of gravel near Astoria Park. He pulled the car to a screeching halt. The thirty-foot concrete towers of the sewage plant rose eerily across the water. On the boulevard, a few hookers caught the evening commuter traffic, negotiating business through the windows of double-parked cars with dealership stickers from Long Island.

"What the hell's going on?" Marenko demanded. "A delayed reaction to what happened back there with Dana?"

Georgia sucked in her breath, like someone about to plunge down a roller-coaster.

"This isn't about Dana," she managed to choke out.

"What then?"

"Did you ever take me to meet your kids?"

"Huh?" Marenko's black eyebrows knitted together. "They're with Patsy on Long Island most of the time. I only see them myself a couple of weekends a month. And your schedule doesn't always coincide . . ."

"—Did you ever *offer* to take me along?"

"You got Richie to take care of," he shrugged. "Seems to me you don't need to hang around more . . ."

"—Bullshit, Mac. That's not the reason. And you know it. I don't meet your kids. I don't meet your brothers. I don't meet your parents because I'm just recreation to you. Someone you take to the movies and to bed. You don't expect to have any kind of future with me."

"Oh, Jesus—here it comes." Marenko hit the steering wheel. "We've been together what? Four months? And already you're looking to put a noose around my neck." He sank back in his seat and looked at the interior ceiling as if there were a god in the stereo system who could give him the answers. "What the hell is it with women? Isn't being physically faithful commitment enough? I ain't whoring around, you know."

"And I'm not some teenager you can waltz with a few times, then hand off to another partner. I'm going on thirty-one years of age, Mac. I'm not asking you to march me down the aisle . . ."

"—Well, don't." He gave her a hard look, his blue eyes as cold as the North Atlantic in February. "'Cause I've been there, sweetheart. The death-do-us-part crap, the his-and-hers towels, the Lamaze classes, the mortgage, and then the boot and you're looking at an empty fridge and school photos of your kids, and you can't even pitch a ball to 'em anymore without making an appointment."

Marenko ran his hands roughly down his face. He closed his eyes and grunted in disgust—with himself, with her—she couldn't tell. When he opened them again, his voice turned soft, but his words were steely. "I'm not doing it again. Not ever." He shook his head. "If you thought it was gonna be different with me, forget about it. I'm not your guy."

"I think I'm pregnant." The words came out like an exhale. At first, she wasn't sure he'd heard. His frozen silence, however, told her he had.

"You sure?" he whispered finally.

"No. Not yet."

Another long pause. "What're you gonna do?"

"My problem, right?" Georgia gave a bitter laugh. "What am *I* gonna do?"

"I didn't mean it like that." He sighed, then reached across her. She thought he was going to pull her toward him and tell her things would be okay. Instead, he opened the glove compartment and pulled out a pack of Marlboros. He'd assured her three weeks ago that he'd quit smoking. Again.

"Oh great," said Georgia. "Kill yourself with cancer. That'll solve all our problems."

He rolled down the windows. The sulfur stench of the sewage-treatment plant across the river seeped in. Georgia didn't think they showed this particular view of the city in any "I Love New York" ads. Marenko lit the cigarette and took a drag.

"So much for your will power," she sneered.

"Hey," he said angrily, taking the cigarette from his lips. "If I had any willpower, I wouldn't be in this mess."

"A mess for *you*—right? *You've* got a problem. *I'm* the problem. You're just like Rick a decade ago. It's all about you, isn't it?" She opened her car door and got out. She needed air, and this was about all that qualified. She didn't even know where she was supposed to be walking.

Marenko threw down his cigarette and got out of the car. He kept pace beside her, patting the air in an effort to get her to calm down. "Scout, look."

"Get away from me."

"Listen to me. I'm *not* Rick, okay? I won't desert you." He grabbed her arm. His touch was firm and strong. She tried to pull away, but couldn't. He guided her toward him and put both hands on her shoulders, then stared down into her eyes.

"I'm sorry—all right? I didn't know what you were going through. God, it's been a hell of a day for you, hasn't it?" He bit down on his lip and looked away. Words were never easy for him. "Look, I care about you. I do. It's just . . . so sudden, I don't know what to say." He wiped a callused thumb across her tear-stained cheek.

"How about saying I'm your girlfriend once in a while?"

He straightened. "To who?"

"To everyone."

"To the guys in the bureau? After all the time you've put into getting them to take you seriously? You really want me to ruin it for you like that?"

"No," she sighed. "I guess not."

"Besides," he added, "it's nobody's goddamned business what we do together."

. . .

GEORGIA'S SON, RICHIE, was shooting hoops on the driveway of their brick bungalow in Woodside, Queens, when Marenko pulled up to the curb. The ten-year-old's face broke out in a wide grin. He barely noticed that his mother looked like she'd lost a fight with a two-ton wrecking ball.

"Mac," shouted the boy, running to the curb. He was wearing denim cutoffs that fell below his scraped, knobby knees and an oversized Knicks shirt.

"Hey, Sport," Marenko called to Richie. "How ya' doin'?"

Richie tossed Mac his basketball. Marenko caught it one-handed, then whipped it back. Richie dropped it, then chased it across the driveway while Marenko fetched Rosen's files from the trunk. You could tell Richie and Mac weren't from the same gene pool.

"Are you staying for dinner?" asked the boy. "Grandma's making burgers."

Marenko hefted the box under one arm and glanced at Georgia. She couldn't read his expression.

"If you want to, Mac," she offered.

"Connie's here, too," Richie added as he scampered around back to the patio.

Marenko's gait slowed. "She know?" he mumbled, nodding to Georgia's belly.

"My mother? Are you crazy? She's got enough on her mind."

"I meant Connie."

"I mentioned it."

"Christ." Marenko gave her a sour look.

"She's my best friend, Mac. I tell her everything."

"Yeah? She tell *you* everything?"

Georgia frowned, thinking about their lunch today.

"Uh-huh," said Marenko. "That's what I figured."

They walked around to the back of the house. A new above-ground pool took up most of the yard now. Sunlight glinted across its surface like razor blades. There was a concrete patio in back as well, covered by an orange-and-yellow tin awning. Georgia's mother was at the far end of the patio, lifting the lid off the grill and shifting the charcoal briquettes. She wore one of those pink-and-purple parachute-fabric sweatsuits that looked too dressy to work out in, yet too casual for much else.

"Hey, Mrs. Skeehan," Marenko called out in a husky voice. Margaret Skeehan turned and beamed as he put the box down, then walked over and gave her a kiss on the cheek. "I want my revenge on the pool table," he teased her. Georgia's mother was a champion pool player. She won matches not only because she was good, but also because no one ever believed they could get whupped by a fifty-five-year-old grandmother.

"Anytime you think you're man enough," she ribbed him. Marenko had lost a bucketful of pride the last time he'd played Georgia's mother.

Marenko looked across the patio at Georgia. She had hung back by the box of Rosen's case files—she knew her mother would be alarmed when she saw her. "You want me to get you some ice for your hand?" he offered.

"I'm all right," Georgia insisted. Margaret walked over and took in her daughter's torn, filthy clothes and reddened hand.

"My goodness, you're not," she said. She called into the kitchen. "Connie, can you bring out an ice pack?"

The kitchen screen door opened a minute later and Connie stepped out, carrying an ice pack in one hand and a plate of raw hamburger patties in the other. She was wearing a skimpy white tank top and cutoffs. Her hair was pulled back into a ponytail, her full breasts jangled freely and her brown skin looked like warm caramel in the late-day sun. Georgia caught Marenko taking her in and pretending not to at the same time.

"How you doin', baby girl?" asked Connie, putting the platter of meat down and handing her the ice pack. She had just redone her fingernails, too. Day-Glo orange, same as her toenails—a shade only Connie could get away with. "God, I'm sorry."

"Nothing for anyone to be sorry about," said Georgia, cutting her off. She didn't want Connie to think she'd told Marenko about their lunch today. Yet even so, she noticed Connie trying to read something in Marenko's face. Mac felt it, too. He seemed to shrink under that piercing dark-brown gaze. This wasn't about the Empire Pipeline, Georgia realized suddenly. This was about something much, much closer to home.

"How many burgers should I put on the grill?" asked Margaret.

"Five," Richie piped up.

"Uh, four," Marenko corrected. He turned to Richie and tousled the boy's dark, wavy hair. "Sorry, Sport. I really gotta go tonight. Some other time." He made a quick round of apologies to everyone. On the driveway, he shot a couple of hoops with Richie, then gave Georgia a peck on the cheek—not his usual sensual kiss. The absence of his lips on hers made her feel hollow inside. He didn't look back as he drove off.

. . .

"I told him, Con—about the pregnancy, I mean."

Georgia said the words softly later that evening, after dinner. The sun had just set and the sky was still bright—white with a tinge of blue, like an undershirt washed with new blue jeans. Richie and Margaret had gone inside, and Georgia and Connie were sitting at the picnic table under the orange-and-yellow tin awning. Georgia had a huge dark blue binder in front of her, and she was quizzing Connie for her sergeant's exam. From the living room, she could hear snatches of *Wheel of Fortune* blaring from the television.

"I thought you might have," said Connie. "How'd he take it?"

"Let's just say, terminal cancer would've gotten a better reception."
Georgia sighed. "Sometimes I feel like everything I touch, I ruin."

Connie took the binder out of Georgia's hands and pushed it to
one side. "How can you say that? Look at that beautiful son you've got
in there."

"Yeah," said Georgia. "And I almost walked out on him—remember?" Connie was the only person Georgia could ever admit that to.
Sometimes, she had trouble admitting it to herself.

"You were just overwhelmed. You pulled through."

"You mean you *pulled* me through."

Georgia caught the edge to her own voice and looked away, embarrassed. She owed so much to Connie, and yet there were times she felt
more jealousy than gratitude about it. Connie was one of the strongest
people Georgia had ever known. Though she spoke little about her
childhood, Georgia knew it was a sad one marked by her mother's nervous breakdown and a succession of foster homes. Yet Connie had pulled
herself up from that with a grace that seemed almost effortless. In fact,
everything about Connie had a buoyancy and ease to it that Georgia envied, from her relationships with men to her advancements at work.
Connie moved through the roughest seas like all she had to do was kick
her feet and swim, whereas Georgia always felt like she was dog-
paddling the rapids just before Niagara Falls.

"Okay," said Connie. "So I *pulled* you through. Big deal. It all
worked out in the end."

Georgia made a face. She wasn't in the mood to be jollied along right
now. "What worked out, Con? That I ended up almost thirty-one, un-
married, still living in my mother's house?"

"Least you *got* a mother's house," Connie shot back.

"Sorry, Con. I didn't mean . . ."

"—Forget about it. I'm just trying to remind you of all the things you
do have—a home, a child, a good career . . ."

"—Not anymore," Georgia corrected.

"Huh?"

A car alarm squealed somewhere down the block. Georgia rose from the table. She leaned on one of the white wrought-iron awning supports and looked out across the backyard. She could smell the chlorine evaporating from the pool.

"I killed that doctor, Con," Georgia said softly, rubbing a hand down the painted wrought iron. It flaked like dandruff across the concrete. "I used my Leatherman to break into his house to get his garage-door opener. Dana died horribly, and it's all my fault. The Bronx marshals might have covered for me, but Willard and Arzuti will eat me alive over this now that A and E is taking the case over."

Connie didn't speak for several minutes. She lifted one of her long, bronze legs up beside her on the picnic bench and played with a silver chain around her ankle. She'd always loved unconventional jewelry—toe rings, belly-button rings, cuff earrings. She talked about getting a tattoo—one of those thorn garlands around an ankle or a rose on her hip. Georgia tried to discourage her. She thought tattoos looked seedy—especially on women.

"Did you tell Chief Brennan?" Connie asked finally.

"I lied, Con. That's all I've been doing all day. Carter and I said we went up to Dana's because he was Rosen's ex-partner. We never told anyone that stuff you told us about the bomb threat against the Empire Pipeline."

"Good," she said. "Because I've been assigned to the case myself now. I can't have that stuff coming back to me."

"So the bomb threat's for real?" asked Georgia. Connie stared silently at laundry flapping across the backyard neighbor's clothesline. The jeans had baked as stiff as cardboard.

"I can't say. And if you were in my place, that's all you'd say, too."

Georgia laughed. "No worries about that." She flopped back down at the table and pressed a glass of lemonade, beaded with sweat, against her forehead. She fiddled with the silver chain tucked into her T-shirt. "When Brennan finds out I lied to him, I'll be kicked out of the bureau."

Connie reached across the wooden picnic table to Georgia. Georgia thought she was going to pat her arm and tell her everything would be all right. But there was a toughness to Connie's eyes as she yanked out the smooth, shiny black stone on the silver chain around Georgia's neck.

"You remember what this is?" Connie asked, holding the stone up to Georgia's face.

"An Apache's tear," Georgia mumbled, giving Connie a puzzled look. "You bought it for me maybe six years ago when you went to New Mexico."

Connie let the stone fall to Georgia's chest. "Damn straight, girlfriend." Connie's dark eyes took on the same look Georgia had seen the night Connie gave her a heart-to-heart after scraping Richie's peas off the kitchen floor. "It's obsidian," said Connie slowly. "Volcanic glass. Formed by fire. Hard as a rock, yet sharp as a razor if you try to break it. To Apaches, the rock symbolized their bravest warriors who threw themselves off cliffs rather than surrender to the enemy." Connie leveled a finger at Georgia now. "I gave you this necklace not just to *make* you strong, but to remind you that you *are* strong."

"I won't be very strong when I'm pregnant and unemployed."

Connie rolled her eyes. "Don't give me that pity-party shit . . ."

"—Then stop pretending I'm you. I'm not. I can't bend the world to my will. I can't make every man's head turn in my direction or get the guys on my job to treat me as their equal." The truth was tumbling out—though it was a truth Georgia suspected that Connie already knew. "I *wish* I had what you have, Con," Georgia said softly. "I really do."

A hint of a smile—a sad one—played across Connie's lips. Then she cupped a palm over Georgia's unburned hand. "You do, baby girl. You just don't know it yet, but you do."

. . .

It was almost nine by the time Georgia and Connie had talked themselves out and Connie left. Georgia and Richie took turns reading a scary *Goosebumps* story, then she put him to bed and settled in to read through Louise Rosen's case files.

It was tedious work. There were charts and records and memos dating all the way back to 1980. Georgia wasn't even sure what she was supposed to be looking for, but she knew Carter was probably feeling the same way right now. She pictured him in his brownstone living room in Brooklyn, tan walls covered with African artwork and masks, surrounded by the same paper mountain. His wife, Marilyn, was no doubt giving him hell for the mess.

Rosen was meticulous, at least. Her files were dated, and Georgia's box seemed to run through 1987. Carter probably had the more recent FDNY case files. The paperwork had a pattern to it. There would be one or more injury reports, several pages of the firefighter's medical records, and then a determination. *Denied* was usually the word stamped across it.

But there was one piece of paperwork that didn't fit the pattern. It was a memo on FDNY letterhead, dated September 15, 1984. It was addressed to Alphonse Pinelli, chief of the Division of Safety, and signed by Edward I. Delaney, a lieutenant in the same department. Pinelli had long since retired and died. But Delaney had risen to chief of operations. He was now one of the top uniformed officers in the FDNY. Georgia scanned the letter now:

Dear Chief Pinelli:

I am respectfully submitting my findings regarding my year-long investigation into the fire and alleged line-of-duty injuries related to the incident that occurred at 2300 hours on August 21st, 1978, at box alarm 3407 in Brooklyn.

Please refer to the attached medical records, fire reports and work charts for further details of this incident. My report was put together with the help of eyewitness accounts, including detailed records from the captains of Ladder 121 and Engine 203, and firefighter Seamus Hanlon of Ladder 106.

The name stopped Georgia in her tracks. Seamus Hanlon was now the captain of Engine Two-seventy-eight here in Woodside. It was her father's old company. She read on.

As you will see, the men of Ladders 121 and 148, and Engines 203 and 252 have a strong case regarding the aforementioned fire.

Respectfully submitted,
Lieutenant Edward I. Delaney,
Division of Safety

Georgia stared down at the closed copy list at the bottom of the page. She expected the usual cc's to various staff chiefs at headquarters. But the final cc made her pause:

Cc: Director of Operations, Empire Pipeline

Georgia could think of only one reason why an internal fire department report would be made available to someone at Empire Pipeline: *because the pipeline had something to do with the men's disability requests.* She searched the rest of the box but could not find the supporting materials Delaney had made reference to in his memo.

Seamus Hanlon works five minutes from my house, Georgia reasoned. *It's only 10:30 P.M. If he's on duty, I could take a quick ride over there and ask him about this memo.* It would be her last chance to do so. Tomorrow, she'd have to turn this box of records over to Arzuti and Willard.

She called the firehouse. A firefighter informed her that Captain Hanlon was on duty. She should have been pleased. And yet, as she sat on her bed, surrounded by stacks of yellowing files, she felt a reluctance to step inside that firehouse that she couldn't simply shrug off to fatigue or laziness. She called Carter and told him about the memo and her plans to visit Hanlon.

"Are you okay with that?" he asked. "That's your father's old firehouse. I know Hanlon was a close friend of uh..." Carter's voice trailed off. He knew that talking about firefighter Jimmy Gallagher was as painful to Georgia as talking about Cassie was for him. In recent years, since her father's death, Gallagher had become her mother's soul mate and the only steady male presence her son, Richie, had ever known. His death in the line of duty a few months ago had devastated them all.

Georgia fingered the stone around her neck. *Apaches' tears. Hard as a rock. Sharp as a razor.* She swallowed hard when she thought about Jimmy and tried to ignore the odd hollowness that came over her.

"I can handle it," she told him.

. . .

12

ENGINE TWO-SEVENTY-EIGHT was in a two-story red-brick firehouse on a quiet block of mom-and-pop stores in Woodside, Queens. Georgia hadn't seen Captain Seamus Hanlon since Jimmy Gallagher's funeral in April.

A firefighter copied Georgia's name into the company journal—a daily log of the engine's activities, emergencies and visitors, as well as a list of names of the men on duty. Somewhere in this firehouse, George Skeehan's name and the shift that took his life at age thirty-nine were hand-copied into a log.

Georgia gazed past a corkboard of firefighter snapshots to a bronze plaque halfway up the metal stairs. It was a relief cast of her father in a firefighter's helmet and turnout gear, along with the date of the ceiling collapse that killed him. Georgia knew it was there, set into the diesel-smeared white tile wall. But she didn't trust herself to look at it—even after all these years. Some things, it seemed, don't get less painful with time.

Seamus Hanlon's pale blue eyes crinkled softly when he bounded down the stairs and found her waiting for him at the bottom.

"God strike me dead if I don't think of Jimmy Gallagher every blessed day," he said as he hugged her. Georgia could smell the soot of a recent fire on his light-blue uniform shirt. Captain Hanlon was a bulky man, not fat so much as broad, with thick walruslike jowls accentuated by a mustache the color of cigarette ash. His crew-cut hair—the same color—stood up like a wire brush on the top of his head. Coupled with the bags beneath his eyes, it gave Seamus Hanlon the appearance of an over-the-hill boxer with a score to settle.

"How's your mother holding up?" he asked.

"As well as can be expected." Georgia sighed. "She misses him a lot."

"God knows, we all do."

Georgia recalled now that the captain had lost his own wife to cancer not too long ago. "How are you . . . ?" she started to ask, but Hanlon cut her off.

"You work a lot of overtime," he said with a sad smile. "Kids are all on their own now. House is as empty as a bad gambler's pockets." He nodded to the kitchen. "You hungry? We got leftover sausage and peppers from dinner. You're always welcome."

"No, thanks," said Georgia. "I had dinner. But I would like to talk to you—maybe in your office."

He rocked on his feet and jingled some change in his uniform pants. "And I thought you were here to tell me a couple of good Gallagher stories. I could use a few these days."

"Oh, we can do that, too," she said.

He led her up the iron mesh stairs past the bronze plaque of her father. "I wish I'd known him," Hanlon said softly, nodding at the plaque. The face chiseled out of bronze was rugged-looking with curly hair just like Georgia's and mischievous eyes. It was her father, and yet not her father at the same time, and it made her ache the same way old pictures of him did.

"In some ways," said Georgia, "he was a lot like Jimmy."

"That I can believe. I know Jimmy thought the world of your dad."

At the top of the stairs, Hanlon turned into a narrow office across from the firefighters' bunk room. The walls were beige, pockmarked by ink-black smudges and gouges in the plaster that crumbled like glazed sugar. A steel bed frame and a file cabinet piled high with dusty volumes of fire department regulations hugged the wall opposite the desk and computer.

Hanlon flopped into a swivel chair with duct tape covering the rips in the armrests. "Jimmy was a character, I tell you. Most of the time, he worked in Manhattan, but he did a few overtime tours out this way. One time, we had this young kid, Eagan, who was trying to learn the bagpipes. Kid sounded like he was torturing a cat. The guys were going crazy listening to him every tour. They tried hiding his pipes, stuffing them with paper. Kid kept playing. One day Jimmy comes in, hears that God-awful sound and starts singing."

Georgia laughed. She'd heard Gallagher sing. Or rather, try to.

"Jimmy was many things, but he was no Irish tenor." Hanlon grinned. "Kid took the pipes home that night. Never heard another word. We owe our eardrums to an Irishman who couldn't hold a note if it was Gabriel's trumpet and he had both hands wrapped around it."

Georgia smiled sadly. "He was a great man."

"Aye, that he was. As dear to me as my own brother, Michael—God rest both their souls." Hanlon sank back in his seat. They were both quiet a moment. Then he clapped his hands together. "So what can I do you for, Georgia?"

"I need to know about a report you helped Ed Delaney prepare for the Division of Safety. It was back in 1984 when you were a firefighter at Ladder One-oh-six."

He rubbed a thumb and finger across his thick mustache. "That's a long time ago you're talking about."

"Do you remember the report? It had to do with a fire that took place in August 1978 in North Brooklyn."

He picked a rubber band off his desk and toyed with it. "Georgia, what in God's name do you need that for?"

"It has to do with a case I'm working on," she said. "Were you at that fire?"

Hanlon shot the rubber band across the room. He seemed to be aiming for the clock on the wall. It was the kind of goofy thing Marenko would do to distract himself from something unpleasant.

"I was at that fire," he said softly.

"Can you tell me about it?"

He leaned back in his chair and stared at the peeling paint rippling across the ceiling like a bad sunburn. "It was at a warehouse on Bridgewater Street in Greenpoint. My company, Ladder One-oh-six, responded on the third alarm. By the time I got there, it had been turned into an outside operation. The men who went in came out. The rest of us never went in. Chief Nickelson—he was the deputy chief on the scene—he ordered a surround and drown. They brought in the tower ladders and got the job done in under six hours."

"Did the Empire Pipeline have anything to do with the fire?"

"I seem to recall that they thought a leak in the pipeline might have touched off the blaze. It ran near the warehouse, I believe."

"Were any men injured at that fire?"

Hanlon raked the back of his hand across his lips. His pale blue eyes had a razor's edge to them. "Nobody went sick at the scene, if that's what you mean."

"How about later?"

Hanlon's face grew dark. He palmed the bags beneath his eyes. "It was a long time ago, Georgia. The men are dead. Can't bring 'em back. Nobody really knows what happened that night. Leave it be."

"Why?"

"*Why?*" He stared at her now. "Because I busted up my liver *not* leaving it be. Almost lost my job."

"Over the fire?"

"Nah." Hanlon got up from his chair and walked over to the room's only window. The bottom half had an ancient air-conditioning unit inserted into it with plywood fitted around the casing. It rumbled like an elevated train. He stared out at a potholed street.

"A lot of stuff started happening in my life right around that time." Hanlon didn't meet her gaze. "Things got out of control. Lieutenant Delaney—*Chief* Delaney now—he helped me shake the monkey off my back, if you know what I mean." Hanlon turned to her now. "I've been sober fifteen years," he added with a nod that suggested it was still a battle of wills every day.

Georgia recalled faintly that Jimmy Gallagher had referred to Hanlon as a "hellraiser" in his youth. "Hellraiser" was Gallagher's gentle euphemism for an alcoholic.

"It happens to a lot of guys on this job," Georgia reassured him.

"Yeah, well..." Hanlon sighed. "I want to help you, lass. For Jimmy's sake. For the memory of your father. But this fire—I don't really recollect the details anymore. And I'm not sure I want to. It was such a long time ago."

"Do you know if any firefighters applied for line-of-duty disability pensions as a result of that fire?"

"Applied? Yes. Received? No. There were these two doctors back then." Hanlon made a face. "We called them the hitmen of the One-B Board. They turned down line-of-duty pensions like they were St. Peter at the gates of heaven."

"Louise Rosen and Charles Dana," said Georgia. Hanlon started.

"Yeah," he said warily. "How did you ... ?"

"—They both burned to death within the last twenty-four hours."

"Holy Mother of God. Accidental?"

"We don't know yet," said Georgia. She wasn't about to divulge specifics that might compromise the case. "But that's why I'm here. Would you know any firefighters who'd want to do something like that to them?"

"No disrespect to the dead, lass, but I could fill a union hall with the men who got shafted by those two."

"Any particular names pop out?"

"It was so long ago. I just don't remember anymore."

"How about the report you helped prepare on this warehouse fire back in 1984?" Georgia pressed. "Is there any way to get a copy? All I have is Ed Delaney's cover letter."

"I'd have to go through Delaney, and right now, I'd feel funny asking him," said Hanlon. "You've heard the rumors, right?"

Georgia gave him a blank look. She'd been a little preoccupied for rumors.

"Word is, Chief Delaney is Mayor Ortaglia's top pick to replace Lynch as fire commissioner. I don't think this is the time to ask him about the report." He saw her crestfallen face. "I still have a couple of contacts at the Division of Safety," Hanlon offered. "Maybe I can get *them* to dig it up for you."

"That'd be great," she said.

Downstairs, near the door to the firehouse, Hanlon grabbed a photo off the corkboard and pressed it into Georgia's hand.

"For your mother," he said, then turned and hustled back up the stairs as if he didn't trust himself to say more.

When Georgia got outside, she looked at the snapshot. It was of a group of men and boys on a fishing boat on Long Island Sound. Their names were scribbled on back. Irish names, mostly: *Hennessy, Dugan, O'Rourke, Mahoney*... Seamus Hanlon was there. He looked about ten years younger. His jowls were less fleshy, his hair less gray. His arm was around a shorter, stocky man with hair just beginning to turn silver, holding up a two-foot perch. It was a great picture of Jimmy Gallagher—the way Georgia would always remember him, all sunshine and roguish good humor. Hanlon had given it away for the same reason that Georgia's mother would probably stick it in a drawer and never look at it again. For the same reason that Georgia would not set foot again in Engine Two-seventy-eight for a long, long time.

Some things were just too full of memory to go back to.

. . .

13

THE MORNING LIGHT caught the Federalist columns of Grand Central Terminal at an angle as Georgia crossed Forty-second Street and headed for the doors on the lower level. Above, she had only the vaguest notion of the symphony of arches in steel and glass. But even when she didn't let her eyes wander to the canopy of marble above her, she always sensed she was in the presence of a great building.

There were taller, more opulent New York buildings than Grand Central Terminal. Yet those were built primarily as monuments to the greed of men or the fear of God. Here was a building laid out nearly ninety years ago for a practical purpose—to move people and goods into and out of the largest city in the world. It was an engineering feat as much as a work of art, for beneath the Beaux Arts stone exterior lay a two-and-a-half-mile stretch of tunnels, some at a depth of as much as a hundred feet—ten stories below street level. It had taken ten years to build Grand Central Terminal. And when it was done, nearly three million cubic yards of the city's bedrock had been excavated—enough landfill to put a new island in the East River.

A crush of morning commuters streamed through the doors on their way to midtown office buildings. Georgia was one of the few rushing in the other direction. She walked down a short flight of stairs to the main concourse. Pale, peach-toned marble shone beneath her feet. One hundred and twenty feet overhead, a sea-foam green ceiling sported the bronze zodiac constellations of a New York sky at dusk.

She walked through the nearly football-sized concourse, past a sweeping marble staircase and sixty-foot windows, to the stationmaster's office. The task force meeting was supposed to start in a conference room there at 0900.

The conference room had none of the grandeur of the main part of the building. The ceiling was low, the walls, Sheetrock. There was a portable chalkboard at one end of the conference table and a coffee machine at the other. In between were several faces Georgia recognized and several she didn't. Carter was there. So was Fire Marshal Eddie Suarez. He was a compact man with a weight lifter's bullish torso and a black mustache that probably dipped a half inch below department restrictions on facial hair. But Suarez was one of the bureau's best marshals, so nobody said a word.

Suarez was seated next to his new partner, a newly appointed fire marshal whom Georgia hadn't met yet. He had to be about her age, though there was still something unformed and boyish about him—as if his cheekbones and jaw were still waiting to burst through a late adolescence and give his face definition. He rose from the table and extended a hand.

"I'm Andy Kyle," he said. "You must be Marshal Skeehan." He looked her in the eye. Firefighters rarely did that on a first meeting. Some were too shy to. Some were too busy looking at her breasts. And some just couldn't get it through their heads that a woman could be their equal.

"Georgia," she offered, shaking his hand. There was no swagger about him, and yet there was a confidence there that she found fascinating. She could see it in the thrust of his hand, the crisp, clean way he pronounced his vowels, his simple, understated choice of linen jacket and silk tie. Andy Kyle wasn't your typical firefighter.

"I've heard a lot about you," he told Georgia.

"I was afraid of that," she said, only half kidding. He laughed.

Georgia grabbed some coffee and took a seat beside Carter. In front of every chair was a booklet of photocopied Grand Central emergency procedures. She thumbed through hers now and smiled when she got to a memo concerning evacuation. The preparer was listed as C. Ruiz. *Connie.*

"Your girlfriend," said Carter, nodding to the name while he sneaked glances at a *New York Daily News* under the table.

"Yours, too," she teased him. He acted as if he had no idea what she was talking about. He would never admit he had a crush on Connie.

Georgia peeked at the article Carter was reading on his lap. It was in the sports pages. *No Place Like Home,* read the headline. Beneath it was a color photo of a man in an expensive suit with prematurely white hair. Carter caught her eyeing the article.

"Says here," he mumbled, "that the city's looking to build the Jets a football stadium of their own." Carter was a big Jets fan. Marenko loved the Giants. At least *that* rivalry was a friendly one.

"Who's the white-haired guy?" asked Georgia.

"Some dude from the mayor's office in charge of land acquisition." Carter pointed to the name, but didn't attempt to pronounce it: *Gus Rankoff.* He was listed in the article as Mayor Ortaglia's economic development advisor. Carter folded the paper and placed it on the table now. The session would soon be starting.

"How'd your visit with Hanlon go last night?" he asked her.

"Hanlon didn't remember much about the fire," said Georgia. "He's going to try to track down the original report for me through the Division of Safety. But it may not come before we have to turn the whole case over."

The door to the conference room opened now, and two men walked in. The first was a short, egg-shaped man with a face too small for his body and hair so black, it looked as if he dyed it daily. He wore a navy blue suit that looked like a designer's cut, yet he hadn't bothered to get it properly tailored, with the result that the pants were a little too short and the jacket sleeves too long. He introduced himself in a soft, monotone voice as Lieutenant Sandowsky, commander of the NYPD's Arson and Explosion Squad. The second man didn't have to introduce himself. Georgia stiffened at the sight of the thick red mustache, the blond hair receding at the temples and the thickening gut over the waist of his pants.

"Well, well, if it isn't Starsky and Klutz," said Chris Willard with a broad smile on his face. "I understand they couldn't scrape Dana off the floor when you were done with him. We find any screwups you *haven't* told us about, we'll be sure to let your chief know."

"I'm sure you will," said Georgia stiffly.

"Do me a favor, Skeehan?" said Willard. "Next time you feel like investigating a fatal fire, try getting a guy who's fatal *before* you meet him."

The men at the table snickered. Georgia searched for a snappy comeback, but couldn't find one. There was nothing funny about the image she had in her head of Dana on the floor of that flaming garage, crawling toward her, his skin hanging from his burning arms. There was nothing funny about the possibility of Brennan kicking her out of the bureau for breaking and entering, either.

Willard must have sensed he'd gotten to her—just like at the burn unit the other day. He smiled viciously as he pulled out a butane lighter and flicked it on. "Hey guys," he said, nodding to the flame dancing above the lighter. "You know what this is? A witness who just talked to Skeehan."

"You know, Detective," a voice piped up over the guffaws, "I think Marshal Skeehan is dealing with enough grief over this incident without you getting your laughs at her expense."

The table of heads turned. Georgia's mouth dropped open. Andy Kyle was either the bravest or the dumbest fire marshal she'd ever met.

"Her *expense?*" Willard mocked the word now, gave it a slight feminine lisp, as Georgia knew he would. "Who the *fuck* are you, kid?" Somebody murmured the answer, and Willard's eyes became slits. "Oh, the little Yale college boy from Scarsdale playing fire marshal. Family's in tight with the mayor, Daddy's some hotshot lawyer, so you think you can say whatever you want. Well, *fuck* you. I don't give a damn about your family *or* your money."

Kyle leaned forward in his chair, unfazed by Willard's bluster.

"You got a problem with me, Detective, take it up one-on-one. I don't hide behind my family," said Kyle, looking about the room. "Don't hide behind yours."

"Now guys, guys," said Lieutenant Sandowsky, rubbing a hand nervously over his shoe-polish hair. "Let's cut this out and get down to business."

The rest of the lecture passed by in a blur. All Georgia could think about was the confrontation between Willard and Kyle. Although Georgia was sure that Kyle meant well, his misguided attempt at chivalry had given Chris Willard all the motivation he needed to sink her career.

On their walking tour of Grand Central, Georgia pulled Kyle aside. They were on a platform with unfinished concrete walls, lit by construction bulbs. Kyle had just unwrapped a stick of gum. He held out the pack to Georgia, and she declined.

"Look, Andy," she began. "I know you were trying to help back there. And I appreciate it. But please, in the future, let me handle my own problems."

Kyle crumpled the wrapper. They were on the platform by themselves now. The group had already descended a yellow metal staircase. "But that detective . . ."

"—is a son of a bitch," Georgia cut him off. "But you took a momentary embarrassment and turned it into a permanent grudge. Willard's going to go out of his way now to highlight any screwups I made on the Dana case."

"I'm sure you didn't make any screwups," said Kyle. He dropped the foil gum wrapper onto the platform. Georgia frowned.

"That's your first mistake: to be sure of *anything* on this job." She picked up the wrapper and stuffed it back in his hand. "And by the way, this it metal. Anything metal gets under the third rail, it can short the whole track out. So don't make assumptions."

Kyle looked at her for a long moment. Then he shook his head at the wrapper in his hand. "I guess there's a lot I don't know yet, even after five years as a firefighter." He took a deep breath. "Look, Georgia, I said what I said because I don't like to see people pushed around. That's my father's style, and I hate it. It's not mine."

"I wasn't *being* pushed around," she insisted. "Not really."

"I'm sorry. I guess I misinterpreted the situation."

Nobody from Woodside ever used words like *misinterpreted.* Georgia wondered how two people could grow up in the same twenty-five-mile radius from Manhattan and speak so differently.

"Fair enough," said Georgia. "Then let me give you some advice: Keep your mouth shut and your ears open. Don't solve other people's problems. And don't apologize. The guys I work with save 'sorry' and 'thanks' for the really big stuff. The rest of the time, they speak in four-letter words."

"Okay, sor—Gotcha."

"That's better."

They caught up to the group just as they were heading back to the bustling concourse. Carter pulled Georgia to one side.

"Willard's gonna be looking for every opportunity to stick it to you after that little episode this morning."

"I know," said Georgia. "Did he at least give you an update on the Dana case?"

"I got diddlysquat from both him and Sandowsky," he told her. "But I heard Sandowsky talking on his cell phone at one point, and it sounded like the PD's got guys all over JFK and LaGuardia airports looking for something . . ."

"—The Empire Pipeline runs to both airports," Georgia reminded him.

"I know, but they said nothing to me. All I know is, they still want our cause-and-origin report on Rosen by six P.M. today."

"We're gonna look like idiots putting that report together with nothing to go on."

"Nobody's giving us anything," said Carter. "Heck, Brennan's so eager to wrap this up, I keep thinking somebody ordered him to minimize the publicity on this thing."

"Maybe they did," said Georgia. "But our names are still going on that report. You think perhaps someone at the crime lab could help us?"

"Couldn't hurt to pay them a visit after this," said Carter. "Speed things along." He touched her elbow and nodded to one of the men in their group. Georgia had noticed him when they first sat down in the stationmaster's office. He was a handsome man in his mid-thirties, a little hefty, but with a nice head of blue-black hair. He spent a lot of the tour talking to Suarez.

"Hey, guess who that is?" asked Carter.

"You got me," said Georgia.

"Nick Marenko—Mac's brother. Suarez told me. The guy just made detective in the PD's transit bureau. Why don't y'all go say hello. Bet he didn't realize who you are."

They were headed back to the stationmaster's office, but Georgia hustled a little ahead and came up on Nick Marenko now. He was tall like Mac, but bigger boned. His eyes were brown, not blue, but in the shape of his face, she thought she saw a family resemblance. She was surprised she hadn't noticed it before, especially when she watched him walk. He had the same, slightly cocky swagger of his brother.

"Detective?"

He turned and flashed her the famous Marenko smile.

"I'm Georgia Skeehan." She thrust out a hand and he shook it. His face was pleasant, but his eyes were flat, like the eyes you give to a waitress taking your order. "Mac may have mentioned me to you," she stammered, hoping to jog his memory.

A tiny crease settled between his black eyebrows.

"You, um, work with my brother?" he asked politely.

He doesn't know who I am, Georgia realized with a jolt.

"Yeah, I . . . I was on that big case with Mac several months ago."

"Sure," said Nick, smiling. "I remember that case. The Spring Street arson, right? I think I saw you on television."

Georgia waited for some further spark of recognition, but there was none. She searched for a graceful retreat. "I . . . I just wanted to congratulate you on your promotion to detective."

"Oh . . . thanks. I think Mac's out on Long Island today, but I'll tell him I saw you."

GEORGIA SAID LITTLE in the car as they drove to the NYPD's crime lab in Jamaica, Queens. Carter didn't seem to notice at first. He kept flipping radio stations, seeing if he could find out any more about the Jets football stadium project. The air conditioner was still barely functional, so Georgia rolled down the windows. Somewhere nearby was a bakery plant. Its yeasty smell softened the scent of Dumpsters and exhaust that seeped into the car.

"What's eating you, girl?" Carter asked her finally. "Ever since you spoke to Mac's brother, y'all been looking like you stepped on a honeybee and you still got the stinger in your toe."

"Don't ask, Randy. It's better this way."

The lab was a drab, fortresslike building, made even drabber by a Tuesday-morning sky of dulled chrome and air as tactile as cobwebs. A row of pigeons stared down at them from the roof of an adjoining auto body shop as they got out of their Caprice. Just being here was like a needle prick to Georgia's skin. The FDNY used to have its own lab, run by her good friend Walter Frankel. When he died, the lab died with him. It was at moments like these when she really missed him.

"What's the matter?" Carter pressed as he and Georgia sat in a couple of stiff chairs in the lobby, waiting to speak to the forensic chemist handling the case. "Y'all want more of Mac than he's ready to give?"

Georgia tossed off a small, hard laugh. "I think the problem is, he gave too much of himself already."

Carter frowned in the direction of the lab doors. "You're not pregnant, are you?"

"I should've known, right?" Georgia muttered, picking up a magazine and flipping through it. "Mac'll follow anything that resembles a ball. Stands to reason his sperm would do the same. Probably had John Madden announcing the play-by-play."

"Humdinger of a situation," said Carter, shaking his head. "Here I've been, hoping you wouldn't stick with that son of a gun, and now, I'm gonna have to hope that you do."

"You don't like him much, do you?"

Carter said nothing for a long while. He could do that—live in all that silence and be comfortable with it. Georgia suspected this was a rural trait. New Yorkers considered it tantamount to holding one's breath. Do it for more than four minutes, say, and you'd become unconscious, which to New Yorkers, was the same as being from somewhere else.

"I reckon I always thought you could do better," he said finally.

The doors to the lab opened now, and a short, dark-skinned man with a close-cropped black beard walked toward them. Georgia recognized him instantly as the chemist who'd given that lecture on flashovers in May. He wore a turban on his head the color of port wine, and underneath his white lab coat, the loudest pink-and-green floral shirt this side of Waikiki. He pressed his palms together and nodded his head slightly as Georgia and Carter rose and introduced themselves and explained that they were there on the Louise Rosen case.

"Skeehan, Carter, yes. Your names are familiar," said Ajay Singh. He had a singsong Indian accent that, coupled with his loud shirt, made Georgia think of the convenience-store owner in *The Simpsons*.

"We were at your lecture in May," Georgia explained.

"Yes, yes. Good to see you again. I have just finished reviewing the evidence. Come."

They followed Singh through a maze of windowless hallways and cubicles, all done in government-issue grays and greens. At another door, Singh held up what looked like an ATM card and buzzed them into the lab. There were powder blue tiles on the floors, stainless-steel counters along the walls and banks of microscopes and specimen slides. Singh beckoned Georgia and Carter over to a personal computer.

"Have you done any work with fire modeling?" he asked them.

"Not really," said Carter.

Singh typed in some codes on the computer screen now. "I take the known variables about a fire—the dimensions of the room, the fuel load, the amount of initial ventilation and suspected point of origin—and I plug them into a computer program to try to replicate the fire," he explained.

"Can the fire model tell you what happened?" asked Georgia.

"Sometimes," said Singh. "But where it is really useful is in telling an investigator what did *not* happen. It narrows the possibilities."

"This got something to do with the Rosen fire?" asked Carter impatiently. Randy Carter was old school. He still believed that a smart, experienced investigator didn't need a lot of high-tech gadgetry to solve most cases.

"Yes," said Singh curtly. He had obviously dealt with a lot of old-school cops before. "And I think you will be surprised by what you see, Marshal."

Singh punched in some keys and brought up what looked like a three-dimensional topographical map.

"This is Louise Rosen's bedroom before the fire," Singh explained. He pointed to abstract squares and rectangles of color, representing the doctor's bed, dresser, chair, lamps, window and door.

"In this initial representation, we need to identify the three factors that make up the fire—the so-called fire triangle," Singh explained.

"Heat, oxygen and fuel," said Georgia.

"Correct," said Singh, clearly pleased that he had, at least, one interested party. "Insufficient heat, and the fire won't ignite. Or it will smolder, but not flame. Insufficient fuel and the fire will burn itself out. Insufficient oxygen and the fire won't spark. Or it will die out until it can get more oxygen. Then it will explode all at once into a backdraft. But if you have the right quantities of heat, oxygen and fuel, then the fire will . . ."

"—flash over," offered Georgia.

"Not necessarily," said Singh. "If the room is very large, well ventilated or has a very high ceiling, there will be no spontaneous ignition of all the contents of the room. Things will burn—yes. But in order for a flashover to happen, the gases in the ceiling must be hot enough to radiate back down and ignite other fuel sources not in direct contact with the flames."

"Isn't that what almost happened in the Rosen fire?" asked Carter in a tone that suggested Singh had just used a lot of fancy language to tell them the obvious.

"That's what you *think* happened," said Singh. "But factoring in the ten-foot ceilings, the size of the room and the fire load, it is impossible for a spark in a chair cushion to have produced a fire of that magnitude. Watch."

He pressed a button to start the program. Georgia saw a small orange triangle form in the center of the upholstered corner chair. A timer at the top of the screen recorded the elapsed seconds. Within twenty seconds, the triangle colors started turning a darker shade of orange. Singh explained that the darker the orange on the screen, the hotter the temperature of the flame.

At one minute, a V pattern began to form in the corner of the room as hot gases traveled across the ceiling. The triangles darkened in color and spread across the room. Colored bands in shades of yellow recorded temperatures at different heights in the space. Georgia frowned. The uppermost band showed temperatures of six hundred degrees. Five minutes later, the temperature along the ceiling had climbed by only fifty degrees. It was as if the fire had somehow maxed out—burning briskly but never getting hot enough for the room to flash over.

"I've seen flashovers occur at six hundred and fifty degrees," Carter mumbled defensively.

"Not in this room," Singh corrected. "Factoring in all the variables, I have estimated that ceiling temperatures would have to reach eleven hundred degrees Fahrenheit for a flashover."

A blue dot now appeared on the model and widened. Georgia noticed the temperatures dropping. Singh had obviously programmed in the arrival of the firefighters. The screen froze on this last image. Georgia stared at it in amazement.

"But the room did come close to flashing over," she insisted. "We've got the physical evidence to prove it." She glanced at Carter. He gave her an I-told-you-so look and shrugged.

"That's why y'all should never trust a computer."

"The program does not lie," Singh explained with irritating confidence. "There was not enough fuel load in that chair to start a fire of that magnitude. It is not arguable."

"How about if we assume there were a lot of pillows on the chair?" asked Carter.

"It would alter the outcome very little," said Singh. "For this fire to reach eleven hundred degrees, you would need something with a significant fuel load in that corner."

Georgia tried to picture the room. The chair was near the window. The broken window. A window without . . .

"—Drapes," said Georgia. Singh and Carter looked at her. "Rosen had these floor-length red drapes in her living room."

"But there weren't any in her bedroom," Carter reminded her.

"Because they were in the street, next to the mattress," said Georgia. "I thought they were blankets. But now that I think about it, they looked a lot like the drapes in her living room."

Singh asked her some questions about the drapes and tried to estimate their size and fuel load for his model. He plugged in the variables and ran the program again.

Georgia and Carter watched the orange triangles darken and multiply again. Only this time, they began to grow quickly in size, feeding freely on the upholstered chair, then enveloping the heavy drapes. The yellow bands recorded temperatures climbing above eight hundred and fifty degrees as the smoke banked down lower and lower to the floor. At three minutes, fifteen seconds, the window glass failed. Twenty seconds later, objects in the room began to ignite spontaneously. The room was quickly approaching flashover.

"If the drapes provided the initial fuel for the fire," asked Georgia, "what provided the ignition? There were no electrical outlets, there was no evidence of any accelerant . . ."

"—The candle," muttered Carter, staring at the screen. "It was on the floor, near the window. It could've lit up the drapes—accidentally or on purpose, I don't know."

"What I don't get," said Georgia, "is what kept Rosen on that bed? Her carbon monoxide levels in her bloodstream weren't that high. There was no evidence she was beaten or restrained."

Singh opened a file drawer in the lab and pulled out a small, sealed vial of what looked like water. "I think she may have been put into a temporary coma by this," he said, handing the vial to Georgia.

"What is it?"

"Gamma hydroxybutyrate—GHB. Commonly called the 'date rape drug,'" Singh explained. "I made this batch myself. It's not hard to do. There are recipes on the Internet."

"But Louise Rosen's tox screen was negative," Georgia reminded him.

"The screen was for alcohol and a standard panel of drugs," said Singh. "GHB disappears very quickly from the body. To find it, you have to isolate small samples of tissue and subject them to rigorous testing. I have ordered new tests, but even these may not isolate any GHB. Dr. Rosen was alive six hours after the fire—long enough for the drug to have begun to leave her system."

"What makes you think she consumed any, then?" asked Carter.

"I recovered some GHB residue from a red plastic cap you found in her bedroom. The cap was from a bottle of McCormick's liquid extract," Singh added.

"What the heck is *extract*? asked Carter.

"You know," said Georgia. "When a recipe calls for vanilla or almond flavoring and you measure out a teaspoon or two?"

Carter gaped at her as if she'd just revealed a fluency in Swahili.

"What? I cook," she said defensively.

"Reheating pizza doesn't count."

"You are correct, in any case," Singh told her. "It would certainly explain Rosen's incapacitated state."

Georgia handed the vial of GHB back to Singh. "So our physical evidence, combined with your fire model, suggests that Rosen was drugged and then burned in a fire started by drapes and perhaps a candle—is that right?" asked Georgia.

"That would be consistent with the evidence," said Singh.

"None of that hooey gets us any nearer to finding out whether we got an arson on our hands," grumbled Carter. "Rosen could've drugged herself, then passed out."

"You are forgetting one thing, Marshal," said Singh.

"What?"

"Charles Dana. I am handling the evidence on this case, too. And I think Dana may have also been drugged and intentionally burned."

"Your fire model tell you that?" asked Carter. Georgia could tell he was still suspicious of evidence he couldn't hold between his fingers.

"No," said Singh. "Your Bronx marshals told me that. And I agree. The tracking along the inside of the automatic garage door was bent. The tool marks are consistent with a firefighter's halligan . . ."

"—*We* used a halligan," said Georgia.

"Not on the tracking, we didn't," Carter corrected. "But the firefighters who put out the fire could've."

"No," said Singh. "The marks were covered in soot. That means the damage to the tracking was done *before* the fire. The marshals and I concur on this."

Georgia took a moment to process what Singh was saying. "So you're telling us that Dana and Rosen were both drugged and perhaps intentionally burned, and the torch is someone with a good working knowledge of fire science, who also happens to possess a halligan . . ."

"—In other words, a firefighter," said Carter, completing her thought.

"That would be my conclusion, yes," said Singh. "I understand that Dana and Rosen worked for the fire department and were unpopular with the men. It appears that the police will be concentrating their search in your backyard."

"Backyard? Heck," muttered Carter. "More like up our backsides."

"Yes, Marshal," said Singh, biting back a small grin of satisfaction at finally getting the upper hand. "And you do not even need a computer model to figure that one out."

15

. . .

IT WAS ALMOST SIX P.M. by the time Georgia finished her cause-and-origin report and headed home on her Harley Davidson. The air was muggy, but the breeze flying past her as she shifted from third gear to fourth lifted her spirits. Sometimes the only place she could think was on her bike, with a fistful of engine between her legs and a stretch of asphalt beneath her.

She'd bought the bike eight months ago, shortly after her thirtieth birthday, though, at the time, she'd never been on a motorcycle in her life—much less a monster that weighed over six hundred pounds. Her mother called the purchase "dangerous and irresponsible"—as opposed to Georgia's job, she guessed, which was dangerous and responsible. Friends joked that she was starting her midlife crisis ten years too early. Mac wouldn't let her drive him around the block on it, though Georgia suspected that had more to do with the macho discomfort of having a girl for a chauffeur than with any real concern that she might kill him.

Only Connie was supportive. "You were a single mom before you turned twenty-one," she reminded Georgia at the time. "Maybe you need to cut loose a little now and then." Connie even sprang for a custom-painted rose on the gas tank—"a bike-warming gift," she'd called it. Georgia loved that rose.

Now, as she maneuvered her bike between rows of cars crawling along the Long Island Expressway, Georgia thought about the report she'd just completed. Under the section labeled "determination," Georgia had scribbled, *cuppi*—short for *cause undetermined pending police investigation.* She couldn't call Rosen's death an "accident"—no matter how embarrassing the eventual findings might be to the FDNY. Ajay Singh was onto something, she was sure of it. Though now that the case was out of her hands, she'd never know more.

And yet there was more. She could feel it this afternoon at One Police Plaza, the NYPD's high-rise headquarters, when she dropped off a copy of the report. There was a nervous energy in A and E's ninth-floor squad room. Lieutenant Sandowsky was in a glassed-in office, along with Arzuti and Willard, meeting with serious-looking civilians in suits. Georgia knew they were civilians—there were no telltale bulges of guns beneath their jackets. Other detectives, normally quick with a friendly dig at the rival FDNY, averted their eyes as she passed. When the elevator arrived to take her back to the lobby, a couple of cops in *Bomb Squad* jackets got off on the A and E floor.

Georgia had planned to head straight home, but on impulse, she took a detour through a semi-industrial area on the borders of Woodside and Sunnyside, a mile or so from her house. Instinct drove her to the spot. It was the only place she could think of where she might be able to put her fears to rest.

Half a block from the highway, the apartment houses and bodegas disappeared, replaced by gray, low-slung warehouses, shoe repair shops and mechanics' garages now closed for the evening. Beyond, the Amtrak rail yards rumbled with silver cars full of Long Island commuters.

Georgia turned down a one-way street with a self-storage building on the corner. Just beyond the concrete-block building, a dark blue sedan with an Albany, NY dealership sticker idled in the center of the street, blocking her path. Beyond the sedan, men in suits and yellow hard hats walked the cracked sidewalks, mumbling into radios and waving what looked like metal detectors across the pavement.

Georgia planted her feet on the asphalt and shifted her bike into neutral to coast a little closer. A tall, bony man with a radio in his hand got out of the sedan. He looked to be in his early sixties, with sawdust-colored hair and the kind of thin lips and humorless pale eyes of a college basketball coach. Voices crackled over his radio—flat, twangy voices—not from New York. Certainly not cops, firefighters or Con Ed electricians. *Who were these guys?*

"This street is closed," the man grunted in a bland astronaut's voice. *Definitely not a New Yorker,* Georgia decided.

"How come?" she pressed.

The man frowned at her. An impatient frown, like he was used to being obeyed, not questioned. Even with six hundred pounds of bike beneath her and a helmet obscuring most of her features, she still didn't look very threatening.

"It's being surveyed," said the man.

Georgia searched the cluster of yellow hard hats for a surveyor's tripod. There was none. Instead, she saw a man in a blue blazer leading a German shepherd along a patch of sidewalk. The shepherd sniffed the concrete with the intensity of an addict doing a line of cocaine.

Surveying, my ass, thought Georgia. "Can you tell me how to get to Skillman Avenue?" She knew the way. But since she had no authority to question anyone here, it was the best she could do to buy time.

The man gave her a blank look just as another figure emerged from the dark blue sedan.

"Two right turns and a left on Forty-first," said the second man with the nasal assuredness of a Queens native. He was short and stocky, with a chunky, square-shaped face topped by a shock of snow-white hair. Although his bushy white eyebrows were frozen into something approaching a kindly expression, his dark brown eyes gave off an entirely different feel. Like the blackness of an elevator shaft. She had seen that face before, though she couldn't remember where. The more she studied him, the more his eyes seemed to penetrate hers like two carbon-tipped drill bits.

"Well?" asked the white-haired man. "What are you waiting for? A police escort?"

"No . . . thanks," said Georgia, backing off. She turned her bike around and headed home, an odd sensation of dread creeping over her. There was only one thing that would bring a bomb-sniffing dog, a bunch of suits from upstate and a man that intense-looking to this patch of drab

real estate on the borders of Woodside, Queens. They weren't there for
what was *on* that street. They were there for what was *beneath* it.

By the time Georgia pulled into her driveway, the sun was beginning
to set. But the sky was still bright and the air had cooled. Above the hum
of air conditioners, Georgia heard splashing water.

She unstrapped her metallic red helmet and followed the noise to the
backyard. Richie was paddling furiously across the pool in the waning
light. Her mother was seated underneath the awning, polishing her
nails. A third figure was chest deep in the water with his back to her.
Two strong, sculpted arms, tanned the color of olive oil, were locked
over the rim of the pool. A head of blue-black hair dripped down to the
concrete beneath. *Marenko.* That was all she needed right now.

"Mom, watch this," said Richie, by way of greeting. He hoisted his
rail-thin body onto the top step of the aluminum pool ladder, then
turned to Marenko. "Okay, shoot me, Mac."

Marenko formed his hand into the shape of a pistol and pretended to
fire. Richie clutched his heart and belly-flopped with great melodrama
into the water. Marenko laughed, a deep, rich sound.

"That's funny, Richie," said Georgia. Then she turned to her mother,
pointedly ignoring Marenko. "I'm going to take a shower, Ma. Then I'll
help with dinner."

"I'll give you a shower," growled Mac playfully, cupping his hands
with pool water. But something in Georgia's face made him stop. Instead, he hoisted himself out of the pool, wrapped a towel around his
waist and followed Georgia to the back door.

"So, uh . . . did you get the Rosen report into A and E?" he asked,
stumbling over his words in that clueless sort of way he had when
he sensed he'd done something wrong but wasn't sure what. "I was running around the city all day . . . and I, uh, didn't get a chance to call you."

A small crease appeared on Georgia's brow. His brother had said Mac
was on Long Island.

"I got the report in," Georgia said coolly as she breezed past him into
the kitchen. "They could use it for toilet paper, for what it's worth."

Marenko followed, closing the door. He removed the towel from his waist and began to dry his hair.

"What do you mean?" he mumbled from beneath the towel.

"A and E lied. They don't think the Rosen and Dana burnings are accidental."

"How do you know?"

"I just do."

He stopped toweling and looked up. "What? You're not gonna tell me?"

"Like you tell *me* everything," Georgia shot back.

"Scout, I don't know zip about the case. It's not even the FDNY's case any . . ."

"—You were in Long Island today," she cut him off.

He paused as it sank in. "Okay," he said softly. "So I was. So?"

"Seeing your kids?"

"And if I was?" His blue eyes stared back defiantly.

"Why does everything have to be a big secret with you? Why am *I* a secret?"

"You're not a secret."

She laughed. "Yeah? Maybe you should talk to your brother Nick about that."

He gave her a confused expression. She sank into a chrome chair by the Formica kitchen table.

"See that look? That's the look Nick gave me today when I introduced myself to him at the task force drill in Grand Central."

"Nicky was there?"

"You never told him about us."

"I don't remember what I've told him." He shrugged and paced the floor. "It's not like we have some big heart-to-heart every week, you know." He looked at her from the corner of his eye. "Aw, c'mon, Scout. This case has got you all worked up. You're making a big deal out of nothing. You've always wanted to be taken seriously on this job. Seems to me, you'd be happy that I respect our privacy."

"I am. It's just that . . ." Georgia felt her whole body slump. ". . . You play pool with my mother. You shoot hoops with my son. A wedding, a funeral comes along, so do you." She looked up at him. "My God, Richie *worships* you . . . But your life—it's out *there* somewhere under lock and key."

He took a step toward her. "I don't live with my kids," he said softly. "I don't live with my parents. My life's different, that's all."

"How convenient."

Marenko pulled out another chrome chair from the table and straddled it backwards, his sinewy forearms, tanned and black haired, propped on the seat back, his chin resting on his knuckles. He studied her for a long moment. It was always hard to resist the wattage of that gaze.

"Scout," he pleaded in a soft, husky voice, "what is it you want from me?"

She took a deep breath. "I want to meet your family—your brothers, your parents, your son and daughter."

The angles of his jaw tightened. "What'll that prove?"

"I'll know you're for real."

He pulled back from the chair and thumped his chest. "I *am* for real. Jesus, you're the only woman I think about, the only woman I look at. You think I'd still be here otherwise? 'Cause man oh man—you *are* a handful."

"Then what's the problem?"

Marenko ran a hand through his wet hair, then exhaled slowly and stared at the ceiling, trying to collect his thoughts. "I'm not the kind of guy you can push. I'm not ready, okay?" He stood up. "I'm sorry I can't give you what you want right now. But I'm here. I didn't run away."

He kicked the chair out of the way and pulled her toward him. She didn't resist. The damp, bare touch of his skin felt warm and reassuring. He brought his lips down gently on hers and she felt, as she always did in these moments, ready to forgive anything about Mac Marenko.

"We're both spent," he whispered, stroking her hair. He squinted at the clock above the kitchen sink. Seven P.M. "How 'bout I take a rain check on dinner?"

Georgia nodded. "This stuff can wait. We've got enough on our minds right now." Over Marenko's bicep, she noticed her son toweling off to come in. She sighed.

"I'll go tell Richie."

16

· · ·

RICHIE MOPED AROUND all evening after Marenko left. He picked at his dinner, complaining that Georgia's mashed potatoes tasted like wallpaper paste and her meat loaf was "squishy." By the time he went to bed, Georgia was so exhausted, she fell asleep beside him. She awoke at midnight. The phone was ringing in her bedroom.

She stumbled down the hall and answered gruffly, groggy from sleep.

"Skeehan." The voice belonged to Randy Carter, and it was shaky. "I'm sorry to be calling y'all so late."

"Randy? What's wrong?" Georgia sat on the edge of her bed and wiped her eyes. Then she flicked on the lamp beside her bed.

"It's Connie." His voice cracked. "Something bad's happened. I got a friend in the PD's crime-scene unit, and he just called me 'cause he's heard me talk about her."

"Crime scene? Is Connie hurt?" Georgia's heart pounded in her chest. She felt like she'd just mainlined a hypodermic full of epinephrine.

"A neighbor of Connie's heard gunshots coming from her apartment and called the police. Cops broke down the door—blood everywhere— but they can't find Connie."

"Oh, my God." Georgia stood up. She began to shiver and sweat at the same time. "Who would want to hurt Connie? Do they have any leads? Any suspects?"

"That's the other reason I'm calling you, girl." There was a tightness in Carter's voice Georgia had never heard before, and it scared her almost as much as the thought of Connie lying hurt or dead somewhere.

"They . . . they have the suspect in custody," Carter continued. "Found him in her apartment, covered with her blood."

"Who is he?"

"Skeehan . . . The man they found in Connie's apartment is Mac Marenko."

11

. . .

THEY WERE HOLDING Mac Marenko at the 109th Precinct station house in Flushing, Queens, three blocks from Connie's apartment. The police hadn't charged him—yet. Georgia knew they wouldn't until the firefighters' union could scrounge up a lawyer and a representative—which wasn't going to happen until sometime on Wednesday morning. Until then, he'd kill time in a holding cell—professional courtesy. Marenko was a fellow law-enforcement officer, and his brother, Nick, was NYPD. No cop was eager to bust him.

Georgia got to the station house around 1:30 in the morning. Already, there were fire marshals in the precinct lobby, sipping coffee by a vending machine. They gave each other disapproving looks when she walked by. *Oh, God. The rumors are already starting to circulate,* she thought. Someone called out her name. She turned to see a snub-nosed Irishman with pale brown hair as fine and thin as fishing lure.

"I'm Detective Leahy," the man muttered. "You shouldn't be here."

"I know but . . ."

"—When I want your explanations, I'll ask for them," he said. "Walk this way."

Leahy led her down a hallway, then snapped his fingers in an open doorway at a heavy-set female police detective with red-tinted hair. Georgia vaguely recognized the woman from a bust they'd handled jointly in Chinatown in June. Debbie was her name, Georgia thought. Debbie smiled. Leahy did not. Instead, he spent the next two hours grilling Georgia on her relationships with Connie and Marenko and her whereabouts that evening. He told her nothing about why Mac was found in Connie's apartment or whether they'd found Connie.

It was nearly four in the morning when Leahy finally seemed satisfied that Georgia had nothing to do with the case. He told Debbie to escort her out of the building. Georgia waited until Leahy left the room to speak.

"I really came to see Marenko," Georgia said softly. She couldn't look Debbie in the eye. Bad enough that she'd had to pour out her love life to two strangers. Now, she had to beg a favor.

"You know I can't let you see him," said Debbie. "The place is crawling with fire marshals. I can't just march you in there. Leahy would have my head—not to mention what *your* people would do to *you.*"

Georgia knew the layout of police stations. They were all the same. There was more than one way into the holding pen area. "Take me through the lineup room, then," she pleaded. "No one will see us."

Georgia could feel Debbie's hesitation. The red-haired cop fingered her wedding ring. Georgia knew the woman was thinking about her own man.

"Five minutes," Debbie said sternly. "That's all."

Marenko was slumped in a metal folding chair at the far end of a bare, windowless interrogation room just beyond the holding pen. He was wearing baggy brown pants that looked like they came from Goodwill, and an old white T-shirt that had faded to gray. His hair, normally a glistening black, was dull and matted from grime and what appeared to be dried blood. He was smoking, focusing his eyes on the cigarette between his fingers and the tin ashtray before him on the gouged, graffiti-covered table. A fan, mounted on the wall, sputtered noisily in a vain attempt to circulate the air.

"Mac?"

He looked up in a dazed sort of way, his face a sickly yellow under the bright fluorescent lights, his eyes bloodshot and red rimmed. Georgia had assumed he'd be relieved to see her. Instead, he shuffled his large frame uncomfortably on the folding chair and looked down again at his cigarette, shaking his head.

"You shouldn't have come," he muttered, running the back of his other hand across the stubble on his cheeks and chin. His fingers were stained black from having his fingerprints taken. One of his ankles was cuffed to a leg of the table, and it jingled when he moved. He caught her looking at it now.

"Cops are afraid I might try to tackle 'em and off myself with one of their guns," he said hoarsely, then went back to staring at his burning cigarette.

Georgia scrounged a metal folding chair near the wall and brought it to the edge of the scarred wooden table, facing him. She sat down close enough for their knees to touch. He shifted his legs in response. He didn't seem to want her intimacy right now. Her eyes skimmed the length of his body.

"They took my clothes, loaned me these," he said, sensing her scrutiny.

"Why?"

" 'Cause mine are covered with blood. *Her* blood." Marenko stubbed out his cigarette and put the heels of his palms to his eyes, pressing down on them hard. "It feels like someone took a crowbar to my brain."

"Mac, if you were attacked, they've got no right to assume . . ."

"—I wasn't attacked, okay?" he said gruffly, taking his palms away from his eyes. "There isn't a scratch on me. Zip. I've just got a monster headache is all."

Georgia put a hand on his knee. "Can you tell me what happened?"

"I don't know," he said, shaking his head. "That's what I keep telling 'em. I don't know."

Marenko ran his blackened thumb over a gouged-out moniker in the table. *JA, the iceman,* it read. Some sixteen-year-old hit man with a wish for immortality.

"Somebody heard shots coming from Connie's apartment and called the cops," he said. "Her door was locked, they busted it open and found me in her bathroom, throwing up and covered with her blood. No sign of Connie, no sign of my gun, but two bullets that match my ammo had been fired into her couch. That's all I know, Scout—I swear. I don't know anything else."

"You don't know how you ended up at Connie Ruiz's apartment?"

He kept his eyes on the iceman's graffiti and licked his parched lips. "That part, I know," he said tonelessly.

"And?"

"She called me."

Georgia took her hand off his knee. "Why would *my* best friend call *you*?"

His eyes, the color of stonewashed denim, met Georgia's unblinkingly. "'Cause I know her, Scout."

"*Know,* as in, 'we're both members of the International Association of Arson Investigators'? That kind of know?"

Marenko allowed a small, sad smile to play at the edges of his lips while he fiddled with the overflowing ashtray. Georgia sat staring at him for what seemed like an eternity. The weight of his words sank in gradually, eclipsing the sputtering of the fan and the buzzing of a fly that had found its way into the windowless room.

"I don't believe you," she whispered finally. "I don't fucking believe you."

Marenko winced. He seemed too tired even to defend himself. Instead, he leaned back in his chair, causing the flimsy metal to groan from his weight and the cuff around his ankle to jingle again. He combed a hand through his matted hair and stared at the ceiling. Brown water stains played at the edges of the acoustical tiles.

Georgia rose and kicked her chair aside. It fell sideways and clanged loudly on the bare concrete floor. A phone rang somewhere down the hall, and two cops conversed in agitated voices. The room felt like it was closing in. She needed air.

"You son of a bitch," she spat out. "I hope they nail your sorry ass to the wall."

"It's . . . It's not what you think," he said softly, more to himself than to her, as if he'd given up all hope of convincing her. He massaged his forehead, like a man seriously hung over. "Nothing happened to-night."

"Get your story straight, Mac. You just said you don't remember anything—*remember?*"

"I'd know if I . . ." His voice trailed off and he frowned. "Look, Scout, Connie and I are ancient history. It's not like that between us anymore." He tipped another Marlboro from his pack. "I met her around the time of my divorce. We were both working on the same case. It was over almost as soon as it began." He lit the cigarette and inhaled deeply. "I didn't even *know* you then," he said on the exhale. "You were still a firefighter."

"Then why didn't you tell me?"

He grinned to himself, the old Mac glimmering beneath the fog. "Oh that would've gone over big: 'Hey, Scout, I used to sleep with your best friend.' Either you'd have ditched her, or you'd have ditched me. And for what? Hell"—he took another hit off his cigarette—"Connie must've figured it the same way, 'cause she never told you either."

"What were you doing at her place, then?"

He slid his cigarette along the side of the ashtray and shaved a wad of gray ash off the tip. "She called me up, crying."

"Connie? Crying?" Georgia frowned. She'd never seen Connie cry.

"I know," said Marenko. "She hadn't done that since . . ." His voice trailed off, and he shook his head. ". . . She told me she'd gotten this threatening phone call maybe ten minutes earlier. Not just a crank call— something much worse. I asked her if it was some old boyfriend. She made it sound like it was related to some case she was working on, but she didn't give me any details. All she kept saying was that this guy was for real, that he wasn't kidding around."

A small crease appeared in Marenko's brow—as if he were replaying the events, asking himself if he should have done something differently. "Scout, she was terrified. What was I supposed to do? Tell her to call nine-one-one?"

He shook his head. "The cops are all thinking I either went psycho and killed her, or I have some accomplice I'm protecting. It doesn't help that the door was locked, my gun's missing and the only fingerprints Crime Scene can find in that apartment are mine and Connie's."

"Jesus, Mac, you say you'd remember having sex with her. But you can't even remember how she got hurt? Or whether she's *alive*?"

"No. I . . ." He kept his eyes on the gouge marks in the table. ". . . I keep trying to remember, Scout. It's just some big blank spot in my head."

"Were you drinking?"

"I had one beer—honest—that's all. I checked her locks and windows. We watched a little TV and talked about you. I told her I was gonna leave at eleven-thirty and she should report the threats to her supervisors in the morning and get one of those caller IDs. Next thing I knew, I was covered with blood, puking up my insides, and the cops were busting down the door."

"You smoke anything there besides tobacco?"

Marenko made a face. "I don't do that shit. You know that."

"Connie does."

"Used to," he corrected. *He knew Connie pretty well, indeed,* thought Georgia. "Anyway," said Marenko, "she never did it around me." He stubbed out his cigarette. "Look, Scout, I know I was all messed up when the cops came, and I have no idea why. But I passed my Breathalyzer. I pissed in a cup at the scene and I passed a drug test." He reached for her arm. "Georgia."

She cocked her head at the sound of her name in his husky voice.

"I'm as scared for Connie as you are," he said wearily. "And I swear—dear God, I swear—I don't know what happened."

. . .

MARENKO WANTED GEORGIA to go home, but she didn't feel up to explaining everything to her mother and Richie right now. She decided to spend the rest of the night in the bunk room at the Queens fire marshals' base in Fort Totten, twenty minutes from Flushing. She gave Debbie her cell phone number and asked her to phone when Marenko got released.

"Now, how do I get out of the precinct without getting caught?" asked Georgia.

"I know a good route," said Debbie. "Through the female officers' locker room. There's an exit door across the hall on the other side."

The locker room was nothing like what Georgia had experienced as a firefighter. The toilets were in clean, lockable stalls with seats in the down position. A tampon dispenser hung on the wall, and the shower boasted a curtain. Female officers were commonplace in the NYPD. In the FDNY, out of more than eleven thousand active members, only about thirty were women.

"I've been in the fire department too long," Georgia muttered, as she walked across the unstained carpet. "The men I work with think a lock on a bathroom door is a major feminist concession."

They were nearly at the exit door when Georgia froze at the familiar figure barreling toward her, his tie loosened about his fleshy neck. Beads of sweat dampened the upright shafts of his thinning silver hair. He did a double take when he saw her as well.

"Skeehan," Arthur Brennan's voice boomed. "What the hell do you think you're doing here?"

"Chief, I'm sorry. I was just . . ."

"—Detective Leahy requested an interview with the marshal," Debbie explained without troubling to mention that Georgia was already in the precinct when he made his request. "I was escorting her out."

Debbie's words immediately took the steam out of Brennan. He could bully Georgia all he wanted to, but Debbie was NYPD, and Brennan knew he had no authority over her. Georgia shot Debbie a look of thanks.

"I'd like to speak to the marshal myself," said Brennan. "Can the PD spare an interview room?"

"I'd be happy to check, Chief," she said.

· · ·

The room Debbie got for them was small and hot. Brennan shifted and grunted—looking for all the world like Khrushchev with a bad case of hemorrhoids. A big fat fly buzzed around the room, bumping into the Plexiglas covering on the fluorescent lights. Georgia watched its frantic efforts to escape. She knew the feeling.

"I want to know what the hell is going on," said Brennan. "And I do mean everything." He saw the crease beginning to form on her brow. "And don't hand me any crap about giving your statement already to detectives. I don't care what they asked you. *I'm* asking the questions now."

"Shouldn't Mac . . . ?"

"Marenko, because of his detention, is under union protection. I'm forbidden from talking to him without a union attorney present. *You,* however, have the pleasure of answering to me. First off, I want to know what your relationship with Marenko is."

"But sir, that's priv—"

"Don't hand me that ACLU garbage, Skeehan. I don't give a rat's ass if you do it with a monkey covered with peanut butter. But I want to know if my people are clean. So you'll answer me: What's your relationship with Mac Marenko?"

"We're dating," Georgia answered stiffly.

"You're sleeping together, then."

"Yes."

"And this police officer from A and E who's missing? She's a friend of yours?"

"Yes."

"Were you aware that Marenko was with her tonight?"

"No."

"Were you aware of their relationship?"

"Not before tonight." Georgia could see the wheels turning in Brennan's head. He was sizing up the situation as a lover's triangle gone sour. As much as he had always liked Mac, Arthur Brennan was too politically savvy to stick his neck out on something as personal as this.

"On Monday, you asked Officer Ruiz to brief you about A and E's interest in the Louise Rosen case, did you not?"

"How did you . . . ?"

"Damnit, Skeehan, just answer the friggin' question."

Georgia tugged nervously on her fingers. "Yes, I did."

"And what did she tell you?"

"Sir, I don't think that has any bearing . . ."

Brennan slammed the table. "*I'll* decide what has bearing around here. What did she tell you?"

Georgia took a deep breath. Connie was missing. Whatever it took to find her, that's what she would do.

"Officer Ruiz told Marshal Carter and me that there had been a bomb threat against the Empire Pipeline and that the person who made the threat mentioned a Dr. Rosen."

Georgia looked across at Brennan. There was no surprise in his features. *So it's all true,* thought Georgia. *The commotion at A and E, the men with metal detectors, the dog sniffing the pavement—there really might be a bomb. And Brennan knows about it.* Georgia stifled a shudder. If it was out there, hundreds of innocent lives were at risk. She tried to collect her thoughts enough to continue.

"Officer Ruiz said A and E was investigating the possibility that

Louise Rosen was the Dr. Rosen the blackmailer was referring to," Georgia explained.

Brennan studied her a moment, drumming his fingers absentmindedly on the table. Then he leaned forward, the buttons on his white shirt straining at his belly. "What else do you know, Skeehan? What aren't you telling me?"

Georgia felt her heart migrate into her throat. *He knows I broke into Dana's house. He knows,* a voice inside her screamed.

"Sir, I . . . I've told you everything . . ."

"Bullshit, Skeehan. Bullshit . . . I don't know what went on among the three of you, and I'm not sure I care yet. But *you* are at the center of something, and I want to know why."

Brennan reached into his suit jacket across the chair and pulled a small tape recorder from the pocket. He set it on the conference table and pushed Play.

"It's Robin Hood again."

The voice was slow and deep; the vowels strangely drawn out, like sound in water. It took a moment for Georgia to realize why. The caller was running his voice through a synthesizer.

"You found Dr. Rosen, I see. And Dr. Dana, too. Those bastards deserved a little payback. And now it's your turn: one million in cash by Friday at noon, or I will blow up the Empire Pipeline. I'll be in touch to work out the details. There's just one more condition: the little female fire marshal who helped me get rid of Dana? She does the drop—got that?"

Georgia's shoulders began to quake while her hands did just the opposite, freezing in a clutch of the table rim. She felt as if a giant tuning fork were reverberating through her body. *Who is this Robin Hood,* she wondered? *And why is he involving me in his blackmail schemes?*

"Where did you get this?" she stammered.

Brennan turned off the tape recorder and regarded her closely. "It arrived at Mayor Ortaglia's office this morning."

Just like the tape Connie told me about on Monday, thought Georgia. "Why me?" she asked softly.

"That's what I'd like to know," said Brennan. "*Why* you?"

"I don't know."

"I think you do." Brennan sat very still, looking at her. It was a clas-sic interrogation move—the long, uncomfortable pause. Georgia looked down and bit her lip. She was a rookie—surely not important enough in the FDNY to single out. And yet this blackmailer had. Why? Because she was a woman? Because she'd handled that high-profile serial arson case last April? Or was Ajay Singh right? Was Robin Hood a firefighter? And if so . . .

"Do you think he knows me?" Georgia asked, giving voice to her worst fears.

"Knows you . . ." said Brennan, leaning forward. "—Or knows something about you. He didn't mention Carter helping him get rid of Dr. Dana, Skeehan. He only mentions *you*. Why?"

Dear God, thought Georgia. *Robin Hood knows what I did back at Dana's house. Could he have seen me?*

"Chief, I . . . I don't know if this has any bearing, but I broke into Dana's house. I saw the clicker to open his garage on his kitchen counter, so I slipped the lock. It was a stupid, rookie thing to do . . . Marshal Carter's got nothing to do with this. Nobody does—except me."

Arthur Brennan did something Georgia was totally unprepared for. He smiled. A tiny one—almost imperceptible. He actually looked re-lieved.

"Do you think that's why Robin Hood wants me?" asked Georgia.

"I don't know," said Brennan. "I'll ask the PD to send a patrol car at regular intervals to check on your home and family. In the meantime, you will not mention a word about Robin Hood or the bomb threat to anyone. Are we clear on that?"

Brennan rose. Georgia rose in response and saluted. "Yessir. Thank you, sir."

"Don't thank me. I'd toss you out in a minute if I could. But you're our only link to Robin Hood at the moment."

Brennan dismissed Georgia. She left the office, shaky and light-headed from the encounter. She understood suddenly how panicked

Connie must have been when she got that threatening call last night. Georgia felt the same way herself now. Someone could see her, but she couldn't see him. In one fell swoop, he'd gotten complete control over her life. She had to find a way to get some of it back, to make sense of the seemingly random, catastrophic events of the last few hours, even if all she got back was the illusion of control.

On the way out she spotted Leahy.

"I thought I told you to scram." He gave her an annoyed look. She might be law-enforcement at other times, but here, she was strictly the girlfriend of a suspect.

"I'm leaving now," Georgia told him. "Detective Leahy, do you have any of your people looking for Connie's red Suzuki?"

"Marshal, don't tell me how to do my job. We've already had the vehicle impounded, along with the suspect's. And that's all I'm going to tell you."

A chill traveled down Georgia's spine. Leahy referred to Marenko not by his name, but as "the suspect." He had already pegged Connie's disappearance and possible murder to a love affair gone sour—just as Brennan had. In Leahy's mind, Marenko had killed her because of jealousy, or because Connie was horning in on his new relationship—not because of anything connected to her work as a police officer.

"Just one more thing," Georgia said. "Mac says Connie called him tonight because she got a threatening phone call. He said he thought it might have something to do with a case she was working on."

Leahy gave Georgia a patronizing smile and shook his head. "Sweetheart, you wanna be snowed by lover boy in there, that's your business. But don't ask me to shovel it for you."

"What do you mean?"

"I guarantee you, there *was* no threatening phone call. Anyone can see, he and your girlfriend were having a roll in the hay and things got out of hand."

"He would've told . . ."

"—Yeah, right. You think he's gonna admit he was there getting his rocks off? That'd be like admitting he iced her."

"He didn't."

"That's good. You keep that up, girlie. You'll make a great witness for the defense." He turned on his heel and started down the hall. He had a heavy walk, feet turned out, like a duck.

She called after him. "Aren't you even going to *check* if Connie got a threatening call tonight?"

He spun around and gave Georgia a sad smile.

"We've already subpoenaed her telephone records," he said. "We'll trace her calls—don't you worry. But believe me—I'm never wrong about this stuff. The only incoming calls we're gonna find on Officer Ruiz's numbers will be the ones from Mac Marenko."

19

. . .

IT WAS ALMOST ten on Wednesday morning before the union rep and the fire department lawyer finished the paperwork that would free Marenko—at least for the time being—from police custody. The cuffs were removed, but a million other indignities took their place. Marenko was suspended for thirty days without pay, pending the outcome of the investigation. He was stripped of his badge and his right to carry a weapon. He didn't have a passport, but he had to agree to surrender his birth certificate so he couldn't leave the country. He had to submit to random drug and alcohol tests, which meant he'd be slugging down O'Douls until this was over. And he couldn't leave the state without special written permission.

Marenko's face dropped. "Not even Jersey?" Georgia recalled that his brother Pete was having a family get-together there on Labor Day.

"Most people don't think of that as a punishment," cracked Detective Leahy. Georgia, who had driven over from Fort Totten as soon as she got word he'd be released, shot Leahy a dirty look.

Mac got his wallet and keys back, but it would be a month or two before the crime lab returned his car. He and Georgia left the station by the rear exit doors. Word had already leaked out about Marenko's arrest, but the cops on duty cut him a break and told the media he was being held at a different precinct to give him a head start.

The blinding morning sun caught both of them off guard as they

walked out of the building. Georgia put on her sunglasses. Marenko
brought a hand up to cover his eyes.

"I know you want to go home, Mac. But first, we have to talk."

"You gonna ball me out about being with Connie?"

"No. I think it's best if I explain while we grab some breakfast. Are
you hungry?"

Marenko looked down at his baggy brown trousers and wrinkled
T-shirt. "Scout, I need a shower and a shave bad, and I've got maybe ten
dollars in my wallet."

"But are you hungry?" she asked.

"Are you kidding? I could eat *your* cooking."

"Don't bite the hand that's going to feed you."

They found a diner three blocks away peopled by annoyed Greek
owners and harried Mexican busboys. Marenko chose a spot in the
smoking section in back. He went to light up the moment the waitress
brought their water. Georgia cupped a hand over his.

"Mac, please. I know you're smoking a lot because you're under
stress, but it's first thing in the morning."

He put the cigarettes back in his pocket, but couldn't resist a shake of
the head. "Man, the law won't let me drink. You won't let me smoke. I
might as well be in jail." His eyes traveled down her tight-fitting rib-
knit T-shirt, stopping at the zipper of her faded jeans. "With everything
that's been happening, I haven't asked if you . . ."

Georgia shook her head. "Ten days. No period."

"Well"—he tossed off a laugh—"you can't sue me for child support.
I won't even be getting a paycheck."

"How's that going to go down with . . . ?"

Marenko put his hands over his ears, as if to ward off a blow. "I don't
even want to think about it. Forget the money. What do I tell my kids?"
He shook his head. "I can't believe I would hurt her, Scout," he mumbled, as if arguing with himself. "I've never raised a hand to a woman in
my life. I keep thinking maybe I had a seizure."

"But surely you'd remember *something*," said Georgia.

He ran his fingers through his matted hair. "I don't even know where she is or how I ended up in this state. I'm scared for her. I'm scared for me. And no one believes me. No one."

"I believe you."

His blue eyes locked on hers. Even unshaven and grimy, he could still send an electric jolt to her heart. "Thank you," he said softly. He put one of his large, callused hands on top of hers. "That means a lot . . . You mean . . ."

The waitress appeared at Marenko's elbow. "Do you know what you want?"

Georgia studied the menu. "Scrambled eggs, bacon and coffee. Side of whole wheat, no butter."

Marenko raised an eyebrow. "What's this 'no butter' stuff? You got maybe two thousand calories there. Butter ain't gonna make a difference."

"Well, it's a start," said Georgia. Marenko smiled at the waitress, who seemed to blush under that wattage. He never tried, never even seemed to give it much thought, yet he always had that effect on women.

"I'll have the same," he said. "*Extra* butter on *my* toast."

The waitress took their menus, and Marenko went to the bathroom to wash his hands. When he returned, he had a serious, questioning look in his eyes.

"Chief Brennan was at the station house last night," he said. "He talk to you at all?"

"He did," said Georgia.

"About me?"

"He asked what our relationship was and how Connie fit into all of this."

"And?"

"And what, Mac? I told him the truth."

"Aw, Jeez." He pulled a face.

"What?" asked Georgia, annoyed. "You want me to lie to the chief fire marshal of the city of New York in a murder investigation? A man you consider your own personal rabbi in the department?"

He leaned back in the Naugahyde booth and palmed his tired eyes.

"I'm just sayin'—you know—that since you had nothing to do with the situation at Connie's, you could've just told Brennan we were friends. For chrissake, Scout, he's my boss. How's it gonna look?"

"So in the future, if I know something, I should keep it to myself—is that right?"

"Well . . . yeah." Marenko shrugged. The waitress brought their food.

"There you go. Extra butter for you, sir," the woman said, blushing at him. It looked as though she'd freshened her lipstick, too. Georgia's eyes narrowed.

"Bet they don't feed you like that in *jail.*" Georgia smiled up at the waitress. "He just got out of jail, you know. For murder."

The waitress left the table quickly. Marenko frowned.

"What did you tell her that for?"

"Oh, I'm sorry. I forgot. I'm supposed to keep things to myself."

"Women." Marenko rolled his eyes and stuffed a forkful of scrambled egg in his mouth. He took a sip of water. "So Brennan knows who's sleeping with who—is that what you wanted to tell me?"

"No."

"What, then?"

"It doesn't matter. I'll handle it myself."

Marenko put down his fork and stared at her. "Does it have to do with Connie?"

"I'm not sure."

"If it does, you owe it to me to tell me."

"Chief Brennan doesn't want me to."

"Well, the chief ain't looking at twenty-five-to-life."

"And you just finished lecturing me about keeping things to myself."

"But not from *me,*" Marenko said indignantly. "Scout, I've told you everything I know about Connie and last night. I swear. I couldn't have hurt her. I didn't even *sleep* with her."

"Yeah? Well talk to Detective Leahy. He told me I was a sap for believing that one."

"I told you," said Marenko. "I went there 'cause she was upset over a threatening call."

"Then an audit of her phone records should contain evidence of that call."

Marenko dismissed Georgia with a wave of his hand. "The number that turns up will be worthless. Nobody's stupid enough to make a call like that from a traceable line."

Georgia stared at him. His jaw hardened as it sank in. "Oh, I get it," he said, pushing his plate away. "Finding that call's got nothing to do with getting a bead on who hurt Connie. It's about figuring out whether I'm telling the truth about why I went to her apartment."

"You don't have an exactly stellar record in the truth department now, do you?"

Marenko fiddled with his coffee cup while Georgia asked for the check. "I'm paying," she told the waitress with a smile that said *He just got out of jail, you know.* She enjoyed watching him squirm.

. . .

20

GEORGIA DROPPED MARENKO off at the subway station to catch a train back to his apartment in Manhattan. He forced a brave smile as he leaned over and gave her a warm, soulful kiss.

"You sure you don't want to tell me what you discussed with the chief?"

She smiled. "So that's what the kiss was for—a bribe."

"Not a bribe." He grinned like a little boy caught in the act. "A . . . uh . . . show of faith."

"Let me think about what I'm going to do, okay?"

"Okay." He nodded. "I trust you." He put a hand on the door latch. "One day, maybe you'll say the same about me, huh?"

She laughed. "When pigs fly."

He got out of the car and gave her a wink as he closed the door. "I'm working on it." As soon as he left her, his demeanor turned somber. By the time he trudged down the steps to the subway, his whole body looked as if two concrete blocks were nailed to his shoulders.

Georgia watched him disappear. It felt like a brick to her heart. She still had no sense of what happened last night. And she had to know. It was the only way she could hope to find Connie. She tried to picture Connie's apartment now. Everything in the place was white or turquoise. White rug. Turquoise drapes. White couch. Turquoise pillows. Big white conch shells on the glass coffee table. A big turquoise mother-of-pearl bowl on top of the wall unit.

But there was something flat and static about these images because the apartment Georgia was picturing was no longer there. Now, it was a blood-splattered crime scene. *If I'm going to find her, I've got to face the truth about her last hours there. I've got to see the place myself.*

Connie's apartment was part of a complex of three buildings, each ten stories high, styled in what, years from now, historians will cite as a perfect example of 1960s space-age architecture. The windows were round like portholes on a spaceship; the lobby had a strange, curved ceiling like a space module. Tubular steel, mirrors and white concrete predominated. Connie, never one for understatement, loved the place. But then again, she thought the 1964 World's Fair Unisphere in Flushing Meadows Park was one of the Seven Wonders of the World.

On the drive over, Georgia's emotions seesawed a million times. One moment, she couldn't imagine Marenko hurting *any* woman, much less one he'd been attached to. She pictured him in her basement, shooting pool with her mother, or on their driveway, tossing around a basketball with Richie. But the next moment, she'd get an image of him in the kitchen of Charles Dana's house—callous, hot tempered and demanding. She couldn't help wondering whether this was the real Mac, the one she wouldn't allow herself to see.

Georgia walked into the lobby and opened the door to the fire stairs. Randy Carter was trudging up the first set of steps. Their eyes locked for one speechless moment.

"What are you doing here, girl? This could be misconstrued as compromising an investigation."

"And you aren't?" she replied, bounding up the stairs to meet him.

"I was going to tell you about it, later."

"Well now you don't have to." Georgia surveyed the stairwell above them. "How were you planning to get in?"

"I'm not sure," he admitted. They climbed the stairs in silence. At the third-floor landing, Carter cracked open the fire door. Halfway down the hall, Georgia could see Connie's front door. Yellow crime-scene tape was strung across the entrance. A baby-faced Latino police officer was slouched against the wall near Connie's door, smoking a cigarette and talking to a teenage girl who appeared to be taking out the trash. The officer's black duty holster was so stiff and shiny, Georgia felt certain he was brand-new to the job. He couldn't have been more than twenty-two years old.

"Just follow my lead, okay?" said Carter. With that, he threw open the door to the fire stairs and barreled down the hallway.

"You there," Carter boomed in his best ex-drill sergeant's voice. He flashed his gold shield at the young cop, then quickly put it away before the cop could tell he wasn't NYPD. "You call yourself a police officer, son? I've seen Brownies writing parking tickets who conduct themselves better."

The officer's baby face paled. He opened his mouth to speak while the girl inched away. Carter looked the kid over. His nameplate said "Mercado."

"This ain't no dating game, Mercado. Put out that cigarette. Straighten your cap. Wipe that stupid look off your face. My partner and I have work to do, so you will stand by this doorway and not let anyone in until we're through. Are we clear?"

"Yes, detective," Officer Mercado mumbled.

"I didn't *hear* you," said Carter in a loud sing-song voice.

Mercado lifted his chin and saluted. "Yes, sir."

"That's better."

"That was quite a show you put on out there," Georgia whispered to Carter when they got inside Connie's apartment.

"Yeah, well." He sighed. "I wish it was for something more positive than this. Keep your gloves on and don't move or *remove* anything, you hear?"

"I won't."

The entrance hall looked undisturbed. So did the galley kitchen, which didn't surprise Georgia. Connie probably turned the stove on once a year. On the counter sat a small, silver ashtray with some ash in it. Connie didn't smoke. Georgia knew who the cigarette ash belonged to.

She let Mac smoke in her apartment, thought Georgia, an odd defensiveness coming over her. Georgia made Marenko smoke outside.

They walked past the kitchen into the living room. Georgia knew what was coming and yet she flinched anyway when she saw the eight-by-twelve-inch voids in Connie's white carpet. The police had cut the rectangles for evidence. Georgia didn't need to be told what was on them. The remaining checkerboard of carpet carried traces of the dark red stains. She could still smell the musky, coppery odor of blood in the apartment. She pictured Connie lying on this rug. *Was she frightened? Was she unconscious? What about now?*

"You see Marenko yet?" Carter grunted, his voice as sudden as a firecracker in the perfect silence of the room.

"Yes."

"He confess?"

"He says he didn't do it. He says he doesn't know what happened."

Carter said nothing. He simply walked over to a wall unit where Connie's compact discs of jazz and salsa were lined up along the stereo. There were black powder marks everywhere in the room from where the Crime Scene unit had dusted for fingerprints. There were pinhole marks along the edges of certain splatters suggesting that the police had run string between the pinholes to photograph the splatters' trajectory and dimensions.

On top of the television, Connie's blue binder of materials for the sergeant's exam lay open to the very page she and Georgia had stopped on on Monday night. Georgia's heart twisted like a dishrag to see Connie's pencil scribbles in the margins—some sort of "to do" list she'd put together since their last meeting:

Shampoo ... Lipstick ... Dry cleaning ... Bridgewater ... B-day card for Joanne ...

Georgia knew who the "Joanne" was: Joanne Zeligman, an older woman and the closest thing to a mother Connie had ever had. Georgia was certain the police would have already gone through Connie's address book and spoken to her. She worked as a Tae-Bo instructor at a gym in Chelsea. She would be devastated by Connie's disappearance.

Georgia's eyes passed over the list a second time. The words were etched deeply into the page. Connie regularly broke pencil tips and caused ballpoint pens to rupture. She always pressed too hard. Only that wasn't what made Georgia stare at the page now. It was the fourth entry that gave her pause: *Bridgewater.*

"Randy, does the word *Bridgewater* mean anything to you?"

"There's a Bridge*port* in Connecticut."

Georgia gestured to the binder. "Connie scribbled what looks like a list of errands sometime during the last twenty-four hours she was in this apartment. 'Bridgewater' was one of her errands. When I spoke to Seamus Hanlon the other night—about that safety report in Dr. Rosen's files—he told me it had to do with a fire on Bridgewater Street in Greenpoint, Brooklyn. Do you think Connie was referring to the same Bridgewater?"

"Even if she was, it's just a street."

"Connie was working on the Dana/Rosen case. Maybe she found out something and . . ."

"—Skeehan." Carter cut her off. His voice was harsh and shaky. The crime scene was getting to him, too. He rubbed a hand across his face and walked over to the white couch that now sported two bullet holes and a splatter of blood that looked like barbecue sauce. There was a smear on the wall behind the couch. Carter couldn't take his eyes off it. Georgia walked up behind him, stared at the smear and choked back a note of alarm. It was a bloody handprint—too delicate and long fingered to be Marenko's.

"The door was locked," Carter mumbled. His voice was hoarse and quavering. "The fingerprints are all Marenko's or Connie's. Crime Scene said so. And the blood—it's Connie's too, matched against her personnel records."

"Oh, God," said Georgia. "No, no." She felt light-headed and nauseated. Her hands shook. "It can't be, Randy. He wouldn't. He couldn't."

"Skeehan." Carter turned to face her. "He did."

. . .

RANDY CARTER WALKED Georgia to her car, an eight-year-old Ford Escort, once red, now rust. She took a quick look up at those space-age apartment windows, and her heart sank. She missed Connie already—missed her crazy, expensive, lizard-look shoes and her Day-Glo nail polish. She missed the tender way Connie called her "baby girl," as if that endearment could never apply to anyone else. Georgia fingered the Apache's tear around her neck and tried to take comfort in this small bit of her best friend's presence. Right now, however, it just felt cold and black and dead in her hands.

"Y'all need to go home and get some rest," Carter told her gently. "I'll check in with you later."

She drove the familiar back roads from Flushing to Woodside. Every restaurant reminded her of a place where she and Connie once ate. Every second store seemed to sell shoes Connie either owned or had once tried on. Eight years she had known Connie, and those had been the best years she'd ever shared with a female friend. They met right before Georgia came on the job, at a gathering of women police officers and firefighters. Most of what the women had to say scared Georgia—the stories of harassment, the bitterness, the frustration. Georgia felt more uncertain of the job than ever at that meeting.

Until she met Connie.

Connie was a kid then—a rookie cop still in uniform, the only one who ever managed to look feminine in all that gear. She had a mouth on her that would make most veterans crawl under a table. But she had a terrific sense of humor, and it allowed her to sail through any situation. Connie was respected right from the start, and a lot of it had to do with the fact that she never took what the men said to heart. Pretty soon, they stopped taking it to heart as well.

Connie, I need your advice so much right now, thought Georgia. She replayed the chilling, synthesized voice of Robin Hood again in her head: . . . *You found Rosen . . . And Dr. Dana, too. Those bastards deserved a little payback . . .*

Here was a killer who knew something about fire science and tools, and had used them to orchestrate the horrific, fatal burning of two fire department doctors. And now, he was talking about detonating a bomb that could do the same to hundreds of innocent New Yorkers. Connie was the only person Georgia could have spoken to about all this. Not only did she understand Georgia better than anyone. She was also familiar with the case—perhaps even more so than Georgia.

Connie had written down the word, Bridgewater. Georgia couldn't get that word out of her mind as she drove past the red-brick quarters of Engine Two-seventy-eight on her way home. The red enamel apparatus door was open, and the engine was inside. She parked at a meter up the street. She didn't want to set foot in that firehouse again so soon, but lately, there were a lot of places she didn't want to go that she had to.

Seamus Hanlon was on duty. A firefighter at house watch paged him, and he sauntered out of the kitchen. His watery blue eyes turned wary when he caught sight of her. He forced a smile beneath his mustache, but he didn't invite her up to his office this time. Instead, he beckoned Georgia around to the front of the Seagrave pumper, facing the street, away from the men. At first, she thought it had to do with Marenko's arrest. But she could see in his face that he didn't yet know about that. By tonight he would, though. Everyone in the FDNY would.

"I was wondering if you'd been able to find out any more about that Division of Safety report," said Georgia.

Hanlon lifted a black work boot on the chrome bumper and bent down to tie his shoelace. "There is no report, lass."

"You mean they lost it?"

He straightened up. "I mean there is no report . . . No report you're gonna get, that is."

He leaned on the fire engine now and stared out across the small boulevard of grocery stores, bars and discount clothing shops. The sun blinded him, and he put a hand up to shield his eyes. He didn't look at her.

"Georgia." He rolled her name out like an exhale. "If I tell you something, for the love of Jimmy Gallagher, will ya listen?"

"I'll listen."

"I tried to get you that report. There's some heat on it. Major heat. It was strongly recommended that you and I both drop it."

"Who? Who strongly recommended this?"

"I can't say. But I'll tell you this—these are good people, Georgia. You don't want to hurt 'em for some ancient history that won't amount to a heap of sod."

"Two doctors were horrifically burned—murdered—Captain," Georgia said angrily. "The NYPD thinks a firefighter's behind it. If you know something, you'd be impeding a criminal investigation not to tell me."

He gave her a disappointed look. The bags under his blue eyes sagged as if pulled down by two lead weights. "You think I don't want to help you? Georgia, I *am* helping you. You chase that report, they'll destroy you. And it won't solve your case, believe me. The men from those North Brooklyn companies are all dead now—all except for Vinnie Battaglia—and I guarantee you, Battaglia didn't kill those two doctors."

"How can you be so sure?"

Hanlon pushed himself off the engine and walked over to the cork-board of snapshots by the house-watch desk. His eyes scanned the collage of photos of firefighters and their families—in the firehouse, on fishing trips, at ball games and barbecues. He squinted at a half-hidden shot on the upper-right-hand corner of the board and pulled it out. It was a photo taken in the firehouse kitchen at the annual company Christmas party. The counters were covered with homemade lasagnas and turkeys. A scrawny, misshapen Christmas tree stood in the corner and one of the firefighters, dressed as Santa, sat near it with a little girl on his knee and a bunch of other children nearby.

Hanlon pointed to a figure behind the firefighter Santa, a man with a shaved head in a wheelchair. His eyes looked glazed, and his shoulders were slumped.

"That," said Hanlon, "is Vinnie Battaglia. Taken last December. He worked in Engine Two-seventy-eight for a couple of years after he left Ladder One-twenty-one in Brooklyn and before he started getting sick. We still invite him to our Christmas party every year."

Georgia squinted at the man in the photo. His head had an odd tilt to it; his eyes looked unfocused. His skin was sallow, and his shirt hung on his scrawny frame. If Hanlon had said he was seventy-five, Georgia wouldn't have argued.

"He has Parkinson's and brain cancer. He can't get out of the wheel-chair," Hanlon explained. "And by the way, lass—in case you're won-dering—Vinnie is my age: fifty-four." Hanlon tacked the photo back on the corkboard.

"Did all the men at Bridgewater die of illnesses?"

"Only the ones who went into the warehouse got sick," said Hanlon. A shadow passed in front of his face. "And not all of them died of disease."

"What did the others die of?" asked Georgia.

Hanlon didn't answer. A two-tone electronic chime interrupted their conversation. Engine Two-seventy-eight had a run. Within seconds, the men were sliding down the brass pole and shrugging into their gear. Hanlon seemed relieved to be able to exchange his thoughts for actions and reflex. "It doesn't matter anymore, lass," he said as he stepped into his boots and bunker pants and slipped on his turnout coat. "Nobody wants to go back to this one—nobody. And you shouldn't either."

. . .

22

THE PIER WAS a weathered gray, as unreliable and full of gaps as an old man's teeth. Fishermen and crabbers still used it, but they were long gone by noon when the tide rolled out and the ocean bared her secrets like an aging whore. In sand the color of a Manhattan sidewalk, Robin Hood could see a graveyard of paper cups, fast-food wrappers and plastic bags that ballooned like jellyfish in the sun. And Hood could see something else, too. Another secret, visible only when the ocean inhaled like a fat man sucking in his gut to see his toes.

Hood hoisted a tackle box under one arm and a folding canvas chair over the opposite shoulder and began to slog through the squishy sand underneath the pier. It wasn't the pier that brought people here. Or even the beach. It was memory—of days etched in the smell of hot dogs and Coppertone, of nights bathed in neon and the clickety-clack of a roller coaster. It didn't matter that the place was only a seedy skeleton of its former self. People lived in their memories. Hood certainly did.

The spot Hood was looking for was only a hundred feet from shore, underneath the pier. Black stains ran halfway up the soggy pilings, and seaweed and old fishing lures snagged the beams like hair around a drain. But with the tide out, the water was no more than ankle deep. Perfect for the kind of fishing Hood had to do.

There was no one to notice. It would be night before the teenagers and tourists flocked again to this patch of waterfront in the shadow of the red-brick projects. For now, there were only a few ancient-looking black men on the boardwalk, playing cards and drinking malt liquor out of paper bags. Here, beneath the pier, Hood was nearly invisible to them. Light fell in slats through the rotting boards and dropped bait festered and broiled in the August heat.

Hood quickly spotted the small orange flag, swimming with a coating of slimy green seaweed. It was located under the pier so that no boat could mistakenly hit it. Not that any boat would know it was here. No civilian maps marked the location. Even some of the topographical maps of the area missed it.

Hood settled the chair into the marshy sand, placed the tackle box on the seat and undid the latch. Seagulls hovered and complained in the salty air above the pier, and waves farther out made a cupping sound as they hit the shore. The tide would be coming in soon. Everything was ready. Hood stroked the block of soft, white putty, the size and shape of a spaghetti box, then fingered the metal ring attached to the block by a cord. The whole thing had taken just five minutes to assemble—and it was guaranteed to work, even in water.

Hood pressed the block into position, pulled the ring and offered a parting glance at its long tail of cord, striped with light from the pier slats. It reminded Hood of a piece of bait—which it was, after all—a teaser to keep them dangling on the end of a hook. Like all good fishermen, Hood knew that to catch a big fish, you had to use the right bait.

23

. . .

RICHIE WAS IN the living room, watching television, when Georgia arrived home. He was dressed only in ratty denim cutoffs. His dark hair was sticking out at odd angles and there were Oreo crumbs on the couch. It was just after noon, and he clearly hadn't combed his hair or brushed his teeth all morning. His eyes had that dull, glassy look children have when they've been watching too many hours of cartoons.

"Why aren't you at camp today?" she asked him.

"I didn't feel like going."

Georgia bent down to feel his forehead. No fever. She wished it were that simple. *He knows,* she realized as she watched him hug his knees to his chest. He looked as if he were trying to crawl inside himself. Georgia wanted to crawl right in there with him, pull a blanket over their heads and wake them both when he was twenty-one. Instead, she did the next best thing. She kicked off her shoes and curled up next to her boy, wrapping her arms protectively around him. They sat like that for several long minutes without speaking. She could hear the slight wheeze to his breathing and smell the little-boy sweat on his skin.

"Where's Grandma?" she asked finally. Georgia's mother was a bookkeeper for a local dentist. Dr. Arigoni was his name, but everyone in the neighborhood called him Dr. Agony. The man had all the finesse of a transmission repair specialist, but he was kind to her mother and the hours were good.

"She stayed home with me today. She's in the kitchen." Georgia could hear it now: humming. Her mother always hummed when she was upset. Usually some kind of elevator music. Today, it was "Raindrops Keep Falling on My Head."

"Grandma told you?" Georgia asked softly.

"I heard her talking to you on the phone early this morning," he mumbled, his eyes on the cartoon figures darting across the television. A *Rugrats* rerun.

"Richie . . ." Georgia stumbled about. *Oh boy,* she thought. *There are no child-rearing manuals on this one.* "Nothing's certain yet. Please, honey, don't do this to yourself."

"Is Mac in jail?"

Georgia's heart fell into her stomach. "No. He's not in jail. Connie's missing, but everyone is trying to find her. Mac, too," Georgia added in a voice so bright, it sounded as if they were all searching for a lost glove instead of the bloody body of her best friend.

Richie pushed back and searched her face. "It's a mistake. Right, Mom? Mac wouldn't hurt Connie, would he?"

Georgia looked into her son's honey-colored eyes, and she felt her throat close over. It was the same question she'd been asking herself all morning. And she didn't have the kind of logical, carefully thought out adult answer she'd been hoping for. But she did have a gut feeling—one that even that bloody handprint in Connie's apartment couldn't entirely dislodge.

"I don't think Mac would intentionally hurt Connie," Georgia said slowly. "I don't know *what* happened, but I'll do the best I can to find out."

Georgia looked up from the couch and saw her mother standing by the open kitchen door. Margaret Skeehan's eyes were red rimmed, and she seemed to be trying to force a hopefulness to her face that made it appear unnaturally tight. Georgia kissed Richie on the head and rose. She followed her mother into the kitchen.

"Ma," Georgia said hoarsely as the door closed behind them. It was all she could manage to choke out before the tears started to stream down her face. Margaret pulled her daughter toward her and held her tightly. It was the same fierce, protective hug Georgia had just given Richie. They were all closing ranks.

Georgia sank into a chrome chair at the kitchen table and poured out her grief and confusion. Margaret listened, her hands interlaced in front of her as if she didn't trust them to do more.

"I've been saying rosaries for Connie all morning," Margaret said finally. "I don't even know what to think anymore. Even police cars passing by make me nervous."

Police cars. Brennan had ordered protection on the house. "Ma?" Georgia said softly. "I want you to be extra careful around strangers right now. Don't give out any information over the phone and don't let Richie talk to anyone you don't know."

"What's wrong?" Margaret put a manicured hand on top of Georgia's. She always did have beautiful hands—painted nails, soft skin smelling of Ponds cold cream. Georgia's hands were always so ragged and scraped from her work, she didn't even like to look at them.

Georgia took a deep breath. "It's probably nothing, Ma," she lied, forcing a smile. "But with Connie missing, I just think you and Richie need to be careful."

"You too, dear. Especially when it comes to Mac."

"But Mac couldn't have . . ."

"—Darling," said Margaret, "I like Mac—you know I do. But this?" She sighed. "This is not something you should be involved with. Connie was your best friend."

Georgia started to argue, but caught herself. She sensed her mother had been rehearsing this speech all morning.

"Even if it's true that Mac is innocent," Margaret continued, "there will be a cloud over him for the rest of his life. Please, Georgia—you're tired and confused. But please think about that—for your sake and Richie's."

Georgia was too weak to argue. She went upstairs to take a shower and lie down. She managed about an hour and a half before she was awakened by a knock on her door.

"Honey?" said Margaret Skeehan. "There's a fire marshal down-stairs. He says he's been ordered by Chief Brennan to fetch you."

A fire marshal? Georgia palmed her eyes. If it were Carter, her mother would have said. Even Eddie Suarez is a familiar name to her. She slipped into a blouse and pants, combed her hair and walked down-stairs.

Andy Kyle was sitting on her living-room couch doing coin tricks for her son. He was dressed in a linen sports jacket and tie that looked casually expensive, a pair of corn-colored khakis and a cotton button-down shirt with a subtle stripe of olive green. He flipped the quarter in his palm to Richie and rose from the couch. He smiled when he saw Georgia, then seemed to think better of it, and wiped it away.

"Marshal," he said, taking a step forward. "I'm sorry to hear about . . ."

"—What are you doing here?" Georgia asked, cutting him off.

"Chief Brennan asked me to escort you to a meeting."

"*Escort* me? Why would you need to *escort* me?" It was a snotty question, delivered in a snotty tone and Georgia had no idea why she felt the need to say it except that whatever it was Chief Brennan wanted, she didn't appreciate hearing about it from this brand-new, wet-behind-the-ears fire marshal.

She expected Kyle to become surly. Mac certainly would have if she'd used a tone like that on him. But Andy Kyle just leveled a cool, confident gaze at her.

"If you'd prefer to run behind the car, that's fine with me," he offered with a slight grin. "But you might get pretty sweaty by the time we hit Brooklyn."

Then he politely thanked her mother, said good-bye to her son and began to walk out of the house. Georgia, feeling a little chagrined herself now, grabbed her duty holster and gun, gave a quick hug to Richie and her mother and followed Kyle to a blue department sedan parked by the curb. He unlocked her door and opened it. She went to speak, but she was stopped by a grin across his boyish face.

"Now what's so funny?" she asked.

"You were just about to lecture me about why I'm not supposed to open your door for you."

"Well . . . yeah."

"If I run over you, are we even?"

Georgia smiled in spite of herself. "Okay, I'm in a pissed-off mood. I admit it," she said as Kyle got in and pulled away from the curb. "I've had a tough night. I've got no right to take it out on you. Sorry."

"Uh-uh." Kyle shook his head. "'Sorry' is only for the big things, remember? Proper responses here include any four-letter word, a derogatory and preferably profane comment about my parentage, ethnic background or procreation capacities, or a complaint about the union contract."

Georgia laughed. "You're all right, Andy—you know that? A few more years in the FDNY, we'll have you talking like you actually come from this friggin' city."

Kyle got on the Brooklyn-Queens Expressway. Georgia assumed he was taking them to headquarters, but he passed the turnoff and kept heading south.

"May I ask where we're going?"

"Coney Island, but I don't know anything else," said Kyle. "Brennan didn't want you to drive, I guess, because he thought you'd be exhausted from . . ." Kyle's voice trailed off. At the first traffic light, he studied her profile. Georgia could feel his eyes on her. She checked her reflection in the rearview mirror in response. She felt acutely aware of a pimple that was beginning to develop on her left cheek and of having every one of those two thousand calories Marenko spoke about at the diner this morning sitting on her hips.

"How's Mac holding up?" asked Kyle. "Everybody at base heard about his arrest. You must be going through hell right now."

Georgia shrugged. She was certain Marenko would be livid with her for discussing anything about him to this rookie.

"Georgia, I *know* about you and Mac. You don't have to play dumb with me. Eddie Suarez told me."

"And how would Suarez know?"

"He says it's written all over your face every time Marenko enters a room."

Georgia stared out her window without answering, hoping to hide the flush in her face as the Caprice crawled along in bumper-to-bumper traffic. Rows of houses gave way to industrial lots, junkyards and an open artery of rail tracks. To her right, just across the East River, the skyscrapers of Manhattan shimmered in the early-afternoon heat, sparkling like the Emerald City of Oz.

"Look, I'm not trying to pry," Kyle told her. "Here's why I'm asking." He pulled a slip of paper out of his shirt pocket and handed it to her. The name Bernard Chandler was scribbled across it, along with a phone number in Manhattan.

"Mac's going to need a good lawyer," Kyle explained. "Bernie Chandler's one of the best criminal defense attorneys in New York. At eight hundred dollars an hour, he'd better be."

"Mac hasn't got that kind of money," said Georgia.

"Bernie's a partner in Berenson, Chandler, Kaufman and Kyle, Georgia. The 'Kyle' is my father, Jerome. Best lawyers in the city. If something's happening—contracts, real estate, high-profile criminal case or divorce—they're involved. Don't worry, Bernie will work out a deal with him. It will be very affordable, I promise."

Growing up, Georgia thought having clout meant that your dad was a desk sergeant who could fix a parking ticket. This was an entirely different level of clout—from a man she hadn't even treated especially well. She refolded the paper. She didn't know what to say.

"I appreciate this, Andy. Really. But I know Mac. He'd never accept a handout. He's too proud."

"It's not a handout," said Kyle. "It's a hand, and you don't have to tell him it came from me. That's why I didn't write the law firm's name on that sheet of paper. You can just give him Bernie Chandler's number and tell him you heard he's a good attorney. Make up where you got it. Bernie won't let on. He's expecting Mac's call."

Georgia tucked the slip of paper into her black hip bag. She watched Kyle at the wheel now. With his classy clothes and blandly handsome features, he looked like he should be driving them out to the Hamptons in his father's Mercedes instead of rumbling along the streets of Brooklyn in an old city-issued Chevy.

"I don't get it," she said finally. "With your polish and connections, you could've been anything, Andy. How come you joined the fire department?"

Kyle shrugged. "I always wanted to be a firefighter, I guess. Money and power never meant that much to me. The people in my life who had it always seemed to abuse it. I thought, being a firefighter, I could really help people."

"So how come you switched over to the marshals? People see you with a gun, you stop being 'helpful' in most of their eyes."

"The way I look at it," said Kyle, "as a firefighter, I could only help one person at a time. As a marshal, I can help a whole community by putting the bad guys out of commission. It's the big picture that matters to me, Georgia—not the individuals. They come and go."

"Not all of them," said Georgia, patting her bag and thinking about Kyle's efforts to help Mac.

"No, Georgia." Kyle's brown eyes lingered on her now. "*Not* all of them."

They were nearing Coney Island now. She saw the high-rise projects first. Their boxy façades covered in little rectangular windows loomed like a child's building blocks over the southern tip of Brooklyn, blocking the ocean. About the only thing Georgia could see beyond them was the latticed steel of the old Parachute Jump rising two hundred and sixty feet in the air—an Eiffel Tower with a pizza on its head. Kyle fished around on the floor for his cell phone and punched in a number.

"Chief Brennan said I should call when we got down here," Kyle explained.

He got the chief on the line as they turned off Stillwell Avenue onto Surf. Georgia stared through the windows at the massive crossbeams and loops of the Cyclone roller coaster and the Wonder Wheel Ferris wheel. She hadn't been out this way since she and Rick were still together.

Kyle exchanged a bunch of "yes, chief"s with Brennan, then disconnected. "The chief says I should drop you off at the boardwalk near the pier and he'll arrange for you to get a ride home later."

"Did he tell you what I'm supposed to be doing out here?" asked Georgia.

They both caught sight of a truck from the FDNY's Hazardous Materials Unit—"Mop and Glo" firefighters jokingly referred to it— parked at the foot of the boardwalk. On the beach beyond, men in head-to-toe white hazard suits walked the gray sand. The water that lapped around their feet had the rippled thickness of melted chocolate. When the sun hit it, it gave off a swirling sheen of rainbow colors. *Gasoline.* But with more of a bite. *Jet fuel.*

"Looks like whatever the chief brought you down here for," said Kyle. "I'm pretty sure it's not a beach party."

. . .

THIS IS NO fifty-gallon boat leak, thought Georgia as she gazed past the yellow band of tape blocking off Coney Island beach. The water resembled a bottle of salad dressing someone had forgotten to shake. Waves poured over the sand leaving rings like chocolate milk.

Georgia's eyes scanned the beach, settling on a collection of men. She watched the tall, gaunt figure with the sawdust-colored hair speaking angrily into his cell phone. Then she saw him gesture to the man with the snow-white hair she had also seen in Woodside. *What's going on here,* she wondered?

She pushed her way through the crowd of onlookers to a cluster of men at the foot of the pier. Chief Brennan was among them. His silver hair was slick with sweat, and his nose and cheeks had already turned the color of canned ham from the sun. "We've got problems," he mumbled, taking her aside.

"A leak in the pipeline?" asked Georgia.

"Estimate of the spill is about five hundred gallons," Brennan grunted. "Hazmat has managed to keep it contained largely to Coney Island's beach. We've got people from Empire here now, repairing the broken valve by the pier."

Brennan nodded to an unmarked camper on the street. "Gus Rankoff from the mayor's office has asked for a face-to-face with you," said Brennan. "He's over there by the camper, talking to Chief Delaney."

Rankoff, thought Georgia, squinting at the thickset man with the white hair talking to the FDNY's chief of operations. Now she remembered where she'd seen him before. It was in a photo in Randy Carter's newspaper article about the Jets football stadium. Rankoff was in charge of the project.

"Delaney and John Welcastle, Empire's chairman, will also be in the meeting," said Brennan, gesturing to the gaunt man on the beach.

"Chief?" Georgia asked. "Does this have to do with Robin Hood?"

Brennan gave her a stony look. "You're an errand girl, Skeehan. Just remember that."

He walked her to the camper, which was basically an air-conditioned conference room on wheels. There were charts and graphs of the Empire Pipeline on the walls. A personal computer stood across from a conference table. The blinds were drawn. Rankoff and Delaney were already inside. Welcastle joined them after a minute. From the men's vague looks, Georgia knew right away that neither Rankoff nor Welcastle recalled meeting her the other day in Woodside. Georgia decided not to bring it up. They probably didn't recognize her without her helmet.

"You have a very important job to do for this city," Rankoff said, shaking Georgia's hand and shooting her one of his dark, penetrating gazes.

"I'm not sure I know what's going on," said Georgia. She focused on Delaney now. She knew the chief of fire operations only by reputation, but he was a former rescue company captain, highly decorated. She'd trust him over any mayoral aide. But Delaney said nothing. Instead, Rankoff clapped his hands together.

"Marshal Skeehan," he said. "We have a situation so grave that nothing we say here must leave this room—understood?"

"Yessir," said Georgia. She had expected Delaney to be in charge of a pipeline leak emergency. She was surprised to see that the man calling the shots here appeared to be Rankoff. He seemed the least connected to the situation.

"The pipeline did not undergo a stress fracture. It was sabotaged," said Rankoff. "The valve was blown apart, and there's evidence that

C-four plastic explosives were used. The mayor's office was informed this morning that some kind of incident would happen today . . . We don't know if this will be the *only* one—or the first of many."

"Robin Hood," muttered Georgia. Rankoff offered the slightest nod. Georgia felt as if chipped ice were flowing down her spine. If Robin Hood could sabotage an obscure valve on the Empire Pipeline this easily, then no part of it was safe. This time, it was a fuel spill that didn't take anyone's life. *But next time?*

"He's a firefighter, isn't he?" she asked, turning to Brennan and Delaney.

"A and E is looking into that possibility," said Delaney. "But, Marshal, you must understand, we're out of that end of the investigation." Delaney's posture was ramrod straight—there was no mistaking he was ex-military. But he had a firefighter's sincerity in his deep voice. Georgia wondered if the rumors Hanlon had told her were true about his being considered for commissioner.

"Chief Delaney is telling you, Skeehan, that the progress of this investigation is not your concern," Brennan growled.

Rankoff cleared his throat. He didn't want to get involved in department politics right now. He fixed his gaze on Georgia. "Chief Delaney has obtained a computer simulation that I think will bring home just how serious this situation is."

Rankoff nodded at the computer screen. Georgia and the others crowded around it. Delaney sat down at the computer, put a CD-ROM into the system and typed in some keys. Someone turned off the lights. Outside, Georgia could hear the rumble of trucks and the crash of the surf. But in here, she could hear only the beeps and clicks of a program powering up.

"I obtained this program from a scientist in the NYPD's crime lab," explained Delaney. Georgia didn't have to be told that it was Ajay Singh. "I asked him to program a hypothetical pipeline explosion, using Empire's twelve-inch pipe diameter, its pipeline pressure of twelve hundred pounds per square inch and its delivery rate of four thousand gallons of jet fuel a minute. We selected a typical neighborhood that the pipeline might run through—semi-industrial with light manufacturing and a smattering of small, residential buildings and retail stores."

Delaney pressed Enter and a flat, two-dimensional representation of Delaney's "typical" pipeline neighborhood came on the screen. It was like looking at an ant farm. There was the "above ground" section—the asphalt streets, the concrete warehouses, the low-lying masonry-sided apartment buildings and wood-shingled row houses. And there was the "below ground" section—a green cylinder representing the pipeline. A random scattering of cars, trucks, pedestrians and streetlights had also been programmed into the setting. A box in the upper-right-hand corner showed time, wind speed and temperature. Delaney had programmed a light wind—five miles per hour—and an ambient temperature of seventy-five. Wishful thinking. It was easily twenty degrees higher today.

"I asked the crime lab to make the explosion equivalent to about a stick of dynamite, just large enough to cause a failure of the pipeline," Delaney said.

He clicked Run. Immediately, an amoebalike mass—in shades of orange and yellow representing temperature variations—appeared on the green line below the ground.

"That's the ignition of the jet fuel," explained Delaney.

It took only a fraction of a second for it to rip through the asphalt, causing a partial collapse of the street above. But within the first minute, everything changed. Cars caught fire and exploded. Streetlights and windows shattered. The tar-paper roofs of row houses and warehouses lit up like candles on a cake, each feeding the next. The cartoon figures lay dead—the computer not able to simulate the horrible burns that would surely cover their bodies.

Georgia looked at the time and temperature gauge in the corner of the screen. Already the temperature of the flames within a hundred yards of the pipeline failure was almost two thousand degrees—as hot as a blast furnace. But that was only the beginning of the destruction.

Every new burn fed the vortex of gases and heat. Wood-shingled buildings a half block away turned bright red on the screen, indicating they had ignited spontaneously from the radiant heat. Georgia watched as pools of fuel oozed like blood along the pavement. Above the pools flickered a wave of orange.

"Is that right?" asked Georgia. According to the simulation, the flames were averaging a height of about a hundred and thirty feet—as high as a thirteen-story building—more than twice the height of the buildings in the simulation.

"That's *average* flame height," Delaney explained. "Dr. Singh at the crime lab said some flame tips could reach a height in excess of twenty stories."

"How far would the destruction extend?" asked Brennan.

"The spill would fan out in a V shape over an area roughly the size of a football field," said Delaney. "But the heat damage could extend to twice that area. With something as tenacious as jet-base fuel, a ten-block cone of destruction is not out of the question."

Georgia watched as the minutes ticked past. Flaming fuel pooled in sidewalk gutters beyond the seat of the explosion. It rolled under cars and ignited them. The vapors found their way into the basements of buildings, presumably making contact with pilot lights from burners and exploding out windows. Temperature spikes climbed to over twenty-one hundred degrees. Georgia knew that that kind of heat could melt aluminum window frames, brass doorknobs and the asphalt shingles off of roofs. Even surrounding streets showed patches of radiant heat in excess of five hundred degrees. No one could survive that.

"The crime lab ran the simulation for twenty minutes," Delaney told them. "When it was over, there was nothing left but the brick outer shells of some of the buildings and the pavements. Everything else was gone."

Delaney shut down the program and switched on the lights. Rankoff's dark eyes flashed at Welcastle. He stared at Welcastle for a moment until Welcastle pursed his thin lips and looked away.

"You can see why we've been urging Empire to do whatever is necessary to prevent this disaster from taking place," said Rankoff. "The city can't afford the psychological toll right now—never mind the physical."

"I don't understand," said Georgia, looking from Welcastle to Rankoff. " Is the city urging Empire to *pay?*" An extortion scheme using explosives would normally be handled in cooperation with the Feds, in this case, the Bureau of Alcohol, Tobacco and Firearms. "Wouldn't you want the ATF to . . . ?"

"—Marshal," Brennan growled, "you are not here to render opinions on the mayor's decisions. You are simply here to receive instructions."

"As Chief Delaney has so aptly demonstrated," said Rankoff, rapping a fleshy knuckle on the computer video monitor, "a fire in the pipeline would be an unacceptable risk at this time. The mayor has determined that he can't afford such a risk. There are projects that could be negatively impacted by the kind of public situation that might occur by calling in the ATF."

"I gather this has never happened before," said Georgia.

"In forty years of supplying petroleum products to New York City, we've only had one *leak,*" Welcastle explained.

"When was that?"

"About ten years ago. In Staten Island. It took us a few days to repair back then—our leak-detection system wasn't as advanced. Now, we'd have the line instantly shut down and the leak fixed within a couple of hours."

"So a leak of the magnitude we just saw couldn't happen?" asked Georgia.

Welcastle shook his head. "Even if we instantly shut down the system, we can't do anything about the fuel already *in* that section of the pipeline." The chairman ran a nervous hand through his sawdust-colored hair. "Chief Delaney's scenario is not incorrect."

One pipeline leak in forty years. Georgia mulled that record over in her head. *So what was that 1984 Division of Safety Report about?*

"Mr. Welcastle? Was there ever a pipeline leak in North Brooklyn in 1978? At a warehouse on Bridgewater Street?"

The crow's feet thickened around Welcastle's colorless eyes. A nervous energy seemed to radiate through his lean body. He licked his thin lips without answering. Georgia saw him shoot a look around the room. No one spoke. Georgia turned to Delaney now.

"Chief? You wrote a report on that fire, I believe."

Delaney's ex-military posture seemed to slump a little. "I have no memory of such a report," he said thickly.

"You are mistaken, young lady," said Welcastle tightly. "There was no leak on the pipeline *ever*—with the exception of the incident I just told you about. We have teams of engineers as we speak, scouring every inch of the pipeline for evidence of tampering," said Welcastle. "We're using X-ray monitors, infrared scanners—you name it. So far, we've come up with nothing."

"Can't you just shut down the pipeline?" asked Georgia.

"This is not a simple process," said Welcastle. "The airports are absolutely dependent on us to supply jet fuel. Without it, New York businesses, shipping and mail delivery would grind to a halt. The city would lose millions."

"And then we'd have to go to the public and explain why we've shut everything down," Gus Rankoff added. "Most New Yorkers don't even know we *have* a pipeline. That's why it's imperative that we handle this situation as quietly as possible. No task forces. No Feds. No press. And most of all, no blowups on the pipeline. Empire will supply the million in cash. We have no choice."

"You see, young lady," said Welcastle, "*I* know my pipeline's safe. But I'm damned if I'm going to try to convince eight and a half million New Yorkers of that."

. . .

CHIEF BRENNAN OFFERED to get one of the fire marshals at Brooklyn base to take Georgia back to Woodside, but she begged off in favor of the subway. She needed time alone to sort through the events of the past couple of days—Rosen's and Dana's deaths, Connie's disappearance and, perhaps most of all, why Robin Hood would choose her to set up the blackmail of Empire. This last complication scared her. She found herself staring into the faces of strangers on the subway, wondering if behind one of their bored stares were the watchful eyes of Robin Hood. Every firefighter gave her pause now. Their casual glances and innocuous remarks seemed fraught with new meaning. *Are you the one? Did Connie figure you out? Is that why she wrote the word Bridgewater in her binder? Is that why she's missing?*

In the rumble of the subway, Georgia kept coming back to the same ancient link: a twenty-five-year-old fire in Greenpoint, Brooklyn, that no one seemed to want to talk about. *Who would know about a warehouse fire that old?*

Greenpoint was an industrial waterfront neighborhood, heavily Polish in makeup. There were lots of warehouses in the area and probably plenty of fires over the years. This one would mean nothing to most people. *But Mac knows Greenpoint,* thought Georgia. Marenko had spent half his childhood there before his family moved to Long Island. When Marenko first became a fire marshal, Brooklyn was his base of operations. Georgia fished out her cell phone and dialed his number. He picked up on the first ring.

"If this is another goddamned reporter, you can take your story and shove it up your . . ."

"Mac, it's me."

"Oh."

"That bad, huh?"

"Story's all over the friggin' news," he said. "I haven't even been charged yet, and everyone's acting like I'm going to the chair. Christ," he said softly. "I had to tell my kids. I feel so torn up inside."

"I'm really sorry."

"Yeah, I know. Thanks."

"Listen," said Georgia. "I need to ask you about something. I was in Connie's apartment this morning."

Silence. "You . . . shouldn't have gone there," he muttered. Georgia sensed him shuddering on the line.

"I know," said Georgia, thinking the same thing herself. "But, Mac, Connie wrote something in her sergeant's binder. She wrote the word *Bridgewater.* Does that mean anything to you?"

"Only Bridgewater I know is a street in my old neighborhood in Brooklyn. Why?"

"Because there was a fire at a warehouse there in 1978 that seems to tie into a lot of stuff I'm working on right now—including Connie's disappearance. And no one wants to tell me anything about it."

"I don't know about it, either," said Marenko. "My parents had moved us to Long Island by seventy-eight. But I betcha some old-timer out of Ladder One-twenty-one would know. That's their response area."

"I'll call the firehouse. In the meantime, can you talk to some folks in the neighborhood and see what you can find out about this blaze?"

There was a pause. "Scout," Marenko pleaded. "I'm about as desperate as a man can be to find out what's going on. But I don't see how some twenty-five-year-old fire's gonna tell us anything."

Georgia hung on the line without speaking.

"There's something else, isn't there?" he said. "Something you're not telling me."

"C'mon," Georgia coaxed. "You sit in your apartment brooding all afternoon, you'll go crazy." His apartment was on the sixth floor of a tenement walkup in Manhattan's Hell's Kitchen. It consisted of a sagging sofa, a mound of old *Sports Illustrated*s, a weight bench and a view of a fire escape. It would be depressing even if he weren't facing a murder rap.

"Why don't I see what I can find out through the firehouse," said Georgia, "while you talk to some of the old ladies in the neighborhood. They'll love a nice Polish boy like you."

"I'm half Italian," he reminded her flatly.

"So? Fake it."

"What? I'm supposed do a polka or something?"

"No, just stand there and look confused. That shouldn't be hard for you."

He sighed. "There's a bar in Greenpoint called the Baltic. On McGuinness Boulevard and One Hundred Eighty-ninth Street. Meet me there in an hour and a half. We'll compare notes, all right?"

"You can't drink, you know," Georgia reminded him.

"I can inhale, can't I?"

. . .

IN THE TYPICAL seesaw fashion of city fiscal logic, Ladder One-twenty-one and Engine Two-oh-three were closed up in the mid-1980s because of budgetary cutbacks, then reopened in spanking new quarters eight blocks away in the early 1990s. The result, unfortunately, was that there were no old-timers in the new Greenpoint firehouse. They had long ago been scattered to other parts of the city.

Georgia stood at the entrance of the sleek new firehouse, all concrete and beige tile, and interviewed Lieutenant Prager, the officer on duty. Prager was simply too young to know anything about a twenty-five-year-old fire. Georgia was ready to leave when he snapped his fingers.

"Denise Flannagan," the lieutenant said suddenly. "She might know. She's Captain Flannagan's widow. He was the captain of the old Ladder One-twenty-one. She comes around here sometimes with cakes and cookies for the guys. Nice lady. She runs a day-care center out of her row house here in Greenpoint."

Prager didn't have Denise Flannagan's address, but Georgia got it from a phone book and walked the few blocks to a yellow aluminum-sided row house with crepe-paper cutouts of children on the front windows and the squeal of youngsters out back. It was a cheerful house with flowers in the window boxes and balls in the front yard. And yet, on closer inspection, it was a house in sore need of repair. The concrete stoop was crumbling. The iron railing was rusting into the cement. The gutters looked old and pitted, and there were stains along the edges of the roof where it had been leaking. Georgia walked up the long concrete stoop to ring the doorbell.

A woman about Georgia's age answered. She had fine, dark blond hair pulled up in a straggly bun and the greenest eyes Georgia had ever seen. Although she wore no makeup, her skin was smooth and flawless, all except for a certain tiredness about the eyes. She had a baby on her shoulder.

"Excuse me," said Georgia. "I'm looking for Denise Flannagan."

"I'm Tricia, her daughter," said the woman. The baby started to cry. "Can I help you?"

Georgia showed the woman her badge. "I was hoping to talk to your mother about a fire that happened in the neighborhood many years ago." Georgia had to shout over the baby's cries. "Have I got you at a bad time?"

Tricia nodded to the child. "With Kolya, every time is bad."

"Your son?"

"Kolya? No, I'm not Polish, but a lot of the kids we care for are," said Tricia. "My two are in back. My mother and I run a day-care center. We've got six besides mine we take care of. Come in."

Georgia stepped through the front door. There were baby swings and playpens and sippy cups of juice everywhere. In the corner, Barney the purple dinosaur danced across the television screen. Above the television, a crucifix hung on the wall and next to it, a cross-stitch of the same Irish blessing Georgia's mother had in their kitchen: *May the wind be at your back . . . May you be in heaven a half hour before the devil knows you're dead.*

"My mom's just putting a couple of the children down for a nap. Which fire do you want to talk to her about?"

"A fire that happened on Bridgewater Street back in 1978."

Tricia's smile disappeared. "The fire at Kowalski's warehouse?"

"Do you know about it?" asked Georgia.

"My father did." The baby fussed some more on her shoulder. Tricia's hair loosened in its bun and fell down onto her sweaty neck. A little voice called out from the kitchen for cookies. "I'll get you cookies in a minute, Caitlin," she snapped. "Go outside and play." Then she turned back to Georgia. The baby was screaming now. Tricia bounced him on her shoulder in an attempt to quiet him down. "I don't think my mother will want to talk to you."

"Why?"

"Because my father's obsession with that blaze was almost worse than his illness. Both nearly bankrupted the family. We almost lost the house. My mother's still barely able to hold onto it. Look, Miss Skeehan, please don't upset her. She's been through enough."

"I don't want to upset her. But this is really important."

"Important?" Tricia's face hardened. "My father died from this job, Miss Skeehan. Do you have any idea what that's like?" The hoarse, emotional sound of Tricia's voice made the baby stop crying. The two women stared at each other, both breathing heavily.

"When I was twelve," Georgia said softly, "my father went to work one night in Engine Two-seventy-eight in Woodside. He never came home. I still hate the smell of incense and red roses. I hate the sound of bagpipes playing "Amazing Grace." I can't walk into his old engine company and not get a lump in my throat. I miss him every single day, and it never gets any easier. So yes, I *do* know what it's like."

Tricia swallowed hard. "I'm sorry," she said finally. "I didn't realize . . ." She hefted the fidgety child on her hip. "Wait here. I'll get my mother for you."

Tricia took Kolya upstairs, leaving Georgia in the living room—just her and a little boy teething on a rubber pretzel in a playpen in the center of the room. The pretzel dropped to the floor, beyond his reach, and he let out a little squeal.

"I'll get that for you," Georgia cooed to the child. He beamed—a big, grateful grin, just like the ones Richie used to give her at that age.

"You're a real charmer—yes you are."

As she babbled on to the delighted child, Georgia found herself fantasizing about life with a baby attached to her hip instead of a nine-millimeter Glock. She'd bake cookies, volunteer in the PTA and spend her evenings talking to Mac about birthday parties and picnics at the beach. Richie would come to see her as the kind of mother she'd always wanted to be. A real mother. Joined to a real father.

"Miss Skeehan?"

Georgia rose from the side of the playpen. A small, reed-thin woman shuffled forward and extended her hand. It was nearly impossible to gauge her age. In her youth, Denise Flannagan must have been a beauty. She had the same deep green eyes as her daughter. Even wrinkled, her skin had a milky white glow to it—all except for under her eyes, which were dark with shadows. She walked with a slight limp, the result, Georgia suspected, of an arthritic hip. She looked like a kind woman, but she seemed too old to be caring for so many young children.

"Mrs. Flannagan?" Georgia shook her hand. "I'm so sorry to bother you. I don't know if your daughter told you why I'm here."

"She did."

The little boy in the playpen reached out to Denise Flannagan. She picked him up, wincing from the effort.

"You must really love children to do all this," said Georgia over the drone of cartoons.

"Oh, I do." The woman smiled. She felt the child's diaper. It was time for a change. "I raised six of my own. But I think I'd give the day care up if I could. It's getting awfully hard on me." She walked the child over to a changing table.

"Why don't you?" It was a bold question, and Georgia felt suddenly embarrassed for asking it. But Denise Flannagan only laughed—a warm, good-natured laugh—as if words were the least of her troubles.

"Because, dear," she said kindly, "I need the money. I would've lost the house without it."

"But your husband was a fire captain . . ."

"—Who retired many years ago on a small, basic pension. Pat was sick a long time, and the medical plan only covered so much." She finished the diapering, found a rocking chair by the front window and rocked the boy on her lap.

"May I ask what he died of?"

"Well . . ." She sighed. "He had the cancer." She whispered the word *cancer* the way older people in Woodside sometimes did, as if it were an all-purpose illness, synonymous with death and far too personal to make an issue of. Georgia knew right then that Denise Flannagan would never say what kind of cancer.

"But he didn't die of that, you see," Denise added. "Pat was leaving his doctor's office one day, stepped off the curb and got hit by a car. They never caught the driver."

"I'm so sorry," said Georgia. "Your daughter said he was obsessed with the fire at Kowalski's warehouse."

"He was, indeed," said Mrs. Flannagan. "He believed that's what made him so sick."

"Why did he think that?"

"Well," she said, "it was just about the worst beating Pat ever took. Tricia—*Pa*tricia, she's named after my husband—she was a little girl at the time, but she still remembers how bad he looked. He was green when he came home the next morning, and he had these sores all over his body. It was horrible. He couldn't eat for two days. He couldn't keep anything in his stomach." Denise Flannagan had that polite, older-person way of talking, Georgia noticed. She'd never say her husband "vomited."

Tricia came down the stairs now. Denise Flannagan nodded at her. "Isn't that right, dear?"

"What?"

"Daddy was so sick after that fire?"

The baby was fidgeting on Denise's lap. Tricia picked the child up. "I don't want to talk about it." The younger woman wandered down the hall. Georgia heard a refrigerator door open.

"She was very traumatized," Mrs. Flannagan said in the kind of conspiratorial whisper she'd reserved up until now for cancer. "All the children were. But it hit Tricia the hardest, I think. She was so close to her father."

"I know the feeling," said Georgia, thinking about her own dad. "When did Captain Flannagan start to get sick? Was it right after the fire?"

"Not really," said the older woman. "He recovered from that initial bout after a few days. And then, for a long time, Pat didn't pay it no mind. He was so strong and healthy. He smoked—all the men did back then. But he also ran in a couple of New York City Marathons. It was five or six years after the fire that things started happening to him. Small things, at first. He started trying to track down the men who were there. They closed the firehouse, you see. So the men were scattered all over the city."

"Were a lot of the men sick by then?"

"I'm not sure," she said. "There were maybe a hundred men at that fire. A lot of them seemed just fine." The old woman clasped her hands in her lap. The knuckles were bony, the fingers bent from arthritis. "I had the children to think about and when Pat got sick, I concentrated on him—and the medical bills. I was too busy to keep track of much else."

"How long has it been since he died?" asked Georgia.

"It'll be seven years next month, God rest his soul. But he had to retire eight years before that—he was so sick." She cocked her head. "May I ask why you're interested?"

"Because the Bridgewater fire might have something to do with a case I'm working on, and no one seems to know much about it."

"My husband could've helped you," said Mrs. Flannagan. "Before he passed away, Pat was putting together a case history of that fire. He had files and records all over the basement."

"What happened to the stuff?" asked Georgia.

"I just boxed everything up and left it there. Would you like to take a look?"

"I'd love to."

"Tricia will have to show you," she apologized. "I don't take the basement stairs more than I have to. It's hard on my knees."

· · ·

The basement was unfinished. White asbestos sleeves covered the pipes. Mold and dust covered a stack of cardboard cartons by a workbench.

Tricia grudgingly pulled one of the cartons out and plonked it on top of the workbench.

"You don't want me to look through this stuff, do you?" asked Georgia.

"You go to your father's old firehouse much?" Tricia shot back.

Georgia nodded. "Point taken. Look, I won't remove anything without your permission—okay? Can you give me half an hour?"

Tricia grabbed a folding chair from the corner and pulled it open. "Have a seat," she said. "You've got until the babies wake up from their naps."

The dust and mold on the carton made Georgia sneeze as she opened it. On the top was a sheet of lined yellow notebook paper with fourteen names across it. Beside each name was a ladder or engine company number, followed by a date of death.

Georgia noticed right away that each name was from one of four fire companies Ed Delaney had mentioned in his 1984 Division of Safety report. The companies were also the ones in closest proximity to the blaze— the companies that would have gone inside the warehouse that night. And fourteen of the men were dead by the time Pat Flannagan compiled this list seven years ago.

Georgia pulled out a sheaf of papers and heard something thud onto the concrete floor. It was a stack of photographs that had stuck together. Georgia leafed through them now. The top one was a black-and-white fire department photo, the "death shot," as firefighters called it. It was the portrait the FDNY kept on file in case a firefighter died in the line of duty and the newspapers wanted a picture of him.

The firefighter in the photograph was handsome in a bland sort of way. He had a square face and shoulders that suggested he was tall and muscular. He wore firefighter's dress blues, and his faded blond hair was bushy like a character in a 1970s sitcom. Georgia guessed the picture had been snapped around that time. Beneath his thick blond mustache there was a hint of a smile. She guessed the man was about twenty-four years old. The pale eyes were eager—maybe too eager. He'd probably just come on the job. Along the bottom, someone had scrawled his name. Georgia stared at it and her heart stopped. *Michael "Mickey" Hanlon, March 1978,* it read.

If she had any doubt about the connection, the very next photo—a color snapshot—showed a group of men with their arms around one another at a barbecue. There, next to Mickey Hanlon, was a muscular young man with watery blue eyes, a thick mustache and a slight fleshiness beneath the jowls. No one had to tell her she was looking at a much younger Seamus Hanlon.

Georgia put the picture aside and turned her attention to the next photo in the stack. The sight made her draw back in horror. It too, was a black-and-white portrait, though clearly, this one never graced any FDNY personnel file. It was a photograph of a man in a wheelchair with sticklike arms and legs. His grizzled face sported a two-day growth of beard and was hollow and gaunt as if he were sucking on a lemon. The skin on his neck was black and purple, and his eyes had a frightened look. She felt her breath catch in her chest when she read the words on the bottom: *Mickey Hanlon, August 1995.* He couldn't have been more than forty-one years old.

Forty-one? It didn't seem possible. Georgia flipped through to the next photo. Another department shot of a young firefighter, followed by another horrific shot of the man at the close of his life. And then another. And then another. Only the hair color seemed to change. The before-and-after shots made Georgia feel nauseated and clammy. She kept bouncing between the shots, looking for a clue that the men in the "before" shots would become the men in the "after"s. She could tell they were the same men around the eyes, but little else remained recognizable.

Why didn't Seamus tell me? Georgia wondered. *His brother. His own brother.*

Beneath the stack of pictures was a manila envelope. She opened it up to find a mimeographed map of the Empire Pipeline, yellowed with age—the kind Georgia had seen in many firehouses, listing all the locations of valves and shutoffs from Staten Island to Brooklyn and up through Queens. Attached to it was a faded blueprint from the city Buildings Department outlining the original construction of Kowalski's warehouse on Bridgewater Street.

Georgia put the blueprint to one side, puzzled as to why Pat Flannagan would want it. It sat on a corner of the workbench, the paper so thin that the map of the pipeline bled right through it, with the roads and junctions lining up perfectly—and Kowalski's warehouse smack dab over the Empire Pipeline.

Georgia frowned at the blueprint, certain that she'd made a mistake. Buildings weren't supposed to straddle the pipeline—yet this one had. Flannagan had uncovered a nasty little blunder. And then he was killed. By a hit-and-run driver who was never found. Though it wasn't cold in the basement, Georgia felt a shiver travel through her body.

She could hear the babies starting to fuss, so she began putting Flannagan's notes away. A piece of letterhead at the bottom of the box caught her eye. It was from the city's Department of Environmental Protection, a "work for hire" form dated February 1, 1978. The form authorized a firm called Tristate Trucking to remove "unspecified manufacturing by-products" from Kowalski's Carting and Hauling and truck them to a firm called Camden Bonded Disposal in Camden, New Jersey.

Georgia stared at the form. It was dated six months before the fire. Did the DEP *know* there were hazardous chemicals in that warehouse, she wondered? And if so, why weren't the firefighters told?

She heard a set of footsteps on the rotting wood risers at the far end of the room and turned. It was Tricia.

"Time's up," the young woman told Georgia.

"I was wondering if I could hold on to a few things from the boxes," asked Georgia. "I promise to return them."

"*What* few things?"

"This form," said Georgia, holding up the DEP authorization. "A blueprint of a building. And some pictures and names of the men at the fire. I know the brother of one of the men. Captain Hanlon in Engine Two-seventy-eight."

Tricia descended the rest of the stairs. She folded her arms across her chest. There was a hard look to her beautiful green eyes. Georgia could see it now—the same thrust-out jaw of runaways in the Port Authority Bus Terminal.

"My mother's been through a lot, Miss Skeehan," said Tricia. "I don't want her dealing with depositions and subpoenas."

"I understand," said Georgia. "I won't put her through any more heartache. We're all fire department here."

"*All* fire department? That's supposed to make everything okay?" Tricia laughed bitterly. "My dad *loved* the department—loved it like he loved his own kids. All the men did. And what did they ever get in return? My God, Ms. Skeehan, the city never even put up a goddamn plaque in their memory."

21

. . .

THE BALTIC BAR in Greenpoint was a narrow, dingy working-man's
bar with a glowing Budweiser sign in the window. It was a short walk
from the Newtown Creek, an industrial canal of water that flowed—
barely—into the East River. The creek was always black—even when
the sun was shining on it.

Marenko was sitting on a bar stool by the door. He'd showered and
shaved, and was wearing a black polo shirt and tan khakis. But his eyes
looked puffy and dark, and he had already smoked several cigarettes.
Georgia walked over and nodded to what looked like an empty beer
glass in front of him.

"Nonalcoholic," he muttered, catching her disapproving gaze. "Tastes
like cat's piss. You want something?"

"Yeah," said Georgia. "Answers." She opened a large envelope she
was carrying and thrust the stack of photos she'd found in Flannagan's
basement into Marenko's hands. He thumbed through the pictures.

"Holy . . ." He let out a long whistle. "What happened to these guys?"

"The one thing they all had in common was that fire in nineteen
seventy-eight on Bridgewater Street. Louise Rosen had a mention of it
in her files. Seamus Hanlon wouldn't talk to me about it, even though
his own brother was there. And Connie had the name of the street
scribbled in her sergeant's binder."

Marenko put the stack of pictures facedown on the bar next to Georgia. The photos clearly spooked him.

"There's one thing I don't get," said Georgia, putting the photos away. "This fire happened twenty-five years ago. Why would anyone care about it *now*?"

"Maybe it's not the fire they care about." Marenko shrugged.

"What do you mean?"

He slipped off the bar stool and slapped some bills on the counter. "C'mon," he said.

"Where are we going?"

"To Bridgewater Street. I think you should see the site. There's something about it you need to know."

Outside, the sky was the color of liquid mercury. Georgia could feel the air, gritty as pumice on her skin. Storm clouds were gathering in the distance. A gust of wind kicked up candy wrappers and tumbled them across the asphalt. The rain would hit hard when it finally came—maybe cool things down a bit.

Georgia and Marenko cut across a small park that was more concrete than grass. Children rumbled by on skateboards, cherry ices in their hands red as spilled blood. Cars roared along the streets and music blared from open windows, exhaling the heat of the day.

They turned down a street of body shops and scrap-metal yards. Up ahead, Georgia could see the concrete bulkheads of the Newtown Creek.

"Me and my three brothers, we used to play down here as kids," said Marenko. "Used to pitch rocks into the creek. My grandmother still lives about four blocks from here." He told her about the unexploded World War II bombs and spent shells they found in the neighborhood. He pointed out the concrete stacks of the sewage-treatment plant across the street from several large white hatboxes—oil storage tanks. He seemed to know every crack in the cement like it was a birthmark on one of his kids.

"A regular *Leave It to Beaver* childhood you had here," said Georgia.

"Yeah." Marenko laughed. "Not the healthiest of places, Greenpoint. It's got the largest sewage-treatment plant in the state, a sanitation depot, an abandoned incinerator, a dozen or so chemical manufacturers—all within the space of maybe half a mile. As a marshal, I think I was inside every one of them at one time or another. Hell, there's even a fifty-acre oil spill below much of this neighborhood—seventeen million gallons. Can you believe it? When I was a kid, some of it leaked into the sewers and blew out the manhole covers."

"Sounds pretty horrendous," said Georgia.

"I guess." Marenko shrugged. "But when you're a kid, you kind of see it as an adventure. Anyway, not a whole lot's changed around here since then." The smile faded from his lips. "I wonder if thirty years from now . . ." His voice trailed off. He shoved his hands in his pockets. He was already gearing himself for a future in which life was measured in decades of lost time.

Georgia put a tender hand on his right shoulder. He reached over with his left hand and held it there an instant.

"I'm scared, Mac," Georgia whispered, giving in to the strength of his touch.

"Yeah . . . well." He shrugged off the moment without meeting her gaze. He wasn't going to go there. Georgia sensed it was all he'd been doing in the quiet of his apartment: picturing himself behind bars, a white cop from the suburbs of Long Island in prison, cut off for decades from family and friends. He was too good of an investigator not to know what he was up against. All the prosecution had to do was say the words "lovers' triangle," and the rest would fall into place. Marenko himself had helped put guys away on less physical evidence than what was facing him now.

"I almost forgot." Georgia opened her hip bag and fished out Bernie Chandler's name and phone number. She handed the slip of paper to Marenko. "Here. Chandler's supposed to be an excellent criminal defense attorney and he's reasonable. In case it turns out that you need . . ."

He stopped in his tracks and frowned at the slip of paper. "—Where'd you get this?"

"A friend of a friend." Georgia shrugged. She was a lousy liar, and Marenko knew it.

"Cut the crap, Scout. You ask around some holding pen for a drug dealer's attorney?"

"No. And besides, what difference does it make where I got it? Chandler's supposed to be good. He'll work cheap and—not for nothing, Mac—you don't have a lot of options."

"Then tell me where you got it."

"You are such a pigheaded . . ." She threw up her hands. ". . . Andy Kyle gave it to me, all right? His father's a partner in the same law firm as Chandler."

Marenko crumpled up the slip of paper and tossed it on the sidewalk, next to a chain-link fence with a heap of crushed cars behind it. "I don't need some rich kid's handouts."

He walked ahead. Georgia retrieved the paper and caught up with him. "I told Andy you'd say that. That's why he didn't write the law firm name down."

Marenko turned to her and raised an eyebrow. "You and Kyle have been doing quite a *lot* of talking, I see. What else you tell him about me, huh?"

Georgia shook her head at the irony. Marenko could discuss her all he wanted to with Connie. But let Georgia say one word to a fellow fire marshal, and *he* was indignant.

"Mac, get real for a moment. Andy Kyle knows about us. All the marshals at Manhattan base know. Your privacy ended the moment you woke up bloody in Connie Ruiz's apartment. Andy was trying to help—nothing more—and the sooner you get that through your thick head, the better." She grabbed Marenko's hand and stuffed the paper into it. "Grow up a little, okay? You may need this."

They walked the rest of the way to Bridgewater Street in silence. The sun's brutal edge had passed, but the air was pearly with the hint of approaching thundershowers.

"Here we are." Marenko nodded to a vacant lot surrounded by a chain-link fence topped with razor wire. Smashed beer bottles sparkled like diamond chips on the decaying sidewalk in front, next to a lead-colored fire hydrant. "This is where the fire happened—right here at the former site of Kowalski's Carting and Hauling."

"There's nothing here," said Georgia.

"Yeah? Well, look long and hard, sweetheart. Because this is gonna be the fifty-yard line for the new football stadium Mayor Ortaglia's fixing to build."

"Where'd you hear that rumor?"

"Ain't no rumor." He nodded to the weed-choked lot. "There were four guys here an hour ago. Surveyors, Scout. They told me straight. When I checked around the bars, I heard the same thing. The city already owns several parcels of land around here, and they're buying this one. The Empire Pipeline runs beneath here, but I guess that's not moving. They'll have to build around it somehow."

"Or over it," Georgia muttered, thinking about Flannagan's blueprint of the warehouse. She peered through the rusted fence, more certain than ever that the fire that took place here twenty-five years ago was in some way tied in to Rosen's and Dana's deaths, to Robin Hood, and maybe even to Connie.

Marenko leaned his back on the fence, put a foot up and studied her. His eyes were as blue as two lapis-lazuli gemstones. "Scout—what are we doing here?"

Georgia didn't answer. Thunder rumbled in the distance. The sky darkened to an ominous shade of gray.

"C'mon, man, this isn't a game," he pleaded. "This is my life you're talking about."

Georgia looked down at the pavement, not trusting herself to gaze at him now. "It's all conjecture," she said, shaking her head. "A and E has the case. The only stuff I know for sure, I'm not supposed to talk about."

"But if it'll help us find Connie . . ."

"—I don't *know* if it'll help us find Connie!" she snapped at him. "How can I *know* that, Mac? How can I have looked at her apartment and *know* that?"

Marenko closed his eyes as if he'd been hit. Then he turned and clutched the chain-link fence and thumped his forehead lightly against it. The rusted metal reverberated down the panel.

"You're right." He sighed. "How could you know? Jeez—*I* don't even trust myself right now. How can you?" He reached into his khakis and pulled out a pack of Marlboros and a lighter. He tried to hide the trembling in his fingers, but it took him several attempts to get a spark.

They walked back toward the park in silence. Two teenagers were skateboarding near a fountain that had been turned off in some fiscal cutback and never turned back on. Across from the fountain was a large gray Roman Catholic Church. A banner announced a celebration for the Feast of Saint Hyacinth on Friday. Marenko nodded toward the church.

"I was an altar boy there."

"Yeah?"

He grinned. "Don't look so surprised."

"Saint Hyacinth—who was she?"

"He," Marenko corrected. He stepped up on the lip of the fountain and peered into the base. On top of a pile of decaying leaves, Georgia saw several empty liquor bottles in paper bags and some fast-food containers.

"I think his name was Jacob, but in Latin, it was Jacinthus, which means 'hyacinth,'" Marenko explained. "He was this Polish saint who was supposed to have saved a bunch of people when a bridge collapsed. I like him, as saints go, 'cause he put his life on the line to help people. He was kind of like the firefighter of saints."

"What's the feast like?" asked Georgia.

Marenko stepped down off the lip of the fountain. "My grandmother always helps out at it. It's usually a big parade followed by a picnic. You've never seen so many different kinds of Polish sausage in your life. And the bread. Nobody makes bread like the Poles."

He took another hit off his cigarette and slowly exhaled a stream of smoke. He ran a hand down his face. Georgia felt she could almost read the thoughts running through his head—the fears and the longings. She shouldn't have dragged him back to his old neighborhood today. Too many memories.

"There's a bomb," Georgia blurted out. She wasn't sure why she had said it. Maybe she just wanted to make him understand why she'd brought him here.

"A bomb?" He turned to look at her now. "Where?"

"Somewhere on the Empire Pipeline. A and E knows about it. *Connie* knew about it."

Marenko looked puzzled. "How do *you* know?"

Georgia sank down on a wooden bench with a slat missing and put her head in her hands. She poured out the whole story, starting with Connie's revelations about Robin Hood, and ending with how she'd been tapped by this Hood character to do the payoff.

Marenko listened intently. "Robin Hood wants *you* to make the drop? Son of a bitch—why?"

"I don't know, Mac. And I'm scared. First, Connie's gone, and now this." Marenko put a reassuring hand on her thigh. "So you think this warehouse fire on Bridgewater Street is the link, huh?"

"Something was stored in that warehouse—something that wasn't supposed to be there," Georgia explained. "I think it basically poisoned the men to death. And now, with the new football stadium going up, I think Robin Hood knows the evidence will be covered over forever, and he's looking for payback." She opened the manila envelope she'd been carrying and showed him the DEP form she'd taken from Flannagan's basement.

"From the looks of this form, the DEP knew about the problem six months before the fire," said Georgia. "But either they wouldn't or couldn't get the stuff out in time."

Marenko furrowed his brow at the yellowed slip of paper. "Tristate Trucking, huh? I got a friend at HIDTA who could run Tristate through his computer." HIDTA, pronounced *high-da,* was short for High Intensity Drug Trafficking Area, a multi-agency program set up by the federal government to compile computerized information on criminals.

"Problem is," Marenko added, "Robin Hood can't possibly be one of the firefighters from Bridgewater. From what you're telling me, they're all dead."

"But he could be related in some way, Mac. I think he's a firefighter. He knows fire. He knows the tools. *And* he knows the pipeline. But I can't find out any more about the incident. Everyone is shutting me down."

"What does Empire think of all this? They're coughing up the mil, after all."

"They've got their own secrets to protect," Georgia explained. She pulled the blueprint of the warehouse out of her folder and showed it to him.

"The warehouse is gone, but now, the city's fixing to build a stadium here," said Georgia. "Maybe Empire doesn't want their past screwups on this site to become public knowledge. It could make everyone skittish about letting the line run alongside a proposed stadium."

A clap of thunder rattled the still air. The sky turned the color of tarnished silver. Marenko stamped out his cigarette. "Maybe you should talk to Brennan."

"He won't listen to me."

"Then I'll do it."

"No," said Georgia. "You've got enough problems. I'll find a way."

A couple of fat raindrops dive-bombed the pavement. Marenko rose. "We should go. You're gonna get soaked. C'mon, I'll walk you to the subway station."

"What about you? Aren't you going back to Manhattan?" He shrugged, and Georgia suddenly remembered. "Are you going to go visit your grandmother?"

He kicked at a piece of loose concrete on the cracked pavement without answering.

"Don't worry. I'm not going to ask to come along," Georgia assured him. She rose and checked her watch. "I should be heading home, anyway."

Marenko put a hand on her arm. "She calls me 'Stashoo,'" he muttered.

"Who does?"

"My grandmother. It's a Polish version of Stanley. My father's name. And, uh, technically, mine, too. 'Mac's' a ... a ..." He grew red faced and put his hands in his pockets.

"A nickname. I know," said Georgia. "I peeked at your driver's license once. You never got it changed?"

He made a face. "I can't. My grandmother would have a coronary. She says Mac's a cheeseburger, not a person."

Georgia giggled.

"You think it's funny? First day of school every year, the teacher would call out, 'Where's Stanley Marenko, Junior?' And the kids would be on the floor when I raised my hand. And when I played football in high school? My grandmother would cheer for her 'Stashoo.' Let me tell you, with a name like that, you get good with your fists real fast."

"Well . . . go see her, *Stashoo.*" Georgia gave him a playful punch on the arm. "She's probably worried about you."

"She doesn't know," he said. "Nobody in my family told her. And that's the way I intend to keep it."

Georgia lifted herself up on tiptoes and gave him a kiss on the cheek. "Visit her anyway. You'll make her day." She turned to leave, and he grabbed her wrist.

"Come with me," he said huskily. More rain was falling now. A scattershot of hard drops darkening the pavement.

"No," said Georgia, shaking her head.

"Why not?"

"Because it makes you uncomfortable."

"But it's what you wanted, isn't it?"

"Not this way, Mac. Not because you feel pressured into it."

Marenko wiped a hand down his face. The rain was falling harder now. Georgia could feel it beating on her shoulders.

"Jesus, Scout. I'm standing here, asking you and you're not . . . If you want to come, you should come."

Georgia folded her arms across her chest and stared at him. "Why?"

He lifted his gaze to the clouds swirling above like smoke. "Because the sky is gonna piss down on us . . . Because my grandmother's house is closer than the subway . . ."

"—So long, Mac." She began to walk away. He ran a hand through his wet hair and cursed.

"Because I couldn't have gotten through the last twelve hours without you, all right?"

Georgia turned and saw something flicker in Marenko's eyes she'd never seen before. Something raw and sincere. It filled her more than any words.

"Shouldn't you call first?" she asked. "Just showing up with me might make your grandmother uncomfortable."

Marenko laughed—the first real laugh he'd tossed off since Connie's disappearance. It was a deep, rich sound and it always made her ache with longing.

"Scout, the pope in drag couldn't make Ida Marenko uncomfortable."

28

. . .

RAIN. FLOWING IN rivulets down the gutters, turning the pavements as slick as polished granite, chasing the squealing children from the park. Rain washes the streets—of garbage, of heat, of people. But not of memories. Memories, Robin Hood noticed, seemed to blossom like clover in the rain.

Bear had loved the rain. He never minded being wet. He used to say that feeling the icy runoff of a fire hose down the back of his turnout coat on a ninety-degree day was the sweetest sensation in the world. Even after he got sick, Bear loved being out in the back of their row house during a soft summer shower. He loved lightning and thunder. He had a laugh like thunder—rumbling deep down in his gut so that you could feel it like a dog's growl when you got near him.

Hood grabbed a sandwich in a small deli and stared out windows fogged with condensation. Cars roared by, kicking up a spray of water along the curb. It had rained like this when they were burying Bear at the cemetery, too—rained so hard the hole was nothing but mud and everybody's shoes were ruined. Water stains, mixed with lime, running in wavy white lines on black patent and flat leather. Hood remembered the ruined shoes more than anything else that day. Funny what you re-member.

Don't let them forget. That's what Bear had always said. *Don't let them forget, or I'll have died for nothing.* So Bear told the tale and the child learned it note by note and breath by breath, as if that terrible night belonged to them both.

The night air was fit for the breath of a dragon. A hot August evening when just sitting puts sweat on your skin and the air feels as damp as an errant mist off Long Island Sound. Back then, the city was reeling from municipal cutbacks and neighborhoods were burning up like candles on a cake. Three or four fires a night were the norm. Big fires, too. But this? This was no big deal. "A walk in the smoke," they called fires like this.

The 10-33 came in around 2300 hours. A 10-33 is a smoke condition. Twenty-three hundred hours: eleven P.M. Everything in the fire department is on military time. A passing oil delivery truck noticed a few wisps coming out of Kowalski's warehouse on Bridgewater Street. Ladder One-twenty-one and Engine Two-oh-three were first due. Captain Patrick Flannagan was in charge of the ladder, Lieutenant Frank Lopasio, the engine. All the men working under them were experienced hands—all except for Mickey, the twenty-four-year-old proby, or first-year firefighter. He was brand-new to Ladder One-twenty-one. Gerry Mulrooney, with twenty years on the job, took Mickey under his wing.

"Stick with me, kid, and do as I tell you, you'll be all right," he growled. "Ain't a fire been made that can put me in hell 'cause I'll just piss it out."

Kowalski's Carting and Hauling was sprawled across two acres on Bridgewater Street. It was surrounded by a chain-link fence topped off with razor wire. The gates were padlocked. The men took bolt cutters and snipped off the chain. Inside the fence, the pitted land resembled a moonscape. Nothing grew—not a cluster of dandelions or a thatch of crab grass. All around them were rusting hulks of fifty-five-gallon drums and piles of discarded tires. It had rained the night before, and small puddles swirled blue, green and purple in the men's flashlights, viscous like bubbles in a lava lamp. But the smoke poking out of the roof vents in the warehouse looked innocuous enough. It was gray—not black. A good sign.

The men split up. Flannagan's firefighters in the ladder, or truck, company needed to break into the warehouse, search it for victims and break windows to allow heat and smoke to escape. Lopasio's men in the engine needed to unfurl the two-and-a-half-inch hose line, hook it up to the hydrant and then get the hose into the warehouse to put out the fire. Since getting a hose into a structure is always a slower operation than doing a search, the first-due truck company often works without any water backup.

Mickey went to fetch a mask and air tank, and Mulrooney frowned.

"Kid, ya gotta learn to eat smoke or you're in the wrong business." Mulrooney wasn't wrong, either. In those days, rigs carried only two or three masks and air cylinders, and those lasted fifteen minutes at best. Taking smoke was part of the job—and no one could do it better than Gerry Mulrooney. He stood up in fires that would make other men throw up or pass out.

The steel door to the warehouse was padlocked. The men used the bolt cutters again to open the door. A wad of thick, gray-green smoke wafted over them. It smelled like rotten eggs and bitter almonds and stung their throats like salt in a raw wound. "Take some air out here," Mulrooney coached Mickey. "Then get down low and don't panic. It's just smoke. It won't kill ya."

Captain Flannagan took the lead, crouching low, his flashlight attached to his helmet, passing a dim light over the dark, hazy interior. Behind him were his four company firefighters. He stopped in his tracks and got on the radio to Lopasio outside.

"Hey, Frankie. Tell Dispatch and Chief Nickelson we need a second alarm."

None of the firefighters had to ask why. From floor to ceiling, the warehouse was stacked with fifty-five-gallon drums, some with skulls and crossbones on their labels. Worse still, the drums were plonked randomly in the warehouse so that there was no straight path from the front to the back. The only route appeared to be a zigzag.

Flannagan crouched low and headed to a dim shape that appeared to be a window. He ordered Gerry Mulrooney to take it with his halligan. Mulrooney lifted his halligan and swung hard at the window, but the halligan bounced off. It was covered with a sheet of unbreakable Lexan plastic. One of the men took the pronged end of the halligan and tried to pry the Lexan off, but the plastic never budged.

By now, the firefighters were breathing hard. Their eyes and throats burned from the smoke, which had blackened and was shot through with shafts of acid green. Tears and black snot poured down their faces. Wiping their eyes and noses did nothing but make it worse. They still couldn't see the fire, but it didn't matter now. Their skin tingled like a bad sunburn. Captain Flannagan ordered a retreat, but when they turned for the door, the smoke that had been haze just moments before, turned as thick as the sea on a moonless night. The men couldn't see the door. They couldn't even see each other. All they could see were steaming drums that glowed phosphorescent blue, yellow and purple—bright enough to cut the smoke.

"Stay together," Flannagan choked out. He radioed Lopasio that they were lost, but Lopasio's men were already in the warehouse as well. And they, too, were lost. Engine Two-fifty-two and Ladder One-forty-eight had arrived as backup. They told the two companies to stay calm. They would extend a lifeline from the entrance door and feel their way forward through the maze. Mickey started to hyperventilate. Mulrooney tried to calm him.

"You're doing great, kid. Stories for your scrapbook. Fuck it, I'll buy you a beer tomorrow and we'll laugh."

And then it happened. Like kernels of popcorn in a microwave, the drums began to explode and hurtle through the air. The men saw fire now—lots of it. Flames, some blue as well as orange—danced across a viscous sea of slippery, yellow-green muck.

Battalion Chief Nickelson arrived on the scene. He got on the radio. "All units, back out of building ASAP. We're going to a surround and drown." An exterior operation. Once the men were out, tower ladders would douse the building with water from the outside. The building would be a total loss.

It was too hot and smoky for the firefighters to stand. On their knees and their bellies, covered in an oozing slime they could barely see, the firefighters of Ladder One-twenty-one held on to one another and tried to crawl out of the warehouse. Barrels flew overhead, crashed, exploded and rained down upon them until they were soaked through to their underwear.

The men knew what they had to do. They formed a human chain. Flannagan, as captain, took up the rear. He would see that all his men got out before him. Mulrooney yanked Mickey by the collar of his turnout coat and put him between Flannagan and himself—the most protected place on the chain. O'Rourke took the lead, big enough to push objects out of the way and Battaglia, somewhat smaller, fell in behind him. The five men moved forward efficiently, without panic, though their eyes were swollen shut from the smoke, their throats were raw and their lungs were as taught as stretched rubber bands.

"Cap, I'm having a beer when we get back," croaked Mulrooney over his shoulder. "And I don't give a fuck what Chief Nickelson says."

"I hear you, Gerry," Flannagan gasped.

They made it out—all four companies. The men who first went in, and the others who extended lifelines to get them out. They fell on the dirt and vomited where they lay. Twenty men in black rubber turnout coats as slick as babes straight from the womb. They tried to drink and gagged from the burning in their throats and chests. Other fire companies hosed them down, but already, the men's eyes were pink and swollen, their skin covered with tiny red bumps that looked like measles. Mulrooney insisted on getting to his feet without assistance, only to stagger three steps before falling again. "Ach," said the forty-three-year-old in disgust. "I'm getting old. Can't take a little smoke no more."

Although a hundred men responded to the fire at Kowalski's Carting and Hauling that night, only twenty went into that warehouse. When they came out, Nickelson ordered the tower ladders to rain down water from above. The warehouse was not to be saved.

The men weren't either.

Gerry Mulrooney had trouble swallowing six months after the fire. His doctor diagnosed throat cancer. He was dead within two years. He was the first.

Sikorsky in the engine company was next. He noticed a brown spot on his arm eighteen months after the fire. He ignored it—and died of a heart attack following surgery for malignant melanoma four years later. Brain cancer took Chris McGinty in Ladder One-forty-eight inch by inch. It was still taking Vinnie Battaglia the same way. Bobby Niernoff in Engine Two-oh-three thought he'd beaten "the big C," as the men called it—until Lou Gehrig's Disease turned him into a quivering bunch of neurons that made cancer look almost preferable. Frank Lopasio let a fire take him before three separate diseases could.

Mickey developed thyroid cancer and beat it, only to learn he had stomach cancer and multiple sclerosis. "I wanna go out with something left in me—the way Gerry Mulrooney did," he vowed. He was already a beaten-up shell of a man when they say he put a revolver to his mouth and ate a bullet. Mickey Hanlon was forty-one.

The rain stopped. Outside the delicatessen, taillights made the puddles shimmer with a deep red glow, and steam clouds rose from subway grates. Hood watched people begin to trickle back onto the sidewalks. Soon, the tragedy would be behind Hood. Not the deaths—the deaths would always be there. But it wasn't simply the deaths that made Hood grieve. Or even that the men had died forgotten. The tragedy was that they had died for nothing. They saved no lives in the warehouse that night—only the reputations of a few powerful men. It was the injustice of that equation that made Hood burn.

And now—thought Hood—others will, too.

. . .

LIKE MOST PEOPLE who have reached the ripe old age of eighty-nine, Ida Marenko was usually home. Mac didn't call. He just sloshed through the downpour with Georgia until they ended up at a tidy, aluminum-sided row house on Kent Street, soaked to the bone. Fortunately, Ida Marenko had a tin awning over her front door and they caught their breath underneath it.

"I can't meet your grandmother like this," said Georgia, breathing hard from the dash. "I'm a mess."

Mac pushed back a clump of wet, black hair from his face and grinned. "I kinda like it," he said. Georgia noticed now that her white blouse had turned semi-see-through from the rain.

"Great. She'll think I'm a streetwalker you just rescued."

"She won't think that." He pushed the doorbell. A short, stocky woman answered. She had hair dyed strawberry blond and swept up in a neat bun. She wore a loud floral-print dress with matching chunky jewelry and had long fingernails done up in bright red nail polish that matched the tint of her lips. An eighty-nine-year-old coquette. She frowned at the huge, dripping man before her for only a second.

"Stashoo, my God!" she cried, wrapping her short, thick arms around his waist as he towered over her. She didn't seem to mind that hugging him was like hugging a wet Saint Bernard. "So long I haven't seen you." Then she pushed him back roughly and narrowed her gaze. "Who died?"

"Nobody died, *Babcia.* I was in the neighborhood and I got caught in the rain." He did a quick size up of her clothes. "But I see you were going out."

"Out—*pffft!*" she said, waving her arms as if she were dispersing smoke. "Some old farts I have dinner with once a week. Early-bird senior special. They'll eat without me." She laughed. She had Marenko's exuberant laugh. "Some won't even remember if I was there or not." She peeked around the door now and caught sight of Georgia. Then she hit Marenko on the arm. Hard. Georgia saw him wince. Ida Marenko was like a four-foot-eleven-inch linebacker.

"You bring a nice young lady, leave her standing there in the rain, and you don't introduce? What? You were raised in a cave?"

"Babcia, this is Georgia Skeehan. She's my . . . uh . . . my . . ." Marenko stumbled. Ida turned to Georgia, a wide smile on her bright red lips. She beckoned her inside. Georgia could smell the woman's Lily of the Valley cologne from a foot away.

"Are you dating my Stashoo?" Ida asked as they walked in the door.

"I am," said Georgia, extending a hand. "Pleased to meet you, Mrs. Marenko . . ."

"Ida, dear. Call me Ida." She turned to Marenko. "Is 'girlfriend' such a hard word?" Ida nodded to the belt secured around Georgia's waist with its holstered nine-millimeter. "Are you a marshal, too, dear? Or do you just like to keep my Stashoo in line?" Nothing escaped Ida Marenko's attention. Georgia laughed.

"I'm a marshal."

"Come," she beckoned. "We must get you dried off."

Stepping into Ida Marenko's immaculate row house was like entering another era. The front foyer sported a plastic Jesus with a dish of holy water below his upraised hand. Scatter rugs and plastic runners covered a plush cream-colored carpet that looked as if it had never been walked on. The living-room couch and love seat, done in Wedgewood blue satin brocade, were covered with plastic. The drapes were velvet. There were doilies under the lamps, and photographs covered almost every wall and table surface in the house.

Ida brought Georgia two fluffy towels and a short-sleeved blouse to change into until her own blouse dried. The blouse was pink like the underside of a pig's belly and had large white flowers all over it. The collar was trimmed in lace, the buttons were pearl and there were darts at the seams.

"It won't fit well, I'm afraid," said Ida. "I am built like a Polish peasant and you, dear, have a lovely young figure. But you will feel more comfortable being dry."

"Thank you," said Georgia. "That's very kind of you." She dried herself off in the bathroom and slipped into the blouse. Ida obviously loved pink. The entire bathroom was pink—even down to the crocheted skirt of a plastic doll on the back of the toilet tank. Her skirt hid an extra roll of toilet paper.

Georgia found Marenko sprawled in a chair in the kitchen beside a large Formica-topped table. Clearly, this was where all the real living in the house took place. He was toweling off his hair.

"What's *Babcia* mean?" Georgia mumbled.

"*Bob-che,*" said Marenko, pronouncing the word slowly and phonetically, so Georgia would get it right. "It's Polish for 'grandmother.' Ida was born in Poland."

He looked up from his toweling, took in her blouse and grinned. The blouse had darts for a large bustline. Trouble was, Georgia was small-breasted. The excess material made her chest look like a beach ball someone had forgotten to inflate.

"Don't say anything," Georgia warned.

"Can't talk about what ain't there, right?" Marenko teased.

"You like pierogies, Georgia?" asked Ida, pulling a skillet out of a cabinet.

"We just came to say hi. You don't have to feed us," said Georgia.

"*Pffft.* You don't eat, I think you don't like me."

"But you're all dressed to go out."

"Out." Ida rolled her eyes. "They will dress me like this to bury me, too. Only Rosemary probably won't let them do my nails. And she'll put some God-awful crucifix around my neck, big as the one they nailed Jesus to."

"Rosemary's my father's sister," Marenko explained. "Babcia's daughter. She's sort of . . ."

"—She'd make the Vatican Council look like a bunch of hooligans," said Ida as she took out several small, homemade turnovers of pale white dough and began to fry them in butter and onions in the skillet. The smell made Georgia's stomach rumble with hunger. She hadn't had anything to eat for hours.

"Aunt Rosemary's very straitlaced," Marenko explained.

"*Baah,*" said Ida. "Shoulda had my tubes tied after your Uncle Leonard."

Georgia giggled, and Marenko laughed with her. "Told you you couldn't make my grandmother uncomfortable," he said.

Ida Marenko clearly hadn't heard about Mac's legal troubles, and neither Mac nor Georgia said a word to her about them. Being here, after all that had happened to him these past twenty-four hours, was like a little haven from the storm. Marenko relaxed in his grandmother's presence and blossomed under her charm. His whole face brightened. His body became loose limbed as he draped himself across a chair and put his feet up on another. He pulled off his wet socks, and Ida stuck a finger in a hole on the bottom of one of them.

"I fix that for you before you leave," she said.

"You don't have to do that," he protested.

"*Baah,*" said Ida. "You leave my house, get hit by a car and they see your socks? I will never be able to go out in public again."

Both Mac and Georgia ate everything Ida put in front of them, adding heaping tablespoons of sour cream to their hot potato pierogies and wolfing it all down with glasses of ginger ale. Marenko teased his grandmother, and she alternately doted on him and scolded him as if he were six again. Georgia couldn't ever recall seeing him as happy and at ease as he was in her kitchen. He didn't even get antsy for a cigarette. They both lost track of time—until Georgia's pager went off. She frowned at the number, then paled. *Chief Brennan.*

Marenko saw the number, too. A darkness fell across his features.

Georgia saw the weight return to his shoulders, saw the tightness in his face. Here, in his grandmother's kitchen, he'd been able to forget for a while. But it was all coming back.

"Use the phone by the refrigerator, dear," Ida told Georgia. Then she said something to Marenko that Georgia didn't catch. Mac left the kitchen for a moment and came back with a chess set, which he began to set up on the kitchen table.

"You play chess?" Georgia asked him.

"*Pffft,*" said Ida. "He's no Boris Spassky. Ten years I teach Stashoo and still, he doesn't always remember which way the pieces move. That's his Italian side."

"Babcia." Marenko strung out the word and rolled his eyes. Georgia turned her back on them and dialed Brennan's office. He was in a meeting, but as soon as Georgia identified herself, she was transferred through.

"Skeehan." He said her name as if he were swallowing steel splinters. "What the hell did you think you were doing today?"

"Chief?"

"In Greenpoint. At Flannagan's house."

"How did you . . . ?" But before Georgia could finish the question, she already knew. Tricia had called Hanlon at Engine Two-seventy-eight. Hanlon had called Delaney, and Delaney had called Brennan. *I'm dead.*

"I thought I was very clear about what was expected of you on this investigation," said Brennan.

"You were, sir," said Georgia. "It's just that . . ."

"—Do you understand the magnitude of what we're facing here?"

"I do, sir. That's why I had to check out this fire. It think it may be the key to finding Robin Hood. Perhaps if I could show you some of Captain Flannagan's findings . . ."

"—Oh, you'll show them to me all right," said Brennan. "I'm on my way to the Knights of Columbus Hall in Bay Ridge right now. And you're going to meet me there ASAP."

"Bay Ridge, *Brooklyn?*" asked Georgia. It seemed an odd location for a meeting with Brennan. The chief wasn't even *from* Brooklyn.

"William Lynch was moved over to the NYPD this afternoon. He's their headache now," Brennan grunted. He had always hated Lynch. "Chief Delaney has been appointed acting commissioner in his place. Some of the men from his old division are putting together a celebration in his honor. *You,* however, are not there to celebrate."

"I understand."

Georgia scribbled the news on a pad of paper and held it up for Marenko to read. Marenko squinted at the page, then began to fill his grandmother in on the intricacies of department politics, as labyrinthine as any chess match.

"A piece of advice, Skeehan?" said Brennan. "William Lynch may have appreciated your renegade style in this department. But Ed Delaney's an ex-marine. He follows orders and he expects everyone else to do the same. You want to stay in this department, you'll learn that, pronto."

Brennan hung up. Georgia took a deep breath and walked over to the game. "I've got to go meet the chief in Bay Ridge," she explained, forcing a smile to her lips. She didn't want Marenko to see how unnerved she was by the call. It paled in comparison with his own situation.

Marenko rose from his chair. "You want me to come with you?"

The light in his eyes faded and his face turned blank, as if a curtain had been drawn over his emotions. It was a protective reflex, Georgia knew. Marenko was going back "out there," where practically everyone he knew regarded him with suspicion. He had to be strong and show nothing. Yet right this minute, the thing he needed most was to be a little boy again in his grandmother's kitchen.

"Stay here," Georgia said softly, putting a hand on his arm and easing him back down in his chair.

Marenko was about to object, but she interrupted him. "I can't take you with me. It wouldn't look right," she explained. "I'll just change back into my blouse . . ."

"—*Pffft,*" said Ida, jumping up from the table. "You put on wet things, you catch cold. Wear my blouse. You give it back another time."

"Oh, Ida," said Georgia. "I couldn't do that."

"What, you couldn't? You wear. You return. This way, I see you again, yes?"

Marenko grinned. "That's my Babcia. Always got an angle."

"Shut up," said Ida, swatting his arm. "Or I'll make you visit your Aunt Rosemary. She'll have you saying Hail Marys for a week."

. . .

30

GEORGIA COULD HEAR the whine of bagpipes and squeal of a fiddle even before she stepped up to the steel front doors of the Knights of Columbus Hall in Bay Ridge, Brooklyn. High and reedy, the sound wafted past the firefighters' double-parked cars, then lingered in the pearly mist like a battle cry across a Gaelic glen.

The rain had stopped. Two firefighters with crew cuts sat on the front steps of the hall, staring out at the street of tidy stucco homes with televisions flickering in the windows. They eyed Georgia with curiosity as she picked her way past them and went inside. Ed Delaney's party was a firefighters' event. Wives and families were not invited. Georgia was likely to be the only woman in attendance.

The alcove was dark. It took a moment for Georgia's eyes to adjust to the dim light and the nicotine haze that wafted over the Irish clan symbols on the walls and the tartan plaids that looked like couch fabric in somebody's den.

Beyond the alcove was a long, narrow room with a bar along one wall and a quartet of musicians in the opposite corner, hammering out a frenetic Irish tune that sounded to Georgia as though the bagpipes, banjo, fiddle and flute were playing their own separate melodies. There were maybe fifty men—all white—gathered in small clusters about the room. The only women were the six step dancers in plaid skirts near the musicians. The dancers, all very young and unsmiling, were staring zombielike at the opposite wall, their hands plastered to their sides, their legs moving so fast, it looked to Georgia as if their upper and lower bodies belonged to different people.

Georgia scanned the room for Chief Brennan while other eyes scanned her. She was waiting for the day when she could walk into a gathering of firefighters, and not have every head turn and every opinion already formed.

The isolation of being different got to Georgia more than anything—the loneliness of working with people she never knew outside the job. It kicked in when she heard firefighters talk about a bar they were going to meet up in after work or a fishing trip they were planning or a night at a ball game. She'd picture them, surrounded by clouds of cigarette smoke and the warm, musky smell of beer, telling their raucous jokes, laughing loudly and professing their loyalties to one another.

She didn't necessarily want to hang out with them on a steady basis. But once—just once—she would have liked to feel welcome. She knew that could never be. Most weren't hostile toward her—just uncomfortable. They didn't know how to socialize with a woman who wasn't family or a girlfriend. Their fraternal world was not open to her, and in the fire department, there was no life without it.

"Hello, Georgia," said a voice behind her now. She turned and was startled to see Andy Kyle grinning at her, drink in hand. "Nice blouse."

Georgia looked down at the accordion folds of pink floral rayon that rippled where an ample bust was supposed to be. She frowned. She'd forgotten that she was wearing Ida Marenko's blouse.

"I got caught in the rain and borrowed this," she explained. She cocked her head at him. "Man, you must be connected to be at something like this."

He laughed. "Did it ever occur to you I'm just here to drive the chief?"

"Brennan?"

"In the back room." He pointed to a small hallway with a scarred oak door on one side. Then he swirled the ice in his drink. "This, by the way, is just club soda, in case you were wondering. Brennan's waiting for you. And he's got Delaney and a man from the mayor's office with him." He furrowed his brow. "Are you in some kind of trouble?"

"Yeah, probably." She could feel the vibrations of the step dancers across the planking.

"Anything I can do?" He gazed at a manila envelope in Georgia's hand. "They were talking about taking some papers from you. Has this got something to do with the Rosen case you were working on?"

The papers. They were Pat Flannagan's only copies. She'd promised Tricia she'd get them back to her. Without them, she'd have nothing to back up her suspicions about Bridgewater. Unless she could find out what had been stored at Kowalski's warehouse and by whom.

"Andy? Can you do me a favor?" Georgia pulled out a pen and scribbled Marenko's cell phone number across it. "Can you call Mac? Tell him Georgia needs him to call his friend at HIDTA and run a check on Tristate Trucking. Can you do that for me?"

"Tristate?" He squinted at the slip of paper. "What do you need to know about them for?"

"Look, Andy. This is really important. You talk about wanting to help people in a big way on this job—here's your chance. A lot of lives could be resting on this."

He tucked the slip of paper into his shirt pocket. "Sure, Georgia. I'll call Marenko," said Kyle. "But you be careful in there, okay?"

In the back room, Ed Delaney was seated behind a desk, next to a poster for a Knights of Columbus charity picnic. This should have been a night of celebration for him, but he looked worn-out. Gus Rankoff, behind him in a chair, next to an American flag, drummed his fingers on the pants of his suit. Brennan, pacing nervously, scratched at the sunburn on the top of his head—a souvenir from today's little excursion to the beach.

Georgia suspected that this bomb threat was keeping them all on twenty-four-hour alert right now. The highest levels of the NYPD and FDNY were probably in a state of near-frenzy over this thing, though so far, they were doing a good job of keeping it out of the press and away from the rank-and-file. For Georgia, the panic wasn't so easy to contain. She had to face Robin Hood.

"You have some explaining to do, Skeehan," said Brennan when she closed the door. No one offered her a seat. Georgia took a deep breath and, as succinctly as she could, began to pour out everything she'd been able to find out about the Bridgewater fire and how it appeared to relate to Robin Hood. Delaney's face betrayed nothing as he listened to her story. In the main hall, the music had turned sweet and sorrowful, mimicking the vast, barren hills of Ireland and the ceaseless winds off the sea. The wailing tenor of the bagpipe came at her as if it had been borne on a North Atlantic breeze.

"Chief, er . . . Commissioner," Georgia corrected herself, "if I could just get ahold of that Division of Safety report you wrote in nineteen eighty-four, perhaps we'd be able to find the definitive link."

"I don't have the report," said Delaney. "And from what I recall of it, it wouldn't help you anyway."

"Skeehan," Brennan warned. He'd stopped pacing at the mention of the report. "Do you realize who you are talking to?"

"It's all right, Arthur," said Delaney. "The marshal is just being thorough." He looked embarrassed—not, Georgia sensed, because she'd pressed him, but because he couldn't give her what she asked for. She looked into Delaney's brown eyes and saw a hesitation there, as if his words didn't match his feelings. *He wants to help me. But he can't. Why?*

Georgia opened the clasp of her manila folder now and spread the pictures of the Bridgewater firefighters on the desk before Delaney. "Chief, look at these men. They were firefighters. Just like you and me. And they died horribly from something in that warehouse."

Delaney thumbed through the photos. His face paled. Georgia noticed his fingers tremble and slip when he slid the stack of photos facedown across the desk to her. He shook his head.

"Those men are dead, Marshal. Robin Hood can't be among them."

"He could be a brother, a son, an uncle. I think he's related. And I think I know why he wants Empire to pay. The pipeline runs right underneath the former warehouse site on Bridgewater Street. A leak—even a very small one—could have started that blaze. And now, as I understand it, that site has been slated for the new football stadium."

The room went silent. Rankoff's eyes, dark as port, glinted almost as much as the fluorescent lights bouncing off his white hair.

"Marshal Skeehan is a remarkably good investigator," said Rankoff. "Yes, Marshal." He turned to her. "The land along Bridgewater Street is being seriously considered for the new stadium. And I will most certainly bring all your concerns to the mayor's attention—if I may hold onto these papers for now?" He nodded politely to her.

"I promised I would return them to Tricia Flannagan."

"And so you shall—*after* I show them to the mayor." Rankoff's smooth voice brooked no argument. He took the materials from her.

"One question troubles me," said Rankoff. His dark eyes seemed to hold her in his grasp like two magnets. "In his taped message, did Robin Hood ever *mention* this Bridgewater fire?"

"Well, no . . ."

"Was there any reference to Greenpoint? To a warehouse?"

"No, sir. But I think if Chief Delaney could find that report . . ."

"—Acting *Commissioner* Delaney," Rankoff corrected, "has just expressed to you that he has nothing to corroborate your concerns about that fire. The firehouses are gone. The men are dead. The city is doing everything it can to find Robin Hood and stop this bomb. You are stirring up issues that are unrelated to the task at hand, and I am sure I speak for the commissioner when I say that this is an inefficient use of your resources."

Georgia's mouth dropped open. She bounced a look from Rankoff to Delaney to Brennan. No one seemed taken aback that Rankoff had just gone over Delaney's head and in effect ordered Georgia to stop the investigation. Georgia couldn't believe it. A civilian, going over the head of a thirty-year veteran of the FDNY, the chief of operations and now the acting commissioner of the entire department. Who *was* this guy?

Georgia stared at Delaney—a challenge of sorts. *Are you going to take this?* Delaney shifted in his chair. Georgia saw something flicker in his warm brown eyes. A hint of gratitude, mingled with fear. He looked as torn as Georgia had after she'd left Connie's apartment with Randy Carter. He rose partway from the chair.

"I'm going to have to close the matter, Marshal," said Delaney. "Unless, of course, you can find me something solid to link this fire to Robin Hood."

Georgia found Andy Kyle after the meeting. He was sitting by himself on the front steps outside the building, staring at the ribbons of clouds snaking razorlike across an opal-colored moon.

"Did you get hold of Mac?" she asked.

"I did." He patted the concrete stoop next to him, urging her to sit. She obliged. "Mac said he'd look into Tristate . . . and he, um, said thanks." Kyle kicked a stone at his feet. They both knew what he was talking about.

"You did a nice thing, giving him Bernie Chandler's number."

"Let's hope he doesn't need it," said Kyle. "How did the firing squad go?"

"I'm not sure," said Georgia. On the plus side, no one had mentioned charges—perhaps because the department needed her too much right now. Then again, she'd been stripped of all her evidence regarding the Bridgewater fire and Delaney had told her to stop investigating it. *Or had he?* He'd said to stop investigating unless she could find a solid link. Georgia might have tossed off the inconsistency—except for the fact that every statement Delaney made in that room appeared to be under duress.

But how do I investigate a fire if the men are dead and the firehouse they came from no longer exists?

"You know, Georgia," said Kyle now, "my dad knows a lot about real estate firms in the city. If you tell me what you're looking for, maybe I can get some information on Tristate for you."

"That's very kind of you, Andy. But you're brand new. I don't want to get you involved in something that could be bad for your career."

He laughed. "Hey, if it's a lost cause, I'm your man. In college, I was the guy who was dumb enough to launch a Mideast peace march."

"Always trying to save the world, huh?"

He shrugged. "I'm more realistic now. I pick my battles a little better."

"What?" asked Georgia. "You eat dolphin-friendly tuna?"

Kyle laughed. "Yeah, that kind of thing."

"Believe me, Andy, this is bigger and uglier than you want to get into."

Their conversation was broken by the rumble of a fire engine pulling up to the curb in front of a fire hydrant. Five men in dark blue firefighters' uniforms got out. Kyle nodded to them.

"Wanna bet they'll knock back a few cold ones for old Ed?" He shook his head as the firefighters wandered past. "I'll bet they didn't log *this* little excursion into their firehouse journal."

The firehouse journal—of course. Georgia straightened up. Why hadn't she thought of it? Everything about the Bridgewater fire would be in the daily company log. And those logs would probably still be in the old boarded-up firehouse. It wouldn't be that hard to get inside. The Bureau of Fire Prevention still used the building for storage. Georgia herself had gone there about six months ago to retrieve some paperwork for a case she was working on. There was bound to be a way to get in there again. The logs might offer the definitive link Delaney seemed to need to override Rankoff on this case.

"The Bureau of Fire Prevention still keeps records in the old Ladder One-twenty-one, don't they?" asked Georgia.

"Maybe," said Kyle.

31

. . .

THE GREENPOINT, BROOKLYN, firehouse once occupied by Ladder One-twenty-one and Engine Two-oh-three had been built of brick and timber a hundred years ago, back when, as the saying goes, the buildings were made of wood and the men were made of steel. It had a low-slung room in the rear—a former stable—and a three-story airshaft for drying hoses when they were still covered with canvas instead of polyester. It had a brass sliding pole, a coal-fired burner and a recessed area in the officers' quarters for a spittoon. There was history in every piece of crumbling mortar, a history that resonated with the hooves of horses and the bark of Dalmatians along the cobblestoned streets of this riverfront community.

Now, it was a ghost of its former self. The garage was empty of rigs. The red paint on the apparatus door peeled like a bad sunburn. Some windowpanes were broken, some boarded over. And the flagpole in front hadn't had an American flag hoisted on its riggings for more than a decade.

Georgia scanned the deserted block. It was eight P.M. The heating contractors and auto-body shops that bordered the firehouse were all closed at this hour. The row houses—two blocks farther down—had their blinds drawn and their air conditioners on high. To the north, the dark, stagnant waters of the Newtown Creek slithered like a slow-moving python into the East River.

The firehouse was locked—accessible only by keyless entry, a code

Georgia had, thanks to a quick call to Lieutenant Prager at Ladder One-twenty-one's new quarters. Georgia trotted out her tale about needing some records in Fire Prevention, and Prager looked up the coded entry for her. She knew he'd have the combination. It seemed inconceivable that the new Ladder One-twenty-one wouldn't have access to its former quarters.

She pushed the four digits into the panel by the side door now and flicked on a switch. A pale sheen of fluorescent light buzzed to life four-teen feet overhead. The brass sliding pole had tarnished from lack of use. The white tile walls were caked with layers of soot and diesel exhaust. Georgia ran her hand over the greasy squares of glass inside the appara-tus door and shivered. She wasn't cold—just anxious. She wanted to browse through the journals and go home. The sooner, the better.

Georgia's footsteps echoed across the concrete floor with a starkness that reminded her of a subway tunnel in the dead of night. The only other sound was a steady *thump-thump* of water leaking from a corner of the first-floor ceiling into an old tin coal bucket. She longed for the sounds of a firehouse to fill up the space—the curses and guffaws of fire-fighters trading insults with one another, the disembodied drone of dis-patchers over the department radio, the clacking keys of a teletype machine spewing out a status report of a fire in progress. She felt the ghosts of every firefighter who'd ever worked here.

The building looked just as the firefighters had left it when the place closed down in the mid-1980s. On a bulletin board, there were yellowed notices about firehouse barbecues and newspaper clippings that were beginning to crumble. In the drawers of the house-watch desk Georgia found old memos and a faded Polaroid of a man Georgia recognized from one of Tricia's photos. A big, burly man with sandy hair and a goofy grin. In the snapshot, he was munching on a foot-long sandwich. Beneath it, a firefighter had scrawled, *O'Rourke gives mouth-to-mouth to a* real *hero.* Beneath that, in different handwriting, someone had writ-ten, *What hero? All I see is a fat guy eating like he's going to the chair.*

Georgia started her search in the basement. There were no firehouse journals there—only some discarded furniture with cigarette burns on the armrests. The walls were slick with moisture, the pipes were covered with powdery white asbestos and the place smelled of mildew. Georgia headed back up the stairs and took a rusting metal staircase up another flight to the second floor.

The hallway was dingy. Huge water stains radiated from the ceiling, and plaster hung like torn scabs. There were three tin coal buckets along the floor, but they were mostly empty—not like the one on the first floor with its steady *thump-thump. Must be a leaky pipe down there,* thought Georgia.

She bypassed the locker room and walked into the firefighters' bunk room. There were no cots anymore, but Georgia could still see the marks on the walls from where the metal head rails had been. There were boxes on the floor and a couple of filing cabinets in a corner, but these were all marked "Bureau of Fire Prevention."

She wandered back down the hall and opened the frosted-glass door to the officers' bunk room. Here, too, the beds were gone, replaced with more filing drawers and cartons. The window, facing the front of the building, was covered over with plywood. She did a quick search among the boxes and filing cabinets, but there were no journals. Her heart sank. *What if the new companies simply took the old records with them?* She couldn't look at those records without an explanation—and any explanation would need to be cleared through Chief Brennan.

The officers' bathroom was on her right. She flushed the toilet, and was pleased to see it still worked. She'd been in the FDNY too long not to take advantage of any working toilet with some privacy.

As she unzipped her pants and relieved herself, she caught a reflection in a cracked mirror on the wall. It was another door, on the opposite side of the bathroom. She flushed the toilet, then opened the door to find a steep, rusted-metal ladder leading up a short flight of stairs. She climbed the ladder, nearly bumping her head on the sloped roof and running into a massive bank of cobwebs. The space at the top was only about four feet high with a small oval window overlooking the street. But it was big enough for its purpose. Staring back at Georgia were rows and rows of haphazardly stacked journals recording the daily history of Ladder Company One-twenty-one and Engine Company Two-oh-three. No one took them, Georgia suspected, because no one knew they were here.

She pulled one down and fingered it. It was a very old one—from 1910—a big cloth-bound ledger, the size of a coffee-table travel book and just as heavy. The pages were brittle and mildewed with age. Inside, in beautiful script, were entries recorded in military time: *1400 hours: Fed and watered the horses . . . 1800 hours: Attended to splinter in Nozzle's paw.* Nozzle was probably a Dalmatian. Dalmatians were used because they had a calming effect on the horses, plus they had the speed necessary to run ahead of them and clear the streets.

Georgia searched through the books until she found the more contemporary journals. It was easily ninety degrees in the crawl space, so she grabbed all the journals she could find from 1978 through 1984, stuffed them into an old canvas tool bag she found lying around, and dropped them down the ladder. In the officer's bunk room, she thumbed through the 1978 one first. It was filled with the mundane daily entries of firehouse life. *10:00: Captain Flannagan drills on forcible entry.* Forcible entry was a nice word for breaking down doors and windows. *13:00: BI.* BI was building inspection, checking buildings for code violations or fire risks.

She flipped ahead until she reached the right day, August 21, 1978. But the entries told her nothing. There was a mark in the journal for a 10-33 at 23:00—a smoke condition at eleven P.M. But there was no mention of injuries. The men may have *been* sick when they left that fire. But in the macho code of the day, no one "tapped out"—went on medical leave.

Georgia idly scanned the pages for the months after the fire. *November 12, 1900 hours: Firefighter Gerry Mulrooney collapses in kitchen . . . January 9, 1979, 1300 hours: Firefighter Mickey Hanlon complains of trouble breathing after a training exercise.* In the months and year that followed Bridgewater, Georgia saw dozens of odd illnesses and physical complaints she'd never seen in the time preceding the fire. Suddenly, men who had never gone on sick leave—not even when they suffered second-degree burns or bone fractures at a job—were falling apart.

She read the firehouse journals from the early 1980s. The complaints of strange illnesses continued. In 1983, she counted twenty-two separate reports of serious health complaints. In the 1984 journal, there were frequent mentions of Lieutenant Edward Delaney of the Division of Safety interviewing members of the two fire companies. Still, there was nothing in these pages that really told her anything.

And then, as she turned one of the pages, something tumbled out of the journal—a canary-yellow index card, eight inches by five inches in size. Georgia recognized the card right away. It was a CIDS card—CIDS being short for Critical Information Dispatch System. Firefighters filled these out when they encountered a hazardous or unusual condition during a routine building inspection. CIDS cards were sent to the borough's fire dispatchers and entered into their files. In the event of a fire, the information was relayed to the chief on the scene to alert firefighters before they entered a building.

Georgia scanned the CIDS card now. Its corners had become dog-eared, the yellow had mottled and there were coffee stains on the back. But the business name and address were clear: *Kowalski's Carting and Hauling, 327 Bridgewater Street, Brooklyn.* She could hear her heart beating in her ears as she searched out a date. *November 1977.*

But what was a CIDS card doing in an old firehouse journal? Even if the building no longer existed, the card still belonged with Brooklyn Dispatch.

Georgia noticed that under the section labeled "Transmitted Data," some long-ago firefighter had neatly hand-lettered in the squares: *Approximately fifteen thousand 55-gallon drums of unspecified chemicals stacked in Z-shaped configuration inside warehouse. Strong solvent odors. Hazardous and incendiary conditions. Recommend immediate removal. Firefighters should not attempt interior firefighting operations.*

November 1977? Georgia frowned at the card now. That was nine months before the fire took place—three months before the Department of Environmental Protection authorized the barrels to be trucked out of there. Why didn't the fire department close the warehouse down? Why were four fire companies allowed to go inside when this CIDS card—

filled out nine months prior to the fire—specifically said not to? Was it a simple oversight?

She looked down at the box labeled *Ownership of Property.* A cold, clammy sensation settled along Georgia's spine. She expected to see the name Kowalski. But she saw a name that made her heart feel the cool certainty that this was no simple filing mistake: *Tristate Trucking.* The very company charged with trucking the fifty-five-gallon drums out of the warehouse six months before the fire was also the warehouse's owner for at least three months before that. Tristate knew the hazards—and did nothing.

Georgia opened up her black leather hip bag and shoved the CIDS card inside. The zipper on her bag pierced the silence. There was something wrong with that silence, she realized now. The steady *thump-thump* of water in the tin bucket at the foot of the stairs had stopped. Georgia sat still and listened, expecting to hear the drip start up again. But instead of a thump, she heard the sound of metal scraping across concrete. Someone was moving the bucket. Her breath stilled. Her heart curdled in her chest.

"Who's down there?" she called out. She reached for her gun, then flattened herself behind the open door and listened. It could be a fire-fighter sent over to retrieve some old files. But even as she called out the words, she knew: firefighters are loud walkers and loud talkers. She'd have heard a brother coming before he ever made it this far into the building. That meant that whoever was here probably wasn't supposed to be.

Christ, thought Georgia. *Of all the times for the building to be vandalized.* She took the safety latch off her nine-millimeter Glock semiautomatic. Her stomach twisted like a washcloth being wrung of moisture. She didn't want to be forced into making an arrest, not here, in this boarded-up firehouse. Not with all the explanations she'd have to come up with. Plus, she didn't want any intruder to think she was alone. That could be the most dangerous miscalculation of all.

She heard a set of footsteps on the concrete and the rattle of what sounded like a tin can.

"We are New York City Fire Marshals," Georgia called out. "We are armed and prepared to shoot. You have ten seconds to vacate the premises, starting now." She began to count backwards.

The footsteps echoed across the concrete floor. The intruder was walking away. *He's leaving.* She felt a small sigh escape her chest. She had finished her count, but something made her hang back, made her not want to leave the safety of this little space behind the open door. She tried to take a deep breath, but her lungs burned with the effort. The air seemed heavy and devoid of oxygen, and an airport-fuel smell wafted toward her now. The smell grew stronger as the steps grew fainter. And in that instant, Georgia knew.

Kerosene. *Oh, my God. That's why he's moving away from me,* Georgia realized. *He's going to torch the firehouse.*

A second later, the door downstairs slammed shut and a loud *whoosh* roared below Georgia. Almost immediately, thick, acrid smoke began pushing up the stairs, cutting off the light like a giant black inner tube someone had inflated in the hallway. Georgia holstered her weapon and kicked the officers' bunk room door shut. Even so, smoke began to seep through the space between the floorboards and the bottom of the door. The flames would take longer to get going—they always did with kerosene. But even so, there was no interior escape. To walk out that door meant certain death. Georgia would die in a thick cloud of carbon monoxide before she made it to the top of the staircase. And even then, there was nowhere to go. The first floor was saturated with kerosene. She pulled out her radio.

"Mayday, Mayday," she said into the receiver. "This is Fire Marshal Georgia Skeehan. I'm trapped at a ten-seventy-five at the old Ladder One-twenty-one. Repeat the OLD Ladder One-twenty-one on Clay off Franklin."

Just choking out those words brought an uncontrollable fit of coughing to her lungs. The room was filling up with smoke fast. A dispatcher's voice told her help was on the way. Georgia couldn't answer him. A gray haze hung over the room now. It was banking down, inch by inch. She ran over to the plyboard-covered window and tried to pry off the sheet, but it was nailed down tight. She searched the room for an axe or a crowbar, but there was nothing in the room except cartons of paper. Her eyes began to smart from the smoke. She coughed hard, and it felt like a punch to the chest.

The crawl space, thought Georgia. *There's a window up there.* Smoke had darkened the room so much, she had to grope forward by feel, but she sensed the tile sill of the bathroom and reached around for the crawl space door.

She could feel the flames crackling through the floor beneath her and curling up the stairwell—climbing higher and higher in the search for oxygen. The first floor was burning up now. It would take only a minute or two for the second floor to start to flame as well.

She forced herself off her knees just long enough to reach for the knob of the crawl space door. Then she climbed the ladder to the top of the space. But even the crawl space was filling with smoke, and temperatures were beginning to leapfrog. The small oval window at knee level was single-paned glass. Georgia leaned back and kicked the heel of her shoe at the center of the glass. It shattered on impact. She had never heard such a delicious sound. She kicked until all the fragments were gone, then pushed herself to the edge. Directly below the oval pane was a small ledge. But the next drop was a distance of more than twenty feet to the street.

Smoke was pouring over her shoulder, constricting her lungs like a tourniquet and stinging her eyes. Georgia hoisted herself feet first onto the narrow ledge outside the window. Her hands clawed at the loose mortar in the bricks. She prayed it wouldn't give way. She hadn't been to mass in years, yet suddenly, before she knew it, she was mouthing the Act of Contrition she'd learned from the nuns in grade school: *O my God, I am heartily sorry for having offended thee and I detest all my sins.* The words came unbidden. They came, she realized, because she was sure she was going to die.

And then she saw it—the flagpole, planted next to the firehouse at the end of the ledge. It was unused, and there was no telling how stable it was. Still, it was a pole—not vastly different from the brass poles Georgia had slid down as a firefighter. She inched slowly toward it now. She hadn't slid down a pole in two years; and this one—with its metal rods and riggings—wasn't exactly made for sliding. But it was all she had. She could hear sirens in the distance, but her panic wouldn't allow her simply to stand here and wait for rescue. Georgia inched her way to the edge of the ledge, leaned over and grabbed the metal cylinder. Then she hugged it to her body, wrapped her ankles around it and gave in to the tug of gravity.

She hit the ground with a thud. A metal bolt ripped Ida's pink rayon blouse. A hoisting line abraded the flesh along her inner right arm. Georgia was scraped up, but not seriously injured. She stepped back just as a fire engine and truck were rolling to the curb.

She forced her stinging eyes to look up at the building now. Black smoke was pushing out every window, and flames were crackling through the roof. It would take probably no more than about twenty minutes to bring the blaze under control. But by then, a hundred-year-old firehouse would be reduced to a smoldering ruin and a century of firefighting history would be wiped out.

Georgia sat down on a stoop across the street, feeling her lungs burn with each breath of the clammy exhaust-choked air. The journals were gone, and with them, countless generations of men who had given their lives to this city.

And with them, the ghosts of nineteen men who refused to die.

IT WAS NEARLY NINE P.M. before Georgia was able to wrap up her statement on the fire. She was relieved that the Brooklyn marshals bought her story about being in the building to look through some old records in Fire Prevention. What troubled them was the physical evidence.

They found no signs of a break-in, yet Georgia was certain she'd closed the door to the firehouse behind her. From the odor of the fuel and Georgia's description of the relatively slow spread of flames, they knew the torch had used kerosene instead of gasoline to start the blaze. Kerosene, because of its lower volatility, is the choice accelerant of professional arsonists. Yet the fire itself had all the earmarks of an impulsive act of vandalism. The fuel was carelessly splashed, as if the torch just wanted a big fire and didn't care what burned.

But most troubling of all to them was the fact that Georgia had insisted she'd called out her presence in the building and given the arsonist time to flee. If the torch had just been looking for an impulsive thrill, he would have thought twice about adding murder—especially the murder of a law-enforcement officer—to his rap sheet. To the Brooklyn marshals, the case was perplexing. To Georgia, only one explanation—an explanation she couldn't give them—made chilling sense. The torch wasn't trying to burn down the building; he was trying to burn down the woman inside.

The Brooklyn marshals let her shower at their base and drove her home. One of the men even loaned her a clean pair of sweatpants and a

T-shirt so she wouldn't frighten her mother and son when she walked in
the door. It was a good thing he did, too. Richie and Margaret were
waiting anxiously for her. Margaret looked exhausted. Richie, who normally disappeared into his room for long stretches, hovered protectively
nearby. Georgia tried to shrug off the afternoon and evening with just a
word or two about the investigation, but Margaret noticed her daughter
pulling all the telephone cords out of the walls after she had changed
into shorts and one of her own shirts.

"What are you doing, dear?"

"I just want to be home, Ma. Here. Safe. I don't want the outside
world intruding."

Richie seemed to loosen up now that his mother was home. He began
to regale her with the latest stunts from a Jackie Chan movie. Margaret
fell asleep on the couch, then woke with a start and opted to go to bed.
Georgia gave her a kiss on the cheek.

"Things will be better tomorrow, Ma," Georgia told her, forcing a
smile.

"I hope so, honey." Margaret sighed. "I've been saying that ever since
Jimmy . . ." Margaret's voice trailed off. They both knew what she was
going to say: *Ever since Jimmy died.* Margaret wasn't ready to accord
Jimmy Gallagher the light, breezy caress of memory that Georgia felt
sure he'd have wanted. She missed him too much. It made Georgia think
of that picture Seamus Hanlon had given her from the corkboard of Engine Two-seventy-eight.

"Ma? What happened to that picture I left for you? Of Jimmy and
Seamus Hanlon on that fishing trip?"

Margaret shook her head. "I put it with Jimmy's mass cards and
medals. I can't look at it, Georgia."

Georgia put a hand on top of her mother's. "I understand."

After Margaret went to bed, Georgia made popcorn for Richie while
he acted out a scene from the Jackie Chan flick, his body a long, lean set
of sticks with a face still chubby enough to make Georgia want to nuz-
zle him in her arms.

"Okay, so then Jackie Chan does this." Richie kicked his foot out sideways. "And then the bad guy does this." He spun and moved his hands in short chops in front of his face. There seemed to be no dialogue in the movie, or at least none he wanted to convey. Georgia attempted a karate chop herself and ended up flipping the popcorn bowl in the air. The boy laughed. That small, childish giggle lifted her spirits for the first time in days.

They were scraping kernels off the floor when Richie caught her eye, a serious look on his face.

"Jimmy DeLuca saw a picture of Mac's arrest on TV."

The statement stopped Georgia cold. She put down the popcorn bowl and sat back on her heels, staring at Richie. Jimmy DeLuca was her son's best friend. She didn't want him having to explain something like this to other children.

"How did you feel when Jimmy told you?" Georgia asked, willing her voice to sound nonchalant. She went back to scooping popcorn kernels off the floor, but she watched him from the corner of her eye.

Another shrug. "Okay, I guess," said the boy. He straightened up, then walked over to the kitchen counter and hoisted himself on top. Georgia hated it when he sat on the counters, but she decided against correcting him right now. "I told Jimmy that Mac was innocent—like in the movies. Jimmy thought it was kinda cool that I knew somebody who'd been arrested for murder. It was like knowing a rap star or something." Richie curled his fingers and extended his forefingers and pinkies, then moved them like a rap singer's stage gestures. "Yo, check it out."

"Oh, terrific." Georgia rolled her eyes. *Come the fall, the entire PTA at Saint Aloysius will be whispering that Richie Skeehan's mother is dating a murderer.*

"I'm sorry you're in the middle of this, honey," said Georgia. "If anyone gives you a hard time about this, you tell me—okay?"

"Okay." He hopped down off the counter. Georgia swept up the remainder of the popcorn and threw it in the garbage. "Can we play a board game?" he asked.

Georgia was about to tell him she was too tired and it was past his bedtime, but when she saw his hopeful face, she changed her mind. "Oh, all right. Which one?"

"Life."

Richie loved the game of Life. Everybody got married. All the little pink and blue kid pegs had a matching set of pink and blue parents. Nobody died suddenly or thought about walking out on their kids or cheating on their lovers. Nobody got arrested for murder. And the worst trouble that could befall you was some uncle leaving you a skunk farm that you had to pay $10,000 to get rid of.

They played until just after ten-thirty—well past Richie's bedtime, but Georgia sensed he needed this time with her right now. She was just about to send Richie up to bed when the doorbell rang. Georgia furrowed her brow. She wasn't expecting anybody.

"Go upstairs," she told him. She'd temporarily tossed her duty holster on top of the television in the living room. She got her gun from it now, telling herself that what happened at the old firehouse in Greenpoint hadn't affected her. She was just being cautious—that's all. It made perfect sense to answer your front door with a gun trained on it. Perfect sense.

She cracked open the front door. It was Mac. He was wearing a baseball cap pulled low across his face and mirrored sunglasses.

"Hey there, Stashoo. Nice disguise," she teased, trying to recover from the wave of panic that had seized her just moments before. Her body temperature had risen at least ten degrees. Her face felt flushed. Sweat gathered under her armpits, across her brow and in between her breasts.

He stepped inside, pulled off his sunglasses and stared at the gun in her hand. "Who you planning to shoot?" he asked gruffly. "And what's wrong with your phones? Christ, I heard about what happened in Greenpoint and I wanted to make sure you were okay. I couldn't even get you on your cell phone."

Georgia lifted her right hand and examined the gun still clutched tightly in its grip as if it had walked over by itself. She returned it to her duty holster and locked the door. All three locks—even the chain.

"Friendly tonight, aren't you? What's going on?" he asked. "And what the hell were you doing in that firehouse anyhow?"

"Trying to get something solid to tie Bridgewater to Robin Hood," Georgia said in hushed tones. She knew Richie was listening.

"You okay?" he asked, holding her by the shoulders and looking into her eyes. There was a distance to his own bright blue wattage. Something was on his mind.

"Hi, Mac," a little voice called from the top of the stairs.

Marenko turned and forced a smile to his lips, but the edgy glint never left his eyes. "Hey, Sport, how ya doing?" Richie came down the stairs. Marenko pulled off his baseball cap and swatted the boy playfully on the shoulder. Richie gaped at him with a mixture of curiosity and awe.

"My friend saw you on TV."

Marenko's face dropped. "Fu—."

Georgia gave him a dirty look. He caught himself just in time. He threw his baseball cap and sunglasses on a table near the door and regained his composure. ". . . Sport, I'm uh . . ."

". . . Honey, go upstairs," Georgia interrupted. "I'll be up in a moment to put you to bed."

"Can Mac put me to bed?"

"What?" Georgia bounced a look from Richie to Marenko.

Marenko bit back a grin. Georgia could tell he was flattered. Instead of making Georgia happy, however, it filled her with a dull ache. Richie was bonded to a man who might not be in their lives much longer.

"Relax, *Mom,*" said Marenko, kissing her cheek as he sidled past her and up the stairs. "My good night's are G-rated."

···

It was ten minutes before Marenko came back downstairs. In the interim, Georgia cringed at the loud, wet-sounding release of air from Richie's "Captain Underpants" whoopee cushion. She listened to her son's latest rap tape, and she heard Marenko talking to the boy about how the Mets were "kicking ass" this summer.

Georgia shook her head at Marenko as his footsteps thudded on the landing. The pictures on the walls seemed to shake when he walked past. She was glad her mother was a heavy sleeper.

"What?" he asked.

"Do you act this way around Michael and Beth, too?"

His back straightened. His kids were always a sore topic. "Act *what* way?"

"Like an overgrown delinquent."

He made a face. "I just like to horse around, that's all. Richie likes it. All boys do."

He flopped down in a chair across from the television. Georgia noticed he didn't sit next to her on the couch. He was keeping his distance tonight for some reason. "I wouldn't have come over at all if you hadn't turned off your cell phone and unplugged every friggin' phone in this house," he added. "I was really worried about you."

"I ruined your grandmother's blouse."

Marenko dismissed it with a wave of his hand. "She won't care. She's got twenty more just like it. The point is, *you're* okay." He ran a hand through his hair, matted down from the baseball cap. He gave her a dark, tentative look. Something was on his mind. "Did you, uh, speak to Chief Brennan tonight?"

"Yeah. And Ed Delaney. And this guy from the mayor's office. They don't want me investigating the Bridgewater fire or the Empire Pipeline anymore." Georgia still had the CIDS card in her hip bag. She retrieved it and showed it to him. It smelled of smoke, like everything else in the bag, but it was still legible at least.

"Somebody knew what was in that warehouse nine months before the fire," she explained. "The card could've been misfiled or someone could've chosen to deliberately hide that information . . . Did Andy call you with my request?"

"Yeah." Marenko frowned at the card, then handed it back to Georgia. "Tristate's out of business—went out of business right after the fire. But, man, what a sleazebag operation it was. The firm was responsible for illegally disposing of thousands of gallons of PCBs, benzene and toluene. Very, very toxic stuff. Since the nineteen seventies, benzene and toluene have been classified as known human carcinogens. It's almost a guarantee that that's what the men at Bridgewater were exposed to."

"Yeah, but the DEP was trying to clean it up."

"They were *supposed* to notify the EPA. They were *supposed* to get the soil tested and cleaned—not sneak the barrels out and hope nobody in the neighborhood found out they were living down the street from a major environmental disaster. That's my old neighborhood, Scout. Practically my grandmother's backyard. My family's health and well-being were traded in a back-room deal because the city was afraid of ending up with another Love Canal on their hands."

Georgia sank back onto the couch. "It's a dead end, though, I guess, since Tristate's out of business."

"Yes and no," said Marenko. "Tristate's assets went into receivership and were bought out by a construction firm called Northway. They're a big developer in the five boroughs. My friend at HIDTA tells me that Tristate probably only went belly-up to avoid liability after the fire. It's possible the people who owned Tristate and the people behind Northway are one and the same."

"Do you know who owns Northway?"

"The firm's a limited partnership," Marenko explained. "As I understand it, that means the limited partners hold all the assets, but they don't have to disclose themselves if they don't want to." He pulled a slip of paper out of the back pocket of his khakis and handed it to her. "There's an address and telephone number in Brooklyn on there. You can call Northway tomorrow and see if they'll give you any more information."

"You don't want to call?" she asked him. "I'm going to be at work tomorrow, and there's no telling how busy . . ." Georgia stopped in midsentence. Marenko was leaning forward in his chair, arms on his thighs, picking at a hangnail. He was blinking hard and avoiding her gaze.

"Mac? What's wrong?"

"I'm gone, Scout," he said hoarsely. "My brother Nick gave me the heads-up. The cops are closing in."

"They found Connie?"

Marenko shook his head, but kept his gaze on the floor. "I don't know *what* they've found, but I know it's bad. I don't think anyone can help me."

Georgia went over to him now and sat on the arm of his chair, stroking the side of his face.

"Don't say that," she told him. "You'll pull through. We'll pull through together."

He kept his eyes on the floor, but it looked as though it was taking all his effort not to break down. "Aw, Christ." His voice cracked and he got to his feet. "I gotta get some air."

He walked into the kitchen. A moment later, Georgia heard the back door slam. She didn't follow right away. Mac Marenko defined himself by his ability to control his emotions and his circumstances. The kindest thing she could do for him right now was to let him find a way to reclaim it.

She allowed several minutes to pass before she went outside. He had kicked off his socks and shoes and was sitting on the rim of the above-ground swimming pool with his legs in the water. He hadn't bothered to roll up his khakis. They were soaked to the knee.

It was a muggy night with the moon drifting in and out of sight like a beach ball caught in an undertow. The air had a thick, compressed quality, muffling the squawk of car alarms and the squeal of tires in the distance. Georgia hoisted herself up to the pool rim next to Marenko and stuck her bare legs in the water. They sat together in silence for several long minutes, watching swatches of patio light flicker and scatter on the surface of the pool.

He looked up at the lead-colored clouds skating across the sky. "I'm sorry, Scout," he said softly, laying out the words as if each were made of stone. "What I wouldn't give to do Tuesday night over . . . to do a lot of things over."

"You'll come out of this," she told him. "You'll see."

"But I can't remember. I keep trying to. I lie in bed and I can't sleep, I'm trying so hard. And I can't remember *anything*." His voice cracked again. He closed his eyes and blew a long gust of breath from his mouth.

She reached out a hand, dampened from the pool, and pressed it over his. His eyes were glassy in the passing moonlight. His face was filled with a rawness she'd never seen before. It sent her pulse racing. She ran a hand through his tangle of shiny black hair and felt a burning in her loins as he brought his lips down on hers. His hands were wet from the pool and she felt the coolness of the water seep through her T-shirt when he snaked them down her back, then along the contours of her hips and in between her thighs. Her breath quickened and her nipples hardened in response.

And suddenly, the world spun. She felt the tumble, gave in to it completely. The water was cool, not cold, and the splash felt as refreshing as champagne bubbles on her lips. She laughed as she bobbed to the surface. Her T-shirt and bra had turned translucent.

Marenko let out a whoop as he pulled off his wet black polo shirt and threw it in the grass. Then he grabbed her and pressed her against his bare chest, kissing her face and growling playfully as he slid a hand beneath her shirt and unhooked her bra. She could feel his erection bulging beneath his wet khakis as he grinned boyishly and pushed his wet hair back from his face.

"You did that on purpose," she said.

He winked at her. "Maybe I did."

They made love on the sparse grass in the shadow of the pool, as reckless as two teenagers. Georgia left her wet T-shirt on in case they got caught. Marenko kept his soaked trousers around his knees. When he lowered himself on top of her, Georgia felt the beads of water and sweat slide between them and the slipperiness of it made her hunger for him even more. He pushed hard and urgently inside. This wasn't Mac's usual lovemaking, which was tender and gentle and unhurried. This was something else—something more instinctive and animal. And Georgia welcomed it if only because, for a moment, it pushed away the darkness for both of them.

When it was over, he rolled off of her and pulled up his soaked trousers. Even in the shadows of the pool, Georgia could see that the light beige fabric was covered with mud and grass stains. He reached for his black polo shirt and wrung it out. Usually, they lingered after making love. Then again, usually they didn't do it in the backyard by the pool with her mother and Richie asleep upstairs.

She took one look at his soggy, mud-caked clothes and sat up. "You can't go home on the subway like that."

"I'll be all right." He shrugged, tossing the wet shirt over his shoulder. "It'll dry off." He checked his wristwatch. The brown leather strap had darkened almost to black from the water. "I can't stay here like this, and you've got to go to work tomorrow."

"I'll put your clothes in the dryer."

"Nah." He pulled her to her feet. "It's just water. The air's warm." He kissed her gently on the lips. "And I'm warm." He winked at her. She ran her hands down the sides of his wet khakis. The cool, prickly sensation made her feel like making love to him all over again.

"Let me just slip into some dry clothes then," said Georgia. "I'll see you off." She left him on the back patio smoking a cigarette while she went inside to change. She crept upstairs quietly and stripped down in the bathroom. She pulled off her soaked underpants and noticed it. Blood. Her period. Ten days late, but here nonetheless.

She should have been elated. But instead, she felt empty and let down. She didn't want another child right now. And yet, with all the death and ugliness and uncertainty surrounding them and their future together, it had felt good to have this little spark of life to connect them. Now, that was gone and nothing else about their future seemed certain. She sank onto the tiles and started to cry.

"Scout?" The kitchen door slammed. She heard his footsteps lumbering up the stairs. "Hey," said Marenko, picking her up off the bathroom floor and wiping her tears. He closed the bathroom door. He didn't want Richie and Margaret to find them. "What's the matter?"

She rested her head against his bare chest with its fine, dark dusting of hair. "My period," she sobbed. "I got it."

"You did? That's great." Marenko brought a hand under her chin and lifted her eyes up to his. He gave her a small, questioning smile. "Don't *you* think it's great? You couldn't want a baby right now—I mean, with all that's going on."

"No." Georgia sighed. "I guess not." She rose and stepped into dry clothes while he leaned against the towel rack and watched her with hungry eyes. She shivered, feeling the cold dampness of her body—the aloneness of it—for the first time.

"I can't believe you slept with Connie and didn't tell me."

Georgia had no idea why she blurted out the words then. Exhaustion, maybe. Or maybe disappointment. Marenko was clearly relieved that Georgia wasn't pregnant. She couldn't help seeing that as a form of rejection. It was something he'd never understand.

He wiped his face on one of the towels and caught her eye as she combed her hair in the bathroom mirror. "I told you, Scout. It was before I knew you. I knew it would cause trouble if I mentioned it. I was right about that one, wasn't I?"

She turned from the mirror now to face him. "She was in love with you, you know. She was supposed to move in with you. You broke her heart."

His jaw tightened. "She was gonna move in while her apartment was painted—for a couple of weeks—that's all. And besides, how would you know how she felt? You never even knew we were together."

"She never told me your *name*, Mac. She only told me you were a cop she'd met through work. But she told me the details. Don't you think I've been putting it together?"

"So you've been putting it together—so? I'm supposed to walk around on eggshells because of it?"

"Why did you break up with her?"

His blue eyes stared back defiantly. "Why don't you just ask about my divorce while you're at it?"

"I'd like to."

"Forget it, Scout. Whether it's Connie or Patsy, what's done is done. I don't go around crying in my beer. That's not my style."

"This isn't about 'style,' Mac. You're facing a murder rap. I need to know."

"Nothing I can tell you will help you find Connie. You don't *need* to know; you *want* to know. And I don't want to tell you—end of discussion."

They stood staring at each other for a long moment. Then, gradually, it dawned on Georgia what was happening here: they were boxing at shadows because the real threats looming over them were too terrible to face. Marenko must have felt it, too. He pulled Georgia close and cradled her head in his hands.

"Scout, please," he begged in a husky voice. There was fear in his eyes. "Let's not argue like this. Whatever you know or don't know—it may not matter pretty soon. This may be our last . . ."

"—Don't." Georgia put a finger to his lips. "You don't have to say anything—okay, Mac? Just stay with me a little while longer."

· · ·

Manhattan base, the seat of all arson investigations in the borough, was housed above Ladder Twenty on Lafayette Street, just west of the Bowery in lower Manhattan. When Georgia arrived at her desk in the squad room on Thursday morning, she saw three marshals at the back window fighting over a pair of binoculars. She didn't have to be told what they were looking at: *the blonde.* The woman's bathroom faced the back windows of the firehouse, and she didn't believe in curtains. Eddie Suarez never hesitated to point out that she was blond all over.

"Don't you guys ever get tired of looking?" asked Georgia.

"It's like shoes for you chicks," said Suarez, a smoldering Newport Light hanging from his lips. "No matter how many pairs you got, you still want more."

"I think I'd always want that pair," muttered Sal Giordano. He was a heavyset bowlegged marshal who wore a hideous black toupee and neckties wide enough to park a boat beside. His belly was pressed against the window as he watched the woman slip a tight-fitting white cotton tank top over two voluptuous breasts.

"Boobs," growled Don McClusky, the third marshal at the window. "Boobs are the downfall of Western society." McClusky was in his late forties with the build of Buzz Lightyear, the swagger of John Wayne and the philosophical integrity of a pimply-faced reject from the Michigan Militia. "Those A-rabs with the red-checkered tablecloths on their heads—they've got one thing right," said McClusky. "Cover a woman up. Keep a man's mind on what's important."

"Yeah," said Suarez. "That's why the Middle East is such a calm and happy place."

None of the marshals said a word to Georgia about Marenko. She was sure they talked about nothing else when she wasn't around, but it was as if a wall went up when she walked into the room. A big part of it, she suspected, was simple awkwardness. The men she worked with were used to covering over their feelings with humor. Problem was, facing a murder rap just wasn't funny. She started to sort through some odds and ends she needed to tie up on minor investigations while she waited for Carter to arrive. Her partner was never late. Her phone rang. She picked it up.

"Manhattan base. Fire Marshal Georgia Skeehan," she answered.

"I'm outside, girl. Y'all need to come down right away."

"Randy? What's wrong?"

"We'll talk in the car."

. . .

Carter was perspiring heavily when Georgia found him parked in their usual squad car. Trucks rumbled along Lafayette Street, their diesel fumes lingering ghostlike in the stale summer air.

"I heard about last night," he said as she got in. "Are you okay?" She nodded. "Things are crazy 'round here," he said. "I think Connie was right about a bomb on the pipeline. This morning, I passed by Police Plaza and I saw bomb squad trucks near the entrance, all lined up like they were ready for some kind of maneuver."

"Is that what you wanted to tell me?"

"No." Carter nosed the dark blue sedan onto the FDR Drive and headed uptown. "It's going to hit the news and the firehouse gossip lines any minute, so I figured we'd disappear for a little while, get some air."

"What's going to hit the news?"

He turned from the wheel and looked at her, his deep-set basset-hound eyes full of sorrow. "Skeehan, they found some stuff in a Dumpster in the basement of Marenko's apartment building."

"What stuff?"

"Connie's bloody clothes. Marenko's gun. Some neighbor in his building called up the Midtown North Precinct, hysterical. The cops checked it out. It's definitely her blood and his gun."

"Did they find Connie?"

"No." He sighed, fiddling with the vents. The air-conditioning still wasn't working properly. "But the Queens D.A. figures he's got the murder weapon and all the circumstantial he needs to put together a case." Carter stopped fiddling and stole a sideways glance at Georgia. "The PD arrested Marenko early this morning," he said softly.

Georgia closed her eyes. She kneaded her hands in her lap to keep them from trembling. Her tongue suddenly felt big and fat, as if she had a thumb in her mouth. She couldn't get it to work. The humid air felt as deprived of oxygen as a smoke-filled corridor. She had to take deep breaths to keep her lungs from choking.

"They're sure?" she croaked hoarsely. "That Mac put the gun in that Dumpster?"

"Listen to me, girl. You must know yourself—you need a key to get into his building. That pretty much narrows the list of suspects." *It sure does,* thought Georgia. *Even I don't have a key to Mac's building.* She stared out the window at the East River on her right. A promenade meandered above the shore, dotted with elegant wrought-iron street lamps. Dog-walkers and joggers strode along it beneath a pewter-colored sky.

"Where is he?"

"Riker's Island," said Carter. Georgia stifled a shudder as she pictured the gray behemoth jail colony in the middle of the East River.

Carter pulled off the highway and parked on a side street just west of the FDR Drive. But he didn't get out of the car. Instead, he fished something out of his suit jacket and handed it to her. It was a copy of a phone bill.

"In case you're thinking of visiting him, y'all might want to see this first. It's a present from Detective Leahy. I told him I wanted to be the first to know if Marenko was going down—for your sake—so I could break it to you, as your partner."

Georgia looked at the bill. It was a printout of every incoming and outgoing call on Connie's phone lines Tuesday night—even her cell phone calls.

"These numbers"—Carter pointed to two calls made to her home line between seven and eight P.M.—"these were sales calls. One was a cable company and one was for a subscription to *Newsday*. Leahy checked out those numbers. They're legit."

Carter's voice got very soft and southern. His bridge-jumping voice, reserved for only truly terrible situations. This certainly qualified. "Connie never got any threatening calls that night, Skeehan. Marenko lied."

Georgia took a deep breath. "I feel like such a fool," she said thickly.

"You're not a fool," he said gently, patting her hand. "C'mon, let's get some air."

They walked across a footpath to the promenade.

"I'm afraid to ask," said Carter. "Any news on the pregnancy?"

"I got my period last night."

"Thank the Lord for that." His shoulders seemed to loosen.

Georgia kept staring at the phone records in disbelief. There were two outgoing calls, both made from Connie's cell phone. One number she recognized instantly as Marenko's. The other number was unfamiliar. Connie had dialed it about ten minutes before she'd phoned Mac.

"Whose phone number is this?" Georgia asked Carter.

"Leahy spoke to the woman. She's an older lady," said Carter. "She said she didn't know anyone named Connie Ruiz. She didn't remember the call. The woman ran some kind of day-care center, Leahy told me. Connie hasn't got any kids. It must've been a wrong number."

A day-care center. In the 718 area code.

"Was her name Flannagan? Denise Flannagan?" Georgia asked.

Carter frowned. "Yeah. That sounds right."

Connie interviewed Denise Flannagan, thought Georgia. *Connie wrote down the word* Bridgewater—*and then she disappeared.* That fire. Everything kept coming back to that fire.

"Who's Denise Flannagan?" asked Carter.

"She's the widow of a fire captain in Brooklyn," Georgia explained. "Her husband was the captain of Ladder One-twenty-one. He was at the Bridgewater fire—the same fire Connie had scribbled a mention of before she disappeared."

"So?" said Carter. "That fire was mentioned in Louise Rosen's files. Maybe Connie was checking out Rosen's connection to the bomb threat. That's got nothing to do with Marenko."

"Except the bomb's no rumor, Randy." Georgia palmed her tired eyes. "Connie was right. It's real." She stared out at the promenade. It was ten A.M. Thursday. There were perhaps hundreds of people walking around this city who might have just twenty-six hours to live. Brennan and Delaney couldn't seem to help her. Even Hanlon was running scared. Yet Georgia needed help—now more than ever.

"Let's take that walk, Randy. There's something I haven't told you—something I think you should know."

34

. . .

GEORGIA AND CARTER leaned over a wrought-iron railing on the East Side promenade and watched a salvage barge float by under the bright orange-and-blue footbridge to Wards Island Park. Georgia told Carter everything—about Robin Hood, about Gus Rankoff and the mayor's plans to build a football stadium on the Bridgewater site, about the sabotaged valve in Coney Island and the CIDS card she found at the old firehouse the previous night—before someone decided she shouldn't have.

"Why in the heck did Robin Hood put you in the middle?" Carter wondered aloud. "It makes no sense."

"Maybe he knows me."

"Or wants to," said Carter gravely. "You got a lot of publicity after you wrapped up the Spring Street fire. No telling who took a hankering to you after that. Either way," said Carter, "you've got none of the higher-ups in your corner. The mayor's not gonna be keen about looking into toxic waste dumps on a site he's aiming to put a football stadium on."

"What about Brennan?" asked Georgia. "Doesn't he care?"

"Even if he does, he's got to answer to Delaney who's got to answer to the mayor. Everyone's gonna protect his own turf."

Georgia stared out at a rusty tugboat slicing up the cement-colored water. "Somebody was doing more than protecting his turf last night, Randy."

"Yeah," he grunted. "That's what I'm thinking, too."

"It had to be Robin Hood," said Georgia. "I know he's connected to the Bridgewater fire. A lot of bad stuff happened there, Randy. The families are still in pain. I met Denise Flannagan's daughter, Tricia. I saw the venom she felt for the FDNY. A million dollars of payoff money won't erase that. Whoever this Robin Hood is, I think he'll take the cash and still blow up the pipeline no matter what the police do. A lot of people are going to die."

Carter leaned on the railing and looked at her. "You want me to do something to help you? Tell me what, and I'll do it."

Georgia sighed. "I can't visit the Flannagans about that call Connie made. The department will have my head if I do anything that looks remotely related to this fire—especially after last night."

"I'll go, then," said Carter. "I'll say I'm following up on Connie's disappearance. I won't even mention the Bridgewater fire."

"Okay," said Georgia. She fished Marenko's scribbled address for Northway out of her bag. "Maybe while you're in Brooklyn, you could check this out, too. This is the company that took over the assets of the firm that owned that warehouse. Maybe you can find out who the owners are so we can talk to them."

"Will do." Carter shook a finger at her. "Stay out of the office this morning, Skeehan. Nobody's going to expect you to function. I'm going to put in a call to Suarez and Kyle and ask them to cover for us, all right?"

Georgia nodded. "That'll give me time."

He narrowed his eyes. "For what?"

"Connie found out something about Robin Hood's identity before she disappeared—I'm sure of it, Randy. If we're going to find Robin Hood, I've got to find Connie."

"Y'all can't accomplish what the entire PD hasn't been able to."

"They don't know Connie."

"Maybe," Carter ventured softly, "you didn't totally, either."

"But I know somebody who does."

. . .

35

JOANNE ZELIGMAN WORKED at Gorman's Gym on West Twenty-first Street. It was a boxing gym in a former loft—nothing fancy enough to qualify as a health club. But Joanne worked there for the same reasons that Connie loved going there—it was all about sweat, not spandex.

There were no juice bars, ferns or hot tubs. And when someone took a pulse, it was the other guy's—to see if he was still alive after they'd given him an up-close view of the canvas. Tae-Bo was about the only thing the gym offered that wasn't designed to bloody another human being.

Joanne was there, which was a good thing. Georgia didn't have her home phone number and wasn't sure it was listed. She was in an upstairs room with a few punching bags and fingerprint-smeared mirrors scattered around the perimeter. She was dressed in baggy sweatpants, frayed at the hems, and a faded blue T-shirt soaked with sweat. She must have just finished a class. Georgia assumed that Leahy would have checked her out after Connie's disappearance, so she would have known Connie was missing. And she would have known, too, who the suspect was.

Joanne represented a side of Connie Georgia never really saw. A tougher, more street-savvy side. She was older, for one thing—somewhere in her late forties or even early fifties perhaps, but it was hard to tell. There was a raven-haired beauty beneath the veneer, but she did nothing to bring it out. Her once-black shoulder-length hair was streaked with gray and usually tied off her face in a brittle ponytail. She

paid no attention to clothes and ridiculed Connie about her own preoc-
cupation with expensive shoes. She had a grown son Georgia rarely
heard anything about. There were marriages in her past, as well as drugs,
alcohol, and stints as an actress, a folk singer and a commune dweller.
But she had shed all that now and seemed content with sweating out her
demons in Gorman's.

"Joanne?" Georgia called out hesitantly in the doorway.

Joanne looked over, wiping her face on her loose T-shirt. A steely
edge came into her eyes.

"She's dead, isn't she?" Joanne asked.

"I don't know," said Georgia, stepping nearer. "The police . . . found
some of her clothing in, uh, Mac Marenko's apartment building. But no
one's found Connie."

Joanne reached for a water bottle, took a slug and regarded her
coolly. "Then why are you here?"

Georgia started. She hadn't expected such a chilly reception from the
only other person who knew Connie as well as she did. Then it came to
her. In Joanne's eyes, at least, they weren't really allies.

"Joanne, please—don't turn away from me. You and I—we're
the two people with the best chance of finding out what happened to
Connie."

Joanne thrust out her jaw skeptically. "You care for Connie's sake?
Or Mac's?" she asked.

"Both."

Joanne shook her head. "You can't have it both ways—not on
this one."

"I want the truth just as much as you do," Georgia insisted.

Joanne put down her water bottle and turned to a large, duffle-
shaped punching bag behind her. She pounded her fists in it several
times. "Did he confess?" she grunted between hits.

"Not yesterday. I haven't seen him today."

Joanne steadied the bag. Then she took a gulp of water from her bottle and wiped her mouth with the back of her hand. "He was the one,
you know—the one she really thought would work out."

"Don't you think I've figured that out?" asked Georgia. "Don't you think I know Mac was the cop she flipped over a couple of years ago? Neither of them told me, Joanne. *Neither of them.* And I'm burning with anger and guilt because of it." Georgia made a fist and hit the punching bag—hard. "I don't need you to rub salt into the wound."

Georgia turned and headed for the door. Joanne stepped in front of her.

"Don't go, Georgia," she said. "Connie wouldn't have wanted that."

The two women stared at each other for several long seconds. On the main floor below, Georgia could hear the hollow echoes of fists hitting punching bags and feet hitting bare planking. There were shouts and curses, gruff voices and monosyllabic commands. Not unlike a firehouse.

"I'm sorry," said Joanne. "I don't mean to come down on you. Connie wouldn't want that. All she wanted was your happiness."

"I know," said Georgia. She closed her eyes. She could hear the words as if they were coming from Connie herself. She stepped back against a padded wall by the door, across from the mirror, and sank down. She felt drained. Joanne sat down beside her. The fight had left them both.

"It must have killed her when Mac and I started seeing each other," Georgia said softly. "I wish I'd known. I would've stopped the relationship right then and there."

"That's probably why she didn't tell you," said Joanne. "She never told you anything if she thought it might upset you."

"She told me everything," said Georgia defensively. "Everything except this," she corrected.

"She tell you about her tattoo?"

"Connie didn't have a tattoo," Georgia insisted.

"Oh no? She had a rose tattooed on her butt about a year ago—kind of like the one on your bike. She never told you because she knows you hate tattoos."

Georgia put her head in her hands. "She didn't trust me?"

"Of course she trusted you," said Joanne. "But like I said, she didn't want to upset you." Joanne brought an arm up to her face and wiped off a line of sweat that had collected on the ridges across her forehead. She wore her life on her face—the crow's-feet, the lip lines, the gray that sprouted like weeds from her black hair. Her face told of a woman who had made so many mistakes, she was a walking advertisement for human frailty. But maybe in the end, that's what Connie needed. Maybe in Joanne Zeligman's imperfections, Connie saw a haven of acceptance for her own.

"I can't bring myself to believe she might be dead." Joanne sighed. "She sent me a birthday card right before this. I've kept it in my locker in its original envelope. I'm so afraid it's the last contact I'll ever have with her." Joanne bit her lip and got to her feet. She wasn't going to break down in Gorman's Gym.

B-day card for Joanne . . . Georgia remembered that Connie had scribbled that in the same place she'd scribbled *Bridgewater.*

"Joanne? Do you mind if I take a look at the card?"

Joanne shrugged. "A detective looked at it when he came to interview me. There's nothing there. But you're welcome to see it."

Joanne walked Georgia to her locker and fished the card from her top shelf. On the front was a picture of two little girls with ribbons in their hair, holding hands. *For a Dear Friend on Her Birthday,* read the gold lettering. Inside, Connie had scribbled a short note about how much she cherished Joanne's friendship. Georgia ran a hand over the ballpoint scrawl. Connie always pressed down too hard. Feeling the ridges of her writing was almost like feeling her. Georgia's hand trembled as she fumbled to put the card back in its envelope.

"It's beautiful," Georgia said. She didn't trust herself to say more. She went to hand the envelope back to Joanne when her fingers felt the press of another set of ridges—on the envelope, this time. When Connie addressed Joanne's birthday card, she'd obviously been writing something else, too—on a sheet of paper on top of the envelope. Connie had pressed down so hard, the ghost of it was now on the corner of the back of the envelope. Georgia fished a pencil and a scrap of paper out of her bag. She put the paper over the indentations and lightly rubbed the pencil over the area until the shadings forced the words to life. Her insides turned to dust. Her breath left her as if a baseball had just been lobbed at her sternum.

. . . *When O'Rourke becomes Robin Hood?* Though the sentence had obviously been much longer, that was all the scribble that had registered.

"Are you all right, Georgia?"

Georgia lifted her gaze and looked straight into the woman's raw face. "Did Connie ever mention someone named O'Rourke to you?" Georgia showed her the impressions.

"No. Never. I don't even understand what that means."

"It means," said Georgia, "we may just have gotten a break in her case."

. . .

36

O'ROURKE. IT WAS a common name, as was any Irish name in the New York City police or fire departments. Hell, there were probably thirty O'Rourkes between the two agencies. Yet even as Georgia told herself that, she kept picturing the photographs in Captain Flannagan's basement. She remembered a grisly one of a big man with a head misshapen by surgery. She recalled the faded snapshot of that same man she'd seen the night before at the old firehouse, taken when he was still healthy and fair-haired, eating a meatball sandwich.

O'Rourke is dead. They're all dead, she told herself. *Seamus's brother, Mickey. Tricia's father, Pat. They're all dead except for Vinnie Battaglia, and he's nearly dead, too. Only their widows and brothers and children are left to mourn them.*

Their children . . .

Outside Gorman's gym, the Manhattan sky was blackening over again and a wind was kicking up grit on the pavement. Georgia walked north and found an air-conditioned office building atrium with banana plants and ferns. She took a seat beside the tropical foliage and dialed home. Dr. Arigoni, her mother's boss, played golf on Thursday mornings, so her mother never went in before eleven on Thursdays. Richie would be at camp. Hopefully, neither of them had heard the news yet.

"Ma?" said Georgia when her mother picked up.

"They've found her," Margaret whispered. It was as if she'd been steeling herself for this moment. She couldn't bear any more losses.

"Ma, calm down—they haven't found her yet," said Georgia. She paced the marble floor of the atrium, searching for the right words to tell her mother about Mac. She never thought she'd be delivering the worst news of her life surrounded by a bunch of banana plants and ferns.

"Dear Lord," said Margaret when Georgia had finished. "This is going to break Richie's heart."

"I know." A hot poker of guilt burned in Georgia's gut. "Please don't tell him anything when he comes home from camp today. Keep him away from the television, okay? I want to let him down slowly."

"I understand."

Georgia took a deep breath. "Ma? I've got to ask one last favor. You know that picture I gave you the other day of Jimmy? The one from Seamus Hanlon?"

"Yes," said Margaret. Georgia could tell that just hearing his name brought a dull ache to her heart.

"I need you to look at it for a moment."

"Georgia, I told you. I can't."

"Ma, this is really important. Can you get it?"

"It's an old picture of him. It must be at least fifteen years old."

"Yes, I know," said Georgia. "But it isn't Jimmy I want you to look at."

Margaret sighed. "Hold on." Georgia heard her footsteps on the stairs. Her mother came back down a moment later. "I've got the picture in front of me. What is it you want?"

"There are some names on the back. They match up with the people in the picture. One of them, as I recall, is named O'Rourke. Can you figure out which one?"

"*Hmmm,*" said Margaret. Georgia could hear her mother mumbling off the names, then mumbling them again when she figured out where they were in the photograph. "Yes, I think I've found him. It says 'Carl O'Rourke' on the back and, according to this photo, he's . . . *hmmm* . . . well . . ."

"Well, what?"

"He doesn't look very much like an O'Rourke. More Italian, if you ask me. He's got tanned skin and dark hair. And he's no more than about ten or eleven. What could you possibly want with a little boy?"

"He's not little anymore, Ma."

. . .

Carl O'Rourke. He'd be about twenty-four now, thought Georgia. And Seamus Hanlon knew him—took him fishing with a group of firefighters when Carl was only a kid.

Seamus Hanlon was off duty today. He lived in Little Neck, Queens, near the border of Long Island. The house, a split-level, was on a quiet, tree-lined street with late-model American cars in the driveways. It was vinyl sided in powder blue. There were Hummel figurines in the bay window and an American flag over the front door. Hanlon had served two tours in Vietnam, and he had never stopped being a soldier on some level.

Randy Carter had taken the Caprice, so Georgia was forced to rely on the Long Island Railroad and a brisk walk to reach Hanlon's house. By the time she stepped onto his driveway, lightning was streaking the sky and a scattershot of drops had started to fall.

Hanlon's garage was half open and the trunk of his eighty-eight Oldsmobile was sticking out the door. The captain was at the rear of the garage, hunched over a workbench, drilling into a piece of lumber. From the looks of the other materials on the bench, he appeared to be making a dollhouse. Georgia knew his four children were grown, some of them married. She wondered if the dollhouse was for a grandchild.

Hanlon didn't notice her until she walked right up to him. He shut down his drill and lifted his safety goggles. His eyes, as soft and faded as an old pair of blue jeans, regarded her curiously.

"Georgia? To what do I owe the pleasure, lass?"

She nodded toward the wood on the bench. "I'm never too old for a dollhouse."

Hanlon smiled. "It's a hobby of mine." He shrugged. "This one's for my granddaughter, Jenna. But I make 'em all year for kids in hospitals and foster homes. Then at Christmas, I dress up as Santa and give 'em out."

"That's really nice, Captain."

"Seamus," he corrected. "No need for titles. I'm off duty." He looked down at the dollhouse. "Anyway, it keeps me occupied since Alice . . ." Hanlon's voice trailed off. He couldn't bring himself to say "died." *Just like my mother,* thought Georgia.

Hanlon clapped his hands together. "But you're not here for a dollhouse, are you, lass?"

"No."

"You're going to ask me about that fire again, aren't you?" He threw his goggles on his workbench. "I can't help you, Georgia. I've told you that already."

"Seamus—please. A lot more is riding on this than you know about."

He smiled sadly and shook his head. "No, Georgia. A lot more is riding on this than *you* know about."

"Then tell me."

"I told you. I can't." He walked over to a door separating the garage from the house. He started to open it. "I've got to go."

Georgia glanced at the driveway now. The rain had begun to splash down with the force of pebbles.

"I walked here," said Georgia. "From the train station. You're not going to send me back out in that, are you?"

"No," he said. "I'm going to drive you back to the station." He grabbed a set of car keys just inside the door.

"Answer me one question—*one* question, will you?" Georgia pleaded. "Why didn't you tell me about your brother Michael?"

Hanlon froze. "Leave Mickey out of this," he said tersely.

"Why?"

"Because I said so," he growled.

"I saw the pictures in Pat Flannagan's basement," Georgia explained. "I would think with all that happened to him, you'd want to do right . . ."

"—*Do right?*" Hanlon threw his car keys across the workbench.

His fists opened and closed as if he wanted to hit something. Georgia stepped back.

"*Do right,* you say. Tell me, Georgia—what *is* doing right?"

"Not turning your back on your brother. Not closing your eyes to what happened to him," she replied.

"You think I closed my eyes? Jesus." He slapped the work bench, then swung around and looked at her, his face full of rage and confusion. "Mickey went from being a kid who could lift the front bumper of a car to a man of forty who couldn't pick up a spoon, couldn't use the bathroom." Hanlon's eyes glistened with tears and he blinked them back. "Christ almighty, he had so much cancer, they took out his insides. He had to use one of them *bags* around his waist. All his dignity, all his manhood—it was gone by forty."

"I know," said Georgia softly. "But you can do something about that now."

"I can't do anything," said Hanlon.

"Because you're afraid," she said with disgust. "Like everyone else in this godforsaken bureaucracy. You're afraid to take matters into your own hands."

"I *took* matters into my own hands, Georgia. Lord almighty. And I've been suffering for it ever since." Hanlon's hands trembled as he wiped them down the sides of his denim trousers. "I did the one thing Mickey asked me to do. He asked to go out with something left in him. And I gave him that. God help me, I did."

Hanlon's voice cracked and he turned away from her. He tossed the roof of the dollhouse to one side of his workbench in disgust. "Can you understand what I'm saying, lass? Can you understand? That's all the *right* I could do for my kid brother."

Georgia felt frozen with the enormity of Seamus Hanlon's confession and his conflict over it. She took a step toward him and put a hand on his shoulder. "I'm so sorry, Seamus. I didn't mean to bring up . . ."

"—Forget it." He shrugged her off and took a deep breath. "It's over. I never told anyone—not even Alice. Mickey wouldn't have wanted me to." He pulled a handkerchief out of his pocket and blew his nose.

"Times like this, I wish I could have a beer." He laughed. "Or a case or two."

"How 'bout a soda? Can we get a soda?"

"Sure," he said hoarsely. "I've got a few cans in the fridge."

Georgia could tell a big family had once lived in Seamus Hanlon's house as soon as she stepped into the kitchen. The refrigerator was huge; the kitchen table was long and built to take the bumps and dings of a noisy clan. But it was empty now. Dust gathered on the counters and when Hanlon offered her a soda, she saw that there were only a couple of cans and some Chinese takeout cartons on an empty refrigerator shelf. Hanlon caught her assessment.

"No one in the house but me these days, I'm afraid. My daughter got married last year. My youngest son, Tim, is stationed in Germany. My boy Brendan's working nights to make detective, and Doug—Jenna's father—just joined the FDNY."

"You must be proud of all of them," said Georgia.

"Oh, yeah," said Hanlon. "But it's quiet here sometimes. I'd be lying if I said I didn't miss 'em." He drained his soda and put the empty aluminum can down on the counter with a smack. "Look, Georgia. I know what you want: that Division of Safety report. And I don't have it."

"—But you could get it," she said.

He shook his head. "It wouldn't bring Mickey back. And there's too much heat on it, besides."

"Ed Delaney told you that, didn't he? Because he knows. He *knows* a leak on the Empire Pipeline caused the Bridgewater fire—a leak Empire failed to report. He *knows* Tristate Trucking was storing PCBs, toluene and benzene illegally inside the warehouse. And he *knows* the city was aware of the situation at least nine months before the fire and did nothing about it."

"If you know all that, lass, what do you need the report for?"

Georgia stared at Seamus Hanlon. She could hear the hum of his refrigerator and the ticking of a grandfather clock in the living room.

"I didn't, for sure," she said finally. "You just confirmed it."

Hanlon closed his eyes and shook his head in disgust. "So you know—so?" he asked. "Ed Delaney tried to do something about Bridgewater nineteen years ago. He couldn't then and he can't now. You can't either. Let it go."

"I can't."

"Why?"

"I have my reasons." Georgia put her soda can down and stared at him. "All right. You can't get me that report. But tell me this at least: There was a boy in that photo you gave me of you and Jimmy. He was maybe ten—a kid named Carl O'Rourke. Was he . . . ?"

"—Albert O'Rourke's son—yes, Georgia. O'Rourke was one of the Bridgewater firefighters. I think he'd just died around the time that picture of Carl was taken."

"What was the boy like?"

"You never met a nicer kid. Kind. Decent. Give you the shirt off his back. One time, my boy, Timmy—he was about five maybe—lost this little pinball toy he'd gotten in a box of Cracker Jacks. Carl had one, too. Wanted to give Timmy his, since he was maybe four years older. That's just the way Carl was. Me and Jimmy, we took a real shine to the kid—his sister, Mary too, though she was a little older. We tried to do what we could for them, especially since their mother was already out of the picture."

"Do you know anything about them now?"

A shadow passed across Hanlon's features. "I haven't seen either of them since they were kids. I don't know anything about Mary. And Carl—I've only heard."

"What did you hear?"

Hanlon sighed. "That he got involved in drugs." Hanlon shook his head. "I guess you could sort of see it coming. He was such a soft kid. Maybe even a little fragile. O'Rourke really doted on his children. After he died, they were never quite the same."

. . .

GEORGIA DIALED RANDY Carter's cell phone as soon as Seamus Hanlon dropped her off at the train station.

"Where are you?" he asked her.

"Little Neck, Queens." She told him about the Carl O'Rourke–Robin Hood connection and her visit with Hanlon. "How 'bout you? Any luck with Mrs. Flannagan?"

"Mostly dead ends," said Carter. "Tricia left this morning for a week's vacation on Cape Cod."

"Damn. Does she have a cell phone or something you can reach her with?"

"Nothing, according to her mother. But she said Tricia will probably call home at some point and she'll get me a number." Carter could sense the disappointment in Georgia's voice. "Skeehan, you've got to remember that Tricia may not know who Connie is, either."

"Connie writes the word *Bridgewater* down, calls the family of the fire captain at that fire and then disappears? No, Randy. It's no coincidence. Tricia Flannagan knows something. How about Northway?" Georgia asked. "Any luck?"

"I just got through with them," said Carter. "Short of a subpoena, there's no way for us to find out who the limited partners are. But it turns out Northway has an advisory board—and guess who two of their advisors are?"

"Who?"

"John Welcastle, chairman of Empire Pipeline. And Gus Rankoff."

"Rankoff and Welcastle are connected to Northway?" said Georgia in amazement. "The firm that bought out Tristate?"

"Now y'all know why they don't want you to be looking too hard into that fire."

"Oh, my God," said Georgia. "We've got to tell Chief Brennan."

"Skeehan," Carter stopped her, "Northway is the general contractor for the new football stadium. The mayor *wants* this stadium. Do you honestly think Brennan is going to mess with that?"

"What do we do?"

"We leave Northway *alone*—that's what we do. Nothing good can come of taking on those suckers. But we can try to run down this O'Rourke fellow, find out if he's Robin Hood. Get him before he busts open this pipeline like a piñata on a string."

Georgia looked at her watch now. One-thirty P.M. They had less than twenty-four hours, and there was still no word even about the money drop.

"I'll pick you up at Penn Station," Carter offered. "We'll run some computer checks on this O'Rourke fellow back at base."

Silence.

"Come on, Skeehan. Y'all got to walk back into the squad room at some point," he reminded her. "The sooner you get it over with, the better."

· · ·

Suarez, Giordano and McClusky were at Manhattan base when Georgia and Carter arrived. But for once, they weren't discussing the blonde. They were in the kitchen, conferring on a subject far more juicy. They didn't notice Georgia and Carter as they passed by the open kitchen doorway. They were too busy unwrapping their sandwiches from the deli across the street.

"See?" said Sal Giordano in his thick Bronx accent. "That's why dames don't belong in the FDNY. Screws up the whole works. Me? I'm not gonna lose any sleep if Marenko gets a one-way ticket up the river.

Man should keep his pecker in his pants, if you ask me. But Skeehan? She's gonna be crying and carrying on all over this place. Gonna need a truckload of Kleenex just to get through a tour."

Carter put a hand on Georgia's arm, motioning her to forget their chatter and go to the squad room. But Georgia shook him off. She was no one's entertainment. She stood and listened as Eddie Suarez chimed in.

"Truth is, I feel kinda bad for Skeehan," said Suarez. "For a chick, she turned out okay, ya know? Even though she lost me a chunk of change in that betting pool. Man, I never thought Marenko would get into her pants that easy."

"So who you think she'll sleep with next, huh?" asked Giordano through a mouthful of sandwich.

"You're safe, Sal," said Suarez. "Trust me."

"I'm with Giordano," McClusky muttered. Three years as partners, and McClusky still couldn't pronounce Sal's last name. It always came out "Jerdano" instead of "Gee-or-dano." Any name that wasn't Irish McClusky regarded as foreign.

"I think the female element messes with a man's head," McClusky rambled on. "Marenko might be free today if this department had had the balls to keep women out of a job they're physically and psychologically unfit for."

That did it. Georgia pushed Carter aside and marched in. "Who the *hell* do you guys think you are, anyway?"

"Skeehan," stammered Suarez. He looked at the doorway and saw Carter standing in the frame, frowning. "We didn't know . . ."

She cut him off. "You have the audacity to dissect me and my private life like I'm some TV-show contestant? You want to talk about whiners and complainers? Not for nothing, look at yourselves."

She leaned over the kitchen table and pointed a finger at Sal Giordano. "You, Sal . . ." Giordano froze, his half-eaten sausage hero suspended in his hand. His mouth was full, and he'd forgotten to chew.

". . . Your mother-in-law rules your house and you're miserable and scared to death, but you haven't got the guts to confront her. So you come in here and complain about it."

She turned to Suarez next. He averted his gaze and toyed with the plastic saltshaker on the table. "You, Eddie . . . I've heard every blow-by-blow description of your divorce settlements—*both* of them. I know what your lawyer earned off you last year. I know what size shoes your second ex-wife wore and how much money they cost you. And you?" she turned to Don McClusky who was attempting, unsuccessfully, to inch his way out the doorway. ". . . You can't get it through your thick, John-Wayne, Buzz-Lightyear skull that your fifteen-year-old son would rather play his violin than blow some poor defenseless deer's brains out with you every October. And Goddamnit—that doesn't make him gay. What it makes him is a hell of a lot smarter than his old man."

She straightened up now. She could feel other eyes on her. The supervisor on duty, Rudy Hoaglund, was in the doorway, next to Carter, along with Andy Kyle. Behind them, several firefighters from downstairs were also eavesdropping. She didn't care anymore. She was tired of the whispers. She was going to have it out with them now or go down swinging.

"I've *never* brought my private life into this base. I don't discuss my son, my mother, my sex life or my past with you, and I'm not about to start now. So if you want to snicker about me like a bunch of pimply-faced adolescent boys who only get it in their wet dreams, go ahead. But do me a favor at least?" She slammed the table and they all jumped. "Have the courtesy to do it *outside* the job."

She turned to the doorway and, as if on cue, the men parted. She was a head shorter than most of them, and she felt acutely aware of that as she passed by. She made a right out of the doorway. She couldn't face the squad room—not yet. She needed a place to cool down. On the pretense of looking at case material, she disappeared into the file room—a narrow, windowless enclosure with metal filing cabinets along one wall and a table on the other. Every marshal had a drawer or two of his own cases.

She positioned her back to the door and popped open her case-file drawer. It was a low drawer. The men hated the low drawers because they were hard on the back bending over, hell on the knees squatting down. Georgia got around this by sitting cross-legged on the floor. She pretended to study the records before her, if only to steady the shaking in her fingers.

The door opened. Georgia turned, assuming it would be Carter, but it was Andy Kyle. He closed the door behind him and leaned against it, all confidence and good humor. He never looked ruffled.

"You stole my heart in there." He grinned.

"Yeah?" She turned back to her filing and shrugged. "Seems to me, I just set the cause of gender equality in the fire department *back* about twenty years."

He walked around to the other side of her and squatted on his haunches, forcing Georgia to look at him. He wore no outward displays of his background and privilege—no college rings, no expensive wristwatches—but there was a sort of inward carriage about him that set him apart. He held his back very straight and there was a soft look in his brown eyes. He had none of Mac's swagger, and that, in itself, had a sort of charm for her right now. *Andy Kyle has a crush on me*, Georgia realized. It would be so easy to return the feelings. *What's wrong with me that I can't fall in love with a decent guy like him?*

"You're right, Georgia," said Kyle. "I don't have to fight your battles for you. You knock 'em dead on your own."

"Just call me Slugger."

He straightened up and elected a more comfortable position leaning on the table. "Bernie Chandler went to Riker's this afternoon to see Mac," he said softly.

"For Mac's sake," Georgia said coolly. "I'm glad."

"You're not going to go see him?"

Georgia looked up from her files. "I don't know."

"I'd tell you not to give up on him, but I'm the king of lost causes." Kyle pursed his lips as if he didn't know whether what he'd said was funny or just plain sad. "I, um . . . talked to my father last night about Tristate Corporation, Georgia. You know they're out of business?"

"So Mac told me," she said. "They were bought out by Northway—

a firm headquartered in Brooklyn. Your dad wouldn't happen to know anything about Northway, would he?"

"I can ask him," said Kyle. "Can you give me a hint what I'm looking for?"

"Ask him if any of the owners from Tristate still hold significant stakes in Northway. Ask him why John Welcastle, chairman of Empire Pipeline, and Gus Rankoff from Mayor Ortaglia's office are on Northway's board of advisors."

Kyle frowned at her. "Tristate must've done something pretty bad for you to be this interested."

"They killed firefighters, Andy. I can't think of anything worse."

He nodded. "I'll see what I can find out."

Carter cracked open the file room door. "Skeehan—Ajay Singh from the crime lab wants to talk to you. He's on line two."

"Dr. Singh? What does he want?"

Carter was about to speak, when he noticed a set of legs in gray linen trousers leaning against the file room table. He opened the door wider. He hadn't realized Kyle was in the room. Carter was like all the long-time marshals—he never trusted a "new fish," as he called a recently made marshal.

"Better talk to him yourself," Carter told her.

Georgia walked into the squad room and picked up her phone. "Fire Marshal Georgia Skeehan," she answered.

"Marshal Skeehan—yes. I had a question for you. It concerns Officer Ruiz."

Georgia's heart quickened. She leaned into the phone. *Oh, God—no. The police have found Connie's body.*

"Yes?" she said brusquely.

"Did Officer Ruiz like to bake?"

"*Bake?* As in cookies—that sort of thing?" asked Georgia.

"Yes."

Georgia was so relieved at the question, she began to laugh. "Doctor, if she made popcorn in her microwave, it was a national event," she said. "Why are you asking me this?"

"Because I found a red screw cap from a bottle of McCormick's vanilla extract in her kitchen. I could not find the bottle. I found no other spices. Her assailant had emptied the garbage before the police arrived."

"Dr. Singh," said Georgia, feeling a small blip of hope rise inside of her, "was there any GHB residue on the cap?" Maybe Mac was telling the truth after all. Maybe the same person who drugged Rosen and Dana drugged Connie and Mac as well.

"I am afraid not," said Singh. "But it was an interesting coincidence. I thought I should ask you about it."

38

. . .

As soon as Georgia hung up the phone, Randy Carter was at her desk. "Come on," he said. "Let's get out of here. I've found Carl O'Rourke."

"Where?"

"I'll tell you when we're in the car, okay?"

It was raining hard again by the time Carter nosed the Caprice onto the northbound lane of the FDR Drive. The windows began to fog up, and Georgia wiped a rag across the glass.

"So where is the mysterious Mr. O'Rourke?" she asked.

Carter gave her a long, searching look. Rain pelted the car roof as if someone were pouring rice on it. "Cops arrested him this morning for parole violation. He's got a rap sheet a mile long—burglary, grand larceny auto, drug possession. And yes—even arson."

Georgia cracked open her window in an attempt to defog the windshield. Water poured down along the inside of the glass. "What was the violation?"

"Assault. He got in a bar fight at three A.M. this morning." Carter cleared his throat. "He's at Riker's, Skeehan."

The wiper blades thumped like a racing heartbeat across the windshield.

"I know what you're thinking," said Carter. "Y'all gonna want to see Mac while we're out there."

Georgia scratched a tic-tac-toe board in the condensation on the passenger-side glass and tried to force Marenko from her thoughts.

She'd been trying to do that all day, to no avail. She pictured his arrest this morning—cops thumping on the steel front door of his sixth-floor Hell's Kitchen walkup. She saw Mac, bleary-eyed and bare chested, in ratty track shorts, opening the door, saw him spread-eagled on the ground, frisked, then handcuffed while the police reeled off the Miranda warning Marenko himself had recited a thousand times.

Would he have cursed them? Fought them? No. Georgia had a sense he'd be almost docile—docile and scared, the fight gone, replaced by shame and fear as he was paraded past the cracked-open doors of nosy neighbors. She was glad he didn't live with his children. He would have died rather than let them see him like that.

There would be no bail for a charge of murdering a police officer. They would lock Marenko up at Riker's until his trial. It was a place Mac, like most marshals, knew well. He'd likely gone there dozens of times to interview suspects and investigate cell mattress fires—a crime that could slap an additional five years on an inmate's sentence. But those visits were wrapped in a shield of gold, not a bracelet of steel. This would be a whole different ball game.

She knew where they'd put him: Tier 3C, the North Infirmary Command, the smallest of the men's jails at Riker's, but the one where he could be most closely monitored. It was protective custody—PC or "punk city"—to the inmates. As a white law-enforcement officer, he didn't stand a chance anywhere else. The cons would give him a "buck fifty"—a knife wound across his face, requiring one hundred fifty stitches to close—just to prove they could. Marenko had been a bare-knuckle street fighter in his youth, and he was used to standing his ground. But Georgia suspected that even Mac's well-honed street sense was no match for the brutality of a city prison.

In Tier 3C, he'd be on his own—in a steel-mesh cage with just forty-eight feet to pace around in, a wafer-thin mattress on a steel bed frame, a steel toilet bowl attached to the wall and a big NO SMOKING sign at the door. Like most prisons these days, smoking was prohibited. He'd go stir-crazy within a matter of days.

If he was guilty, he deserved far worse. If he was innocent . . .

"Do you know why Dr. Singh called me this afternoon?" Georgia asked Carter.

"Uh-huh. He found a cap from a bottle of that doohickey extract at Connie's apartment."

"Doesn't that make you wonder? Just a little?" asked Georgia.

"If there was GHB in the cap, it would. But there wasn't." Carter's voice was calm and reasonable. Georgia wanted to feel his certainty—or not feel it with equal ferocity. But try as she might, she found herself in a limbo between belief and disbelief.

"Y'all want to see him, don't you?" asked Carter finally.

"No . . . I don't know." Georgia exhaled in disgust. "Besides, you don't want . . ."

"—Never mind what I want," said Carter. "Seeing as I'm the only one at base who really *does* know all about your son, your mother, your sex life and your past, I might as well make the best of it, right?"

. . .

There was only one port of entry to Riker's Island, and that was over a two-lane, mile-long stretch of concrete and steel from Hazen Street in northwest Queens. Carter and Georgia both turned strangely quiet at the check-in point before the bridge. There, they unloaded their guns inside a box filled with sand to prevent an accidental discharge, then handed their weapons over to the guards. They were given a pass to Housing Area Six South, then allowed to cross the bridge. Above, a steady stream of jets roared their decent into La Guardia Airport, oblivious to the fifteen thousand lost souls beneath their wings, yet so near that Georgia could see the pier of lights pointing pilots to Runway 13-31.

Outside, the air was humid. A silvery coating of condensation kept building up on the front windshield. Carter kept the wipers on, but the intermittent beat of blades squeaking on glass made the atmosphere in the car feel tense and claustrophobic. Not that outside was any better. Beyond the twelve-foot fences topped with razor wire, ten jails—some brick, some concrete—were scattered about like children's blocks over an acreage half the size of Central Park. Georgia could see the North Infirmary Command from the prison road. The windows were a brownish Plexiglas and the ground beneath was littered with colostomy bags that sick inmates threw out the windows to torment the guards. The air smelled of jet fuel and sewage—from the inmates or the South Bronx treatment plant across the water, Georgia wasn't sure.

Georgia always hated going to Riker's—especially in August when the cell blocks sweltered with heat and hate. In her mind she could already hear the ceaseless noise and smell the stench of urine and sweat. She could already feel the desperate animal adrenaline that seemed to permeate every pore of cinder block. But this time was much worse. The trepidation she felt was nothing compared with what Marenko must be going through.

She closed her eyes and pictured him in her pool the night before, his arms around her shoulders, the press of his lips and hands on her body. She couldn't reconcile that man with the one who took Connie's life. But *someone* took it. Georgia held no illusions about that. Connie had been gone nearly forty-eight hours now. If she could have struggled back, she would have by now. Georgia willed herself to keep her mind on interviewing Carl O'Rourke. If they were lucky, he might be the key to everything.

Carter and Georgia were given a large cage for an interview room in Housing Area Six South. It contained a gray metal table and three metal chairs. Beyond the cage, there were white cinder-block walls, video monitors and heavy steel gates. There were no windows or ventilation ducts. Even with fans sputtering, it was easily ninety degrees in there. When a guard led Carl O'Rourke into the cage, Georgia and Carter both did double takes.

"*You're* Carl O'Rourke?" asked Georgia. "The firefighter Albert O'Rourke's son?"

The inmate nodded.

"Man, you don't look Irish," Carter blurted out.

It was true. Carl O'Rourke was a tall, gangly young man with greasy black hair, dark eyes and skin the color of pulled taffy. He looked like he'd once been quite handsome, though he was sickly now. His cheeks were hollow, and there was a yellow sheen to his eyes. Although he'd been picked up on a parole violation, he hadn't been convicted yet, so he still wore street clothes—a faded, stained army green T-shirt and basketball shorts. Up and down his skinny arms were the scars of needle marks. O'Rourke was a junkie. He looked like he might be HIV positive, as well.

Georgia motioned for the man to have a seat. Carl O'Rourke's rap sheet showed that he'd been out of prison for four months after doing a three-year stretch at Greenhaven for arson and burglary. Georgia asked for his whereabouts over the course of the last week. Like most junkies, he was vague and given to a lot of shrugging. He lived off and on with a second cousin. He worked a week or two at a scrap yard. He seemed to be whiling away the days as if it were a vacation from some next stretch of time he'd eventually end up doing.

"I ain't done nothing," he said with a slouch that suggested he didn't care if they believed him or not.

"That's why you're back here, I suppose," said Georgia.

"A man tries to rip me off. Sells me bad product—what am I supposed to do?"

He was posturing—Georgia could see that. Carl O'Rourke had done enough time in prison to know how important it was to act tough. But his eyes—red and sickly as they were—gave him away. The eyes were boyish, maybe even a little tentative.

"We're not here about your assault charge, Carl," Georgia said evenly. "That's a police matter."

"What do you want?"

Georgia leaned across the table. "Who is Robin Hood?"

"*Robin Hood?*" O'Rourke said the words like he was sure he'd gotten them wrong. Then he frowned and shook his head.

"You ever call yourself 'Robin Hood'?" Georgia prodded.

"Ain't he the dude who robs from the rich and gives to the poor?"

"That's right," she said.

"Believe me, lady, if I could rob from the rich, I sure wouldn't be giving none of it away. I'd get myself in a good rehab program—that's what I'd do. Get off this shit once and for all."

Georgia stared at the young man now—at his emaciated frame, the dirt under his nails and track marks down his arms. Robin Hood had been able to murder two doctors in fires designed to look accidental. He'd had access to C-four plastic explosives and knew how to use them. The man before her looked barely able to keep it together between fixes. Carl O'Rourke was no Robin Hood. But there was still a chance he knew Robin Hood's identity.

"You were convicted of arson four years ago," said Georgia. "You want to tell us about it?"

O'Rourke shrugged. "I was shooting up and my sterno flipped over and the building burned down. I didn't do it for kicks or nothing."

"But you must know people who do, right?" asked Georgia.

"In Greenhaven, maybe. But I don't hang with torches, man. They're too weird."

Georgia and Carter exchanged looks. O'Rourke was looking more and more like a two-bit junkie with nothing to offer them. Georgia tried a different tack.

"Do you know someone named Joanne Zeligman?" she asked. O'Rourke's name was, after all, scribbled inadvertently on Joanne's birthday card. Georgia couldn't overlook the obvious—that it was Joanne who knew O'Rourke.

"She a lawyer or something? She got one of them names sounds like she might be a lawyer."

"No," said Georgia. "She's not a lawyer. How about the name, Connie Ruiz? Does that ring any bells?"

"Connie?" In an instant, the convict's swagger had melted from his lean, dark features. His legs jiggled nervously. He drummed his fingers on the table.

"How do you know Connie? Did she arrest you?" asked Georgia.

"*Arrest* me?" O'Rourke bounced a glassy, agitated look from Georgia to Carter. "Are you kidding me, man? She wouldn't arrest me."

"When did you last see her?"

"I ain't seen her but once since I got out of Greenhaven—right after my parole officer called her up, trying to find a place for me to stay. She gave me some bread." He shook his head. "She didn't want me in her life. I can understand that, so I said, 'okay' . . ." His voice trailed off. He looked up at them now, a shade of embarrassment across his features. "Is that what you're looking for? 'Cause I'm starting to hurt here." He rubbed his arms.

"Mr. O'Rourke," said Georgia, "what's your relationship with Officer Ruiz?"

"Our *relationship?*" His glassy yellow eyes looked at her incredulously. "Didn't she tell you?"

Carter and Georgia gave him a blank look.

"Connie Ruiz—Mary Constance Ruiz—is my sister."

Georgia felt her legs go weak, felt the blood drain out of them, just like the time she'd drunk too many gin gimlets and felt perfectly sober—except she couldn't stand up. She looked over at Carter, who seemed shaky himself and was visibly perspiring.

"Connie is your *sister?*" asked Georgia.

"I thought her name was Connie Ruiz," Carter mumbled.

"I guess it is—legally." O'Rourke shrugged. "She was born Mary Constance O'Rourke, but my father sometimes called her Connie. She married this jerk named Ray Ruiz when she was, I dunno, about nineteen. He busted her up good, so she divorced him but kept his name. We always looked Puerto Rican like our mother anyway, so Ruiz worked better for her."

Carl O'Rourke put his skinny elbows on the table and picked at a scab on his left hand. The eyes were soft now—not the eyes of a convict at all. Georgia could almost see the boy Hanlon had described—the one who had offered up his Cracker Jacks toy to a younger child.

"Is Connie in some kind of trouble?" he asked softly. He scratched his arms. "Is she hurt or something? Is that why you're here?"

"We were hoping you could give us some information," said Georgia. The classic noncommittal cop response. They would tell O'Rourke nothing he didn't already know.

"I don't know where she is, if that's what you mean. I swear. I ain't talked to her but once since my release." He leaned forward across the table, the bluster gone. He suddenly looked very young and scared. "Is she dead?" he whispered.

"Do you know anyone who would want her to be?" Georgia came back at him.

O'Rourke put his head in his hands and stared at the table. "I don't know anything about my sister's life."

That makes two of us, thought Georgia. "What can you tell us about her?" she asked.

O'Rourke looked up from his hands. Sweat darkened the neckline of his T-shirt and ran down it in a V. His limbs were in constant motion—hands drumming the table top, legs bobbing up and down, feet jiggling. Watching him suffer withdrawal was like observing a person with Tourette's syndrome. His speech was rambling and disjointed, but in twenty minutes, Georgia learned more about her best friend's life than in eight years of knowing her. She heard about the good stuff—how Connie had nursed her ailing father after he started to succumb to cancer. And she heard about the bad, too—how they had lived in a toolshed one summer rather than go into foster care, a fate that they both eventually had to submit to.

"They raped her, you know," he said softly.

"Who raped her?"

"Some boys in a group home she was staying in. She was sixteen. I was eleven. I couldn't do nothing, but I always felt like I shoulda been able to."

He talked about his own memories, too, of drinking malt liquor on Brooklyn rooftops, of hot-wiring cars and of nights spent lusting after Tricia Flannagan.

"You *know* Tricia?" asked Georgia.

"When we were younger. Not now. Our dads worked together. She was older than me, younger than Connie. Nothing happened between us or anything." He leveled a dark, sober gaze at Georgia now. "My sister's dead, ain't she?"

"We don't know that, Carl," said Georgia. "That's the truth."

He nodded, satisfied that that was all the answer he was going to get—all he believed he deserved. Then he wrapped his arms around his body tightly, and Georgia felt sorry for the young, scraggly man before her—for the hard way he and Connie had lived.

Connie had somehow managed to keep herself together while Carl had fallen apart. Mixed in with Georgia's sorrow was an undeniable guilt. *Connie, I'm sorry,* thought Georgia. *I didn't know how badly you had suffered—how strong you'd had to be. You never let it show.*

"Did Connie stay in touch with Tricia?" Georgia asked.

"I don't know. Maybe. Tricia always knew her as Mary O'Rourke, though. Connie Ruiz—that was her own invention. I guess she was trying to leave all this shit behind."

He shook his head. "She told me last time I talked to her that she'd look into getting me into a good rehab program. I thought maybe . . . if she could find me a good program . . . I'd have a shot at getting clean."

He glanced around the wire-mesh cage, then closed his eyes as if it had just dawned on him how completely his own life had fallen apart, and how unfulfilled his sister's promises would remain.

"You know, growing up, my sister always wanted to be a firefighter." He smiled a sad, sweet smile, showing the boy beneath the broken-down body that would never be whole. "I did, too."

39

· · ·

GEORGIA AND CARTER didn't speak until they'd heard the steel gates
close behind them in Housing Area Six South. They were both stunned by
O'Rourke's revelations. Still, it didn't get them any closer to Robin Hood.

"Y'all still want to see Mac?" asked Carter. Georgia nodded. They
both knew that such a visit would be tricky. Georgia and Carter couldn't
claim official business with Marenko, and Georgia couldn't visit him as a
civilian, either. It was almost five P.M.—visiting hours were over.

Carter tried to sweet-talk a black woman guard on duty. She told him
the best she could do was to put in the request after the guards finished
the inmate count in forty-five minutes.

"We'll stay," Carter told Georgia.

"No, Randy. You take the car back to base and go home. We're at a
dead end. Chief Brennan hasn't called me with any news on Robin
Hood. I think we've done just about all we can do."

"How will you get home?"

"I'll catch a bus off the island. It'll drop me right near the subway. It's
a short ride to Woodside."

"You sure you want to do this?" he asked.

"I'm not sure of anything anymore."

Georgia waited on a stiff bench beside a glassed-in guard's booth,
watching the big clock on the wall count down the time. The hallway
smelled of Clorox, and the strong fluorescent light threw off any sense
of whether it was day or night outside.

"This way," said a black man in uniform opening a steel door with a buzzer after almost an hour. Georgia followed him, hearing both their sets of steps on the bare concrete. He didn't take her to a visitors' room since the room was big and visiting hours were over. Instead, he led her to a cage not unlike the one she and Carter had interviewed O'Rourke in.

Marenko was a detainee, not a convict, so he wore civilian clothes— a ragged, faded navy blue T-shirt with the sleeves cut off and track shorts. His sockless feet were shoved into a pair of sneakers. The blue in his eyes had darkened and dimmed, as if a light had gone off inside him.

He was seated at a metal table in the cage. He put his palms on the table and started to rise to greet her as the guard undid the lock.

"Sit down, Marenko," the guard ordered. "No physical contact or the visit is over. You hear me?" Marenko nodded.

"I didn't hear your answer," said the guard.

"Yessir," Marenko said meekly. He sat back down, his face pale and unreadable.

The guard locked Georgia in, then stood over by a cinder-block wall ten feet from the cage with his arms folded. Georgia tried to forget his presence. She took a seat and stared at Marenko. Her mind had been filled with questions and accusations an hour earlier. Now that she was here, she didn't know what to say. Marenko massaged his forehead.

"I don't know why you'd even want to see me," he mumbled.

"I believed you," said Georgia. "And now, with this new evidence, I don't know what to believe."

"That makes two of us." Marenko ran his hands down his face. He looked like a man who hadn't slept in a week. "Does Richie know?"

"Not yet. I'll have to tell him when I get home. How about your kids?"

He slumped in his chair and looked up at the ceiling of the wire mesh cage. Georgia could see he was fighting for control. When he spoke, it was in a voice so congested, he sounded as if he had a head cold. "I wish some street mutt had just pumped a couple of slugs through my brain a week ago," he said thickly. "That would've been a better ending."

"Don't talk that way, Mac, please," she said softly. "You can't give up like that."

Marenko's shoulder muscles tightened. What Georgia had offered as tenderness, he'd taken as pity. And if there was one thing Mac Marenko didn't want, it was anybody's pity.

"Why the hell are you even here?" he growled at her. "Am I like some car accident you see on the side of the highway and you can't look, but you can't *not* look? Is that it?"

"Is that how you see yourself, Mac? As some *accident*? You *chose* to go to Connie's apartment Tuesday night."

"Because she called me," he said indignantly.

"She never got a threatening call. Why don't you quit bullshitting?"

The guard took note of the rising voices. "Keep it down in there or it's over, Marenko," he ordered.

"Yessir." Marenko shot Georgia a look of daggers. "Look, I've been in touch with Bernie Chandler."

"I know."

"He told me I can't talk to you about the case. He said you could be called upon to testify against me."

"I wouldn't."

"Scout, listen to me. We're not on the same side anymore. Connie was your best friend, and I stand accused of her murder."

"Have they found her body?"

"Not yet. But the cops can make the rap stick on circumstantial alone." Marenko laughed bitterly. "And they've got plenty of that, believe me."

"I know," said Georgia, thinking again of Connie's apartment and suppressing a shudder. Marenko caught the movement like a sock to the jaw.

"Well, if you *know,* then what are you doing here? What do you want from me? A confession? Christ, Leahy was here trying to cut a deal with me, and *he* didn't get one." He feigned a shrug. "I guess I must be fresh out."

"That's not why I came," said Georgia. "I thought you'd know that by now." She started to rise. "I'm sorry. I'll go."

"Wait," Marenko muttered. He made a face like someone who was having gravel picked out of his skin. He kept his eyes on the table as he spoke. "I didn't mean that. I just . . ." He let out a long exhale. "I want you here and I don't want you here at the same time. Do you understand what I'm saying?" He ran a hand through his hair and looked at her now. "I'm trying to do the right thing, Scout. I don't want to screw up your life."

Georgia sat back down. Marenko swallowed hard.

"If it's going to come to this—me in prison," he said. "I want you to move on. I wouldn't feel right otherwise. Hell, I can't even watch your back on that money drop Friday. What use am I to anyone in here?"

Georgia leaned forward. "Mac," she said softly. "I meant what I said when I told you not to give up . . . I didn't just come to Riker's this evening to see you. I came to interview a man named Carl O'Rourke."

Marenko gave her a blank look.

"Carl O'Rourke is the son of Albert O'Rourke, a firefighter who served under Pat Flannagan at Ladder One-twenty-one on the night of the Bridgewater fire."

"Bridgewater again." Marenko rolled his eyes. "That fire has nothing to do with . . ."

"—Carl O'Rourke is the brother of Connie Ruiz."

"What?" Marenko put his palms on the table and leaned closer to her. "But Connie's Puerto Rican."

"Half, it turns out," said Georgia. "Believe me, I didn't know this either until tonight. But this is a link, Mac—a solid link—between Connie's disappearance and the Bridgewater fire she was investigating before she disappeared. And there's something else, too." Georgia told him about Ajay Singh finding the red bottle cap at Connie's and how an identical cap was found at Louise Rosen's.

"I wasn't drugged," Marenko insisted. "I would've known. Connie would've known."

"Maybe Connie was drugged, too."

He frowned as he thought about that. "I passed a drug test."

"You probably weren't tested for GHB."

He shook his head. "Look, Scout—I wanna get out of jail so bad, I'm willing to believe anything. But I think your theories have jack to do with what happened here. Who'd want to kill Connie?"

"Maybe Robin Hood," Georgia whispered. "If Connie was on to him. And she might have been. Can you remember anything about Tuesday night? Anything at all?"

"It's still a black hole," he said sullenly.

"Did Connie make any phone calls while you were there? Did she receive any?"

"Not that I remember."

"What was the last thing you *do* remember?"

Marenko leaned his head in his hands and tried to concentrate. "I was on her couch—you know, the white one with the green cushions?"

Turquoise. Only a man wouldn't know the color turquoise, thought Georgia.

"We were watching television," Marenko recalled. "Some rerun of *Law and Order.* I was drinking a beer. A Rolling Rock. Connie was having one, too. I got up to use the can. I think the bulb burned out in her ceiling light in the bathroom. I asked if she had another. I'd put it in for her. She told me she kept them in a cabinet above the refrigerator in the kitchen, so I went there and got one."

"That's it?" asked Georgia. "That's all you remember?"

"Yeah, but . . ." Marenko frowned.

"But what?"

"The bathroom light fixture had these tiny pain-in-the-ass screws you had to undo, and I think I'd remember if I'd unscrewed 'em. But I don't."

"So?"

"When I came to and I was so sick? I ran into the bathroom to throw up. And . . . the light worked." He shook his head, as if it had never occurred to him until that moment. "Somebody undid that fixture and screwed in that bulb."

"Maybe Connie did."

"Don't you think Connie would be a little too concerned that I'd passed out to be screwing in some bulb? And if *she* passed out, too—as you say—then who screwed in that bulb?"

"Time's up, Marenko," barked the guard beyond the cage.

Marenko flinched as if he'd been struck. He pressed his palms on the table and kept his eyes on them. He was already learning about prison life: keep your hands where the guards can see them.

Georgia rose. "Mac, I . . ."

"—Just go," he muttered into his chest. "Don't say anything, all right? Just go."

. . .

THE TEMPERATURE SEEMED to drop ten degrees as soon as Georgia left Riker's Island. She welcomed the air outside, even though it was bathed in the stench of sulfur and jet fuel. From the back window of the bus, she saw the razor wire and concrete blocks fade. It made her ache to know that Mac was still inside. Connie was dead—she was sure of that now. But that knowledge brought her no closer to finding Robin Hood or stopping the bomb.

On the subway home, Georgia kept thinking about the lightbulb in Connie's apartment. She wondered if Leahy had ever checked it out. Flushing was only three stops more on her subway line.

Just walking back into the 109th Precinct again made Georgia feel sick. She saw the bored, glazed eyes of police officers as they walked by, heard the jingle of handcuffs on suspects being hustled through the doors. She saw the station house in a way she had never seen it as a fire marshal—as frightening, cold and indifferent. She didn't think she could ever see the line between cop and suspect in quite such black-and-white terms again.

"I'm looking for Detective Leahy," said Georgia, flipping her shield at the desk sergeant and playacting a role she'd assumed quite naturally only a few days ago.

"Homicide. Three doors down, on your left," said the sergeant, directing her down a hallway painted the color of moldy bread with scuff marks and gouges along the walls.

Homicide was not unlike Manhattan base. It was a room with fluorescent tube lights recessed in the ceiling, their filaments darkened by a collection of dead bugs. On the far wall, a couple of big windows over-looked a Dumpster behind a fence. The desks—six or seven in all—were topped with computers yet crammed with so much paperwork, one wondered what, exactly, the computers were for.

Leahy was in the far corner of the room, typing on a computer while simultaneously talking on the phone. He was dressed in a rumpled white shirt and tie—no jacket. His fine, brown, fishing-lure hair was damp across his head—from sweat or hair gel, Georgia couldn't tell which. She succeeded in catching Leahy's eye, but he only frowned and turned his back to her, so she walked over and planted herself in front of him. He mumbled a "gotta go. Talk to you later" into the phone and hung up.

"If this is about Marenko, Skeehan, you're out of line walking into homicide. He's at Riker's, where he belongs."

"I know," said Georgia. "I just saw him."

"Then you're a fool, young lady."

"Did you know that Connie Ruiz had a brother?"

That got his interest. He bit his lip, trying to size her up. "Marenko told you this?"

"No. Carter and I found him ourselves. He's at Riker's too, detective. His name is Carl O'Rourke, if you'd like to talk to him. He was picked up this morning on a parole violation."

Leahy made a note of the name on a slip of paper, all the while re-garding her out of the corner of his eye. It was a typical cop look—always scrutinizing. "And you came all the way out to Flushing to tell me this, huh?"

"That's me," said Georgia. "Helpful all over."

He put the note on top of an enormous pile on his desk. He had phone numbers written on brown sandwich bags and napkins and the backs of losing lottery tickets.

"You didn't know about O'Rourke," said Georgia. "Here are two other things you may not have known about." She told Leahy about the cap to the extract bottle. "Singh at the crime lab told me."

Leahy stretched his arms over his head and yawned. Georgia saw sweat stains on his shirt. "No GHB, no proof."

"Okay, how about this." Georgia told him about Marenko's recollection of the lightbulb in Connie's bathroom. "Did you check it for prints?" she asked.

"No. It wouldn't prove anything, anyway, Skeehan. Charles Manson could've changed that lightbulb and it still wouldn't prove he was in her apartment at that particular time."

"But Mac says the bulb had burned out and it was back in . . ."

"—The *accused* can say anything he wants." Leahy shrugged. "His lawyer is welcome to make that case when it comes to court. But it doesn't prove anything, as far as I'm concerned. There's no independent corroboration that anyone else was in that apartment at that time except Mac Marenko."

He fingered a chipped mug on his desk. The coffee in it looked like it had been sitting there since the building went up. "You should be less concerned about Marenko, and more concerned about yourself right now."

Georgia gave him a puzzled look. Leahy put down his mug. "I hear A and E found some tool marks on Charles Dana's back door. They think you broke into Dana's house and you're covering it up."

Georgia froze. Leahy regarded her without looking up.

"I didn't . . . They can't prove . . ."

"Skeehan, I don't care." He spread his palms. "But Dana's case is getting a lot of heat and someone's trying to discredit you big-time. I had some guy from the mayor's office in here last night asking if we'd found out anything unusual about you, going through Ruiz's apartment. He was looking for something to take you down."

"Rankoff," Georgia murmured.

"Yep—that's the guy."

"What did you tell him?"

"I told him you'd been questioned about Ruiz's disappearance soon after it happened. You came up clean and nothing in her apartment said anything to the contrary." He paused and gave her a slight smile. "I *didn't* tell him that you walked through my crime scene later that day with your partner and could've been charged with obstruction of justice." He held her gaze a moment to make sure it sank in.

"Thank you," said Georgia.

"This way, you and I can both pretend it never happened." He rose. "You see, I'm not out to get you—or Marenko. I even tried to cut him a deal in exchange for a confession."

"I'll bet he threw you out," said Georgia.

"No, he didn't," said Leahy. "I told him a confession would save him the embarrassment of a trial and all the media coverage. He seemed to like that idea."

"His kids," Georgia muttered. "He was thinking of his kids."

"Perhaps," Leahy shrugged. "The point is, he was more willing to deal than you might think."

. . .

Richie was in his room, playing a video game, when Georgia got home with a pizza in hand. It was just after seven P.M. She'd called ahead to tell her mother she'd be picking up dinner. They both thought it might ease the pain of what Georgia had to tell her son.

Margaret hummed as she poured three glasses of lemonade and dished out the salad Georgia made. This evening it was, "Do You Know the Way to San Jose?" Her Burt Bacharach repertoire was infinite.

"What's wrong?" asked Richie, bouncing a look from Georgia to his grandmother. He knew the cues as well as his mother did.

"It's Mac, honey." Georgia sighed. "He . . . uh . . . got arrested this morning . . . Connie's still missing and uh . . . the police think Mac's responsible."

The child put his slice of pizza down and stared at his mother, as if her words were a cruel hoax. "But you said it was a mistake. You said Mac didn't do it."

"I know. But the police think he did."

"But *you're* the police." The child's pitch wobbled with panic.

"I'm not a detective, Richie. I'm a fire marshal."

"You arrest people. You could say Mac didn't do it."

"It doesn't work like that." Georgia noticed Richie never asked about Connie. Part of that, she suspected, was denial. If Richie accepted that Connie was dead, then he'd have to accept that Mac had killed her. Georgia shot a nervous glance at her mother, hoping she'd offer up some wise words of comfort. But Margaret said nothing. She looked pretty unsure herself.

"Richie . . . I don't know what to say," said Georgia finally. "This is something a ten-year-old boy shouldn't have to go through." She pushed back from the table and went to hug him. But Richie pushed back, too. He didn't want her tenderness—any more than Mac had at Riker's.

"Please, honey, it'll be all right," said Georgia.

"No, it won't," the boy choked out. "Stop lying to me. Mac's never coming back." He left the table and ran up to his room.

Georgia went to follow, but her mother put a hand on her arm.

"Don't, Georgia," she said softly. "He's not a baby anymore. You can't make the pain go away."

"What do I do?"

"I don't know," said Margaret, her face pale and nearly as frightened as Richie's. "We'll just have to feel our way forward on this one."

Georgia washed the dishes and cleaned up in the kitchen before she managed to pluck up enough courage to knock on Richie's door. He was playing his rap music tapes at top volume. He'd picked some of his angriest selections.

"Richie?" she shouted over the music. "Can I come in?"

He didn't answer, but he turned the volume down—a good sign. If he hadn't wanted her, he would've kept it loud.

Georgia picked her way across the laundry on his floor and sat on the edge of his bed. She kept her gaze on the Mets poster on the wall. She was sure Richie had been crying, and she was just as sure he'd rather she not make issue of it.

"I made a mistake bringing Mac into your life so quickly," she said softly. "It was bad judgment on my part, and I'm sorry." She sighed.

"You two got along so well and I . . . I wanted so much for you to have something resembling a dad . . . I hope you can forgive me." She reached out and squeezed his hand, then rose to leave.

"Mom?" Richie straightened up and rubbed his eyes. "Do you still love Mac?"

Georgia swallowed hard. She'd been with Mac Marenko for four months, and she'd never actually asked herself that question. Did she love him? Now? Ever?

"Yes, Richie," Georgia whispered, giving words to something she'd not been willing to acknowledge in her heart. "I guess I do."

Richie flopped back on his bed. "Me, too," he said, staring at the ceiling. "Me, too."

· · ·

GEORGIA MANAGED TO calm Richie down later that evening and eventually get him to bed. What would happen to them all tomorrow—and the day after that, and the day after that—was another matter. Georgia popped open a beer and sat on the front stoop watching the fireflies dance in the humid night air. Her mother joined her for a while, but eventually grew tired and went to bed. There were no words of comfort for anyone tonight, it seemed.

A car drove down the street, the headlights bouncing off the line of parked cars along the curb. One of them was Georgia's—parked just two car lengths from her front door. She squinted at her windshield now, illuminated by the passing headlights. Something was lodged under one of the front wiper blades. Not an advertisement—more like a big envelope.

She put down her beer and pushed herself off the stoop to investigate. It was a plain nine-inch-by-thirteen-inch manila envelope. It couldn't have been there all day—there had been a lot of rain in the afternoon, and the envelope was dry. There was no address or markings on the outside. She opened it and slid the contents out. The top sheet was a mimeographed copy of a typewritten letter. There was a signature at the bottom. *Lieutenant Edward Delaney, FDNY Division of Safety.* Georgia scanned the rest of the sheets. It was the complete record of the 1984 Bridgewater investigation—not the original, but a very old copy. The paper was faded—almost translucent—and it had yellowed to the color of a smoker's teeth. There was no note inside, nothing to indicate who had sent it to her. But she didn't need a note to know: *Seamus Hanlon.*

Georgia walked back to her stoop and slowly read through the materials. The language was lifeless but the words, even disguised in the most bloodless prose, were chilling. The firefighters who'd been at the Bridgewater blaze described flames in blue and green, smoke so thick they couldn't find the door and bursting drums that flew like missiles through the air.

Piece by painstaking piece, Delaney had managed to assemble the documents, interviews and lab results necessary to prove that then-mayor Hank Berman had orchestrated the cover-up of a huge toxic dump site and lent political protection to the companies most at risk for liability: Empire and Tristate. Nineteen men—soon to be twenty—died horrible, lingering deaths so that a handful of powerful men could save face and protect their interests.

Georgia didn't even know whom to be angry at anymore. Berman was long dead. Tristate had gone out of business. The men at Empire who'd helped facilitate the cover-up were probably retired or dead by this time. Even if someone made restitution at this point, how could any of the firefighters' families recoup what they'd lost after twenty-five years? Indeed, how could Robin Hood?

It wasn't cold out, but Georgia began to shiver as she put the papers away. She stared at the envelope and pictured the destruction Delaney's computer simulation could only hint at yesterday. And she knew: *The money won't be enough for Robin Hood. He's going to explode the bomb.* Hood had viciously burned two doctors who had denied the firefighters line-of-duty pensions. He wasn't simply going to take the money and run.

Seamus. I've got to ask him if he knows any other family members connected to Bridgewater who might want revenge. He gave me the report. He's bound to want to help.

Georgia went inside and dialed Engine Two-seventy-eight. Hanlon sounded breathless when a firefighter handed him the line.

"It's me, Georgia. I just wanted to thank you," she said.

There was a long pause. "You mean for our uh . . . conversation the other day?" asked Hanlon.

"No. I mean for that envelope—the one you left on my car."

Another long pause. "Spit it out, lass. I've just come back from a bad fire, and I don't know what you're talking about."

"The copy of Delaney's report—the one I asked you for," Georgia stammered. "It was on my car tonight. Didn't you put it there?"

"You have the report?" Panic edged up Hanlon's voice. "Listen to me, Georgia. Get rid of it. Don't tell anyone you have it—please. I didn't give it to you. I *wouldn't* give it to you. I want you to live a long and happy life. And that thing? That thing kills men."

"It didn't kill you."

"I was a drunk with a sick brother when it came out. I had so many other problems, I was no threat to anybody."

"It didn't kill Delaney."

"You don't *know* what it did to Ed Delaney. Let me tell you. He tried to make a difference with it, and he couldn't. And then Pat Flannagan . . ." Hanlon's voice faltered. "Burn the report, lass. Burn it. They got to Flannagan; they can get to you." He hung up.

. . .

GEORGIA STARED AT the phone as if Seamus Hanlon's fear could still radiate through the receiver. *Whom was he so afraid of?*

A part of her wanted to shelve the report. It wouldn't help her find Robin Hood—not at eleven-thirty P.M. on the eve of his promised explosion. And yet, *someone* had risked his life and career to get the report to her—someone who knew her car, or had staked it out, or had access to motor vehicle files. Georgia debated calling Carter, but she knew he couldn't help her on this one. He'd already told her to leave Bridgewater alone.

While she was deciding what to do, her pager went off. A tremor rippled through her body when she saw the number: Chief Brennan's cell phone. *Robin Hood has contacted the city about the drop.* She dialed his number.

"Skeehan," he grunted. "I'm at City Hall. Can someone stay with your kid?"

"My mother's here. I'll talk to her, Chief."

"Good. I've just instructed Fire Marshal Kyle to pick you up and escort you to City Hall. You'll be briefed when you arrive. You're to stay at Manhattan base for the duration of this operation."

Georgia frowned at the receiver. *I don't need an escort. And if I wanted a partner, I'd ask Randy.* But she had a sense of why Brennan had chosen Kyle over Carter. The chief wanted someone watching Georgia whose loyalties were greater to the department than to her.

Georgia wanted to ask about the bomb. She wanted to tell Brennan about the report. But she knew better than to trust such important conversations to an unprotected line. She'd bring the report along and show it to him when she saw him. "I'll be ready when Marshal Kyle arrives," she said and hung up.

Andy Kyle picked her up in a department-issued Chevy Caprice about twenty-five minutes later. On the trip into Manhattan, he filled her in on what he knew of the operation so far. "Tomorrow's drop is supposed to be in Chinatown. Robin Hood sent a tape to the mayor's office, spelling it all out. Brennan will tell you where exactly. I understand A and E is setting up the stakeout now."

Georgia raised an eyebrow. Kyle sounded well informed. "Were you just briefed?" she asked him. "Or did you know before this?"

He gave her an amused look. "What you're really asking is, do I have some kind of inside track with the brass."

"Well . . . yeah."

"I found out about this whole operation about three hours ago," he explained. He caught her dubious look. "Georgia, I was a warm body standing around Manhattan base, and I'm new enough to do everything by the book."

"That's true," Georgia had to admit. She ran through the roster of marshals on duty herself. Giordano had too big a mouth to trust on something like this. McClusky was too paranoid. Suarez was dependable, but likely to handle things his own way.

"For what it's worth," Kyle added. "I think this Robin Hood is going through a lot of trouble for a million dollars. People who set up securities frauds make this kind of money with a lot less personal risk."

They were rolling through mid-Manhattan now. Even at half past midnight, the streets were filled with people. Theatergoers in suits. Tourists in shorts, clutching their cameras and pocketbooks tightly. Suburban teens with tie-dyed hair and more body piercings than a voodoo doll. There were rows of yellow cabs, store windows filled with Statue of Liberty replicas and street guitarists hammering out tunes on opposite corners beneath a sky so dark and thick, you could run a butter knife through it.

"I don't think Robin Hood's pulling this blackmail for the money," said Georgia.

"You think he's doing it for revenge," said Kyle. Georgia gave him a startled look. Kyle might have been told the who, what and where of this operation. But the why wouldn't be part of any standard briefing.

"You asked me about Tristate and Northway," Kyle reminded her. "I kind of put two and two together from what my father could tell me about Tristate."

He turned his eyes from the wheel and searched Georgia's face. "That's why Empire's paying this Robin Hood off, isn't it?" he asked. "The city thinks a bomb on the pipeline will make investors and the public skittish about having a river of gasoline so near the new football stadium. It'll open up a can of worms about that piece of land and stop the whole project."

Georgia didn't answer.

"I know." Kyle sighed. He made a face and tried his hand at a heavy New York accent. " 'Don't tell An-dy an-y-thing. He's the neeeww fish.' "

Georgia laughed. "Not even close on the accent."

Kyle grinned. "No. But right on target with the sentiment, right? Hey, Georgia—I'm on your side here. I think the whole payoff-coverup idea stinks."

"You *do?*"

"Yes. I think the city should've told the ATF about this—brought in the heavy guns. I think they should do an investigation into Empire and Northway and stop the stadium project until all these bastards pay restitution for the damage they've done."

She shook her head. "Nothing anyone can do about it."

"Not unless you've got the goods to fry the bastards," he agreed.

But I have the goods, thought Georgia. *Right here. Right in my bag. I can do something about this.*

···

The Federalist columns of City Hall gleamed white under the spotlights as Kyle drove the department car into an underground garage. He and Georgia showed ID to a police officer on duty.

"The lady comes with me," the officer grunted, then looked at Kyle. "You stay here."

Georgia rifled through the gym bag of spare clothing she'd packed and found the envelope with Delaney's report. She tucked it into a notepad to take to the briefing.

An elevator delivered them to the second floor. The hall was empty except for the commotion coming from one conference room with another police guard by the door.

"It's a zoo in there," said the officer as he left her by the doorway. Georgia quickly saw what he meant. The room was large but felt small because of the frenetic activity and blacked-out windows. There were men and women in suits with cell phones at their ears and grimaces on their faces. Some had guns on their hips—police detectives. Others were jotting notes and calling out orders. It looked like the floor of the New York Stock Exchange at the start of a sell-off. A flurry of paperwork was flying across a conference table—maps and charts and memos. But nothing prepared her for the face in the center of the knot: Mayor Franco Ortaglia.

Ortaglia was a small man with thin lips and dark, wary eyes. He had the look of a coiled spring about him. He tried to smile, but the tightness in his pressed lips reminded Georgia of someone with heartburn. He looked over the head of one of his aides and frowned at Georgia as if she were a smudge on a streak of glass he had just cleaned.

"You're doing the drop," he grunted. "*Hmm . . . yes . . . well.*"

Georgia didn't know if she should extend a hand or sink into a corner. Brennan solved the dilemma.

"Take a seat over there somewhere, Skeehan," said Brennan, gesturing to some empty chairs away from the conference table. "We'll get to you in a minute."

Ortaglia grunted out a few directives to some of the people in the room, then disappeared with four or five of his entourage. Brennan walked over to her when he had left.

"We've gotten word from Robin Hood," he said. "The drop is going to be at oh-nine-hundred tomorrow at the corner of Mott Street and

Bayard, by a fire alarm box outside Tung Hoy Takeout. Lieutenant Sandowsky's crew from A and E is there now, setting up the stakeout. You will stay at Manhattan base tonight with Andy Kyle and await my orders. Stick around for a while, in case there's anything else I need you for." He turned to go.

"Chief?"

"What?"

"I . . . I need to run something by you," Georgia stammered. "Something that ties this whole situation to Robin Hood."

"What?"

"I have a copy of that nineteen eighty-four Division of Safety Report. When you have a moment, perhaps you could take a look at it."

Brennan's face paled—even the rosacea on his cheeks. It took him a moment to find his voice. "Where is the report?" he asked finally.

"I have it with me," said Georgia, fingering an envelope inside her notebook.

"Let's take a little walk, Skeehan. You, me and the report."

Georgia silently followed Brennan out of the conference room, down a flight of stairs and through a hallway carpeted in slate blue and trimmed in white wainscoting. She was too nervous to take in the nearly two-hundred-year-old building's long curved windows and ornate, white-plaster moldings.

They came to a door that opened into a formal, eighteenth-century-style room painted in Wedgewood blue. An oil portrait of Thomas Jefferson loomed over the lectern.

"Do you know what this room is, Skeehan?" asked Brennan. The room was large, and his booming voice echoed beneath a cut-glass chandelier.

"No, sir."

"It's called the 'blue room.' It's where Mayor Ortaglia holds all his press conferences and other official events. Do you know why I brought you here?"

Georgia didn't even try to answer.

"Because in this room, I believe, you can feel the power and greatness of the city of New York. And I'm not talking about Franco Ortaglia, either. I'm talking about the city—the entire fucking city." He opened his fleshy palms. "It eclipses the power of the FDNY and the NYPD combined. And it certainly eclipses the power of the Bureau of Fire Investigation."

"It shouldn't eclipse the law," said Georgia, sensing where this was leading.

Brennan raised an eyebrow at her. "You think the Bureau of Fire Investigation exists to put arsonists in jail, don't you?" he asked.

"Well . . ." Georgia ran her hand along the solid white enameled edge of the room's heavy wainscoting. ". . . Yes. I do."

"It exists because the fire commissioner, the mayor and the men who run this city *choose* to *let* it exist. Fires *have* to be put out, Skeehan. Garbage *has* to be picked up, subways *have* to run. But some street mutt puts a match to a can of lighter fluid, nobody *has* to do a damn thing . . . Oh"—he shrugged—"The NYPD can arrest him, and maybe A and E can make a case against him. Or maybe not. Only *we* get to say if the evidence points to a crime or an accident. And we don't do it by divine right. We do it by *privilege.* You abuse that privilege, it gets taken away."

Georgia's hand froze on the wainscoting.

"Can they do that?" she whispered. "Shut down the bureau, I mean."

Brennan frowned, suddenly aware of whom he was speaking to. Georgia caught the twitch in his beady blue eyes. The big, blubbery man with the silver hair and pitted skin suddenly didn't look so imposing. Suddenly, he looked a little scared. He held out a hand.

"Give me the report, Skeehan. That's a direct order."

"But, Chief, our men died because of what happened at Bridgewater. And the city did them in."

He snorted. "What do you think you're going to do? Wave this in front of the mayor? He doesn't *care,* Skeehan. It didn't happen on his watch. All he wants are his seats on the fifty-yard line. *You,* on the other hand, have a lot to lose here."

He took a small tape recorder out of his pocket. "Remember this?" he asked. He pushed Play:

". . . I broke into Dana's house. I saw the clicker to open his garage on his kitchen counter, so I slipped the lock. It was a stupid, rookie thing to do . . . I deserve charges."

Georgia closed her eyes as she listened to her confession being played back at her.

"Think long and hard here about your career, Skeehan," said Brennan. "Yours and Carter's. 'Cause I'll take you both down. You'd be throwing away two careers for a few pieces of paper that can't help those firefighters anyway. It's too late."

Georgia narrowed her gaze at him now. The room seemed to close in. Her stomach went into free fall. "Why would you threaten my career like this? Or Carter's?" she asked softly. "Do you hate me that much?"

"Hate you?" He laughed joylessly. "Believe it or not, Skeehan, I'm trying to do you a favor here—for Marenko's sake, poor bastard—not yours." He waited a moment for that to sink in, then held out a fleshy hand. "Marshal, give me the report," he said softly. "I'm not trying to destroy your career. I'm trying to save your life."

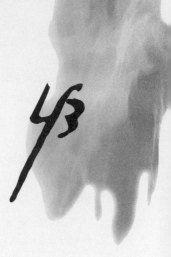

. . .

GEORGIA HANDED OVER the report. She felt she had no choice. Brennan was her superior officer. He had every intention of discrediting her and Carter, too, if she didn't. And what's more, Brennan—like Hanlon—seemed genuinely scared. Someone had gotten to them—and that someone could get to her, too.

"You don't look too happy over there," said Kyle as he drove Georgia to base. "Is Operation Robin Hood going south?"

"No." She shook her head. "This has nothing to do with the drop tomorrow. And besides, I can't involve you."

"Because I'm the new fish," he said glumly.

"No. Because you're a nice guy with a bright future in this department. I don't want to take that away."

"Well, thanks for the 'nice guy' stuff you threw in there, anyway." He sighed.

"That wasn't a brush-off, Andy. I mean it. You've got a lot going for you." Georgia threw back her head and stretched. "I wish I had your self-confidence. Maybe I wouldn't have just copped out back there."

"What do you mean?"

"I had something—something that could really 'fry the bastards' as you said before. And I . . . I lost my nerve." She shook her head. "You wouldn't have lost your nerve."

Kyle was silent a long time. "I guess everybody's different," he said finally. "You do what you can do in this world, Georgia."

"Well"—she tossed off a bitter laugh—"I guess I just showed how little I can do."

...

Ladder Twenty was out on a run when Georgia and Kyle arrived at Manhattan base. They walked past the garage doors and took a small industrial-looking elevator to the fourth-floor marshals' offices. The squad room was painfully bright, yet empty. Everyone was out on assignments or asleep. In the bunk room, Georgia heard Sal Giordano snoring.

"Guess I'm going to be staying up," said Georgia. "You want some coffee?" she asked Kyle.

"Sure."

They headed into the kitchen. Georgia poured two cups. Someone had left Thursday's *Daily News* on the table. The front-page banner read: "Mayor Gives Hacks $10M." Underneath, a subhead read, "Ortaglia declares driving taxi most dangerous job in NY." Kyle thwacked his hand at the story.

"Can you believe it?" he asked. "Mayor Ortaglia's got enough bread to put LoJack tracing devices and cell phones in every gypsy cab, yet he can't buy the FD Handie-Talkies that don't fade out if you jiggle them too hard."

"Guess we don't have the most dangerous job in the world," said Georgia dryly.

"Next time someone's in a burning building, I guess the fire department will tell them to hail a cab."

They lingered over coffee awhile, then Kyle headed for the bunk room. "Are you coming?" he asked Georgia.

"I'm going to check my e-mail first. Maybe by then, Giordano will catch a job and have to wake up."

"Call me if you need me," he said, then disappeared down the hallway.

The squad room was like a department store late at night—eerily empty, yet lit up with a wattage that would rival Times Square. Georgia was alone, yet not alone, and the contradiction heightened her senses until she could practically hear the blood gushing through her veins. Every noise sounded louder, harsher and more abrupt—from the rattle of the window air conditioner in its patchwork of plywood, to the voices of dispatchers over the department radio. Even the rumble of Ladder Twenty backing into quarters downstairs had an undercurrent of tension to it.

Georgia sipped her coffee and turned on her computer. There was only one e-mail—from someone calling himself "247." There was no subject heading. She opened the message.

The first line listed her home address.

The second line listed her son's name and age.

The third line said simply: *Mac Marenko is on Tier Three C, at the North Infirmary Command on Riker's Island. He is the only white face there over the age of 25.*

Georgia stared at the screen. Blood crystallized in her veins. Her whole body felt as if it were encased in rubber bands. Her fingers were wrapped so tightly around her mouse, they felt arthritic. There was no threat—no warning. But the meaning—to Georgia, at least—was simple: *Back off Delaney's report or I'll get to you, your family and Mac Marenko. I know where they are.*

Georgia massaged her forehead and thought through the possibilities. Someone connected to Delaney's report wanted to be very sure she didn't make those findings public. No one in the FDNY would threaten her like this. As Brennan had already aptly demonstrated, there were easier, more subtle ways to control Georgia's actions. That left only one man with the clout to find out so much about Georgia and the power to use it. On the eve of the drop, she had a good idea where he'd be, too.

She left the building without telling anyone. Andy Kyle would've insisted on going with her, and this was something Georgia wanted to handle on her own. She grabbed a cab to Chinatown. Sandowsky and his stakeout crew would probably be there all night, setting up surveillance cameras and recording monitors. A Hollywood movie could be shot in less time.

The cab let her off beside a Pagoda-topped bank, a half block from the corner of Mott Street and Bayard in the heart of Chinatown. It was a narrow street fronted on each side by tenements with wrought-iron fire escapes and store signs in Chinese characters. The corner was quiet at two A.M., but Georgia knew that in seven hours, it would be crowded and chaotic. Robin Hood couldn't have picked a better place for a drop.

Command central was in a Chinese restaurant across the street from Tung Hoy Takeout, a cramped, low-rent joint that Lieutenant Sandowsky and his people had taken over for the operation, much to the annoyance of the owner, who seemed to be perpetually muttering harsh-sounding Chinese words about the police presence in his restaurant. There were listening devices, wires, microphones and video surveillance monitors all over the countertops. There were men in flak vests talking about "deployment" and "rendezvous checkpoints." Operation Robin Hood might as well have been D-Day, the way they were going at it.

"Holding up there, Marshal?" Georgia turned at the sound of a familiar voice. She caught the lopsided, world-weary smile of Phil Arzuti.

"Hey, Phil. You're still talking to me, huh?" Already Georgia had started to catch the cold shoulder from police officers who saw her as the girlfriend of a cop murderer.

"Until this is over, at least." He tossed off a laugh, but Georgia wasn't sure if he was joking.

"Do you know if Gus Rankoff is here?" she asked. "He's an aide from the mayor's office."

"Santa Claus without the beard?"

"That's him." Arzuti tilted his head. "He's in back, talking to Sandowsky."

Georgia maneuvered through the knot of detectives to the kitchen. Rankoff happened to look up. Their eyes met. Arzuti was wrong, Georgia decided. Santa Claus would never have eyes that dark and dead. Shark's eyes, they were. And right now they seemed to bore straight through her.

"Marshal?" Rankoff walked over. "You should be getting some sleep for tomorrow."

Georgia held his gaze. "I find that hard to do when I read my e-mail."

Rankoff smiled as if she had just told a little joke. "Shall we get some air? It's very stuffy in here."

He excused himself and walked Georgia out back to an alley with wooden pallets and stacks of discarded vegetable boxes. Laundry lines crisscrossed the tenement yards like a game of cat's cradle. "You have something on your mind?"

"I understand you're trying to dig up dirt on me to discredit my reputation."

Rankoff frowned. "Who told you this?"

"I have my information from several credible sources."

"I was merely inquiring about you to Detective Leahy and some of the squad at A and E," he explained. "You are going to be undertaking a very serious operation tomorrow. I wanted to make sure you were a stable individual."

"What about *after* tomorrow?"

"After tomorrow?" Rankoff opened his palms expansively and smiled. "It is always good to learn more about people we deal with—yes? In the event one ever needs say . . . leverage?"

"Was that what that message on my e-mail was? Leverage?"

"I don't know what you mean."

"I logged onto my e-mail tonight to find that someone had left me a message listing my home address, my son's name and Fire Marshal Marenko's location at Riker's. What do you call *that*, Mr. Rankoff?"

He sighed. "Perhaps someone is concerned that you are overstepping your authority as a fire marshal. But as long as you continue to focus on the job at hand"—he shrugged—"I see nothing for you to worry about. And who knows? In time, that kind of attention to duty could take a smart young lady such as yourself to great heights." He checked his watch. "Now if you'll excuse me . . ." He turned to go back inside.

Georgia's heart thrummed in her chest. "You need me right now," she called to him. "But what about after the drop, Mr. Rankoff? Is my career—my *life*—going to be dangling by a shoestring? Am I going to have to look over my shoulder to make sure I don't end up like Pat Flannagan?"

Rankoff didn't answer. His face became stony, and his eyes had a dull gleam to them. Georgia wanted outrage. She wanted him to deny her accusations and flail his arms about in protest. But in the end, he offered only a half smile.

"Sleep well, Marshal. Fatigue can make a person careless. And careless people do stupid, dangerous things."

. . .

GEORGIA WAS SO exhausted when she got back to Manhattan base that she fell asleep in her bunk without even rinsing her face. She was awakened by a nudge to her shoulder.

"Skeehan?" It was Andy Kyle. "We gotta go. Right now."

Georgia sat up, smacking her head on the bunk. She'd forgotten she was at work. As soon as she saw her clothes, she remembered. She always slept fully clothed at work.

"What time is it?" she asked. The windowless bunk room gave no indication.

"Just after seven."

"The drop's at nine," she groaned. Her neck hurt from sleeping on the pillow in an awkward way.

"Not anymore, it isn't."

Georgia ran a hand through her tangle of hair. "He changed the time?"

"And the place."

"What?"

Kyle shoved a doughnut in her hand. "Eat up, Georgia. The show's been moved to Grand Central."

"Man, A and E must be pissed after all the setup they went through."

"Yeah, well . . ." Kyle grinned. "Every cloud has its silver lining."

There was no time to waste. Robin Hood had moved the drop time up to 8:15. Kyle hustled Georgia into a car and used his dashboard flashers and horn to snake past gridlocked intersections. It was 7:40 before

Kyle was able to drop Georgia off on Forty-second Street, at the lower-level front entrance to the station. Georgia noticed the legions of un-marked NYPD cars immediately. Operation Robin Hood was big, and—like it or not—she was at the center of it. Georgia sucked back her fear and tried to put on a brave face.

"Do you want me to call Randy for you?" Kyle offered.

"Yeah, thanks," said Georgia. She didn't trust herself to say more. She started to get out of the car.

"Georgia?"

"What?"

"Don't try to prove anything in there, all right? There are worse things than having a deal like this go down smoothly."

"Such as?"

"Such as it *not* going down smoothly. Be careful."

Kyle drove off, and Georgia walked through the station doors. A few days ago, she'd seen Grand Central through the dull, monochromatic lens of a drill. But now, as she entered the sixteen-thousand-square-foot concourse streaming with thousands of commuters, every man with a briefcase, every woman with a cell phone gave her pause. On an average day, half a million people passed through Grand Central. Forget China-town—if ever there was a place for Robin Hood to get lost in a crowd, it was here.

Georgia headed to the stationmaster's office. A woman buzzed her through security doors. In the back room, detectives from Arson and Explosion and security officers from Grand Central were furiously por-ing over structural maps of the building and rail yards, tossing around code words and jargon. Willard and Arzuti were there. They were test-ing some electronic equipment they probably had had to cart over from the egg roll joint across from Tung Hoy Takeout. Lieutenant Sandowsky, his shoe-polish black hair reflecting the fluorescent lights, was talking to Chief Brennan and a security officer from Grand Central.

Brennan beckoned Georgia over. He smoothed out an architectural diagram of Grand Central on the table and pointed a fleshy finger at a small black *S* on the map with a circle around it.

"These are standpipe locations," he grunted. Standpipes are water hookups inside commercial buildings and high-rises that can be attached to a fire company's hose to put out a fire. Without them, firefighters would have to hook up every hose into street hydrants and run them across vast interior spaces and up dozens of flights of stairs.

Brennan pointed at a standpipe box near the entrance to the Lexington Avenue Subway line.

"You will be given two brown paper bags, each containing five hundred thousand dollars of cash in hundred-dollar bills, as per our instructions. At exactly eight-fifteen, you are to walk up to this standpipe box and place the two bags inside. Lieutenant Sandowsky will have the box staked out by plainclothes detectives in Grand Central and the subway station. So once you make the drop, just head straight back to base. Don't give Robin Hood any reason to follow you."

"Is there any way this standpipe riser could be breached internally— through some vent?" asked Georgia.

"A and E ordered all the voids sealed last year, to prevent a terrorist attack," Sandowsky explained.

Brennan unrolled a set of engineering blueprints. "According to the blueprints, the void beneath this standpipe riser has a diameter of ten inches. That's too small for an adult to climb through, anyway."

"Is there another way in?" asked Georgia.

Sandowsky shook his head. "To breach the void, the perpetrator would have to drill through a three-inch-thick concrete ceiling beneath the concourse. We have teams deployed throughout the area in the event an attempt is made. You've got to remember," Sandowsky assured Skeehan, trying to push up the overly long sleeves of his ill-tailored suit, "A and E knows this building in a way Robin Hood never could. You just put the money in the box and leave, Skeehan. We'll handle the rest."

. . .

THERE WERE ANY number of ways to get into Grand Central Terminal—through tunnels connected to high-rises, through shops and restaurants that fanned out from the concourse. There were subway passages
and commuter rail lines. There was even a new subterranean corridor
that ran a full fourteen blocks north of the main building, so it was now
possible to enter Grand Central nearly a mile from the station. Still,
Robin Hood knew, it wasn't the entering that would be difficult. It was
the leaving.

At Fifty-sixth Street and Park Avenue, Hood descended a flight of
stairs into the new north corridor. Commuters streamed past the pink
granite walls inlaid with mosaic tile, checking watches, talking on cell
phones. Most were heading out of Grand Central at 7:45 in the morning.
But Hood was heading in, dressed in a pair of baggy navy blue coveralls,
a white T-shirt, well-worn work boots and a hard hat. Hood carried a
small toolbox and a beat-up backpack with a large ring of keys.

No one paid any attention to the scruffy mechanic unlocking the
door that read *Authorized Metro North Personnel Only.* On the other
side was a narrow concrete platform that looked out over a wide stretch
of train tracks. A scattering of incandescent bulbs offered the only
source of light. There was no air-conditioning and the air had a dank,
close smell to it.

Hood walked down a metal staircase at the end of the concrete walkway. The air was cooler here, another ten feet below the surface. But

damper, too. The concrete glistened with moisture and puddles caught the light, reflecting the faint glow back like the stripes on a firefighter's turnout coat.

Hood scrambled across a set of tracks, keeping clear of the third rail and mindful of the air gusts that might signal an oncoming train. A metal door led to another passageway that sloped slowly downward, heat rising geometrically with every step. Hood had to crouch to keep from hitting the steam pipes overhead. They ran the length of a cement walkway and were covered with crumbling white plaster with faded red signs that read: *Warning: Asbestos.* Hood was soon sweating heavily. Workers who came down to repair pipes were never allowed more than fifteen minutes at a stretch in the steam tunnels. Heat exhaustion was a constant threat.

The pipes extended for perhaps a hundred feet before Hood was able to take another turnoff and slowly ascend again. Here, the ceilings were higher, but more dangerous in some ways, as well. Steam leaks overhead gave the light a hazy quality and the pings of hot, compressed vapor ricocheted like gunfire through the space. Homeless people often lived down here, drawn by the warmth in winter and the chance to use the steam pipes as hot plates the rest of the year. Cut a hole in the asbestos, and you could fry an egg and bacon as easily as on a grill. It wasn't uncommon for the tunnels to smell like a cross between a diner and a urinal, sometimes all in the same breath.

Beyond the tunnels was another set of tracks. A graveyard for broken railway cars. Several silver passenger cars sat alongside a narrow platform strewn with steel plates, hydraulic fluid drums, electrical cables and pipes. A small utility shack of corrugated tin hugged the platform. Hood unlocked it now and walked to a metal door at the back of the shack, set into the concrete wall. It opened into a shaft of darkness— a vertical tunnel, three feet in diameter with a built-in set of rungs leading up. Hood left the backpack and toolbox in the shack and loaded the coverall pockets with screwdrivers, a pair of work gloves, a mirror and a prybar. Then Hood attached a flashlight to the rim of the hard hat and began the climb.

There were forty-three steps until the turnoff. Forty-three steps in solid blackness. Hood counted them off for safety's sake. In the bowels of this labyrinthine structure, almost a century old, it was possible to crawl inside and never crawl out. Every year, Grand Central workers found at least a couple of DOAs in the warren of tunnels beneath the great building.

The turnoff was nothing more than a pipe duct in the ceiling, left empty when other, better, routes were found. It was box shaped, about four feet across and three feet high, and layered with decades of filth and animal droppings. Hood crawled forward on all fours, the flashlight sweeping the space in front until it ended some ten feet ahead at a wall. A dead end, it seemed. Hood shifted position, work boots to the wall, and delivered two swift kicks. A rotted piece of plywood snapped in half and dropped down a forty-foot vertical shaft only ten inches in diameter.

Hood took out the mirror and guided it into the shaft. A mere eight inches above, Hood saw the fire stop that had been put in place to seal off the standpipe void. The fire stop could not be removed by pressing down. A groove of metal held it in place. But it could be easily removed by pressing up—something that wasn't supposed to be possible from a shaft only ten inches in diameter. Then again, no one knew about the pipe duct just eight inches below and slightly to the left of the void.

Hood smiled. They had thought they'd sealed up the darkness below. They had thought nothing could ever rise up and touch them again. But some things just won't stay buried. Some things rise up no matter what you do to stop them.

46

. . .

IT WAS 8:12 A.M. when Georgia walked out the doors of the station-master's office carrying a large, navy blue gym bag weighing about thirty-two pounds. Inside were two brown paper bags loaded with ten bound stacks of five hundred hundred-dollar bills—five hundred thousand dollars each—along with a microchip transmitter buried between the stacks. She had no gun, no Handie-Talkie and no duty holster. If anyone was going to be shooting here, the NYPD was very clear that it was going to be them. All Georgia had was a radio strapped beneath her blouse. It chafed her skin and hampered the movement of her right wrist where the microphone was concealed.

"Your job," Brennan told her again, "is to put the two paper bags in the standpipe box and get the hell out of there."

The standpipe box was at the end of a corridor near the entrance to the Lexington Avenue Subway. Rush hour was at its peak, and the faces streamed past her faster than she could process them. She allowed her gaze to drift sideways to a janitor mopping the marble floors, to two men in Giants football jerseys reading sports scores in the *New York Post,* to a commuter in a business suit sipping a Starbucks coffee and talking into his shirtsleeve. Every one of them looked like what he was: five-oh. A cop. Any halfway-savvy street kid would make them right away. Then again, she wasn't exactly James Bond herself. There had been almost no time to prepare for this drop—which was just what Robin Hood wanted.

Georgia opened the oak door of the standpipe box and was greeted by the familiar brass double-headed serpent—the standpipe hookups. She pushed down on the bottom of the fire stop. It was solidly in place. Then she hefted the two paper bags into the box and closed the door. She pretended to be checking inside her empty bag when she spoke into her sleeve.

"Alpha Position to Checkpoint One," she said. "Breakfast has been served." The money was being referred to as "food" across the airwaves. The drop was "breakfast."

"Ten-four, Alpha," came a voice on the line. It was Willard's. "Now beat it."

Georgia walked across the main concourse of Grand Central. Shafts of morning light streamed through the sixty-foot arches of mullioned glass. A hollow feeling rose in her chest, a churning in her stomach. She couldn't tell if it was a delayed reaction to stress and lack of sleep or an illness coming on. She didn't want to chance the heat feeling this way. She bought a chocolate bar at a kiosk, then walked up a marble staircase overlooking the concourse. She unwrapped the tinfoil and nibbled on the bar. Her radio was still within receiving distance and she caught the voices of detectives checking in with each other, waiting for Robin Hood to appear.

Ten minutes passed. Then fifteen. Georgia finished the chocolate bar. There was no garbage can nearby, so she stuffed the crumpled tinfoil in her pocket. Still no sign of Robin Hood. Georgia heard a voice on the radio spew out a string of expletives. She looked out from the balcony at the floor of the main concourse and caught the familiar figure of Chris Willard, talking into his sleeve and bunching up his lips beneath his red mustache as if he wanted to hit somebody.

"He ate the food," she heard him say over the radio. "The goddamn prick ate the food." *The money was gone.* There was no way Robin Hood could've touched that standpipe door with all those plainclothes detectives standing around. That meant only one thing: He'd found another route into the box.

Georgia went back in her mind to the blueprints Brennan had spread across the table. The vent below the standpipe riser was sealed with a fire stop. The chief had said the vent was too small for an adult to crawl into—only ten inches in diameter. But somehow, Robin Hood had managed it. The vent ended near a walkway on Track Seventeen. And the fastest way to get there, she remembered from her drill, was through a fire-exit door at the back of a restaurant not fifty feet from Georgia on the upper balcony.

She pushed aside the churning in her stomach and raced into the restaurant. Four flights down was Track Seventeen. It was crawling with commuters. Georgia maneuvered through the crowd until she came to a tight knot of detectives in a corner by an open vent. On the floor were the two crumpled paper bags along with a prybar. A heavyset older black man in a frayed denim jacket was being questioned by Willard and another detective from A and E. Arzuti was on the side.

"What's going on?" Georgia asked Arzuti, nodding toward the man.

"Hey!" Willard yelled over. "I thought I told you to scram."

"I'm catching a train, Chris," she shouted back. "I think that's within the definition of scram."

The old man in the frayed jacket looked in Georgia's direction. He had a hapless frown on his face and big, sad, rheumy eyes.

"You're not arresting this guy, are you?" Georgia asked Arzuti under her breath. "I mean, he's not Robin Hood. Just look at him."

"We're just questioning him at the moment," Arzuti replied.

"What happened? I gathered from the radio that Robin Hood got the money internally, somehow."

"We followed the transmitters down here where the vent ended. When we got here, the old guy was crumpling up the bags and pocketing a prybar he said he found inside one of them."

Georgia gave Arzuti a confused look. "Where's the money?"

"No idea. Our suspect here says he was walking by and something loud smashed over the grate on the vent. He saw the bags and pulled them out and they were empty except for the prybar."

"And the transmitters," Georgia reminded him.

"Yes, unfortunately," Arzuti admitted. "That's the one thing we *didn't* want back."

Georgia edged nearer the detectives and squinted at the void. It looked too small for Georgia to squeeze through, let alone this heavy, older man.

"Robin Hood didn't get up that void, Phil," said Georgia.

"I know. Sandowsky is upstairs, poring over the blueprints, trying to find an alternate route. Wherever it is, it's not obvious on the plans." Arzuti spread his palms. "You can't help, Skeehan. This isn't an FDNY operation. You aren't even armed right now."

"I know, I know," said Georgia, holding up her hands. "I'll go back to base."

"We'll keep you posted," Arzuti murmured.

Georgia made a face. "What you mean is, I'll read about it in the newspapers." They both knew how the game worked.

There was a fire-exit door at the far end of the corridor. Georgia opened it and found herself in the middle of a crowd of pedestrians and gridlocked cars on Forty-sixth Street, just off Lexington Avenue, four blocks north of the main building. The hazy heat of the day was beginning to bear down hard.

A blue-and-white city bus rumbled past, and Georgia choked back the smell of diesel exhaust. She was dying of thirst from the chocolate bar. At a pretzel cart, she fumbled in her purse for change to buy a soda, then dropped it all over the sidewalk. She bent to pick it up. People stepped over her as if she were little more than an oversized box that had tipped into their path. She saw their shoes—work boots and sneakers and wing tips and loafers.

And open-toed Ferragamo pumps. The color of desert sand. With gold buttons glistening above the toe opening and a couple of Day-Glo nail-polished toes peeking through the faux-lizard skin.

The world seemed to stop. The noise on the street faded to distant chatter. Georgia rose to her feet, the change forgotten. The crowd rushed past. She searched the backs of heads for a tall, buxom woman with raven hair. But she didn't see her. Her skin felt like it would burst with anticipation. *Why are you doing this?* she asked herself. *She's dead. Get it through your head—she's dead.*

Still, her heart pumped faster and her steps quickened. She looked down for the shoes, if only to convince herself that she was wrong. Her eyes smarted from staring into the morning sun, and she shielded them against the glare. She nearly bumped into a lamppost, her eyes were so focused on people's feet.

And then she saw the Ferragamo pumps. They were on a tall, leggy blonde about fifty feet in front of her. Beneath the woman's beige linen suit, her hips swung with a rhythm that even Randy Carter would recognize. Georgia's mind was slower than her body, because, for an instant, a wave of relief passed through her. *She's alive. Dear God, she's alive.* But her body wasn't fooled. A cold, heavy sensation gathered in her gut, as if some vital organ had been ripped out and replaced with gravel. She wasn't whole anymore.

"Connie!" she called out. The woman turned reflexively and froze. Mirrored sunglasses did little to hide the contours of her caramel-colored face. The crowd ebbed and flowed around them like waves on sand. Georgia couldn't hear the rumble of buses and car horns, the screech of tires, the one-way conversations on cell phones anymore. Everything disappeared except the woman with the dyed-blond hair and the Ferragamo pumps.

Connie's mirrored sunglasses lingered on Georgia's face. Georgia couldn't see her eyes, couldn't read the small parting of her full, cocoa-colored lips, yet her own face was an open book of hurt and betrayal. It was a fitting meeting—Connie, disguised and inscrutable; Georgia, out there on a limb with all her emotions just waiting to be picked off like ducks in a shooting gallery. For a long moment, neither woman made a move. Georgia felt as if she'd just stumbled out of a wrecked car and was too disoriented even to call nine-one-one. Finally, she took a step forward.

The movement had the same effect it would on a rabbit. Connie bolted. The response knocked Georgia out of her dreamlike state. Her adrenaline flushed out her brain. She remembered the microphone still attached to her wrist and spoke into it now as she ran after Connie. In those pumps, there was no way Connie would get far.

"Alpha Position to Checkpoint One. I am on Forty-sixth Street and Lexington. Have just made visual contact with suspect. She is in a beige linen suit, pumps, and her hair is dyed blond. She is Officer Connie Ruiz."

Arzuti's voice came on the line. He was so flummoxed, he forgot her code name. "Skeehan, are you *serious?*"

Georgia squinted. Connie had stopped along the side of the building. *Was she giving up?* Then she saw her whip out a key and stick it into an unmarked door. It opened easily, and she disappeared inside.

"You bet your ass I am, Arzuti. Connie Ruiz is Robin Hood. And she just went back into Grand Central."

. . .

GEORGIA LOST HER. She didn't have a key to open the door Connie had gone through. It was marked *Authorized Personnel Only.*

The money. Connie didn't have the money with her. It weighed around thirty-two pounds, and Connie was carrying only a small hand-bag when Georgia spotted her. That meant the money was still some-where in Grand Central Terminal—but perhaps not for long. Now that Connie had been spotted, she might try to get it out.

And how would I get the money out? Georgia asked herself. *Not on foot.* She'd already been made. Everyone at A and E would be looking for her. *Not by car.* Even if she had a rental in the parking lot of Grand Central, it would take too long to get it out. And, with the gridlock at rush hour in Manhattan, she wouldn't get far. The commuter rails would be too sparsely populated at this hour of the morning. That left the sub-way. And since Connie knew every piece of track in this building, she didn't need to take a public route to get there. She'd find a back way.

Georgia raced down Forty-sixth Street, then found a cobblestoned entrance to Grand Central's underground parking garage. She ran up to the parking attendant, a small, grizzled Latino in a starched uniform shirt, and showed him her badge. "Where does the door at the corner of Lex and Forty-sixth lead to?"

"General storage on the lower level," said the attendant.

"How do I get there from here?"

"Make a right at the door. Take the stairs on Platform F."

"Thanks."

She followed his instructions and soon found herself two stories below the pavements of Manhattan, in a dim and deserted train yard. Bare
bulbs shone at intervals along the grimy concrete walls like torches in a
castle dungeon. On the tracks, five silver commuter cars awaited repairs.
Georgia saw construction lamps, electrical cables and an assortment of
hand and power tools stretched out on the concrete before her. She
picked up a heavy hammer and swung it in her hands. She wanted something for protection.

She scanned the trains. She could hear the constant drip of water
from somewhere in the train yard, and, overhead, a distant clunk and
whir of trains pulling into and out of the station. She tried the door to a
shed on the platform, but it was locked. The rattle reverberated along
the cavernous stretch of tracks.

And then she heard it. A ping—like a crescent wrench hitting a steel
rail. Then all was silent again. Georgia let out a gasp. Her heart felt as if
it would burst through her chest. She lowered herself off the platform
and walked toward the broken car. It blocked the light like a huge
mountain. On the other side, all was shadowy.

Georgia circled the car. The windows were dark. From track level,
she saw the gritty underbelly of the beast—all wheels and gears and axle
grease. An empty aluminum can tipped over inside the car and began a
slow rattle along the floor. Georgia's pulse quickened. Her breathing became rapid and shallow. She tightened her grip on her hammer and took
a step forward in the direction of the sound.

There was a thunderous rattle of empty cans. A man with a long,
wiry beard, greasy hair and a ragged raincoat the color of wet cement
appeared at the door of the car. He had an empty malt liquor bottle in
his hands and he was holding the neck of it like a weapon and swinging
wildly in her direction. Despite the summer temperatures, he was in at
least three layers of clothing. His toes were poking out of his sneakers,
and he reeked of urine and sweat.

"Go on," he shouted. "Get. Get out of here. Goddamn Martians—
taking over the goddamn city is what you're doing."

Georgia said nothing. She held her hammer tight but didn't swing it. She treated emotionally disturbed people—EDPs, in formal law-enforcement terminology, "skells" in firehouse lingo—the same way she would a guard dog. She did nothing to provoke, and all her movements were passive and slow.

As she backed away from the rail car, she caught a movement on the other side of the yard. She turned just in time to catch a figure in navy blue coveralls, work boots and a yellow hard hat stumbling across the tracks. She had changed clothes, but those hips gave her away every time. *Connie.*

Georgia ran across the track bed now, mindful of the third rails and of any oncoming headlights from trains. She hoisted herself up on the other side of the platform. Her clothes were now covered with filth and sweat. Her side was shot through with pain from running. In an adjoining corridor, she caught the flash of a yellow hard hat as Connie ran down a flight of concrete stairs. Georgia followed.

Unlike the rail yard, the halls down here—forty feet below the pavements of New York—were compact and bright. But the temperature was easily over a hundred degrees. And the noise was unceasing. Whistles, pings and staccato bursts like gunfire. Georgia looked down a long, twisting hallway to her right, and an identical one to her left. In both, white clouds of steam rose from huge pipes in crumbling asbestos sleeves. Both were so hot, neither Georgia nor Connie could last long.

Right or left? Georgia knew Connie was right-handed. In a moment of panic, most people choose their favored orientations. But Connie was also a cop. She'd go against her instincts. So Georgia chose the left-hand tunnel. Sweat poured off her skin, loosening her grip on her hammer. Her throat burned, her lips were chapped and a headache throbbed behind her stinging eyes. Her mind started to wander. *Mac is innocent. Mac didn't kill Connie. Richie will be so happy. We'll all be so happy.*

She was losing focus. She tried to shake it off and force herself to move quickly, yet her legs felt like they were strapped with ankle weights and her vision started to blur. Her arm had grown numb from lugging the hammer. She threw it on the concrete in an effort to pick up the pace. *It's no use. I'm starting to drift. I'll die down here without backup.* She reached for the microphone still on her wrist and spoke into the receiver.

"Ten-thirteen," she sputtered, using the universal code for police officer needing assistance. She'd forgotten that her microphone was only hooked to detectives at A and E. It wasn't a radio into dispatch. It was possible that no one was even listening. It was possible the damn microphone didn't even work this far below street level.

"Fire Marshal Skeehan here," she choked out. She was having trouble breathing. "I'm in the steam tunnels below the East Side storage area. I need help."

And then, a hundred feet ahead, Georgia saw Connie struggling to her feet. She had somehow tripped. The yellow hard hat was gone. Her blond hair was drenched with sweat. She half limped, half ran out of the steam tunnel and onto a narrow concrete platform lit only by construction lamps. It was a railroad maintenance walkway, maybe four feet wide, above a set of train tracks. The tracks were dark. They looked abandoned. Connie started down it, then ducked into what Georgia assumed was a side tunnel. Georgia's lungs seared. She was dizzy and near collapse herself. If Connie gained any kind of lead in the tunnel, Georgia would lose her.

She followed Connie to the entranceway. Only there was no tunnel beyond it—just an unused storage area cut out of the rough granite bedrock. The jagged, glistening rock rose fourteen feet to a concrete ceiling. A bare bulb dangled from a construction lamp.

Connie was doubled over at a rear wall, hands on her knees, struggling for breath. Her gasps echoed in the hollow, cavelike room. Her coveralls were soaked with sweat, and her blond hair had turned nearly dark with it. Although she was nearly six feet tall, right at this minute, Connie Ruiz looked very, very small.

. . .

ADRENALINE AND ANGER surged through Georgia's veins, pumping her up so much she felt like a balloon about to explode. She walked up to Connie and pushed her hard against the wall.

"What the *fuck* are you doing?" Georgia screamed. She was breathing hard herself. "Do you know what I've been through? What *Mac's* been through?"

Connie didn't answer. She was bigger and stronger; she could have pushed back. But when she straightened up, her dark eyes were tentative and fearful.

"Goddamn it, answer me." Georgia pushed her again. "You're Robin Hood, aren't you?" she choked out. "You killed those doctors. You set a bomb on the pipeline. Why would you do this, Con? Why?"

Connie gulped some air. Her breathing slowed. She nodded at the wire still attached to Georgia's wrist. "The radio won't work down here, you know," she said in a flat voice. "Your sweat's shorted it out. And you're too far from the receiver."

Georgia stared at her friend in disbelief. "You think I'm asking for *them*?" she said, gesturing above her head to some mythical police command post.

Connie didn't answer. Georgia reached inside her sweat-soaked blouse, yanked out the wires and threw them on the ground. "This is you and me. Right here. Right now." She pulled out the black stone still dangling from a silver chain around her neck. "What was this you gave

me—huh? Bullshit, Con? Another bullshit game? You lied to me at
every turn. You didn't tell me about you and Mac. Or your brother. Or
your father. Jesus Christ, you didn't even tell me you got a goddamn tattoo. You were everything I wanted to be, Con. Why did you throw it
all away?"

"I was everything you wanted to be, huh?" Connie tossed off a small,
bitter laugh. "What? A foster kid? The daughter of a broken man who
died before he turned fifty, forgotten by his own department?"

"That's not what I meant," said Georgia. She shut her eyes tight for
a moment to collect her thoughts. "You brutally murdered those two
doctors, Con. Doesn't that bother you?"

"Do you know what those doctors called my father?" Connie asked.
"A liar. He couldn't stand up, couldn't stop the trembling in his hands
enough to feed himself, and they said he was faking. He was strong as a
bear before that warehouse fire in Greenpoint," she said, her voice brittle with emotion. "That's what everyone called him: Bear. Those doctors
deserved to die."

On the tracks outside, a train rumbled by. The sound exploded out of
nowhere, shaking the room—and then it was gone. A headache throbbed
behind Georgia's eyes. She tried to wipe her face, but her hands were
black with grime.

"Do you know who started the fire that killed *my* dad?" asked Georgia. "A six-year-old. In the basement of a store, playing with matches.
Kid ran out when it started—never had a scratch on him. And my father
burned to death. I still miss him every day. But I don't go around blam-
ing the city or the kid or his family for what happened. I'm not blowing
up pipelines over it."

"You got to mourn your father's death," said Connie. "They gave
him a department funeral. They gave your mother a good pension. You
go to a firehouse, there's a plaque on the wall in his name. Do you know
what happened to *me*? Do you?" Connie shouted, her voice echoing in
the high reaches of jagged rock and cement overhead.

"Yes," said Georgia softly. "Your brother told me." She sighed. "I'm sorry, Con. Truly, I am. But you hurt a lot of innocent people. God-damnit, Connie, you hurt *me.*"

"I know," she said softly.

"And you wanted to, didn't you?" said Georgia.

Connie's eyes glowed with undeniable satisfaction.

"I couldn't take the life I was leading anymore. I wanted an end to the pain. All of it," she said.

"Even if it hurt others."

"Silence." Georgia could read it in her friend's face: *especially if it hurt others.*

"My brother chose drugs as his escape," said Connie. "I tried to erase my life. Start over. God knows, I tried. But Carl was right in the end. One way or another, it catches up with you."

"You could've talked to me about it."

"You looked up to me—you think I wanted to destroy that? That was one of the only good things I had. And then you started seeing Mac, and even what he and I had started to feel like a sham. You had what I lost."

"So you decided to destroy his life," said Georgia, an edge of disbelief in her voice.

"I needed a way to disappear after the pipeline payoff anyway. So I swiped a couple of blood-donor bags and syringes from an EMT. I figured if I doped Mac up on GHB and poured my blood around, you'd forget about having his baby."

Georgia's shocked expression made Connie pause. She swallowed hard. Tears crested the rims of her dark brown eyes. Georgia couldn't ever recall seeing her cry.

"I just couldn't take the pain anymore," Connie choked out. She wiped her sleeve across her eyes. "Not from my father's death. Not from you and Mac." She clenched her fists as she searched for words to convey the depths of her torment. "You were always wishing you could be *me,*" she said softly. "Dear God, baby girl, you never knew how much I wished I could be *you.*"

The damp, cool air made Georgia's sweat congeal on her skin. She took a step forward and stared at her friend's face. She saw the butterscotch skin and full lips as she had always remembered them, marred only by a blinding sheath of blond hair. She saw Connie's failures. But she also saw her own envy and longings reflected back at her. The shame on Georgia's face was not just for Connie but for herself as well.

"You've got every right to hate me, Georgia. I can't explain the things I did. The worst part about them is . . ." she held back the catch in her throat ". . . I really do care for you."

"Connie, listen to me," Georgia begged. "Killing innocent people isn't going to take away your pain. You understand that, don't you?" Georgia felt as if she were talking to someone who'd just woken up from a deep sleep. Connie seemed dazed and unfocused. Even now, all she could do was nod, distracted.

"Con—please," said Georgia in a firm voice. "Please tell me where the bomb is."

. . .

Connie checked her watch. Georgia saw the time: 9:40 A.M. Connie knew explosives. Georgia was sure it would go off at noon without a hitch.

"There's still time to change things," Georgia pleaded with her. "You don't want this to be your father's legacy."

Connie palmed the tears from her eyes. "And then what? I rot in a prison cell and Bear's name is forgotten?"

"I will try to change that, Con. I swear to you. I will do everything I can to make sure your dad—all the men and their families who suffered at that warehouse—are not forgotten."

Connie sank back against the wall and stared up at the construction lamp dangling overhead. Georgia could see she was trying to be strong, trying to suck in the pain. Georgia reached out a hand.

"Come upstairs with me, Con. Tell me where the bomb is. I'll stay with you. I'll make sure no one hurts you."

Connie came off the wall, Georgia took a step forward, and they fell into each other's arms. Then Connie leaned over and buried her face in Georgia's hair. Georgia could feel her tears.

"I'm so sorry things turned out this way," Connie whispered. "Tell Richie and your Ma good-bye for me. Tell Mac . . ." she swallowed hard. "Tell him to take good care of you."

A crack reverberated across the room. It sounded like a backup of high-pressure steam. Then Connie toppled forward into Georgia's arms.

"Connie? Connie, what happened?" Georgia put a hand out to brace her friend's back. It felt wet. Sticky wet. Georgia brought her hand up to the light. Her fingers were coated with blood. "Oh, my God." She looked over toward the entranceway now. She saw the nine-millimeter Glock first, its dull black surface picking up the light from the construction lamp. It was a standard-issue gun for a fire marshal.

"Andy? What did you do?" Georgia stared in disbelief at the frozen figure of Andy Kyle in the doorway. "She wasn't going to hurt me, you moron," Georgia yelled at him.

Connie was losing consciousness fast. Her legs were collapsing. Her breathing became ragged. Georgia tried to lay her down gently. She was moaning. "It's going to be all right," Georgia cooed. Then she rose.

"Get on your Handie-Talkie," she ordered Kyle. "Tell A and E to radio an ambulance down here right away."

Kyle didn't move. He didn't speak. He just stared at the groaning woman spread out on the dirty concrete floor. He seemed to be in shock. He'd probably never shot anyone before.

"Give me the Handie-Talkie," Georgia demanded. He still didn't move. "Goddamnit, Kyle. Give it to me, you dumbass jerk!"

Kyle pulled his Handie-Talkie out of his duty holster. But instead of handing it to her, he flung it out of the room. Georgia heard the plastic crack and shuffle as it skidded down the platform. "She has to die," he said softly, holding her gaze, his usual even confidence returning. "Do you understand, Georgia?"

"Are you out of your fucking mind?" Georgia ran to the entranceway to retrieve the Handie-Talkie. Kyle grabbed her arm.

"No," he said. "Don't you see? Ruiz tells Empire where the bomb is, the whole incident will be hushed up. No one will ever know about Bridgewater Street or the toxic chemicals that were in that neighborhood. They'll build the stadium right over it. Empire and Northway will *win*, Georgia. They'll *win*."

"Let go of me, Kyle. Innocent people are going to die because of what you just did."

She struggled free of his grasp and stumbled onto the platform. The Handie-Talkie was lying next to some mechanic's tools, just two inches from the edge of the dark tracks, six feet below. It crackled with detectives' voices. Cops were roaming all over the building now. All the exits were covered, but there were too many tunnels and crevices to search every one. Georgia bent down and picked up the Handie-Talkie. She depressed the Talk button and heard a click behind her. "Put the Handie-Talkie down and step away, Georgia."

She turned, her hand still depressing the button. Kyle's gun, which had sat limply in his hand since the shooting, now came to rest on her.

"I *gave* you Delaney's report—Goddamn *gave* it to you," he said icily. "And you threw it away."

"How did you get that report?"

"You never checked who Tristate's lawyers were when the firm went belly-up. You should've. Because one of them was my father, Georgia. Jerome Kyle *formed* Northway. He bought out Gus Rankoff and his company, Tristate, then kept Rankoff on as an advisor, along with John Welcastle. I pieced all the details together when I found my father's copy of Delaney's report—the copy I gave to *you*."

"What is this? Some guilt trip you're on?" asked Georgia. "You hate Daddy's money and power, so you want to destroy him?"

"This isn't about my father!" Kyle shouted. "This is about justice. I thought you understood that. I thought you were going to stop those bastards from getting richer off the suffering of others. You let Empire weasel out of this, you'll be helping Gus Rankoff—the man who followed you to that firehouse and tried to burn you." He saw the shock in her face. "That's right, Georgia. Rankoff tried to kill you. I asked my father about it, and he told me. If you protect them, you're just as bad as they are. And you deserve to die." He stepped closer and raised his gun.

Time stood still. Georgia became acutely aware of every function inside her body. She felt the blood gushing through her arteries. She felt a wateriness in her bowels, a fullness in her kidneys, a dryness in her mouth, the beads of sweat mixing with dirt on her skin. Every breath seemed like one of those elaborate cuckoo clocks with hundreds of bolts and gears, all precisely aligned to make the wooden figures dance at the stroke of every hour.

Her mind had gone blank, filled with a sensory overload from her body. She tried to seize on the mental image of her little boy's face. She tried to picture the soft, creamy cheeks, the black hair in need of a trim, the honey-colored eyes, the sticklike body. But it was just a cloudy jumble to her right now. It was almost as if the first step to dying was letting go of the ones you love. She felt like a small bug caught in an emptying drain. She kept getting sucked deeper and deeper into a place where she didn't want to go.

And then she heard the rumble. A train was coming. On the opposite side of the tracks, over a six-foot concrete divide. Kyle heard it, too. He looked over his shoulder and allowed his concentration to waver for an instant. He had assumed that his size and his gun were enough to keep an unarmed, five-foot-four-inch woman in check. He forgot that Georgia was a cop, too.

As the train on the opposite side barreled past, Georgia let go of the Handie-Talkie and sprang forward—not at his chest. She had neither the size nor bulk to knock a man down. But she knew that the right momentum delivered at knee level could topple the heaviest of men. So she wrapped herself tightly around his legs.

His shoulder hit the ground hard. The gun tumbled from his hands, onto the tracks. His cool, confident façade vanished, replaced by a rage in his eyes that made even Gus Rankoff look tame by comparison.

"You piece of trash," he shouted at Georgia as the rumble faded. "I can buy and sell you. And you do this to me—to *me?*"

Georgia spotted a heavy, stainless-steel stilson wrench lying next to a couple of smaller wrenches on the platform. She grabbed it, but Kyle was faster. He yanked it from her hands and swung it at her head. She ducked, but the edge of the wrench caught her in the shoulder and knocked her off balance.

She tumbled. Six feet down. Georgia and the wrench landed on the tracks. Her shoulder and hip ached from the impact. But that was the least of her problems.

A sudden gust of wind blew through the tunnel. At the bend, Georgia could make out the headlights of a train coming her way. She couldn't scale the six feet to scramble back onto the platform. She couldn't make it over the concrete divider to the opposite side. And there was no recessed area to flatten herself against until the train passed.

"Please," Georgia begged Kyle, as she struggled to her feet. "I'll die down here."

Kyle looked down at her now, pity in his eyes. He shook his head. "Too bad, isn't it? But as I told you—it's the big picture that matters to me—not the individuals. Sometimes, for the greater good, sacrifices have to be made."

He ran along the platform, then paused at the entrance to the corridor. "If it's any consolation, I'll see to it that you're buried as a hero." Georgia barely heard the words. Instead, she stared at the bend in the train tunnel. The reflected headlights were growing larger, the rumble was getting nearer. In any minute, there would be a wall of air, then a blinding stab of lights, then impact. The conductor would never see her in time. She saw Andy's gun and the stilson wrench at her feet. Neither could stop a train. They were just two useless hunks of metal.

Metal. Next to an electrically powered track. Georgia grabbed the gun. She had less than a minute to short out the power in the track. She threw the gun sideways at the third rail. It slid underneath the plastic cover, coming into contact with the high-voltage current. Already, she could see the train's headlamps glowing like two cat's eyes a hundred yards in the distance. The gun was now electrically charged. But that meant nothing if she couldn't connect the third rail to a grounded rail and short out the power.

She grabbed the wrench and balanced it upright on one of the track rails. Then she took her hand away and stepped back. The tool crashed to the track bed, one end still on the grounded rail, and the other just centimeters from the tip of the electrically charged gun.

I missed. I'm dead. Panic seized Georgia. The wind pushed hard at her from inside the train tunnel. The ground quaked with the force of twenty tons of barreling steel. The headlights were blinding. *I have nothing metal left on me to short out the circuit and stop the train. Nothing except . . .*

Tinfoil. From the candy bar. Georgia pulled out the foil now. It was already balled up. She pitched the crushed foil at the gap between the stilson wrench and the tip of Kyle's gun. She heard a buzz like a fluorescent light fixture about to fizzle, and saw a spark of bright blue light. Her breath stalled in her chest. Her rib cage felt like it was wrapped in a corset. She was so focused on the screeching brakes of the train as it came to a stop that she barely noticed the thud of feet and crackle of Handie-Talkies on the narrow platform above her until a voice spoke directly overhead.

"I should fucking leave you down there, Skeehan."

Georgia looked up. She never thought she'd be so happy to see Chris Willard. He squatted on the edge of the platform and grabbed at her outstretched hands. "We heard the whole thing over Kyle's Handie-Talkie," he told her as he yanked her up. "We just collared Kyle in the steam tunnel. We'll get a warrant on his father and Gus Rankoff. EMTs are on their way for Ruiz."

"Is she alive?" asked Georgia.

"Barely," said Willard. He squinted at the train not fifty feet down the track. "And now we're gonna have Metro North kicking our asses, too. Looks like you screwed up the whole Harlem line."

. . .

GEORGIA RAN BACK to the storage room off the maintenance platform.
The EMTs hadn't arrived yet.

"I'm here, Con," she whispered, stroking her friend's face. "Help is
on the way."

"You're all right," Connie sputtered. A crooked smile played at the
edges of her lips. Her skin was cold.

"You're going to live, Con. Let others do the same. Tell me where
you put the bomb on the Empire Pipeline." Georgia glanced at her
watch. Ten-ten A.M. They still had a fighting chance.

Connie reached up a bloody hand and pulled Georgia's face closer to
her lips. Georgia's necklace dropped from inside her blouse onto Connie's chest. Connie fingered it now. "Apache's tear," she mumbled, feeling the stone between her fingers. "I want . . . to go . . . the same way."

"You're not going anywhere," Georgia insisted. "Please, Con. Think
about those innocent people. Where did you put the bomb?"

"Flags . . ." Connie choked out. ". . . Cross."

"What flags? What cross?" Connie's chest cavity was filling with
blood. Georgia could hear the thick, gurgling sound.

"Greenpoint," Connie mumbled. "It's . . . gonna be . . . gone."

Georgia reared back. "How many explosives *did* you use?"

"It's . . . where you . . . put them . . . that . . . counts."

The EMTs came into the room now, ushering Georgia out of the way.

Connie stretched out a hand. Her voice sounded like she was gargling. Georgia couldn't even make out what she was saying.

"Connie," Georgia pleaded, her voice ragged with choked sobs and exhaustion, "be strong. Hard as a rock. Sharp as a razor—remember, girl? Remember?"

Mary Constance O'Rourke Ruiz closed her eyes. Her lips parted, and a soft breathy name came out. Not Georgia's or Joanne's or even Mac's. Her last word didn't even sound like a word at all. It sounded like a greeting. A welcome release.

"Bear."

. . .

CHIEF BRENNAN DIDN'T even recognize Georgia when he first saw her. She was sitting in the back of an ambulance, smeared with grime and the blood of Connie Ruiz. She heard an EMT tell Brennan she was in shock. She felt so numb and detached, it was as if the EMT were talking about someone else.

"Skeehan," said Brennan. He had to call her name twice to get her attention. His beady blue eyes looked a little softer than usual. "I have to speak to you now. Do you understand?"

Georgia stared at him as if he were being lip-synched in a bad foreign film.

"Did Ruiz tell you about the bomb?" he asked.

"Ruiz" it was now, thought Georgia. *Not "Officer Ruiz" anymore. Just Ruiz.* Already, they were vilifying her memory.

She squinted at him. Words and thoughts felt glued to her tongue, trapped there like insects in honey. Finally, she managed to utter one word.

"Flags," she told him.

Brennan frowned. "Flags?" he repeated.

"And a cross," said Georgia.

"Jesus Christ," said Brennan, throwing up his hands. "Every god-damn government building, church and cemetery in this city could be a target."

Georgia massaged her forehead. She tried to put her grief over Connie out of her mind and make sense of what she had told her. The only specific Connie had given her was . . .

"—Greenpoint, Chief. Connie said the bomb was in Greenpoint."

"That's it?"

"Someplace with flags and a cross in Greenpoint."

Brennan got on the department radio. "This is Chief Brennan. Transmit a nine thousand box to all units in Greenpoint." Fires were coded according to the number of the nearest alarm box, even if the fire was telephoned in. All fires and emergencies on the Empire Pipeline were given alarm box numbers in the nine thousands to identify them as pipeline emergencies. "Have the fire companies manually shut off all valves in Greenpoint and proceed with standard evacuation guidelines in the area," he added. "And let the PD know we need Bomb Squad there, too."

Georgia tried to wipe off the grime on her watch and see the time. Ten-thirty A.M. The fire companies in Greenpoint had an hour and a half to shut down the pipeline in their response areas and evacuate occupied structures adjacent to it. With the pipeline temporarily shut down, the only material that could be ignited would be the residual fuel left in the pipe. *So why am I not more relieved?* thought Georgia.

Because Connie set the bomb. Connie would've foreseen the procedures. *It's where you put the explosives that counts.* Isn't that what she had said?

"Chief?" Georgia said to Brennan. "When Connie told me the bomb was in Greenpoint, she implied that it was going to be a very, very big explosion—enough to take out a lot of the neighborhood. I think she picked a very specific place to create the largest possible explosion."

"Holy . . ." Brennan hit the side of the ambulance. "How the hell are we going to find the right set of flags and crosses in Greenpoint? Even the fire companies wouldn't know something that obscure. You'd have to have walked every inch of that neighborhood—above and below ground—to find something like that."

"I know someone who probably *has* walked every inch of that neighborhood, sir."

"Who?"

"Mac Marenko."

Brennan blew air through his teeth and thought about it. "It'd take the mayor himself to get Marenko processed out of Riker's in half an hour," he said.

"I'm not just asking because it's Mac, sir. You know he's the right person for this." The chief knew Marenko well enough to be familiar with his Greenpoint childhood and his years as a fire marshal in the borough. No civilian, however knowledgeable about the neighborhood, would be allowed into a fire department operation. And no fire investigator was likely to know Greenpoint quite as well as Marenko.

"All right." Brennan sighed. "Let me see what I can work out."

Georgia waved off any further treatment by the EMTs and a few minutes later followed Brennan into the Met Life Building above Grand Central Station. To save time, Brennan had requested a police helicopter to Brooklyn.

Georgia had never ridden in a helicopter before. As the Bell 407 lifted off the roof of the eighty-story Met Life Building, she strapped on her belt and gazed over Manhattan as if seeing it for the first time. Just to the north, she caught the silver, wedge-shaped tip of the Citicorp Center, and beyond it, the Fifty-ninth Street Bridge across the East River. She thought New York would seem smaller from up here, but instead, she felt the immense grandeur and power of the city far more acutely than when she was in it.

Brennan leaned over and shouted above the pulsating chopper blades. "Mayor Ortaglia made the call himself to release Marenko. They're going to helicopter him to Greenpoint ASAP. We'll sweep the area first, get our bearings, then rendezvous with him at the staging site on Bridgewater."

Georgia nodded. She didn't have the energy to shout. Yet in her heart she felt an undeniable lift at the thought that Mac would soon be out of Riker's. It would have taken another twenty-four hours to get him released through normal channels.

The helicopter crossed the East River now and Georgia saw the flat, tar-paper roofs of row houses in Greenpoint, the granite spires of churches, the low, boxy stores and restaurants, the cars backed up on the Kosciusko Bridge. It was as if she'd spent a lifetime stitching a very small portion of an enormous tapestry, and suddenly, she got to stand back and see the entire work. *So much life. So many stories.* Georgia wondered if Connie would have set that bomb if she could have seen Greenpoint the way Georgia was seeing it now.

Off to her right, she noticed a gathering of fire trucks and police cruisers by an empty lot near the waterfront. Their lights flashed red and blue like sparklers on the Fourth of July. *The staging area.* Just a couple of blocks away, Georgia noticed a large group of people gathered around the steps of a church and in a park across the street. It was the church near Mac's grandmother's house. She recalled now that a saint's feast was planned for today. Some flower name—*Lavender . . . Hibiscus . . . Hyacinth.* Saint Hyacinth. It looked like they were setting up the festivities, maybe getting ready for a parade. Georgia prayed Ida had decided to stay home. The thought of that bubbly old woman caught in the middle of something like this filled her with dread.

The pilot angled the helicopter a little lower, then banked into a turn. Sunlight glinted off the boxy warehouses that anchored much of Greenpoint. Down there, the area seemed so much bigger. But it had been psychological, Georgia realized now. Connie was right: one good-sized explosion really could damage a big chunk of the neighborhood. Georgia just hoped Marenko knew the area as well as he claimed to.

After several passes overhead, the helicopter touched down at Kowalski's lot on Bridgewater Street. Above, the commotion had seemed dreamy and distant. Down here, it was hot, chaotic and scary. Emergency vehicles from both the police and fire departments were double-parked on the streets. Dozens of residents and reporters were crowded behind a barrier.

Brennan walked Georgia through the throngs of uniforms to the command post a block and a half away. Marenko was already there. He was dressed in a gray T-shirt and black sweatpants. His face was tired and pale, but the old gleam was back in those blue eyes. Next to him was John Welcastle, his thin lips moving between Mac and a cell phone he had plastered to his ear. Acting Commissioner Delaney was on another cell phone on the other side.

"Hiya, Skeehan," said Marenko. He wouldn't use "Scout" in front of anyone, but he gave her the barest wink when no one was looking.

"Welcome back to the living," she said, striving for a casualness she didn't feel.

He shook his head. "Don't say that 'til this is over."

Brennan smiled a rare smile. Despite the tension of the situation, Georgia could see the chief was glad to see him. He spread the map of the pipeline out on the bumper of a firetruck. Marenko, Georgia, Delaney and Welcastle gathered around.

"All right, Mac," said the chief. "We've got very little to go on. Ruiz said it's in Greenpoint. There are flags and a cross and it'll take out a chunk of the neighborhood. Any ideas?"

"Flags, huh?" Marenko squinted as if he were trying to picture something. He ran a hand nervously through his hair. "I've been thinking about it on the way over," he said. "I knew where I'd plant this baby if I wanted to take out the neighborhood." He pointed a finger at the map, at a spot a few blocks north of where they were. A nearly rectangular object bordered by Greenpoint Avenue and Provost Street, just a block from the Newtown Creek. Georgia read the words on the map now: *Greenpoint Sewage Treatment Plant.*

"Methane gas," Georgia muttered. A by-product of sewage treatment given off by decaying organic matter. Highly flammable. Even with the pipeline shut down, there was always a chance that the residual jet fuel would be sufficient to spark a fire that would cause a rupture of the methane storage tanks in the sewage plant, and the methane would feed the inferno.

"There are three blue-and-white flags on top of that plant," said Marenko. "Those could be the flags she was talking about."

"How about the cross?" asked Georgia.

"You got me there," Marenko admitted. "But I think if Connie really wanted to take Greenpoint out, she wouldn't have just relied on methane to do the job—not when she had other stuff available, too."

"What do you mean?" asked Delaney.

"You know what's right here?" asked Marenko. He pointed to the west side of Provost Street on the map. "Right here, across from the sewage plant, are three Exxon storage tanks filled with gasoline."

Georgia heard Brennan curse loudly. "What asshole city permit allowed a pipeline full of jet fuel to run between a sewage plant and gas storage tanks?"

"It gets worse, Chief," said Marenko. "Floating right below Provost—below the pavement *we're* standing on—is a seventeen-million gallon gasoline spill. Stuff's been here since World War Two. If you couple that with a pipeline leak, gas tanks and methane vapors—forget a standard two-block evacuation. You'll take out fifteen blocks, easy."

Marenko looked at his watch. It was 11:25 A.M. "There's a goddamn saint's feast going on two blocks from Provost Street. My grandmother's there. She's eighty-nine, for chrissakes. We can't get all these people out in thirty-five minutes. It seems to me we'd be better off trying some kind of controlled detonation of a portion of the pipeline ourselves—sort of a contained burn that we smother with high-expansion foam—just to get rid of the fuel." High-ex foam is used to put out jet-fuel and chemical fires that would be spread—rather than extinguished—by water.

Brennan looked at Delaney.

"I'd have to talk to the PD's people on bomb squad," said Delaney. "But that might be our only option at this point."

"No," Welcastle insisted. "Absolutely not. No one is blowing up the pipeline because they think it *might* blow up."

"This isn't conjecture," said Georgia sharply. "Connie Ruiz had the technical expertise to blow up this entire neighborhood. So the bomb is here—without a doubt." She held his stony gaze for a long moment. "This is one fuel spill you *won't* be able to cover up, Mr. Welcastle."

Welcastle turned away from Georgia. His composure was gone. His hands were trembling. He searched for allies in the group and settled on Brennan. "Chief, my men have been over every inch of this area," he insisted. "There's no evidence the pipeline was dug up or breached in any way. We've sent sensors through the pipe, and they haven't picked up any trauma. I will virtually guarantee you—the line has not been compromised."

"It might not have to be," a voice piped up behind them. Georgia and Marenko turned. A young, black cop in a T-shirt that said BOMB SQUAD was standing before them. He had sunglasses on and he lifted them now, revealing a pair of dark eyes that seemed to pop out a little from their sockets, giving him the impression of always being surprised. Or maybe he was surprised. He seemed to know he'd been speaking out of turn.

"What do you mean 'It might not have to be'?" asked Marenko.

"You could bury a shaped charge pointing to the pipeline without actually touching it, and it would work just as effectively," said the young cop. Beads of sweat glistened across his shaved head.

"Shaped charges—those are used in the military, right?" asked Georgia.

"Yes, ma'am," said the cop, his voice picking up more confidence as he continued. "We used them in the army when I was in the combat engineers. They are also used in oil and gas exploration. You point one at a steel pipe, tack on a blasting cap and a timed fuse and it'll shoot a perfect hole right into that baby. The bomber wouldn't need to dig up the pipe or rig anything touching it. A shaped charge just needs to be on a clear path, pointed in the right direction. It works on the same principle as an R P G rocket."

"That's why Empire's engineers never found a device on the pipeline and never found any dug-up ground," said Georgia. "Because the bomb's not on the pipeline."

"All right, smart guy," said Welcastle to the young bomb-squad cop. "Where *is* this shaped charge, if it's not on the pipeline?"

"That I don't know, sir."

Marenko bit his chapped lips as he studied the concrete towers of the sewage-treatment plant and let his eyes wander to a small inlet leading to the Newtown Creek. "Uh, Mr. Welcastle?" said Marenko. "I think I do."

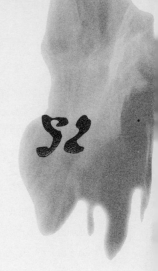

. . .

"Right along Provost Street, there's an old water tunnel," explained Marenko. "Before the sewage-treatment plant opened, the tunnel was used to dump raw sewage into the Newtown Creek. It's empty now—just used as a storm drain mostly. Me and my brothers used to dare each other to go into it. When I was a marshal, I chased a perp in there once."

"You think Connie got into the tunnel?" asked Georgia.

"Absolutely," said Marenko. "It basically runs next to the pipeline. She could've buried a shaped charge in the tunnel and pointed it at the pipeline." Marenko looked at the young black cop from the bomb squad. "What's your name?"

"Tyrell Davies, Marshal."

"Call me Mac," said Marenko, shaking Davies's hand. "You up for finding this thing with me?"

"You bet."

"I think I should go as well," said Georgia.

"No," said Marenko. "You stay here."

"But I can help you find that cross. Connie mentioned a cross, and we haven't found any cross yet."

"If there's a crucifix or something down there, Davies and I will find it," said Marenko. "I don't need you."

Georgia straightened up. She knew what he meant—that it was an extremely dangerous undertaking. He was trying to spare her. Still, after all they'd been through, the words stung. She watched Marenko and Davies get suited up with thick Kevlar arm and chest protection at the command post. Twice, Marenko looked in her direction as he was being strapped into gear. Georgia didn't return his gaze. Part of it was anger that he didn't want her along. And part of it was simple fear. It was 11:32 A.M. They had twenty-eight minutes to find this bomb and figure out how to defuse it. If they failed, Marenko might never come back.

Their plan was to drop into the tunnel along Provost Street by the sewage plant and gas storage tanks. They would be in constant radio contact with the incident command post, two blocks away. Georgia would be able to monitor everything.

A bomb was technically a police operation, but since the bomb was in the Empire Pipeline and the FDNY had jurisdiction over the pipelines, the ultimate authority fell to Acting Commissioner Edward Delaney. He was standing in the incident command post now, surrounded by dark blue uniforms from both departments, as well as a score of men in suits—engineers from Empire and the city's Department of Environmental Protection.

For an operation that was supposed to have been quiet, things had spun hopelessly out of control. The engineers were doing some calculations, and it turned out Marenko was right about the fire's potential. If the pipeline exploded, the residual jet fuel in the line would cause a fire intense enough to spark explosions of the methane at the sewage plant and the storage tanks of gasoline across the street. This, coupled with the seventeen million gallons of gasoline beneath the streets, could generate enough radiant heat in the surrounding area to cause the wood frames and tar-paper roofs on nearby houses to ignite spontaneously and burst into flame—a flashover of sorts on the largest possible scale.

Delaney listened to the engineers and experts, then got on a special red phone linked directly to Mayor Ortaglia. Georgia saw him nodding and speaking gravely into the receiver. His conversation was interrupted by a transmission on the radio. Marenko and Tyrell Davies were inside the sewer line, but they'd come to a fork in the tunnel and they weren't sure which way to go. Their voices crackled like astronauts in space.

They were so near, yet if anything happened, there would be no way to get them out quickly. The engineers and brass from both departments debated whether Marenko and Davies should go left or right. They were at a crossroads. *A cross.*

"Maybe it's the cross," Georgia suggested. "The cross Connie was talking about."

Brennan leaned over the microphone and relayed the message to Marenko.

"Tell him to look for some sort of marking or a disturbance around the bricks," said Georgia. "Connie had to go back probably at least once to set the timer. She would've marked the spot."

A minute or two later, Marenko's voice crackled on the line. "I think we've found it. There's a red spray-painted marking here. It looks kind of like a Maltese Cross."

A cross. A Maltese Cross. In honor of Bear. It had to be Connie's. Davies's voice came on the line now, relaying some of the specifics. The young officer had removed some bricks and could see the bomb. "It's a shaped charge, all right," he radioed. But given the tight, high angle of the device and limited access to the tunnel, there was no way to bring a robot down to disarm it. Defusing it by hand was equally unlikely, he explained. The wires were rigged in such a way that excessive handling would likely set it off. "If we could separate the fuse from the blasting cap, we could disarm it. But we can't do that by hand," he told Delaney.

"All right," said the acting commissioner. He looked at the clock. It was 11:47 A.M. "You can't diffuse it, and you've got thirteen minutes to get out of the tunnel. Can you make it?"

A few seconds passed before Davies came back on the line. "Chief?" he said. "Marshal Marenko says these tunnels still hook up to the sewage plant. If the plant could deliver a major release of water through the tunnel, the force of the flow might be able to blow the bomb out of the tunnel and into the Newtown Creek. Even if it didn't disarm the device, it would allow it to detonate in a safer area. It's a long shot, but Marenko thinks it might work."

"Ten-four. Good work," said Delaney. "Begin evacuation. I'll see what can be done." Delaney grabbed his cell phone and began speaking to the engineers. A smile of relief broke across his face. He shot Georgia a thumbs up. Marenko was right. The plant could release the water as soon as the men were clear of the tunnel. It was 11:50 A.M.—ten minutes to detonation. All Marenko and Tyrell Davies had to do now was get out of the tunnel.

Delaney was still on a cell phone with the engineers when an aide walked up to him and handed him the red phone from the mayor again. Delaney put the engineers on hold and picked up with the mayor. Georgia assumed it was a routine update, but something in Delaney's face stopped her. She saw the acting commissioner's eyebrows knit together and his face become chalklike in color. A look of disbelief spread across his sharp, well-chiseled features. He shook his head and turned his back. Georgia crept closer. She could hear Delaney's end of the conversation now.

"But sir, the two men . . . If I do that . . . Sir, I know you want to keep the pipeline intact, but I believe we can go up to the moment of detonation before . . . I know that's more of a risk, but . . ." Finally, Delaney exhaled and said simply, "Yes, Mr. Mayor. Yes, I understand. I will take care of it."

He turned back to the command post and handed the phone to an aide. He didn't know Georgia had been watching him, but he caught her scrutiny now. He turned his ashen face toward her and swallowed hard.

"Chief . . . Commissioner . . . You can't flood that tunnel yet." She spoke the words so softly, they sounded like a prayer. "Those men are still in there."

Delaney held her eyes for only a moment, then turned and shook his head. "I'm sorry, Skeehan. I have my orders."

. . .

GEORGIA DID SOMETHING she never thought she'd ever do. She put a firm, tight grip on the arm of the most powerful man in the FDNY.

"Five minutes, Chief. That's all it will take. Those men will be out in five minutes."

"The bomb could detonate before then, Skeehan. The mayor's just thinking about the risk to the community."

"He's *thinking* about the negative publicity that could hurt his fucking stadium plans—that's what he's thinking about. Damn it, you *know* that. You've known it all along. No one can be certain if flooding the pipeline will stop that bomb. It's a gamble either way. At least spare those men's lives."

"I can't," said Delaney. He shook her hand off. "I have my orders."

"Orders?" asked Georgia. She no longer cared what happened to her after this. If Delaney let Mac and this young cop die, they could bury the FDNY for all she cared. She was beginning to understand how Connie must have felt. "You followed those goddamn orders almost two decades ago and nineteen men died because of it."

"I didn't know," he insisted.

"But you know now. And what have you done about it, huh? What are you doing about this? Is the brass ring worth that much to you that you'd turn your back on your own people?" she asked.

"I'm doing what I have to in the interests of the department." He reached for his radio to order the water turned on. Georgia's heart felt like a fist in her chest.

"The *department*," she said with disgust. "What the hell is the *department*? An insignia on a letterhead? A bunch of big shiny red trucks and blue uniforms? It's the *people*, sir. It's the men and women who spill their guts for this job, who give their lives for strangers, who run into the buildings everyone else is running out of. And they don't do it because someone orders them to. You can't order courage. Or loyalty. Or pride. Those things come from the heart. What's in *your* heart? Is it a lousy stadium? The mayor's popularity ratings? The next fiscal quarter?"

Delaney's hand froze around the radio. Georgia looked down at it now. It was a large, solid hand—a firefighter's hand. He wore a gold fire department ring on his third finger. The job was his life—had been his life for perhaps thirty years. She could see those years flashing past his eyes now—cutting his teeth as a firefighter in Brooklyn, testing his mettle as a rescue captain. Helping his brothers—watching their backs in building collapses, keeping guys like Seamus Hanlon sober. He hadn't done all that for some politician's popularity ratings. Slowly, Delaney put his radio back in the jacket pocket of his suit and looked at his watch. It was 11:54 A.M.

"Take one firefighter with you to help open the manhole covers," he muttered hoarsely. "I'll give you four minutes to get Marenko and Davies out of the tunnel. After that, the water gets turned on."

"Yes Chief . . . er, Commissioner," Georgia corrected herself.

"After this?" He shook his head. "Not likely."

. . .

Lieutenant Prager from Ladder One-twenty-one volunteered to go with Georgia. He brought along a halligan to pry off the manhole covers, and a life rope, in case they had to hoist the men up. He knew what they were up against. So did Marenko and Davies. It would take at least ten minutes to get out the way they had gone in. Georgia and Prager would have to try to reach them via some other manhole cover—many

of which were welded shut to prevent people from getting into the
tunnels. The men couldn't open the manhole covers from below and
they had only a flashlight to guide them through the darkness, so they
couldn't gauge distances.

"Mac, do you have any idea where you are?" Georgia radioed Marenko now.

"We came in at Provost Street and Greenpoint Avenue," said
Marenko, his voice crackling over the receiver. "My flashlight's picking
up runoff pipes from the sewage plant, so my guess is we're somewhere
between One-hundred-and-ninety-fifth Street and Two-hundred-and-
twenty-first Street, 'cause those are the blocks that span the plant."

"Can you see any manhole covers above you? Maybe if you bang on
one, we can find you."

Prager called out the time. Eleven fifty-five. They had three minutes.
Georgia could feel the noonday August sun beating on her back with almost physical force. Even if they got the men to the surface, there was
no guarantee that flooding the sewer would deactivate—or even move—
the device. They could all die. The whole neighborhood could be torn
apart. Greenpoint would be nothing but a crater on the northern tip of
Brooklyn.

"There's a manhole cover above us," Marenko called out over the
radio. "The ladder's rusted out, so we can't climb up and bang on it.
Tyrell's throwing loose mortar at it."

Georgia and Prager walked the potholed pavement. The stench of
gasoline hung low in the air. In the distance, Georgia could make out
traffic being rerouted off the Pulaski Bridge. And then she heard it. A
sound like uncooked rice on tin foil. Stones. Voices. She and Prager
looked down at the manhole cover before them. Prager took his halligan
and banged on it now.

"Mac—you hear that?" asked Georgia.

"Loud and clear," Marenko answered. "You're right above us. We'll
need a rope. The ladder down here is busted."

"Hang on. We're coming," she said.

Prager shoved the curved end of the halligan underneath the manhole cover and pried it off while Georgia grabbed his rescue rope and searched for something strong on the street to tie the end of the rope onto. She settled on the steel base of a street lamp and tied a rescue knot around it. Then she reeled the rope over to the open manhole and peered down in the darkness. Davies and Marenko were at the bottom.

"Tyrell first," said Marenko. Davies started to object, but Marenko pushed the rope into his hands. Davies grabbed hold and began trying to climb. But his heavy Kevlar bomb gear made it impossible. They both started stripping it off.

"Come on," Georgia pleaded.

"Delaney to Skeehan," said a voice on the radio. "It's eleven fifty-six. I can't hold off much longer."

"Chief—two more minutes. You promised," said Georgia. She heard Delaney's stark command over the radio now: "Commence flooding of the tunnel at eleven fifty-eight."

She had two minutes to save Marenko. Just two minutes. After that, water would gush through the tunnel with the same speed and force as a forty-mile-per-hour car. Marenko and Davies wouldn't stand a chance. The impact would knock them down and sweep them away. They would drown. Then again, that might be preferable. If flooding the tunnel didn't defuse the bomb, the whole space would act as an airshaft. As soon as the shaped charge exploded the pipeline, a fireball would race through that tunnel even faster than the surge of water. Marenko and Davies would be incinerated. And shortly after, they all would be.

Davies grabbed the rope a second time and hoisted himself to the surface. Marenko stood at the bottom, steeling himself to wait until Davies had completed the climb. He could doom them both if he added his weight at this precarious angle.

"Come on, Mac," Georgia pleaded. Marenko grabbed the rope and began to climb while Georgia, Prager and Davies began to pull him up. He had almost reached the surface when a roar like a jet plane engine rushed beneath them. It was the roar of thousands of gallons of water, flooding the tunnel. Georgia grabbed Marenko's arm so tight, she dug her fingernails into his flesh. Prager grabbed the other arm and Davies tried to reach under Marenko's armpits to yank him up. But the force of the water was so powerful, it seemed to suck him from her grip. She clawed at his arm.

"No, Mac. No!" she cried. Not after all they'd been through. She couldn't lose him now. Not now. Not this way. Yet holding onto him was like wrestling with a fish on a line. He was wet and slippery. She'd pull him toward her a little, and the water would suck him right back down. But she must have pulled just enough because Davies suddenly was able to reach under Marenko's armpits and yank him out of the manhole.

The four of them lay on the street, gasping from the effort. They were all wet, but Marenko was soaked head to toe. He tried to get to his feet, yet seemed stuck on his knees. He was shaking badly. Davies and Prager pulled him to his feet. It was noon, and they were on ground zero. No one spoke. The two men each took one of Marenko's arms and half dragged him two blocks down the street, behind the cordon of engine companies readying themselves for the fire.

They had taken only a few steps when a rumble sounded in the direction of the Newtown Creek. Georgia turned her head just in time to catch the explosion. A block and a half away, a thirty-foot plume of water rose from the creek. It exploded out of the black water like a geyser. It was probably the whitest thing the creek had produced in thirty years. Droplets of oily water rained down everywhere and an eerie silence descended on the command post. Everyone seemed to be taking a moment with the enormity of the blast. Everyone seemed to be bracing themselves for what—if anything—would happen next.

Georgia and the men hobbled over to the command post where ambulances were waiting to treat them.

The crowds and reporters had been pushed back ten blocks. Marenko sat on the edge of an ambulance with a blanket over his shoulders. His T-shirt and sweatpants were dripping. When he moved his feet, his sneakers sloshed. Georgia sat next to him. He reached for her hand and held it tight. His fingers shook.

"It's okay," Georgia whispered. "I think we're safe now."

"I'm just cold," he mumbled. It wasn't true, and they both knew it. Fear is the ghost no firefighter can ever afford to acknowledge. Georgia rubbed the blanket around his shoulders.

"You'll be warm soon," she promised. Marenko nodded gratefully. They both knew what she meant: *You don't need to be scared anymore.*

"I was wrong," he choked out in a rasping voice.

"About what?"

"I did need you back there," he said, then added, more softly, "I do need you."

The plant had enough clean water to flood the tunnel for ten minutes. They waited as noon passed. Five minutes. Then ten. The water stopped. The bomb squad began to suit up to fish the fragments of Connie's exploded bomb out of the creek. There would be no more destruction. Cheers went up when the news came over the radio. Georgia broke away from Marenko for a moment and went over to Delaney.

"Chief, that is, Commissioner . . . I want to thank you."

Delaney shook his head. "Forget about it."

"I know you took a risk."

When he looked at her, there was a glassy sheen in his eyes. "Maybe I haven't been taking enough." Then he turned on his heel and walked back into the throng of men who, sensing the crisis had passed, were now talking procedures and paperwork and protocols.

Georgia watched them with a sense of detachment. Already, the panic of the moment was subsiding into a sea of reports and cold, dispassionate phrases that would cover over the moment when Mac Marenko and Tyrell Davies were ready to give up their lives so that others might live. There might be a medal and a ceremony at City Hall, complete with a photo op of them shaking hands with the mayor. Probably Georgia and Lieutenant Prager would be included as well. But the boldness of the act would be buried in bureaucratic blather, in clinical procedure.

Ortaglia would never bring up his premature orders to flood the tunnel. Delaney would never mention that he had overridden the mayor's command and, in so doing, spared two men's lives and possibly cost himself the commissioner's appointment. But Georgia would never forget.

"I'm going to go see my grandmother when this operation is wrapped up," said Marenko. "Want to come?"

"Sure," said Georgia. She laughed as she looked down at their clothes. "Seems like we're always showing up at her door soaked and desperate."

"Hey, this way, she'll feed us."

. . .

THE FOLLOWING FRIDAY, the mayor held a special medal presentation at the Blue Room in City Hall. Marenko, Tyrell Davies, Lieutenant Prager and Georgia got Class One medals, the highest-level honors that can be bestowed on a cop or firefighter.

City Hall and the police and fire departments were anxious to award the medals—anything to detract from the embarrassment of the fallout over the pipeline bomb. The newspapers were having a field day. They couldn't decide which angle to pursue first. Already, they were lionizing Franco Ortaglia for his "courageous, decisive" actions in thwarting a pipeline disaster. He always did have good PR people. But the media was equally intrigued by Andy Kyle. Terrified of prison, he'd already cut a deal to testify against his father and Rankoff in exchange for leniency. It was likely neither he nor his father would do any jail time, though Jerome Kyle would be financially ruined.

Rankoff on the other hand, was looking at hard time. The mayor had immediately disowned him, and the Brooklyn D.A. was reinvestigating Pat Flannagan's hit-and-run death and Rankoff's possible connections to it. Georgia expected to be testifying for months. Yet oddly, throughout all this frenzy of media coverage, two things remained unchanged: The mayor still planned to build a football stadium on Bridgewater Street. And the blaze that had poisoned all those firefighters—the impetus for Connie's rage—remained largely out of the public eye. A twenty-five-year-old fire didn't make good copy, she supposed.

Georgia straightened her dark blue silk blazer and tried to put these thoughts out of her mind as she stepped up to receive her medal at City Hall a week after the incident. Richie was in the audience, along with Georgia's mother. The whole Marenko clan was there as well—Mac's parents, his grandmother Ida, his three brothers and their wives and children, along with Mac's ten-year-old son, Michael, and seven-year-old daughter, Beth.

At one point, Ida waved at Georgia, then elbowed Mac's father hard in the ribs and whispered something in his ear. *Trust Ida to tell them,* thought Georgia. But then she noticed Mac's father, a big, gray-haired man with those same sparkling blue eyes, nod his head. Not a surprised nod or an astonished nod. Just a nod. As if he already knew. *Mac told them. I'm not a ghost anymore.*

She caught Mac's father sneaking a sideways glance at the seats just across the aisle where her mother and Richie were sitting. Then she saw him smile. *And he knows about Richie, too.* She exhaled a long, soft breath. *They know.*

After the ceremony, while Georgia was showing Richie and her mother her medal, she felt a gentle hand on her shoulder. It was Marenko. He looked very handsome in his dark suit as he shuffled about nervously. He rubbed a hand across the back of his neck.

"So . . . uh . . . You and Richie and your ma want to meet my family?"

"I'd love to," said Georgia. She found her gaze drifting to the exit door behind Marenko. A group of the mayor's aides were already on their cell phones, making arrangements to move Franco Ortaglia to the next event. In a moment, he would be gone—and with him, the promise she had made to Connie in that tunnel below Grand Central Station. She turned back to Marenko.

"Would you do me a favor, Mac?"

"Sure."

"Take Richie and Ma. I'll catch up with you later. There's something I have to do first."

Marenko looked shocked. "You're kidding—right? I finally ask you and . . ."

"—It's the asking that matters."

"Women." He rolled his eyes.

She made her apologies, then snaked through the clusters of families gathered around the room, keeping her eyes on the tight-knit circle of men in suits headed for the exit. Mayor Franco Ortaglia was in the center. Georgia would have just one chance at this bluff. If she blew it, she'd never get another.

"Mr. Mayor," she called out breathlessly, pushing through the crowds to reach his entourage. Franco Ortaglia turned. He tried to smile, but he still looked like a man suffering from a bad case of heartburn. He probably thought she wanted his autograph or something for her son.

"Please, sir? Can I speak to you a moment, privately?"

There was a small chamber off the auditorium. Ortaglia hesitated. A short man with a pointy nose touched his watch and whispered in the mayor's ear.

"*Hmmm,* yes, well, Marshal. Perhaps you could make an appointment through channels," Ortaglia suggested. "I'd be happy to meet with you then."

"Hizzoner has a busy schedule," the pointy man added, putting a hand on Ortaglia to usher him out the door. Georgia leaned in closer and caught the mayor's wary eyes. She tried to steady the quake in her voice and remind herself that she was speaking for the men who could no longer speak for themselves.

"You walk out that door, Mr. Mayor, and I'll take the copies of all the documents I have about the Bridgewater fire straight to the *New York Times.* You will *never* build your football stadium."

Georgia had no documents. Delaney's report was gone. The DEP form from Flannagan's files was gone. She had only the CIDS card from the old firehouse. And, although it proved that some firefighter had noted potentially hazardous chemicals in the warehouse nine months before the fire, there was no way of proving that the card had ever made it to dispatch. Still, the bluff seemed to be working. Franco Ortaglia froze. He shot a look at the aide.

"What documents?"

"The report prepared by the FDNY's Division of Safety in 1984 that outlines how this city, Empire Pipeline and Tristate Corporation conspired to cover up a major environmental disaster on Bridgewater Street in Brooklyn—the very spot you want to put your new football stadium on. Gus Rankoff *owned* Tristate, you know."

"I don't know what you're talking about. None of that has anything to do with me," Ortaglia said with disgust.

"You're right." Georgia feigned a shrug. "I'm sure the people of New York won't mind that you've done nothing to clean up that dump and now you want to build a stadium there." She pretended to turn away.

"*Hmmm,* yes, well," said Ortaglia. His thin lips twitched. He nodded toward the small chambers off the Blue Room. "In there. Make it quick."

Georgia followed the mayor and his aide into the room. It had a couple of overstuffed leather chairs and bookshelves of leather-bound city documents. Georgia picked one up to steady the shaking in her hands. She was talking to the most powerful man in the most powerful city in the world, and she had nothing to back up her threats. She'd either succeed or he'd bury her. But she couldn't live with herself if she turned a blind eye—as so many in the department had done before her.

"Remove your jacket," said Ortaglia, nodding to her silky blue blazer.

"Excuse me?"

"Hizzoner doesn't want to hear his words played back for him on *Dateline* next week," the aide explained.

Georgia understood. She removed her jacket and patted her silky white blouse. "No wires—see?"

Ortaglia nodded.

"Who sent you? Delaney?" he grumbled. "Because that prick's not going to be commissioner, so he wants revenge?"

"Chief Delaney has nothing to do with this. I'm acting on my own."

"I could destroy your career," Ortaglia hissed.

"I realize that," Georgia said, trying to control the tremble in her voice.

"But since you just decorated me and I'm one of the few women you *have* in the FDNY, I don't think it would look too good."

"What do you want?"

"Gus Rankoff and his firm, Tristate, were responsible for dumping toxic waste in a warehouse on Bridgewater Street twenty-five years ago. The city covered up the crime and secretly removed the waste—but not before twenty firefighters sickened and nineteen of them died from a fire on that site because no one told them what they were up against."

"*Hmmm,* yes, well." Ortaglia paced the floor. There was no surprise in his face. Clearly, he knew the whole story.

"It's a tragedy," he muttered. "But that doesn't make it my problem. Rankoff and his firm—*they* were the problem. Rankoff's in jail. Jerome Kyle and Northway are being investigated. *I* knew nothing about any of that."

Georgia raised an eyebrow, but already, she suspected it was fruitless to try to accomplish what even the Brooklyn D.A. was unlikely to be able to do. Ortaglia was too politically savvy to get himself linked with anything overtly underhanded.

"How about Empire, Mr. Mayor? Did you know that a leak from the Empire Pipeline sparked that blaze? That the warehouse was built illegally straddling the pipeline and that Empire covered the whole thing up?"

"New Yorkers want a football stadium, Marshal—not a history lesson."

"They won't *get* a football stadium if that report comes out," said Georgia. "That land was never properly cleaned up. It will be the subject of lawsuits for the next twenty-five years."

That got his attention. "What is it you want? To have the site restored to some pristine condition it hasn't been in for two hundred years?"

Georgia clasped her hands in front of her to keep them from shaking. "I want it cleaned up the way it was supposed to have been cleaned up. I want Empire's record more closely scrutinized by an independent panel."

He leaned against a bookcase and ran a finger along the bridge of his bony nose. "I can probably work the clean-up costs for Bridgewater into the overall stadium budget." Ortaglia shot a look at his aide, who whipped out a calculator, punched in some numbers and nodded at the mayor. "As for Empire . . . *Hmmm,* yes, well," said the mayor. "—I can use what just happened to justify the panel. It could even be a good move politically. Shows the city won't allow itself to be pushed around by big business interests." He nodded. "All right."

Ortaglia was done, but Georgia wasn't. "On a more personal level, Mr. Mayor, I'd like the city to erect plaques to the men who died at Bridgewater and install them in the new firehouses, along with a ceremony for their families."

"That can be arranged."

"And in return for never making that safety report public, I want the City of New York to authorize retroactive three-quarters service-connected disability pensions and medical benefits for the twenty Bridgewater families to provide for the widows until their deaths . . ."

"—Absolutely not." Ortaglia pushed himself off the bookcase now. "Are you crazy? Retroactive? We're talking millions of dollars. I can't do that."

"Every one of your staff-chief friends gets a three-quarters disability pension when he leaves the FDNY. Even the doctors who turned down those men's claims got three quarters. A week ago, you authorized *ten* million dollars to put Plexiglas partitions and LoJack warning devices in livery cabs because you were getting political pressure from the minority communities. If you can authorize *ten* million for the cabbies, you can certainly authorize a few million for these families."

Ortaglia banged on the bookcase and cursed. "You goddamned, two-bit civil servant. Where the hell do you get off pulling a stunt like this? I could have your badge—you hear me?"

The aide punched some numbers into his calculator and cleared his throat. Then he showed the mayor the figures. Georgia saw them too.

"You see? The *most* you'll have to authorize is $500,000 per family. *The most.* That's an outlay of probably well under ten million. For firefighters who gave their lives for this city. No one's going to oppose that."

"What do you get out of this? Huh?" he asked.

Georgia thought about walking up that metal staircase in her father's old firehouse and seeing the bronze plaque in his memory set into the tile wall. Men worked in that firehouse who were still in diapers when George Skeehan died. But they were reminded of him every day as they walked up those stairs. Someone remembered. Someone said thanks.

"What do I get out of this?" asked Georgia. "A little bit of peace."

"If I do this—*if* I do this—you may never breathe a word about it to anyone. Ever," said Ortaglia. "That report of Delaney's gets destroyed. The city changes their pensions and cuts these checks and you say nothing—*nothing*—about your involvement."

"Agreed," said Georgia. She held out a hand, and Ortaglia shook it. "I have just one more request," she said.

"What now?"

"There's one check I would like to deliver myself."

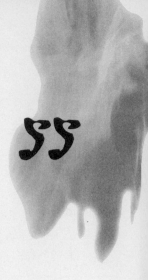

5 5

• • •

THE OLD YELLOW row house in Greenpoint was quiet on this Monday morning in early September. It was Labor Day, and for once, Denise Flannagan did not have to struggle to carry a baby on her arthritic hip or strain her gnarled fingers undoing the buttons on a toddler's pants. Families were off work and at the beach or getting ready for their last barbecue of the season. Georgia could smell charcoal lighter fluid wafting onto the sidewalk from someone's backyard.

Marenko parked his silver Honda Accord in front of the Flannagan house and rolled down his window to drink in the sunny, balmy air. It had been two and a half weeks since his release from Riker's, yet he still greeted the simplest sensations with a pleasure Georgia had never seen in him before.

"I almost lost everything," he told her one night after he and Richie had been dunking each other in Georgia's pool. "That's when I found out what it was all worth." That same evening, he invited her to his brother Pete's Labor Day picnic in New Jersey.

Georgia never mentioned Connie to Marenko. She knew that was an open wound. Yet strangely, for all the grief Connie had caused, Georgia still felt connected to her. She attended Connie's funeral and felt a certain peace when she saw her laid to rest next to her father's grave. She and Carter managed to get her brother Carl into a good drug rehab center, too. Now, with the mayor's new deal, there would be enough money to get him the care his sister had wanted. It was the least they could do for what was left of Albert O'Rourke's family.

Walking up the crumbling stoop of Denise Flannagan's row house, Georgia felt a lift in her step as she rang the doorbell. The sun caught the wrinkles in the old woman's milky-white face as her arthritic fingers struggled to open the door. It took her a moment to place Georgia. She had never met Marenko before.

"Oh," she said, taken aback. "Hello, Marshal. Did you need some of my husband's papers again?"

"No, Mrs. Flannagan," said Georgia. "I came to give you this." She put the sealed official envelope from the City of New York into Denise Flannagan's knobby fingers.

"What is it?" the woman asked warily. Official papers had never meant good news.

"A check, Mrs. Flannagan. For four hundred and fifty thousand dollars retroactive pension. Plus a statement upgrading your husband's pension to three-quarters tax-free for the rest of your life. It's a thank-you for your husband's sacrifices in the line of duty to the New York City Fire Department. There's also an invitation inside to a plaque ceremony for your husband and the other men he served with at Ladder One-twenty-one and Engine Two-oh-three."

"Oh, my Lord," said the woman as she fumbled to unseal the envelope. Tears filled Denise Flannagan's eyes, and she brushed at them. She was a proud woman, Georgia could see. She wasn't used to crying. The years of holding her family together while she watched her husband and his men fall apart had steeled her to be stronger than that. Her hands were shaking. Marenko cupped his big palms around them now.

"You okay, Mrs. Flannagan?" he asked her. Georgia could see a little glassy sheen in his eyes as well.

"Yes, thank you," she said to him. "Oh, please excuse me. I'm so sorry."

"Nothing to be sorry about," Marenko assured her.

"But I just don't believe it," she said. "After all this time? After being ignored for so long—why now?"

"Because," said Georgia. "A thank-you was long overdue."

"I don't know how you made it happen," said Marenko thickly as he nosed his car onto the Brooklyn-Queens Expressway. They were heading to his brother Pete's house in New Jersey. He pretended to adjust his sunglasses. When he thought Georgia wasn't looking, he reached under them and wiped his eyes.

"You did a good thing there, Scout." Then he reached around under his seat and pulled out what looked like a wad of pink tissue paper. "Here," he said, handing the wad to her. "I almost forgot."

Georgia unwrapped the tissue paper now. Inside was a china piggy bank, painted pink with a slot on top and a rubber stopper on the belly. The pig had garish red wings and a goofy smile. It reminded Georgia of something a child might win at an arcade game.

"It's uh . . . nice, Mac," said Georgia.

"You don't remember, do you?" He looked stricken. "I asked you if you could ever trust me. And you said . . . aw." He shrugged. "Forget it."

Georgia held up the pig now, and it all came back to her. It was the ugliest—and best—present any man had ever given her. She started to giggle. "I can't believe you remembered that."

"I remember everything, Scout." He grinned as he ran a hand along her thigh. "Everything."